DRAGON DANCER

BOOK ONE: THE AWAKENING

JULIE KORZENKO

DEDICATION

For Chelsea, may you always fly with the power of a dragon.

OTHER BOOKS BY JULIE KORZENKO

ZEBRA CHRONICLES

DEVIL'S GOLD

ACKNOWLEDGMENTS

I could not do what I do without the support of my wonderful husband, Robert, and my children, Chelsea and Nicholas. I would also like to thank my editor, Janet Bank, for all of her patient assistance in helping me make this the best book possible. I also owe a very warm thanks to my brother-in-law, Ian, for navigating the people mover through the gorgeous countryside of Wales.

Praise for Julie Korzenko

"Fans of Alex Kava, Shannon McKenna, and Suzanne Brockmann will hope to see more…"

~Publisher's Weekly

"With the wonderful characters, a page-turning plot, and interesting facts and details…a definite must-read."~Vix, *Ijustfinished.com*

"…a thoroughly researched and sublimely readable thriller…"

~ Novelspot

RT BOOKReviews Magazine - 2009 Romantic Times Nominee for Best Romantic Suspense

Julie Korzenko

Chapter One

Below the level of full consciousness, Simone Walker enjoyed the brief sensation that everything was perfect. Lavender permeated the air, and she glanced sideways to find her sister offering a cattish grin that pulled an answering smile onto Simone's face.

"What're you doing here?" Simone whispered, languishing in the glow of the complete serenity of sleep.

Rosalyn's smile slipped. "The answer is in the White Book of Rhydderch. You must remember this." Her sister glanced behind her shoulder. "He's almost done. My time is short."

Simone frowned, the quiet of slumber slipping away. "I don't understand."

"One will come to you. Trust him above all else. I'll try to make my way back as soon as possible, but my path will be difficult." Rosalyn pulled her fist tight against her chest and faced Simone. "Do not be afraid, my sister. I love you." She slammed the palm of her hand against Simone's heart with the power of a pistol. "Don't wear black." Simone's head snapped back, and she gasped for air as heat spread through her body. Padlocks sprung open and rage welled from the deepest edge of Simone's soul.

Simone woke into instant awareness, her world shattered. Terror clawed her chest, freezing her breath within burning lungs. She couldn't move. Her bed became a prison.

It'd been a long time, but Simone knew this sense of imminent danger well.

With a rush of panic, she struggled to sit up. Her body refused to move.

Let.

Me.

OUT.

Simone slammed the heel of her palm against her forehead, pushing against a sudden blinding pain hell bent on cracking her skull in half.

OUT.

"I . . ." she struggled to speak. "Don't know how." The screeched words resonated against her eardrums, pulsing and vibrating, escalating the headache and dimming the rest of the world to nothing but pinpricks of light. This was not the husky whisper of her sister. It was deeper, frustrated and angry.

With a deeply drawn breath, Simone concentrated on calming herself. She shut her eyes tight, inhaled and exhaled slowly until the inner voice subsided to a small roar.

A spark of awareness flashed, and she sensed another threat, a powerful evil. Shadows, twisted and gnarled, invaded her room. The moon ducked behind a cloud dousing what little light remained. An invisible force pushed down upon her chest suffocating, demanding, terrifying.

Tears escaped the edges of her shuttered eyes, weaving a wet trail toward the pillow. Her mind skipped back twenty years.

They were back. She'd known they were coming, felt the danger.

Jessie. Simone screamed silently not afraid for herself, this time, but petrified for her daughter. Her shoulder burned and skin tingled with a painful fiery sensation. *Let me out . . . Let me out . . .*

A splinter of ice snaked around her ankle. Glancing down, her eyes focused on a finger of black air slithering up her leg, its tendrils piercing her calf with needle thin claws. The shadows pressed closer.

Simone concentrated and allowed the heat within to grow. It pushed against her skin and shot bullets of pain along every nerve ending. She inhaled deeply. The simmering flame of the voice screaming for release burst with an inner-jolt of electricity. Ribbons of fire spread along her skin, flaring and snatching at tendons, muscle and bone, searching for what she didn't know how to give.

Chill receded beneath inferno.

Fly . . . fly . . . fly

She pulled away from the presence that pinned her in place and followed instinct, but it came with an excruciating price. Simone jumped off the bed, spinning on her heels and scanning every corner of her room. Focused on the unearthly images, her eyes bore into blackness and the shadows began shrinking away, dissolving until there was nothing but the innocent play of moonlight.

Pain shot through her bones, driving Simone to her knees. A voice screeched at a decibel level intent on rupturing her eardrums. *No . . . no . . . let me out.* Gripping the side of her head, Simone rocked back and forth and fought to build back the bubble, imprisoning this strange force and dampening its fire.

Tipping her head back, she screamed--the pressure on her skull too much to handle. Blackness fell and consciousness began to recede. She focused on an image of her daughter's face and streamlined all her energy into pulling oxygen into lungs and not fainting.

The pressure released from her chest and head in a burning wave. She inhaled and wiped her hand against a sweat-soaked forehead. Her fingers shook violently, and it took several seconds before she could disengage herself from the sheets that must have been pulled from the bed when she fell.

With her heart lodged firmly in her throat she ran from her room and down the hallway to Jessie's bed. Flinging the door open, Simone gripped the handle with a fist. Her daughter sat at the computer, earphones on her head singing in an off-tone key that elicited a relieved smile from Simone.

They hadn't found Jessie.

She sighed, ran her fingers through the nest of tangles in her hair then walked over to her daughter. Simone tapped Jessie's shoulder, making her jump.

"What? You scared me." Jessie said, pushing the earphones off her head. "You look terrible. What's the matter?"

Simone thought of reprimanding her for still being awake at midnight and online no less. But life was too short. She didn't want an argument, she wanted love. Bending over she kissed Jessie on the forehead and whispered goodnight. Her heart ached, and she bit back the tears that wanted to spill. "I'm fine. Just a little nightmare."

Turning abruptly, Simone left. She could hear Jessie mumbling about irrational mothers but ignored her. Simone re-entered her room. Collecting her tools, she performed a ritual she hadn't done in twenty years. She walked around and lit the white gardenia-scented candles that lay scattered on her shelves and nightstands. Simone then burned the sticks of frankincense and whispered the spell that banished night terrors.

It wasn't night terrors really, but she wasn't about to stop any of her rituals against whatever closed in on her world. These things might slip in when she slept, but it was only because her guard was down. When they made contact, Simone was always awake.

Embers of the presence that invaded her soul shifted to life, but Simone tightened the bubble and suffocated the weird sensations. Silenced the call. She pulled a faded paperback from the nightstand and stared at the gruesome black and white sketch gracing its cover. An innocent young girl lay prone on a carpet of dried leaves. From her stomach, the shadow of a demon rose toward an oddly angled moon, the figure's misshapen body knotted and wounded. Simone traced the letters that spelled the name of the book. "Possession: A Journey into One Woman's Insanity."

Grabbing her robe from the bottom of her bed, she wrapped it around her. With a sense of dread, Simone crawled beneath her covers and settled into an uneasy sleep.

***

Trent bolted upright in bed. He jumped from beneath the covers, grabbed his gun, and turned in a slow arc scrutinizing each corner of his room. No danger. What had woken him?

His heart raced and pulse thrummed, stronger and faster than he'd every felt. Trent placed his gun back on the nightstand and did a quick mental check of his facilities. Heat streamed across his nerves, his palms burned with fire. He turned them over and scrutinized his hands. Blue iridescent flames licked his skin.

Ancient! I am awake. Come.

"Fuck me," Trent whispered. He closed his eyes and focused on an emerald ball of fire that seared a map into his brain. *Hurry. Danger.*

With a shaky exhale, he opened his eyes and studied the blue fire skating across his palms. Remembering the exercises ingrained in his psyche since childhood, Trent fisted his hands then snapped open his fingers. Power sizzled and crackled against his bedroom walls. He moved in slow steady motion, pulling strands of blue lightning back toward him until he felt his body absorb the energy. Trent sank onto the edge of his bed. "Fuck me."

He tugged on jeans and shrugged into a faded and well-worn MI-5 training sweatshirt and stepped outside onto his private balcony. He gazed across the sculpted stone railing separating the edge of the terrace from the manicured gardens below. Shades of green, muted beneath the glow of first morning, carpeted the rolling hills surrounding the estate.

Castle Draconius.

Once a powerful foothold for warriors and royalty, softened and conformed over time until its fierce spirit and myth-infused foundation vanished beneath civilization.

Ruins of the original stronghold sat in the distance, marring dark green grass with uneven piles of aged, moss-covered stone. The past swept across dew-drenched fields, tugging at Trent -- pulling him toward a battle he'd refused to believe existed.

Malevolence tainted the air.

It skated along his skin, prodding and pushing him toward a destiny he didn't want to accept. But, unfortunately, this fate happened to be his job. And there wasn't a thing he could do about it or his future.

"Bloody hell." Ian appeared on the balcony, stretching and yawning. "Why are we up so early?"

Trent glanced at him. "I've been called."

"The Director's up this early, too?"

With a sigh, Trent shook his head. "She's waking, and we need to be in the States yesterday."

Ian's eyes widened. "Bloody hell."

"Yeah," he agreed. "For some reason I always thought you'd be first."

"Apparently wizards drool and dragons rule." Ian headed toward his bedroom. "I'll grab the books and wind up the chopper." He glanced back and paused, tilting his head and staring at Trent.

"What?"

"You don't look any different. Does it feel weird?"

Trent wanted to yell at Ian that it felt bloody awful but knew his partner was simply curious. He fisted his hands, turned his palms up and extended his fingers, displaying a mesmerizing wave of blue fire. "Look."

Ian moved closer and glanced down. "Fuck me."

With a smile, Trent shook his hands, dissipating the power and punched Ian on the shoulder. "That's what I said. Now go get those books."

Ian turned and headed back to his room. "I'm on it." His tone had dropped from light to thoughtful.

"Ha," Trent allowed a small smile to tilt his lips upward. "Wizards drool . . . funny." He'd known Ian Vale his entire life. Blood brothers bonded by legacies larger than life. They were currently under the direction of a covert section of British Military Intelligence, Section-5. One that would make even the most stalwart believer in ghosts and goblins lift a brow.

***

Several hours of tossing, turning, pillow-punching and frustrated sighs held Simone in a state of half-sleep. An insistent ringing slapped her fully awake. She mashed her palm against her alarm clock but the bell kept making a racket. Picking up her pillow, she muffled the blasted thing. But the noise grew louder the second her bedroom door opened.

"Mama, get up. Sheriff Tippens is at the door."

She pushed her hair back from her face and stared at her daughter through bleary eyes. "Randy? What does that butthead want?"

"Mama! That's Melissa's daddy."

Simone waved and shook her head. "I know. I know. But he's also the ass Aunt Delores divorced." She sighed. "Tell him I'll be down in a minute."

She groaned inwardly. She and Tippens never saw eye-to-eye. She was progressive--he was regressive. They fought constantly. At PTA, at public hearings, at community picnics. Their daughters, however, were inseparable.

Glancing down at her t-shirt and boxers, Simone decided she'd better change. She went into the bathroom, ran water over the puffy tomatoes that used to be her eyes and brushed her teeth. Pulling on a pair of shorts, she grudgingly added a bra and clean shirt to the ensemble. Tippens didn't deserve this amount of respectability at the break of dawn.

Dawn? She looked out the window and sure enough the horizon had barely been lit by the rising sun. Alarm froze her momentarily before she tossed away the sneaker she'd been in the process of putting on and raced out of her room. Jessie stood in the doorway of her bedroom with Melissa by her side. Her face was pale and eyes wide with fear.

"What's going on?" Simone asked her as she headed down the stairs. Jessie shook her head and shrugged, mouthing *I don't know*.

In the kitchen, Delores moved around putting on Simone's coffee pot. This was surreal. Why were these people in her home?

"Randy?"

Simone glanced from her best friend to the Sheriff. Tears glistened in Delores' eyes. Randy stepped up and put a hand on her shoulder. He took a deep breath and glanced back at his ex-wife who nodded at him. Trepidation invaded every single corner of her body. She stepped back not wanting to hear what the sheriff had to say.

"Simone." His voice was soft and uncomfortably mellow. Why didn't he just square his shoulders, puff out his chest and insult her like he normally did. "I have some bad news."

"Well obviously this isn't a social call. Spit it out, Randy." Simone closed her eyes and gripped the edge of the counter. She inhaled and then looked him in the eye.

"Your sister's body was found last night."

Time stopped. The room spun and Simone struggled to hear him through the buzzing in her head. "That's impossible. She was just right here." She pointed to the living room. "Less than twelve hours ago. We were…" Simone's words faltered. What were they doing? Her mind hummed with the memory of her midnight conversation.

"I'm sorry, Simone. I'll need to ask you a few questions but that can wait until after her services."

"What?" She gripped the edge of the counter tighter, ignoring the pain that shot through her fingers. "What happened?"

Delores stepped around the island in the kitchen and embraced her. "It was suicide, sugar. We always knew she was a bit of a soft kernel, didn't we?"

No. She wasn't a soft kernel. Suicide? It didn't feel right. *He was almost done.* Isn't that what Rosalyn had said?

"I want details, Randy. Where was she found?"

"I don't have any other information, Simone. Atlanta PD simply called my office and asked that you be informed. You were the last number dialed on her cell phone. When they contacted me, I confirmed that she was your sister. I know they'll have questions for you. But as a suicide, it's an open and shut case. The paperwork can wait until after you've handled the services."

She picked up a pencil from the misshapen jar Jessie made in art class and ran it through her fingers. The soothing edge helped her focus. "I want to see her."

"I'm afraid that's not possible."

"Why is that?"

"Like I said I don't have any details. But they told me the face wasn't recognizable."

Simone tried to stop the images of a face decimated by gunfire, but it didn't work. "Then how do they know it's Rosalyn?" Her voice came out in a half-sob.

"Her dental records supported the identification."

Simone couldn't stop the tears from falling. She knew Randy meant well, but it wasn't comforting.

"Oh, sugar, don't cry." Delores hugged her tighter. "Bless your poor, broken heart."

Images swirled and words teased her mind. Her last conversation with Rosalyn had been full of riddles and an odd discussion of their childhood. And last night . . . a cat smile. A promise to come back. *Don't wear black.* Simone's heart stalled.

Focus and she'd understand. But reality faded beneath grief, and she slipped to the floor, huddled over to hold the pain close to her chest lest it slip out and taint the rest of her world.

***

Trent strode through the entrance of MI-5 headquarters, ruffling the raindrops from his unruly mop of jet-black hair. He inhaled the scent of polished chrome and heavily cleaned glass. The past twenty-fours had been grueling. He and Ian had barely slept as they'd spent hours pouring over the books and detailing an action plan.

If there was anywhere else on earth that could help clear his fogged mind, he didn't know of it.

Thames House.

Home.

The high ceilings and wall-length tinted windows allowed his six foot three frame plenty of breathing space.

MI-5 employed more than nineteen hundred employees all dedicated to the security of Britain. Terrorists, criminals, political dictators were targets to be monitored, disbanded, apprehended or killed by this elite force of men and women. Trent slid his identification card into the slot beside the paneled door marked Section IV. The heavy wood swung silently open, and he stepped into the hushed interior.

As the door closed, he bent forward for the eye scan and fingerprint analysis that was a prerequisite for all Section IV agents. His division was buried deep within the bustling agency, an arm of MI-5 that never saw the light of publicity.

Identification complete.

Trent entered the chaos. This latest branch created by the current Director General sparked controversy among the members of Parliament. It was innovative, pushing the envelope and accepting the possibility that darker forces existed within the universe other than man.

He'd been raised beneath the blanket of prophecy as had Ian and most of his co-workers, unique in a city of monotony. Each purported to hold a key to greater elements within the universe. Until yesterday, Trent hadn't fully believed.

He shrugged out of his raincoat, tossed it onto a coat rack and pushed up the navy blue and green sleeves of his Preston North End rugby jersey.

"Good afternoon, Agent Arnot. Nice of you to join us today."

Trent glanced down into the steel gray eyes of Kathryn Hilliard, Deputy Director General. "I'm here." His jaw tightened in reflex to the anger that boiled beneath the surface of his tightly controlled emotions.

"Are you ready for debriefing?"

"Yes, Deputy Director." Trent stepped aside to allow her to lead the way into the conference room. With a quick nod, she swept past him.

"Vulture," he said beneath his breath, the trail of her expensive perfume triggering an intense wave of nausea. She'd beat him out of the Deputy Director position in a ruthless race of duplicity which Trent had refused to retaliate against. It rankled, but he knew, in time, her own greed for success would be her downfall.

Ian already sat behind the massive mahogany table. He pushed a cup of coffee in Trent's direction. Their eyes connected, and he nodded at his partner to confirm that he held the data Trent had requested he retrieve prior to leaving Bath.

"Gentlemen and Deputy Director, thank you for taking time out of your hectic schedules for this impromptu debriefing." The Director General's voice boomed out of a large screen at the end of the room. Trent smiled at the grandfatherly image the Director General used to lull young, ambitious agents into a sense of well-being. Only when the razor-sharp scrutiny cut through their pompous pile of self-proclaiming bullshit, did they realize the Director was a tiger in sheep's clothing. He tolerated nothing less than perfection and success. It didn't take long for the inexperienced to learn and mold themselves into the type of men he demanded. With a nod at the video screen, Trent settled comfortably into the leather swivel chair.

"Trent, where do we stand with our evidence against Lord Bromley?"

The MI-5 agent cleared his throat and leaned forward. He focused on Director General Marcus Cornwall and shook his head. "I'm afraid all that surfaced in France was a handful of soil. Laboratory tests indicated that it contained the loamy substance that is prominent in the lands surrounding Blithewoods, the manor home for Bromley, but it's not conclusive enough to issue a warrant."

"I see," the director answered.

Kathryn Hilliard scooted forward. Trent knew by the way her nails clicked against the surface of the table that she resented the Deputy Director questioning him first. "I suggest, Director General, that . . ."

"Have we any profile on these victims? Do we know where he's going next?"

Trent leaned forward. "Yes." He ignored the glare that Kathryn tossed at him. By her flayed nostrils, he knew she struggled to maintain her temper. He flashed a cheeky grin at her, knowing full well that Ian hadn't imparted this aspect of their investigation. "She's awoken. He's going to the States."

A collective gasp skittered through the room. The Director General leaned forward and stared into Trent's eyes. "Are you certain?"

Trent nodded. He'd spent all day yesterday reviewing every aspect of his family's heritage, and the prophecy his mother made him memorize since the second he could read. "I've been called." He glanced around at the other members of the unit which were tied to the same thread in history. "And it wasn't by anyone here."

Kathryn's face blanched.

Trent couldn't help but feel elated. She'd tossed her Dancer heritage in his face each time he'd taken a step beyond her professionally. *She would be his master. She was the Dancer and he only a lowly Ancient.* Her words remained burned upon his mind. He tossed her a smirk and glanced at the video monitor as the Director General began to speak.

"This takes priority above all else. Trent, this is critical. If your hunch is true about Bromley, then *she's* in grave danger. We must protect *her* at all costs. The balance . . . "

"I know, sir." Trent heaved a sigh and ran his fingers through his cropped hair. "This investigation has been nothing if not a practice in patience. Honestly, I can't bloody well tie the bugger to anything. But the victims all hold the same lineage as Ms. Walker. And *she's* there -- within the architect. I can only assume that he is after *her*." Trent split the screen and tossed a picture of Simone Walker onto the video link. "The call is strong. I don't know what's transpired to ignite this but apparently there's truth to the prophecy," he tapped Simone's face. "And this is where it lies."

"If this woman dies, we lose the dragon."

Trent nodded. "And if the dragon breaks free without me, the woman dies."

The Director stared at him, his gaze questioning. "Are you up for this?"

The question made Trent laugh. "Do I have a choice?"

"I suppose not. You must refrain from explaining the prophecy to Ms. Walker. She must be kept in the dark until we have a clear understanding of the outcome of the prophecy. We cannot risk her disappearing from our control."

"Understood, sir."

"Well then, Ancient, I believe you have a dragon to apprehend. Dismissed."

Trent glanced over at Ian. "Time to grab a flight and hop over the pond."

Ian nodded and they pushed away from the table, weaving through the conference room to the exit. "So, Trent the Ancient, explain to me exactly how you're going to convince a Dancer that doesn't understand a thing about this prophecy to let you release her dragon and save her life without her knowing that she even has a dragon that needs releasing or a life that needs saving?"

Chapter Two

Simone stood amidst moss-stained remnants of headstones long since past their own century. The church sat a half mile off the road. A tiny wooden structure nestled on an acre of land sheltered by a curve of blue-tipped mountain ranges that embraced slumbering souls. Grave markers carved with names which decorated most of the major roads were interspersed with the newer, more elaborate, marble statues signifying the progression of life.

She stopped and placed a bouquet of flowers on two headstones bearing her last name. With a deep sigh, she knelt and wondered at the irony of burying her entire family.

Her shoulders slumped in sadness. How could she have ignored Rosalyn for all these years? Better yet, how could her sister have forgotten about her? Life hadn't prepared her for the next task she needed to perform. It seemed twisted--this responsibility of having to bury a woman she hardly knew.

"Mama," her daughter whispered. "Are you all right? The service is about to start. I think we should go stand by the minister now."

"I'm fine, Jessie." She smiled, attempting to lighten the weight of grief. Squeezing the young girl's hand, her heart clenched.

The sun slid behind a single cumulous cloud that hung low in the atmosphere. Simone shivered as daylight dulled, emptying itself of spring's warmth and causing a sprinkling of goose bumps to answer the sudden chill. Was it from lack of sun or fear of the future?

Shadows of two men fell across her feet. She looked up to find Randy and a stranger standing up hill of the burial site. "What are they doing here?"

"Who, Mama?"

"Randy and that man over there."

Simone stared at the taller of the two. He topped Sheriff Tippens by several inches. Tilting his head to the side, he brazenly gazed back. Simone's chest tightened. The air thickened and prophetic fingers trailed up her arms, alerting her to his importance.

She reached for Jessie's hand. Warmth and comfort spread from her daughter's fingers, soothing and calming the ricocheting fear that currently attacked her insides. She glanced sideways and smiled down into the face that held her heart captive.

They turned as one toward the small congregation of mourners. They took their place, and Simone focused on the deep baritone of the minister's voice, allowing it to fold over her insecurity.

Next to her, Jessie vibrated with the innocence of the young. Brilliantly beautiful in bright white pants topped with a shirt splattered in teal-colored palm trees, she shimmered beneath the rays of the sun. She smothered a smile at the contrast her own peach sundress created against the minister's midnight cloak.

As Reverend Parker spoke lovingly from the Bible about a person he'd never met, Simone quickly scanned the area. There weren't many people. A group of women huddled together to the left of the casket, whispering among themselves and casting furtive glances at her and Jessie. She buried the impulse to stick her tongue out at them. Other than that, there was no one else.

She glanced back at the intruder, his stance proud and arrogant, a black cloud marring this beautiful morning. Simone frowned. The stranger stood amidst the azaleas and hydrangeas, leaning nonchalantly against the rough bark of a saw-tooth oak, he oozed superiority and self-confidence and struck a cord of familiarity that felt ominous.

The minister finished his sermon, closed the Bible, and glanced expectantly at Simone. Jessie nudged her side, startling her back to the task at hand. She stumbled forward to place a wilting rose on top of the polished casket. Her mind wandered once more as she realized that the small parade of people flowing past at a snail's pace were all strangers to her.

What prompted her to request her friends not to attend? A sign of her self-condemnation at not knowing the woman who now lay cushioned within the silken interior of the casket? Or had she been trying to hide this side of herself . . . the side only Rosalyn knew?

She now found herself standing beside her daughter, surrounded by people, all of whom had known her sister. Known a woman that Simone barely knew at all.

An elderly lady trailed the line of nameless faces. She wore a long black dress adorned with rows of glittering pearls. The outfit looked vintage. Under closer inspection, Simone confirmed its origin definitely warranted the mothball scent wafting in her direction. The woman's hand, gnarled with age, reached toward her. Bruised with purple veins and sunspots, it shook slightly, but grasped Simone's arm.

"If you have any questions, child, don't hesitate to call." Her voice was paper thin, raspy, and edged with age. She shoved a faded business card between Simone's fingers and patted her gently on the cheek. "Our Rosalyn would have liked your outfit," she chuckled, her laughter quickly lost between fits of choked breath.

Before Simone could answer, the woman hobbled off and was soon enveloped by a group of women.

"Scary," her daughter said.

"You can say that again," Simone agreed, absently shoving the card into her purse. Her eyes narrowed as she caught the profiles of the two men walking down the hill. They approached silently, scanning the grounds for who-knew-what. She cursed.

"Jessie," she spoke sharply. "Go wait in the car."

"Why?" her daughter asked with a slight tinge of a whine.

"Because I said so," Simone pushed her toward the vehicle and gave her a look that quelled any additional comments.

She stood and waited for them to approach. Randy, her own personal thorn-in-the-butt since seventh grade, moved in like a shark sniffing blood. She remembered he'd mentioned questioning her after the services but this was ridiculous.

The taller man, however, continued to hold her attention. He walked with long strides, easily outdistancing the sheriff. His presence pulled at her. She couldn't take her eyes off his face. Her skin began to prick and licks of fire seared the edge of her nerves. With conviction born from frustration and sadness, she slammed a wall up against the unwelcome sensations.

"Simone?" A deep, nicotine-damaged voice called.

She reluctantly turned away from the draw of the handsome man and stared Sheriff Tippens straight in the eye. "Randy, I'm surprised. This is lower than low, even for you."

The sheriff smiled at her, shaking his head. Delores wasn't around, and Simone had no doubt Randy was done with all pretense of compassion.

"Always quick with the tongue, Simone. But this is unavoidable."

She kept her eyes focused on Randy, ignoring the urge to stare at the man standing right behind him. "What can I do for you?"

"There's something about Roslyn that the Atlanta PD held back for investigative reasons."

No duh. She was still waiting on the police report from Atlanta. "Don't be provocative Randy. Spit it out." She closed her eyes in frustration. Simone desperately wanted to run away from these men.

"I have a few questions I'd like answered first," a deep voice broke through her inner ramblings.

The stranger spoke with a husky British accent. Startled, Simone blinked rapidly. She'd spent the past few moments ignoring him, pretending her pulse hadn't escalated to a pace normally reserved for early morning runs. His accent caressed her ears, smoothing his words. Narrowing her eyes, she glanced at him. An Englishman?

"I can't understand a damn thing this guy is saying," the sheriff mumbled beneath his breath.

Simone tilted her head as she scanned the Brit. He was tall, more than six feet, with layered black hair that'd probably been neatly groomed that morning but now appeared as if he'd stuck his finger in a light socket, leaving it disheveled and jagged. Kind of sexy, she thought, and then quickly inhaled when brilliant blue eyes turned to look directly into her face. Definitely sexy. A deep purring sound struck the inside of her ears, distracting her momentarily. "I'm sorry," her voice dripped with sweet southern hospitality that really screamed who-the-hell-are-you. "I don't believe I've had the pleasure of an introduction?"

"Trent Arnot, MI-5." The man reached beneath his jacket pulling out a badge of identification along with a business card which he handed to her.

She didn't glance down but felt the rich embossed letters that protruded from the slip of heavy linen paper.

She swallowed against the unease flooding her system. "Similar to our CIA, right? You've travelled all the way from the land of good ale and even better chocolate. I'm impressed. What on earth dragged you to these parts, Mr. Arnot?"

He frowned at her. Sheriff Tippens glared, and Simone returned both expressions with a sweet smile. She then focused on the stranger who stood as stone, an expression of intense disbelief widening his eyes.

What was he looking for? Sorrow? Fear? Concern? Simone wouldn't allow either one of these goons a glance inside her soul.

"Ms. Walker, have you been apprised of the details of your sister's death?"

One will come.

The man was definitely hot, she thought, silently amused that she was reiterating words from her daughter's current miniscule vocabulary for describing the opposite sex. Jessie would flip at his accent. It made him cute. Vulnerable.

"I have. How is it that MI-5 is investigating a supposedly open and shut suicide?"

"If you'd allow me a few moments of your time, I'll try to explain."

Tired and hot, all she wanted was to go home, take a dip in her pool and rock her troubles away on the front porch. Simone felt lost and slightly unhinged. "Can we do this another time?"

Trust above all else . . .

SHUT UP . . . Simone screamed silently.

"You don't seem to take death very seriously do you, Miss Walker?" Agent Arnot moved close.

Too close.

He'd definitely invaded her personal space. She could feel the heat of him, smell his woodsy aftershave, and despite the coolness her sundress afforded, Simone's palms were clammy and face damp with a light shield of perspiration.

"Oh, I take it seriously Agent Arnot. My parents died in their early fifties, my fiancé at twenty and now my sister at thirty-seven. So just exactly what are you insinuating?"

"Investigating this incident is only one part of my duty." His gaze glinted with danger, an unspoken threat that sent a chill through her soul.

Mine. Yours. Mine. Ours. Free. Fly. Take him. Trust. He's the One. Simone snuffed the voice. Her patience shot. The last thing she needed now was this running commentary from her invisible peanut gallery. "Oh? I suppose the other part would be to research and write a discourse on the difference, or lack thereof, between a redneck and a redcoat?" Simone retaliated.

He grinned and a sparkle of humor touched his eyes. The gaze whisked her away to fantasies of moonlit walks and laughter in the summer rain. She mentally shattered those fantasies, struck by how odd it was to think that way in the first place, and glared into his face.

"Not quite," he said softly.

"Then what?"

"Your protection, Miss Walker, as well as your daughter's."

Simone's mind raced. She couldn't focus on what he said. The man disintegrated into background noise drowned out by the sudden shouting in her head. *He's the one. Free me. Let me out. He's the one. Trust him. Trust him now . . .*

One of his spoken words struck a cord in her mind, muting the private chant.

Simone stepped back. "Premeditated murder?"

"Yes, Miss Walker. Haven't you heard a word I've been saying? You're next." He put his hands on her shoulders, pulling her close. His fingers were strong and firm, their heat sinking through her skin and into the depth of her soul. Agent Arnot bent forward, stared straight into her eyes and demanded her undivided attention with the intensity of his gaze.

"You," he said slowly. "Are the next to die."

He speaks the truth.

Julie Korzenko

Chapter Three

Simone rested her hand on the gleaming silver bar welded securely into the slate steps of her pool and touched one toe into the water. A breeze ruffled the leaves of the large magnolia tree to her left, tossing a light lemon scent in her direction. Memories of a dozen summers mingled with the perfume of late spring. With a shake of her shoulders, she stepped back and jogged to the deep end. Inhaling several short breaths and bracing against the impending shock, Simone dove into the crystal blue water.

She swam the length of the pool and stood at the base of the stairs in the shallow end. "Friggin' cold," Simone slicked back a mane of wet hair and snatched a large raft off the deck. With a quick slip and slide and a few ungraceful butt wiggles, her body rested leisurely upon the raft and began to warm from the afternoon heat.

Pushed by the current created from the skimmer jets, the raft floated back toward the deep end. Simone tilted her face to the sun and closed her eyes. A shrill cry reached from the heavens and tugged her upward, floating higher and higher on the breeze. Simone spread her arms in mimic of the hawk she pretended to be and trailed her fingers along the surface of the water. When her fingers touched nothing but air, she frowned and opened her eyes.

"*Fly,*" a hiss ricocheted through her mind, clearer and more precise than any of the other inner ramblings. "*Fly, little one, fly with me.*"

"What . . ."

"*Quiet. Feel the current. Inhale the air.*"

Simone listened and stared in disbelief at the scene beneath her. A curve of trees cast deep shadows upon the ground, plunging her sunny back yard into muted neutral colors. Upon the surface of her pool, she watched an empty raft circle lazily in the current.

She glanced down the length of her arm. The outline of her skin was soft and tainted an emerald green, nearly transparent. "I'm dreaming."

"Fly."

"You're talking."

"I don't talk. I command."

The presence pushed Simone higher.

"Okay, I'll play along. Who are you?" Soft laughter echoed around Simone. She closed her eyes briefly, enjoying the delusion induced flight.

"I am you. I am him. I am we."

The bizarre riddle ruined the incredible sensation of flight. Simone broke the connection, ignoring the frustrated rage that rumbled deep within her soul, and pulled her arms to her chest, rolling around and releasing herself from the clutch of whatever waking dream this was. "Wake up, Walker," she chanted and felt an immediate discharge and sensation of falling.

Twisting around, Simone face planted into the cold water of her swimming pool.

"Mama," Jessie yelled, running from the house and holding her arms around her waist. "Mama?"

Simone sputtered and spit water out of her mouth, pinching her nose against the stinging pain of inhaled chlorine. She gazed up into her daughter's face, ready to do some pretty bizarre explaining until she realized Jessie was laughing hysterically. "What?" Simone said, treading water and becoming irritable.

"Mama, are you okay? You . . . you . . ." Jessie hiccupped.

"I what?"

"You fell off the raft." She dropped to the ground, giggling and pointing at Simone. "You shoulda' seen yourself. Plop. Smack into the water."

Simone couldn't help but grin, her daughter's giggles contagious. "Hardee har har. I fell asleep." She must be more overworked than she thought, considering for even one second the possibility that she might have been flying. "Get me a towel, you brat."

As her daughter turned and raced back toward the house, Simone stretched her arms toward the sky. Her fingers splayed and sunlight kissed edges of ethereal green. "What the hell?"

***

Almost six and the heat showed no sign of dissipating. Didn't this place ever cool down? Trent tossed his bags on the bed, his keys on the dresser, and collapsed in the chair. His mind focused on Simone Walker.

She hadn't batted an eye. In a state of alarm at the lack of concern she displayed, he ran his fingers through his hair for the umpteenth time that day, ruffling an already unruly mess.

With a jerk, he sat up and yanked the sweat-dampened shirt from his body. Cool air blew through the vents. He closed his eyes as it washed over his chest. Rarely taken for British, his dark hair and slightly olive complexion spoke loudly of his mother's Spanish ancestry. In his line of work, this was often an advantage. He blended well in many European countries. His eyes, however, were an absolute Arnot trait. A vivid blue asset that now stung with lack of sleep and too much pollen.

An image of another set of eyes flashed through his mind. A chameleon. That's what they reminded him of. Green and blue specks of vivaciousness that expanded and retracted alternately, never remaining the same. Soft gray one moment . . . deep green the next. He knew those eyes well.

"Stunning." Trent grinned when he remembered how easily she'd insulted him with her mockingly-sweet smile and wit as sharp as his father's antique rapier. He stood, wishing his mind to rest, and stripped the remainder of his clothes off, throwing them viciously into his suitcase. He padded into the bathroom in search of the shower.

Cold water slapped a bit of sense back into place. "No way in bloody hell does this mean I have to do what the books say." His voice echoed against the tiled wall, mocking him. He exited the bathroom, doubt lodged firmly in his gut.

Trent pulled on a pair of khaki shorts and sat on the bed with his briefcase open. He took a generic beige file folder out and flipped it open. Before settling, he snagged a beer from the ice bucket and quickly downed its contents. The yeasty aroma filled his senses and a quick pang for home tugged at his heart. He inhaled the scent, allowing a quick memory of his local pub to settle him. As the cool liquid filled his mouth, he almost snorted it through his nose, too much carbonation. Swiping the back of his hand across his lips, he focused on the picture that lay within the file.

A landscape of softly rolling hills, a perfect background for the man that stood at the forefront, chin raised to the sky, hand securely . . . no, protectively, resting on the shoulder of a petite young woman. Short silver hair crowned his head, and his profile displayed the sharp features of someone used to getting his way. The woman stood to the background, the man's arrogance screaming silently at her unimportance. He stood to be noticed. In fact, Trent had been unable to identify the stranger beside him. Aristocratic and untouchable, that was the general consensus regarding Lawrence Gideon, Lord of Bromley.

A high pitch peal shattered the silence of the room. Trent snatched his cell-phone off the nightstand and answered it before it rang again.

"Arnot," he barked into the phone, gathering the papers he'd scattered into a neat pile.

"Gideon's out of the Ritz and in a small motel in your general area." Ian's voice sounded strained.

"Bloody hell," he leapt off the bed, and tossed an MI-5 standard issue navy-blue T-shirt over his head. He then tucked another MI-5 standard issue into the waistband of his shorts--a Walther PPK--and quickly donned a pair of leather docksiders. "When?"

"I just got word. Not long."

Trent paused at the door. "Any luck with forensics?"

"I'm heading back over to the lab now. The FBI bloke was right, the Atlanta PD is being more than cooperative."

"Right, then, I guess I'm off to ingratiate myself before we have our next victim."

Ian chuckled. "How are you holding up? Do you hear *her* still?"

Trent tilted his head back and stared at the ceiling. "Ian, I'm not in control."

"How's that?" He heard the concern in his partner's voice.

"It's stronger than I expected. And . . ."

"What?"

"For lack of a better description, she pulls at me." Trent lowered his voice. "Excites me."

Ian laughed. "Well, she is a dragon, mate. I think I'd be pretty damn excited, too."

"Not *her*, you idiot. Walker. Simone Walker."

"Oh," Ian paused. "What does the prophecy say about this?"

Trent rolled his eyes. "You know as well as I do. That when called I must answer. I think there's more though."

"I'll touch base with the Director. But don't forget about that little tidbit your mother had you reiterate in your teens."

"Nah, I still don't believe that. It's too," Trent shrugged at a loss of words. "Weird."

This time Ian really laughed. "Yeah, and this isn't? I'll dig around and see if I can't find some more books. There has to be more than what we know."

Trent smiled at the phone. "Thanks. I appreciate that." He snapped the phone shut, exited the hotel and climbed behind the wheel of his rented Land Rover. A quick call to the sheriff's office assured him that a deputy was in place outside Simone's home. If he lost her now, the damage to the legacy would be permanent.

His mind played over statistics as he sped up Old Highway 5 and turned off onto a secondary road. Tippens had driven him past her home prior to attending the funeral, and his brow creased in concentration as he replayed the directions in his head.

He slowed and verified the number on the small black mailbox, half hidden by an overgrown bush. Pulling off the road, he drove onto a long, serpentine, semi-gravel drive. It twisted and turned around patches of wild blackberry bushes and clusters of large leafed trees that brandished snowball size white flowers. Tall, bushy evergreens lined the end of the drive and stood at attention like proud green soldiers. The soft breeze blew them lazily in the wind, as if their prickly branches were waving him on.

Pulling forward, he rounded the final corner, and slammed his foot on the brake. The Land Rover skidded to a stop, kicking up dusty clouds. A magnificent house rose before a backdrop of brilliant green trees. Beautiful. Its many rooflines were scattered with chimneystacks that sketched a ragged line across the horizon.

Magic . . . this home of hers. He'd known she was an architect, but her file hadn't mentioned the level of talent. An octagonal conservatory skimmed the corner of the home. It reflected all the vibrant colors of the fading sun in its ten-foot glass windows. A massive front porch stretched from corner to corner, broken only by the inviting double doors that were entirely constructed of stained glass. The sheer number of windows was staggering.

Stacked rock cloaked the home in stately fashion. Trent glanced around at the many mini-gardens scattered across the front lawn like forgotten toys. Their haphazard trail testimony to the *free-spirited, color-outside-the-lines, never-go-from-point-a-to point-b-when-you-could-visit-point-c* that his research denoted was Simone Walker. The gardens were living proof. They offered an easy invitation to wander and explore. He shook his head in amazement.

He inched forward, keeping the speed to a snail's pace. The front door opened, and Simone walked out clad in cut-off jeans and a pink tank top. She stood with hands on hips and fire in eyes. "What are you doing here?"

Unfolding his frame from the confinement of the SUV, Trent's gaze soaked in legs already touched with the golden kiss of the sun. Her straight blonde hair swept down past her shoulders and swayed in silky ripples as she descended the short flight of stairs.

"Cat got your tongue, Sherlock?"

"Arnot," Trent grinned. "It's Trent Arnot, not Sherlock Holmes. He worked for Scotland Yard, and I work for MI-5. Different agencies. Different men."

"We'll see about that. It's nice to see you have a sense of humor."

"Why's that?" Trent met her halfway between the driveway and the porch. He tried to focus but her essence pulled him in, threatening to swallow all sense of sanity.

"I like a man with a sense of humor. Your type can be stuffy." Simone arched an eyebrow, challenging a response.

The call heightened the closer he moved. Trent exhaled and used the mental exercises drilled into him by the Director. She quieted and only Simone remained. "And what, exactly, is my type?"

"English."

"That's rather a generality."

"Okay, then. How about an uninvited, irritating Englishman?"

"You're in danger, Miss Walker." He stepped close, noticing that she worked hard at not backing away. The setting sun blazed a brilliant orange halo behind her head. Simone's eyes glittered gold. "And I'm here to protect you."

"Why?"

"It's my job."

"What could an MI-5 agent possibly have to do with li'l ol' me?"

"I work for a special division of MI-5. And right now, I'd rather not detail your sister's murder. But I ask that you trust me."

Simone inhaled sharply and turned to walk back to the front porch. She climbed the few stairs and stood, back ramrod straight, staring through the glass that adorned the front door.

"Prior to this past week, my sister and I hadn't spoken in years."

Trent was momentarily taken aback by this knowledge. He frowned and followed her up the steps. With a hand resting lightly on her shoulder, he turned her to face him. The intensity of color that scattered across her eyes intrigued him, and he bent slightly to peer more closely. Her pupils dilated, soft breaths tickled his cheek as she exhaled.

The lust that slammed into his gut stunned. He dropped his hand and moved away. *Mate.* Urgency pushed against his chest, but he ignored the need.

"What's the matter Agent Arnot? Did you see something in my eyes that scared you?"

"Hardly," he grunted. "Why were you and Rosalyn estranged?"

"Must you know?" Simone's voice was laced with sadness. "I mean, honestly, is it necessary for me to air my dirty laundry for your inspection."

Trent nodded. "I'm afraid so, Miss Walker. There's a man we're following who we believe was involved in your sister's death. He's very dangerous and as of fifteen minutes ago he was parked less than ten miles from here."

Simone's eyes widened. "So what do you want? An invitation to come in, make yourself at home, invade my life?"

He nodded and offered a slight smile. "Please."

They stood still, staring at one another. Trent felt the heat of her gaze and instead of irritating him, it sent sparks of electricity and awareness through his entire nervous system.

The urge to take, dominate and protect battled reality. He ignored the call. Ignored the pull of supernatural forces.

The front door opened, startling the two of them. Trent turned to face a young girl. Jessie Walker gazed at him with the openness and curiosity of the innocent. Pretty. Her mother was going to have a heck of a time keeping the boys away when she blossomed into womanhood. The foundation in place, it needed only a slight nudge from Mother Nature to spring forth the stunning female behind the naïve child.

"Jessie," Simone said. "Get back into the house."

"Who's this?"

"Back into the house . . . now."

"Mama, take a pill, I'm going." Jessie tossed Trent one more curious glance and retreated behind the glass door.

Simone sighed and glanced at him with those ever-changing eyes. "She's a good kid. But she's only thirteen, and I don't want her involved in whatever trouble you are bringing into my home."

"I'm only here to protect. She's in danger, as well."

"How can you expect me to believe anything you say? None of this makes sense. I've yet to receive a report from the Atlanta Police Department. According to them, Rosalyn committed suicide, but apparently you and I both know that's not true." A flush crept up Simone's face, and Trent realized that although her words were angry, she was frightened. And so she should be. "Your hunches aren't a help."

"It's more than a hunch, Miss Walker. I know things." Trent narrowed his eyes when he saw all color drain from Simone's face. She appeared panicked and grabbed his arm with icy fingers.

"What things?"

"I have facts, Miss Walker. Facts which lead me to believe the man responsible for your sister's death murdered several other women allegedly from the same ancestry as you."

"Facts?"

"Yes. Facts."

"Like what?" Simone challenged, color creeping back into her face.

Heat burned into his skin from her touch. The birds stopped their evening song as the gloaming settled in, a snippet of time frozen before reality crashed into fragile walls.

"Like the fact that Marjorie and Des Walker were not your real parents."

Chapter Four

Simone released her grip on Trent's arm. She stepped back, leaning against the stained glass door. Her face searched the vivid blue depths of his eyes. *How could he say she was adopted?* Her heart pounded with shock. He stepped toward her, and she held her hand up in an attempt to ward him off. Her fingers touched the soft, well worn fabric of his T-shirt and instead of pushing they gripped.

"What did you say?" she demanded. Her cheeks burned and anger swirled deep within her chest. She was furious at him. First, he barged in and tilted her world by insisting that her sister had been murdered and now he ripped away her parents. She didn't know who to strike at first, the person responsible for Rosalyn's death or the ghosts of her family. Or him.

"Didn't you know?" Trent stood still. He reached for her fingers and pried them off one by one. "I'm sorry," he said, closing his hand around her fist. "I hadn't considered the possibility that you were unaware of your parentage." The way he quickly averted his eyes convinced Simone he'd been confident of her ignorance.

"No, I'm certain you hadn't." What else did he know about her? Was he aware of the evil that crept closer and closer as the minutes ticked by? Did he have any clue as to the significance of Rosalyn's death, the danger that lurked around the corner, the gray-uglies, the fear of darkness? No. He knew none of this.

His presence, his aura, his entire being suffocated her.

She needed him to leave.

"Are you all right, Simone?"

Her name slipped from his mouth like a soft caress. The warmth of his hand sent shivers up her spine.

"I'm fine." Simone blinked then exhaled with a loud whoosh. "You certainly know how to take a woman by surprise, Sherlock." She pulled her hand out of his grasp, stepped to the side, and walked toward the edge of the front porch. Her hydrangeas were in full bloom displaying white balls tinged at the edge with a deep blush. They covered the bush from the tips of the branches deep into its dark recesses, where Simone imagined the fairies played.

She wanted Trent Arnot to leave her home.

This wasn't going to happen. She could see it in his eyes.

If you won't trust him then use him.

"Well that's the first sensible thing you've ever said."

"Excuse me?"

Simone turned and offered an apologetic smile. "I'm sorry. I tend to talk to myself."

She would take his information and accusations and find the mystery behind her sister's death.

His body, little one, use his body.

She felt her face heat with embarrassment as some very risqué mental pictures appeared within her mind. Simone blanked out the images and put her best hostess expression on her face.

"I guess you can come in. I'm about to cook dinner. I hope you're hungry." As Simone entered her home, its comforting embrace wrapped her in familiarity and strengthened her resolve. She headed into her kitchen confident that the irritating Englishman would follow.

"Your house is astonishing," he called from behind her.

Simone glanced back and stifled a laugh when she saw that he stood in her foyer looking around with the wide-eyed curiosity of a young child. His mouth hung slightly open, and he kept running long fingers through his hair.

She inhaled sharply. Bless his heart, but if he didn't meet all her midnight fantasies, she didn't know what did. *He's yours. Take him.*

"It's me," she said, a little too loud, crossing her arms over her chest and silently berating her unnaturally chatty inner-self. She followed Trent's gaze around the room. Each architectural creation held a piece of her. Whether directed at her own home or one she designed for a customer, Simone's heart remained tightly woven into her craft.

He dropped his arm and pierced her with another of his disconcerting stares. "You? Wow, you must be some woman."

"I manage-" She grinned and motioned him to follow. "But it's really all in the execution."

"The what?" He followed her through the sunken living room and up a step into the kitchen.

"The execution. It's all about searching a person's soul and finding their true desires." Simone's smile widened as he gawked at the layout. She glanced around her kitchen and attempted to envision it from his perspective. The room sparkled and shone with stainless steel. Evergreen countertops pulled the outside in, making the metallic appliances invaders from outer space. Dark cabinetry represented the tree trunks of her inner forest. She'd left many of the wall units vacant of doors in order to ease her cooking and preparation of meals. Moving into the heart of the room, she opened the refrigerator. "Want some tea?"

Trent wandered toward the French doors at the end of the eating area. Satisfied that she'd bought herself a few minutes to wade through the jumbled mess of her mind, she pulled the pitcher of amber liquid from the fridge and filled two tall glasses with ice. It took her several seconds before her hand stopped shaking, and the pitcher poured a steady flow.

"Please, feel free to go outside. I'll just be a moment." Simone wanted him out so the *take-him-take-him* voice would hush.

"I've not had a good cup of tea in twenty-four hours. Just a touch of

milk, please."

Simone frowned at the glasses in her hands. Putting them down, she turned to grab the kettle off the stove and slammed into his chest. With a quick jump, she winced as the countertop bit painfully into her lower back.

"What's that?" He asked, pointing to the ice tea.

"Tea?"

The man was too close, she swore silently. He dropped his head and peered around her shoulder.

"I was afraid of that."

She needed air.

"Mama?" A shrill voice called from the top of the landing. With a sigh of relief, Simone slid sideways and pointed up, indicating she needed to attend to her daughter. A nervous giggle escaped her lips, and she shook her head in an attempt to restore law and order to her raging hormones.

"What's up?" Simone had reached the top of the stairs faster than she'd cashed her first paycheck.

Her daughter stood with her arms crossed over her chest and a glare that demanded the truth. "Who's that man?"

"What man?"

"Mama-" Jessie declared with a laugh. "Have you completely lost it?"

"No, I . . ." The words wouldn't form. "I need to put my hair up. Dinner will be in about an hour, okay?"

"Mama, what's going on?"

"Nothing, Jessie, nothing at all."

"So, who's that man?"

Simone sighed deeply and decided that partial truth would be better than an entire lie. "He's a British investigator."

"What does he want with you?"

Why did children insist on asking questions? *At least she's inquisitive unlike her mother.* Simone rolled her eyes at the inner musing. Perhaps he knew about the book her sister mentioned. What was the name again? Simone swore silently. She needed to go write down everything her sister said to her in that weird conversation they'd had the night Rosalyn died.

"Mama?"

Simone offered her daughter a quick hug. "I don't know, sugar, but I'm about to find out." Simone walked into her room confident for the first time since Trent Arnot pulled his vehicle up the driveway. The only way to play his game would be to learn everything he knew and then determine her course of action.

Knowledge was power.

That's how she designed her homes and ran her business. She needed to apply that to this little wrinkle in her normally perfect world.

"Is everything all right up there?" Trent's deep voice resonated up the stairs.

Simone glanced toward his voice. Who was this woman that wanted to race down those stairs and fling herself into the arms she intuitively knew wanted to hold her?

A woman who needs that man. Take him!

"I'll be right down," she called then dropped her voice into a whisper. "You need to quit jabbering. Is sex the only thing you think about?"

Did I say anything about sex?

Simone sighed and shook her head. "Have you forgotten the full-Monty image?" She headed into the bedroom to change. "I cannot believe I am having this conversation with myself."

An unfamiliar laugh filled her head. It was musical and light and tugged an unwanted grin into place. *He wants you.*

"Of course he does. What hot blooded male wouldn't?" At that the laughter heightened and Simone joined in. "I am truly certifiable." Grabbing a piece of paper, Simone jotted down notes from the last conversation she had with her sister and from the dream conversation. She glanced at the stack of books Rosalyn shoved into her arms when they'd met and sighed. She'd spent too many hours wasted on anger and not enough time developing a meaningful relationship with her sister. All she had left were riddles and books full of writing she didn't understand.

***

Simone stood behind the sink washing the last of the dinner dishes. She glanced out the French doors, taking a quiet moment to appreciate the softened atmosphere as day slipped into night. Trent stood on the deck engaged in animated conversation with Jessie. Hands waved and laughter tripped back through the screen.

With a sigh probably louder than necessary, Simone put the last pan away and walked onto the back deck. Trent turned when he heard her footstep, and the sheen of pure happiness that transformed his normally chiseled features whisked all cognizant thought away. "Your daughter is a Monty Python fan."

Simone stood and stared. His smile faded into a lopsided grin, and he took a step toward her. "I know," she answered. "I have no clue how that happened." She turned and combed her fingers through Jessie's hair. "Time to head upstairs, sugar."

"Really?" Jessie offered a big smile. "I like talking to this guy. His words are funny."

"Scram."

Jessie gave her a quick hug. "I'm gone."

Night crept in and fireflies adorned the surrounding woods like sparkling Christmas lights. Trent reached out his hand, and Simone couldn't prevent the allure that had her moving forward and linking her fingers through his.

His touch was warm and familiar. She frowned, uncomfortable with the tide of feelings spreading through her system.

"She's beautiful," he said softly.

"Yes, she is."

He tilted his head and scanned her face, allowing his eyes to drop and absorb her body with a heated gaze.

"She's not as beautiful as her mother."

Simone shivered at the sudden raspy edge to his voice. She wondered what the smooth and sexy MI-5 agent would do if he knew the direction her mind was taking, a direction that had nothing to do with clothes and everything to do with touch. And certainly the thoughts were inappropriate. But she couldn't shake them thanks to the now silent inner voice. "You're pretty slick, Sherlock. Don't waste your breath on flattery, you're not my type."

"No?" He raised a brow and leaned close. "Your eyes say otherwise."

Time to put that mask back in place and pretend you're dealing with an extremely irate customer rather than a very sexy secret agent. "I think you mistake hospitality for attraction Agent Arnot."

"Too bad, I was kind of hoping you'd find me so irresistible that you wouldn't fight me regarding the protection plan I have in mind."

"Sorry. I don't find you the least bit irresistible." *Liar.* She wanted to tear off his clothes, devour his mouth, and jump his bones. Pictures of the two of them tangled in a white array of bed linens scattered through her already way too imaginative brain. The clarity of the vision brought fear and a startling truth.

She knew.

She was aware of exactly how it felt to lay within his arms, to feel his fingers brush her skin. Her heart stopped then lurched into rapid-fire percussion. And stopped again.

"Are you okay?" He tilted his head and offered a lopsided grin. "You've gone rather pale."

Simone stuttered and offered a sweet--"I'm fine."--praying he hadn't read her mind regarding the jumping bones thing or seen the recognition and panic in her face. "It's been a difficult day."

He gently touched her arm, and she jerked away from his caress. Images swirled and clouded her mind . . . pictures she couldn't understand. Didn't want to understand. "What are your plans, Agent Arnot?"

"Trent, please call me Trent." His expression sobered. "You daughter's too precious a commodity to risk with stubbornness." He moved behind her and pointed around her yard. "Your safety is at risk. You don't know what's out there."

Simone's heart broke. Stubborn wasn't the right word. Leery and cautious were more appropriate. What would straight-laced Agent Arnot say if she were to blurt out that dark, ugly shadows were slowly crowding the house waiting to take her daughter God only knew where?

What would he say to that?

And how about the little déjà vu awareness about his gorgeous body and her wild urge to feel those fingers upon her skin, *again*?

He'd think her insane.

She exhaled a shaky laugh and risked a glance at his face. An eyebrow pinching scowl marred sharp edges and obliterated his sexy grin. "It's not funny."

His voice sounded deep and menacing. "No, I suppose you wouldn't think so." The breath that tickled the nape of her neck felt uncomfortably arousing. She fought the urge to lean back and allow his arms to hold her. "I'm sorry?"

"Never mind, Sherlock. Let's go inside and have a real cup of tea. I think it's time for you to tell me the details behind why MI-5 is interested in me and my family."

Simone pulled away from him. The night pierced her skin, and she shuddered in response.

"Real tea? Without the ice?"

She laughed and nodded.

"I'm staying the night." He stated in a brisk and curt tone.

"No," Simone answered. That wasn't even a consideration. She'd call Randy and make sure that one of his deputies sat in the driveway all night, but this man was not staying in her house.

"Yes," Trent stated flatly.

"You're not staying," she stated emphatically resisting the urge to stamp her foot, the thought of him sleeping beneath her roof sent all kinds of mixed signals, causing her libido to jump into overdrive and her brain to scream stop.

"Yes, I am."

"No, you're not." Simone sighed heavily and stared at Trent, hoping that her eyes were throwing enough daggers to break through his arrogant armor.

"I'm staying," he said.

"I repeat, you're not staying. Randy will provide me with protection."

"If I have to, I'll sleep on your front porch. But I'll be damned if I'm leaving you to the likes of Lawrence Gideon."

"Who?" Bells shrieked through her head at that name. It was so familiar. Simone switched her focus back to Trent.

He moved until he was only a few inches away. His eyes blazed brightly in the soft glow of the solar lights. Simone "The man I mentioned earlier. Did you truly not hear a word I said at the cemetery today?"

"I heard you." *Kind of*.

"What did I say then?"

"You said-" She scrunched her face, trying to remember what he had been going on about. "Blah-blah-blah . . . murder."

"Murder? That's all you got out of that entire conversation?"

"I think it was the only thing I found important." Simone offered a cheeky grin and was taken aback when it wasn't returned. He was angry,

43

she realized.

And he'd every right. She'd ignored the importance of his visit, not wanting to complicate an already impossible situation. Her brain couldn't handle anymore.

Deep inside, past the sorrow and the pain, the truth lay hidden.

Gazing into his face a thin line of heat trickled from her left shoulder, sending shivers along her skin. His eyes narrowed, and he focused on the origination of the inner fire as if he felt it too. Simone frowned, troubled even further.

Fear cleared her vision. *Trust him.*

He was her open door.

Trent turned away from her and stared into the deepening blackness of the woods that cradled her backyard in a horseshoe of green, creating a secluded world of rustling leaves. The cicadas and tree frogs rose to the arrival of night in a crescendo of chirps and croaks that were a lullaby to Simone.

She watched as he clenched and unclenched his fists. His jaw worked furiously over some internal battle.

"Simone." He spoke softly. His tone indicated the gravity with which he wanted her to take his words. "There are powers at play that are beyond your comprehension."

So he thinks. She tilted her head and looked into his sea-blue eyes, remembering her game plan.

Time to listen.

Time to learn.

"Lawrence Gideon is a killer. I've trailed him from London to France and, finally, here to Atlanta. He doesn't just kill his victim. First, he tortures them. Mutilates them. When they are no longer of any use to him, he ends their life. He is especially adept and creative with the use of a knife. We're not certain why he's doing this. The only thing we know for sure is that every victim is related to him. You-" He turned and looked at her. "-And Jessie, are the last two living female descendents of the Bromley line."

"Bromley line?" A snake of apprehension crawled beneath her skin and tickled painfully. Had her sister been tortured? Her words trailed an eerie monologue through her mind. *He's almost done.* Fear sparked at the thought of Jessie succumbing to the same. She felt ill.

"Lawrence Gideon is the Lord of Bromley. The Gideons are a wealthy family. Their estate holdings top more than ten million pounds, which is roughly sixteen million dollars. If I read the genealogy correct, and I certainly don't profess to be an expert in that area, the women would be something akin to your third or fourth cousins."

"Did he torture Rosalyn?"

"Do you really want to know?"

Simone gazed into his eyes. Their depth held truth and honesty, but the flat gaze was laced with memories she imagined he'd rather forget. This was a man who wouldn't think twice about killing his enemy. He'd kill to protect her. She tugged on the ends of her hair not at all pleased by the direction her instincts were taking.

"Let's start at the beginning, Sherlock."

"Your parents?"

"No. I want all the details you have on Rosalyn's death. Where was she, who found her, what were the circumstances. Can you answer those questions?"

"Yes."

"Do you know where her personal belongings are?"

He frowned. "I'm not sure how it works in Atlanta. But I'll be happy to call the officer that walked the crime scene with me and find out where her stuff is. I assumed you'd already received what little she left behind."

"No."

He stared at her, his gaze unwavering. "You're not going to fight me anymore?"

"I'm not going to make you sleep on the front porch, let's just say that."

"Thank you."

"You're welcome."

They stood there gazing at one another. Evening settled with a display of brilliant stars, winking in infinite glory. A slow grin spread across Trent's face, softening his features and fading the tough-guy persona into the background. Simone smiled. "Let's go in and have that cup of tea."

"Good idea." He stepped quickly past her.

She closed her eyes and resisted the urge to grab his arm and pull him back.

Free me. The words floated in her mind, a soft plea. *Free me.*

Simone frowned and followed Trent, she focused on the dilemmas at hand. Her parents weren't her parents. MI-5 insisted her sister had been tortured and murdered. The killer apparently would target her then her daughter next, and her daughter was about to be swallowed by an entirely different type of evil--one she didn't understand.

Simone swore silently. Her life had taken on the disguise of a cheesy thriller. She needed to make certain not to fall prey to movie heroine stupidity and be caught creeping downstairs, weaponless, after a madman.

Chapter Five

A quick chill sent shivers across her skin. Simone did what she always did to combat the cold and lit the gas logs. She didn't care that summer knocked at the door, nor did she care when Trent tossed her a one-browed, what-the-hell-are-you-doing stare. Flames flickered against his face, casting small shadows of dancing ghosts.

Simone noticed the dark hue beneath his eyes and how drawn and haggard he appeared. "Let's talk tomorrow," she suggested.

"Why?"

"You're jet lagged."

"I won't argue with that. But don't you want to know about Rosalyn?"

The sudden thought of more talk and more confusion knotted her stomach. "It can wait." Her shoulder itched and she wanted to go upstairs and sit with Jessie.

He shook his head and glanced at her in surprise. "You're not the slightest bit curious?"

"Would it sound odd if I said I'm a bit afraid?"

Trent ran his hand through his hair and offered a half-hearted shrug. "That's understandable."

"After all that's taken place today, I think I'd like to just spend tonight absorbing what few things you've already disclosed to me. I don't want to go on system overload." Simone offered a smile. "Besides having you here in this house and danger . . . " she pointed toward the front door, " . . . just over there. It all seems a bit surreal."

"I can respect that."

A shrill ring interrupted the quiet atmosphere. Trent swore and snagged a small silver cell phone from his waistband. "Excuse me," he said and headed into the kitchen to take the call.

Simone could hear the deep rumbling of his voice but couldn't make out any words. She sighed and nestled comfortably into a chair that cushioned her body with the softness of a baby's blanket.

"Good night, Mama," Jessie called.

"Good night, sugar. Sweet dreams. I'll be up in a few minutes to tuck you in." She smiled as her daughter groaned and muttered about not being a baby anymore.

"Please don't come tonight," Simone whispered to the house. "Please." The shadows didn't answer.

Trent returned and sank down onto the couch. "That was my partner. He'll be here to relieve me in the morning."

"Around the clock protection?"

"Gideon's close."

Her eyes widened. Things were moving very quickly. "You said that you think Lawrence Gideon killed my sister?"

"Yes."

"Why?"

"Why did he kill her?" Trent shrugged and averted his eyes.

"No. Why do *you* think he killed her?"

"It was the same modus operandi used on the other females, and he was the last one to see her alive."

Frowning, she tried to work through everything but her mind wasn't cooperating. "Do you think we're in danger tonight? I have places I can take Jessie."

"No. I think you're safe. He normally approaches his victims first and tries to develop a relationship. That'll be his plan for tomorrow." Trent leaned forward and braced his elbows on his knees. Tired eyes offered her unspoken comfort.

Simone knew she should ask him to leave. He'd admitted that she wasn't in danger tonight. But suddenly, that seemed like the last thing she wanted. "Want me to show you to the guest room?"

"Yeah," he smiled at her. "That would be great." He winked, and her stomach galloped.

Get a grip, Simone, she mumbled to herself and rose from her chair and indicated with a slight wave that he should follow her down a side hallway.

"The guestroom isn't upstairs?" he asked.

"Nope. It's right here." She opened the door at the end of the passageway and stepped into a large room that contained a king-sized bed, private bath, and amenities normally supplied by an upscale hotel. She loved being able to provide a pleasant space for company to relax in. The room had a beautiful view over her lake, and she walked over to gaze out the window. Moonlight glittered brightly upon the glass surface of the water, tracing a wide path from one grassy edge to the next. A whippoorwill called in the distance. Simone opened the window, allowing the pungent scent of magnolia and honeysuckle to seep in.

"The view is," Trent said, clearing his throat softly, "mesmerizing."

"Thank you. I tried to build the house to take advantage of this gorgeous setting. My room looks over the lake as well."

"You mean there's something beyond the vision of you bathed in moonlight?"

Simone's pulse leapt a mile-wide canyon. She turned to find him framed within the doorway. He leaned lazily against the jamb, arms crossed over his chest, studying her. His eyes were shaded by the darkness that shadowed that corner, and she couldn't read his expression. "You shouldn't say things like that."

"I know."

"Then why did you?"

He moved into the room with long, easy strides. The large suite suddenly felt as confining as a jail cell. "Because you take my breath away."

"You're making me nervous."

"I'm making myself nervous."

"Then stop."

Trent paused. Simone realized he was a breath away from gathering her into his arms. She couldn't allow this to happen. She didn't know this man.

Something buried deep inside disagreed.

A tingle of awareness infused her, preventing her from moving. She gazed into a face that should be strange, but it wasn't. An unearthly screech filled her mind. It rattled her to the core, and she strove to hide her alarm behind a polite smile.

He's the one. Free me.

The silent chant increased in speed until she mentally screamed for it to shut up.

Simone realized Trent hadn't moved an inch. His breath was slightly ragged, and the tangy scent of his aftershave assaulted her senses. She still couldn't decipher his expression.

"I'll leave you," she whispered and quickly skirted past him before he reached out to stop her.

***

Trent inhaled deeply. The absence of Simone enabled him to draw air into his starved lungs. He hadn't lied; she truly took his breath away. He swore softly and violently at the empty room, pacing in a tight circle, then moved to the space she'd vacated and studied the view beyond the windows.

Banging his fist against the wall, he wished fervently that he were in London and could work out this gut-wrenching frustration with an evening of highly energetic sex. Something told him that the convenient, sex-only relationship with his neighbor, Isabel, would no longer satisfy what he craved. He wanted Simone Walker. He burned to caress her skin, to slowly peel back that protective layer that screamed Miss Independence. He wanted to dominate, to claim her for himself. To succumb to prophecy.

With a feral growl, he strengthened his resolve against the seduction her presence offered, and the invitation her eyes unwittingly displayed. It wasn't honest, though. He needed to separate emotion from his job. Their union would be completed as dictated by the prophecy, but his heart would remain under his control, no matter what.

With another emotional punch to himself, Trent left the guest room. He went out the side door and jogged to his car. Grabbing a flashlight, he walked slowly down her driveway. He'd noticed the deputy's car parked across the street earlier and wanted to verify that he'd be there all night.

When he reached the side of the police vehicle, Trent was astounded at what he saw. The man inside was sound asleep. Deep rumbles vibrated out of his chest and a slight line of drool trickled down his open mouth. With a snort of disgust, he ran back up the drive. He entered Simone's house and walked through the entire downstairs. Every window locked. Every door dead bolted.

He picked up his phone and dialed the Director General. A gruff voice answered. "This better be bloody good, Arnot. It's three a.m."

"Sorry, sir. I need guidance." Trent sat on the edge of the bed.

"Ian reported earlier that there were some complications with the awakening."

Trent sighed. "I would like permission to explain to Miss Walker the details," he paused and searched the room for his words. "All the details, sir, of this investigation including what is happening to her personally."

"Request denied. Is that all Arnot?"

Trent bowed his head and swore with silent anger. "Yes, sir. That's all. Sorry for disturbing you."

"The awakening is the biggest phenomena in centuries. It *is* all encompassing. You have permission to contact me any time of day. Good night, agent."

"Good night, sir."

Disappointed, Trent decided he'd better attempt to sleep or else he'd be worthless tomorrow.

***

Free me.

The constant hammering of those two words against her brain set Simone's nerves on edge.

"Go away."

Simone sat on the edge of her bed running the business card she'd received from the old lady through her fingers. Fear for her daughter had her reaching for the phone and dialing the number. It was late, but she didn't care.

A shaky voice echoed across the line. "Hello?"

"Mrs. Lackingbird, this is Simone Walker. I met you today." A brief silence and then she heard a soft sigh.

"Is everything okay, dear?"

Tears pricked at the back of her eyes, and she scrunched them close. "No. I don't think so."

"What can I do for you?"

"Do you know if Rosalyn was searching for a book called The White Book of Rhydderch?"

"Tell me what's happening."

Simone calmed the frustration that rattled her chest. She wanted answers. "I believe Rosalyn thought the answer to the problems that I'm experiencing is in that book."

"That's correct."

Surprised, Simone sat up, paying a bit more attention to the old woman. "Do you know what I'm talking about? Did Rosalyn speak with you about my shadows?"

Silence.

"Mrs. Lackingbird?"

"When you find the book, call me. It needs to be read in conjunction with another volume. Then the answer will be revealed."

More friggin' riddles. Simone sighed and decided that at least she had a plan of attack. "I'll do that. Good night."

"Good night special one."

She hung up shaking her head at that last comment. Special? What a laugh.

Free me!

Crazy was more like it.

***

Trent bolted out of bed, fighting to gather his bearings.

Danger. His sixth sense dove into overdrive. She called to him in licks of fire that stretched invisibly through the air.

He pulled on shorts, grabbed his gun, and exited the room. Pausing beneath the stairs, he closed his eyes, and focused on the sounds of the house. A soft moan drifted down the serpentine banister.

Trent held the gun before him and crept up the spiral staircase, following the cries. His nose flared and shivers of apprehension skittered like a million spiders up and down his back. Where were they?

A wail pierced the quiet, and he raced to the nearest door. With a soft nudge, it swung open. Back to the wall, Trent cautiously entered the room.

The room cloaked itself in black, and he could barely discern the figure of Simone. She appeared to be hunched over the bed. Moving with the grace and silence of a trained hunter, he stepped closer to her.

She knelt on the floor, her arms draped across the sleeping figure of her daughter.

Soft whimpers escaped her lips, and her shoulders were shaking beneath a force he couldn't see. Tucking the gun away, he placed a hand upon her back, bending to whisper her name. She shuddered and turned anguished eyes in his direction.

Pools of fear were reflected in their watery depths, wrenching an unexpected response. He wanted to kill. His instincts screamed to destroy the source of her fear.

Death caressed his neck, and he whirled around to seek his hidden enemy. His gun back in hand, he raced to the door. With a flip of a switch, the room was bathed in the light of the overhead ceiling fan.

Nothing.

What was she afraid of?

Sweat poured down Simone's face, and she shook her head at him, trying to shoo him out. Trent walked back to her and knelt at her side. She tried to speak, but her voice failed her. He wrapped a protective arm around her, pulling her away from the bed and cradling her shivering body. Whatever endangered this family, it wasn't anything he could shoot.

A nightmare? No, Simone was awake. His skin prickled. Trent scanned the room carefully noting each corner, every shadow. Nothing. But his brain registered danger. And the dragon had called.

Simone clung to him, her touch burning his bare skin. She nestled against his chest, absently stroking her fingers along his arms. A trail of fire followed each touch. He could feel the tears trickle from her eyes, and his gut tightened in anger. What stalked her?

He patted her back and murmured soft platitudes against the silken strands of her hair.

He glanced up to look at Jessie. She slept peacefully.

Simone stiffened. His heart lurched, and he loosened his hold making sure she was all right. Finally, a long shuddering breath escaped her lips. She blinked rapidly and slipped from his embrace.

"You shouldn't be in here."

"I thought you were in danger." He rose and reached down to help her to her feet.

"No. I must've been sleepwalking." She smoothed her hair back. The movement pushed her breasts against the wafer thin T-shirt that barely covered her. A knot of desire blasted through his resolve.

He needed to leave.

"I'll go check the doors." Trent hastily retreated from the room. Now, he swore, he was the one sweating. His skin burned. His soul screamed. Prophecy strangled. But it wasn't time.

He pulled open the front door and stepped into the night, gasping for air.

Lightening slashed the sky with white streaks of vengeance. A massive blast of wind hurled itself around the house, tipping unsuspecting trees nearly to the ground. Danger, the thunder rolled.

He tilted his face to the wind, the pull of confusion and tug of anger mimicked the jagged bolts of white light and bellow of thunder. He didn't know if he questioned the strange occurrence upstairs or the maddening enticement of Simone. Trent raised his arms and released his power in a roar of frustrated rage, sending streaks of iridescent lightning into the night.

Chapter Six

Simone sat on the edge of Jessie's bed. She struggled against lying down and submitting to the exhaustion hammering her body. Her daughter slept. Tonight's danger faded quickly, and it amazed her that she'd managed to avoid the horrible stab of pure evil that normally permeated these occurrences.

What had she done differently? The bubble finally worked.

Her mind replayed the actions of the past few hours. The only anomaly was the appearance of Trent Arnot. *He's the one.* Had he somehow scared the gray-uglies away? *Are you deaf?* Or had she managed to recite a few words that actually had an impact? *No, I think simple.* Simone sighed in exasperation. "Please be quiet." She mentally pounded against her dead brain cells, willing them back to life. If she could understand what happened, she might have a chance at protecting her daughter.

What was this force? *If you free me, I will tell you.*

What did it want? *YOU!* The pain that sliced through her head stunned Simone. Anger rattled her soul, inflicting invisible wounds.

"Stop it. Stop it, now."

It ceased, and she breathed a sigh of relief.

She smoothed the hair on Jessie's head, amazed that the child hadn't felt any of the traumas that unfolded within her room. Simone prayed fervently that it would continue this way. She silently beseeched the night to grant her the continued perception of her unseen enemy, and the lasting innocence of her daughter.

Simone rose and walked around the bed, peering closely into the shadowy recesses of the room. She was confident that whatever made an appearance this evening was long gone. The stench faded, and her gut ceased to burn. She paused at the door, placing her forehead against the wall.

What had Trent witnessed?

Her chest tightened, and she inhaled deeply. "Don't panic, Simone," she whispered against the hard surface, her breath warming the cool wallpaper that depicted small bouquets of pastel flowers. Her stomach clenched, and Simone battled the urge to cry. Another layer of troublesome thoughts weighed upon her shoulders.

"Simone?"

With a start, she snapped her head up to find Trent standing on the other side of the threshold. She'd forgotten he wore no shirt. His shoulders spanned the width of the opening, and the bedroom light shone softly on a tanned chest that was scattered lightly with black curls. They wove around his nipples and dove in a deep-v toward a part of his anatomy she definitely couldn't think about at the moment. The feel of his skin beneath her fingers still singed her nerve endings.

"Simone," he repeated softly. "Are you all right?"

"I'm fine," she lied. "Jessie had a nightmare, and it took longer than expected to calm her down. I'm sorry if I woke you."

Trent narrowed his eyes and threw her one of his I-can-see-right-through-you stares. His gaze dropped lower, skirting her scantily clad figure. The cropped T-shirt and low-cut boxer shorts, she knew, were too revealing. She closed her eyes and willed her body not to respond to the very heated glare that was now focused on her.

Her nipples, however, decided to ignore her. They hardened and pushed against the lightweight cotton. The brush of the fabric and overwhelming nearness of the man before her burned a line of fire to her core. She gulped and opened her eyes.

"I'm going downstairs," Trent whispered hoarsely. "Before I do something we'll both regret."

She nodded, gripping the edge of the door with shaking fingers. Simone watched as he descended the stairs. He threw one last look over his shoulder. The desire in that simple glance slammed into her, driving her forward, across the hall, into the safe haven of her bedroom.

What was she doing?

Fool. You are such a fool. There was no anger in the silent words this time only resignation.

Simone closed her door and leaned against it.

Why did she suddenly feel that life as she knew it wasn't enough? That she was missing an integral link? That suddenly her full house was a card short? She cursed Trent Arnot violently and stalked into her bathroom, slamming the door behind her.

***

Simone knew he watched. She willed her hands not to shake as she dropped the last spoonful of freshly ground coffee into the canteen. The aroma of the rich Hawaiian blend permeated the kitchen, causing her mouth to water in anticipation.

"What're you doing?" A deep voice rumbled behind her.

"Making coffee."

"In that?"

Simone frowned. Okay, she admitted silently, her old camping coffee pot was a bit worse for the wear, but it certainly didn't deserve this level of disdain. "Yes," she stated emphatically, turning to face him. "In this."

"It's a bit-" He grimaced lopsidedly, making Simone grin. "-Rustic. Don't you think?"

"Just wait, Sherlock. This'll be the best damned coffee your mouth has ever tasted."

"I'll reserve judgment."

"Okay, and while you're doing that, you can tell me everything you know about Lawrence Gideon, Lord-Almighty of Broo-ha-ha. I specifically want all the pertinent information regarding Rosalyn, myself and my daughter."

"I need caffeine first."

Simone flipped the gas stove to high, placed the lid over the camouflage green metal pot that was covered with small dings and divots from the many camping trips she and Jessie had gone on, and walked into her office. She couldn't help but smile when she heard the footfall of her ever-faithful British Agent following closely on her heels.

He was sexier than any 007 she'd watched cavort across the silver screen. And, he was hers. Well, not really hers, but a few moments of induced fantasy were healthy for any female, Simone decided. Trent Arnot was a walking, talking ticket to the current blockbuster playing in her head.

"What does your T-shirt stand for?" Trent asked.

She glanced down at the black top and shrugged absently.

"It's an architect's rendering of a medieval castle."

"Hmmm, interesting."

"My staff," she smiled. "thought it appropriate."

"Why?" He frowned and stared into her eyes. She was suddenly embarrassed and shook her head.

"It's not important."

"I'm curious."

"If you really must know it's an inside joke regarding my knight in shining armor."

Trent raised his brows and leaned against the wall of her office. "Tell me," he grinned, "about your knight in shining armor."

"He doesn't exist. However, my crew is constantly on the lookout for him. I figure when they finally find me a man willing to show up in armor and riding a white steed, I might consider dating him."

"I see. You're waiting for your prince."

"No," Simone answered with a smile. "I'm waiting for my king."

Suddenly, it occurred to her that she'd allowed him to see more than she was comfortable with. She quickly sat behind her massive antique partner's desk and signaled for him to take the vacant chair opposite her. She watched him absorb the half-done sketches that littered her walls. He frowned when a patch of pictures caught his attention.

"That's Roz," she said.

"Hmm, I recognize her." He walked to the small cluster of color photographs that were pinned beneath a large blueprint. His hands were pushed deep into the pockets of his shorts. "She looks different. I just can't pinpoint what it is."

"I can," Simone whispered.

Trent turned and burned her with an intense look. With raised eyebrows, he silently begged her to continue.

"She's innocent. She hasn't been tainted."

"Tainted?" He walked back to the desk and sat down. "What do you mean by that?"

"Oh," Simone shook her head and flicked her hands in the air, dismissing her words as silly. "It's nothing. Just ignore me."

"Everything means something, Simone. What do you mean when you say tainted?"

She sighed wishing with all her might that she could inhale and snatch back those words.

"I mean tainted by life." She tried to explain. "You know? Bitter. The horrible knowledge of an ugly truth. The acceptance that the world hasn't held up its end of the bargain."

"Is that how you feel?"

"No." She answered quickly. "Quit playing Freud."

Trent chuckled and sat back. "I love the way your eyes change color. One minute gray, the next green. Amazing."

Simone stared at his own set of alluring sexy-as-sin eyes. They touched a part of her soul in the way no man's had ever done before. She felt like she was afloat within a vast ocean; alone, afraid, yet disturbingly secure within the knowledge that he was there . . . a constant protecting force.

A hiss and spark pierced the silence, and she swore loudly, leaping from behind her desk and racing into the kitchen.

"The coffee," she yelled, hoping that Trent didn't take her sudden exit to be more than what it was. She'd be the last one to openly admit the intensity with which he affected her.

Simone moved around the kitchen in remote control mode. She poured two steaming cups full of the aromatic liquid, liberally lacing each mug with cream.

"Here you are," she said, hurrying back to her desk and placing the hot cup before Trent.

"No sugar, I hope." He peered into its vanilla depths and frowned slightly.

"Nope. Not a crystal's worth." Simone settled back into her chair. Their eyes connected and an arc of electricity snaked across the table, shocking her into silence.

"How'd you know I liked cream?"

"I--" She fumbled with her words, tripping and garbling her response. "Guessed. It wasn't too hard. You take milk in your tea so you must like cream in your coffee. Right?"

"I suppose," he said, his voice soft and eyes suddenly distant.

Simone scrutinized her nails. The tone of his voice left a trail of goosebumps along her skin. *He's yours.*

"Look at me." Trent demanded.

She slowly lifted her head up.

He sat back, leisurely draping himself within the leather armchair. His presence exuded confidence and a knowledge that he was always right. Simone narrowed her eyes and made a silent promise to prove that he didn't know anything. He didn't know her.

"What?" Simone felt the power. It burned its way across her left shoulder and touched Trent's mind. He narrowed his eyes as if he felt the pull of the strange force.

"I hear her."

Simone jumped. "Who?" *Me, little one. He hears me.*

He seemed shaken. "Jessie. Is she up?"

"No. No, I don't think so." He watched her intently. She fought against picking up a pencil and running its cool, sleek familiar touch through her fingers. She wasn't going to fidget.

"I must have been mistaken." Trent leaned forward and gathered her hands into his, pulling her closer. She leaned into the desk's sharp edge and smiled back at him.

He didn't scare her.

Yeah, right.

"Fine," she quipped. "Tell me everything about my sister's death."

With a jerk she pulled away from him and grabbed the nearest pencil. It slid into her palm and through her fingers like water. She loved the feel. With quick motions, she sketched an ancient Catholic cross onto the pad before her. She didn't know why, but the ornate corners and intricate design had been plaguing her mind like irritating gnats. She needed to put it down on paper.

Trent excused himself with the promise that he'd be right back. She barely heard him. The call of the drawing beneath her was louder than any spoken word. Her pencil sketched, erased, shaded, and outlined the cross with expert strokes.

"That's bloody impossible," Trent spoke in a rush of words.

She glanced up, released from the trance of creation.

"What is?"

"That." He indicated stabbing at the scratch pad. "Look at what you've drawn."

She looked down and furrowed her brows. The cross was beautiful, and she wondered if the jewelers next to her office might be able to duplicate it.

"It's gorgeous." she sighed. "It'd make a great gift for Jessie, don't you think?"

"It made a great gift. It was given to Mary Queen of Scots."

"Mary?" she repeated, slightly baffled.

"That's a perfect rendition of the cross she carried to her death. Whatever possessed you to draw it?"

Simone was stunned. She didn't know how to answer his question.

"I often see things in my dreams that I need to create on paper. I call it my muse. An idea, or picture of a room, or piece of furniture floats in my brain for days. And when it materializes into a visible sketch, I put it on paper. That's what I did with this cross."

She laughed nervously and closed her sketchpad. "I must have seen this in Jessie's history book and a corner of my brain held onto the image."

"Normally, I'd say you're right. However, the fact that Lawrence Gideon has just acquired this piece from a British Museum for a private showing has my sixth sense tingling."

"You're stretching coincidences once more, Sherlock. It ain't nothin' but a thang," she drawled thickly, dismissing the matter with a shrug of her shoulders. Kind of freaky, though.

"I disagree. May I please have that sketch?"

"Why?"

"Because, Simone, it could become extremely relevant to my investigation."

"A sketch of a cross? You've got to be kidding me."

"Right now, I'm not feeling particularly funny. Hand over the pad, please."

"Oh, for crying out loud, this is ridiculous." Simone snatched up her sketchpad, ripped the offending page out, and threw it across the table at Trent.

"If you don't put any relevance into this picture, then why do you have a problem giving it to me?" Trent retrieved the paper, made a quick notation on the back of the page, and shoved it into the file folder he'd retrieved while she'd been busily drawing.

"Because, we need to be researching pertinent facts not traipsing down the mystical lane of crosses."

"We? Since when have you become involved in this investigation?"

"Since," she smiled benignly, "you so rudely barged into my life and confirmed my sister was murdered. You don't think I'm going to sit back and allow a crazed killer to threaten my daughter and not do anything about it, do you?"

Trent sighed and opened the manila folder. He pulled out several black and white photographs along with a stack of typed paper. He handed everything over to Simone.

"What're these?" she asked, picking up the photographs.

"Those are shots of your distant cousins. Each female, each within five years of your age."

She flipped through the stack. The women were all of various heights and shapes. Some were disconcertingly beautiful . . . others just average. None of them bore any resemblance to her or her daughter.

"What do these have to do with Rosalyn?"

"They were her cousins as well."

"And what do you want me to do with them?" She asked, waving the cluster of black and whites in the air.

"Say a prayer."

"For what? Do these women need redemption?"

"Not anymore. They're all dead."

Simone paused and slowly laid the pictures on the desk. "Did that man kill them all?"

"Not all. Have you ever heard of the disease porphyria?"

She pursed her lips and thought for a moment.

"No. What is it?"

She was becoming increasingly nervous. Murder? Disease? What next.

Blocking the fear, she looked across the table and studied Trent. She was trying to ignore the fact that her pulse raced into hyper-speed every time Agent Arnot leaned forward and brushed his arm against hers. She'd thought the desk would act as a barrier between them. She'd been wrong.

His legs and arms were easily long enough to softly touch her bare skin, leaving tantalizing burns of a desire and need she'd never felt before. His voice, as he explained the details of this disease she'd never heard of, was deep and uncomfortably soothing. Simone tried to concentrate on what he was saying but failed.

She stared at his lips.

She wanted this man to kiss her.

When she looked up, her gaze was met by a lazy, seductive, I-know-exactly-what-you're-thinking grin.

"You didn't hear a word I just said?" He sighed.

"I was doing some internal search on this porphyria thingy."

"Hmm, is that what you were doing?"

"Yes." Simone couldn't prevent the flush that rapidly fanned up her face.

"You were licking your lips." He waggled his brows, and his grin spread into a full-fledged smile that displayed an array of startling white teeth.

"I was not," she laughed.

"Yes. You were."

"I'm sorry I tuned you out." Simone quickly changed the subject. "I was afraid. When that happens, I seem to automatically think of something else. It's a defense mechanism."

"What exactly were you thinking of?" Trent licked his lips suggestively, and she fought to smother her laughter but didn't succeed as it burst forth in an extremely unladylike snort. He grinned and held his hand up. "Truce. I'm sorry, that was absolutely unprofessional. Let's get back to work. Why were you afraid?"

"I," she paused and inhaled deeply. "I believe you. This is very difficult to absorb, but for my daughter's safety, I have to trust you. Those girls are all dead. Am I next and then Jessie?" Her voice cracked. She swallowed and tried to calm the terror that filled her soul.

"I'll not let him near you or Jessie. Simone, listen to me." He leaned forward and forced her to focus on his words. "I will never let anything happen to you. I promise."

"What is porphyria?" she whispered, shaken to the core by his response. It touched something she wasn't willing to acknowledge.

"Porphyria is a bizarre blood anomaly that has been dated back to the early monarchy."

"Let me guess. Mary Queen of Scots?"

"Yes. It's genetic. Lawrence Gideon is a descendent of Mary's and . . ." Trent paused and Simone knew what he was going to say.

"And, so am I right?"

"Right."

"I don't have this porphyria." Wouldn't she know if she were sick?

Trent stared directly into her eyes. She felt rather than saw the tension escalate. He remained motionless, and she couldn't determine specifically what direction his thoughts were taking.

"Porphyria is a blood disease?"

"Correct." He grabbed his briefcase off the floor and extricated a file. "It's relatively unknown probably because the symptoms are so varied from person to person as well as strain to strain. According to my research, each individual reacts differently."

Simone leaned forward and accepted the stack of papers he handed her. She scanned them with an eye familiar to pulling pertinent information from excessively written paragraphs. Her clients were always writing flowery descriptions of their vision for their new home. Her mind trained on what was important within the sentences. "It says here that there's no cure?" Another jolt of fear stabbed her gut. She needed to have Jessie tested immediately. "Look at all these treatments marked experimental." She glanced at Trent. "Are you telling me that we're no further along than the fifteenth century in defining this disease?"

"They didn't even understand it existed in the fifteenth century. Scientists and historians have determined through the current blood line that more than likely porphyria was the root cause for the reign of the mad kings."

Simone shook her head. "Mad kings?"

Trent cocked a brow. "Did you sleep through history class?"

"Obviously."

He grinned. "Straight forward and honest. You're my kind of lass."

She rolled her eyes. "Continue."

"Right. Back to History 101." Trent fiddled with a pen he picked up from her desk. "Going as far back as Caligula, madness has been an element of the monarchy from Rome to Denmark. But beginning in the fourteenth century, there was a predominant number of demented kings from Charles VI all the way through George III. The incestuous marriages that were common through Europe propagated the disease."

Simone narrowed her eyes. "Madness?" She swallowed against the thought that all of these night terrors were actually manifestations of a mentally unstable mind. Like her ancestors. Not to mention her inner voice that had suddenly taken on a personality of its own.

Trent nodded and flipped through his notes. "Let's see -- this lists several types of cerebral symptoms. Delirium, confusion, anxiety, insomnia, sensory loss, seizure and hallucination are only a few. Also there's some neurological indicators. Muscle weakness, paralysis, pain in the arms and back not too mention dyesthesia which means," he turned a page. "Numbness, tingling and burning sensations." Glancing up, he frowned. "Why?"

Sitting back in her chair, Simone turned slowly and gazed out the window. Her shoulder burned and the constant tingle along her nerve endings suddenly became more than a nuisance or unexplained phenomena.

"Simone?"

"What else does this disease encompass?"

"Abdominal pain, nausea, loss of appetite, fever, sweating, blistering, tissue scarring. All kinds of symptoms."

Before she could delve into him with a barrage of questions, his cell phone interrupted them. He flicked the annoying little silver phone from his belt and answered the ring with a brusque hello. He listened for a second, nodded, and snapped the cell shut.

"That was my partner."

"Watson?" She formed a bubble, sending the fear away.

He sighed and shook his head. "Ian."

"Trent and Ian? How British."

Not taking the bait, Trent rose from the desk and walked around to stand next to her chair. She didn't like this new proximity. It put her at a disadvantage.

"Lawrence Gideon is on his way here." His tone denoted the seriousness of his statement.

"Are you sure?"

"Positive."

"Okay, then. I suppose it's time to put my pleasant face on. Are you staying or hiding?"

"As much as I like the idea of sliding beneath your bed and playing Peeping Tom, I think I'll stay. This creep doesn't have any clue who I am or that MI-5 is even investigating his whereabouts."

"Which means that I shouldn't have any idea who he is, right?"

"Correct."

"So really what you're saying is that I get to be your Watson."

"You could put it that way." He grinned and ruffled her hair like she was nothing more than a little girl.

"Keep your hands to yourself, sugar." Simone stood up and ran her fingers across her head, trying to straighten the mess he'd created. Trent laughed and headed out of the small office. She followed and wondered silently when he'd begun leading. Had he been manipulating her into this position the entire time? Was this his plan?

She jumped when the door chimes pierced the quiet morning.

Trent grabbed her arm as she moved past him toward the door. "Listen, about porphyria, Gideon's is very advanced. Don't be shocked by what you see."

"Let go. I've got this." She softened her words with a smile, not knowing why she felt irritated all of a sudden. It must be nerves.

With a quick look at Trent, Simone walked to the foyer and opened the door.

The man on the other side stood beneath the shade of her porch. He was tall, very slender and Simone swore she could see ripples of evil flow off him like an invisible waterfall. Her breath caught, and she fought to calm herself. *Out. Let me out, right now. Little one, you need to let me out.* She silently hissed the voice into submission and concentrated on Lawrence Gideon.

"May I help you?"

"Simone Walker?"

"Yes. And you would be . . .?"

"Miss Walker my name is Lawrence Gideon and to make a tedious story bearable, I'll come directly to the point. I am in the process of producing an accurate family genealogy, and it appears, Madam, that you and I are related."

Yuck, her brain screamed. She didn't want to be related to this shell of a snake. That's what he reminded her of as his voice hissed from deep within a raspy chest. She almost expected to hear his tail rattle.

"I see," Simone nodded, acting as if she were deep in thought over this news. "How may I help you?"

"It would be a great pleasure if we could spend a few hours discussing what you know of your heritage to determine whether or not my facts are true."

Right now, all she wanted was to slam the door in his face. It must be nearing ninety degrees, and Lord Ugly was draped in a full-length black raincoat, leather gloves encased his hands, and a black felt hat was shoved over his forehead. The little skin that was exposed was ghastly pale and covered in angry red boils.

"I have some time before work. Won't you please come in?"

Simone stepped back and allowed him entrance to her home. He stepped across the threshold and an overwhelming sense of doom wrapped around her chest. It suffocated. She felt as if the gray-uglies were lurching from every crack in her home, racing forward to strangle her life and pull her down into whatever pit of evil they dwelled within. Her vision dimmed, and she swayed slightly. *Danger. Use me.*

Lawrence Gideon reached a hand out and steadied her. His touch singed her skin. She felt a sliver of light shine from deep within her soul but this time it didn't burn. It warmed and spread throughout her body, blanketing the fear. She felt calm and capable of handling this situation. With a slight shake of her head, Simone turned to Trent.

Chapter Seven

"Mr. Gideon, I'd like to introduce . . . " she began, but stopped at the dangerous glint in Trent's eye.

He stepped forward, wrapped a possessive arm around her waist, and extended his hand.

"Lawrence Gideon, what a pleasure it is to meet you. I'm Trent Arnot, Miss Walker's fiancé."

Simone froze. His accent reflected the perfect twang of the south.

"Fiancé? My research hadn't uncovered that fact." Lawrence Gideon narrowed his gaze, a sullen expression slipping into place.

"It's a recent engagement," Trent interjected.

"Very recent." Simone agreed, glaring at his back.

Trent turned and gazed into her eyes. The warning was there. Don't blow this cover, he silently conveyed. She smiled tightly and led them into the dining room. "Please, make yourself at home."

Gideon pulled a high-backed chair away from the mahogany table and sat down. He ran his hands over the top of the worn leather of his briefcase then flipped it open, every movement precise, as if he'd done this a million times before.

Simone couldn't take her eyes off the man. She imagined him watching the life fade from her sister's eyes and anger burned. How dare he? It took basketball-sized brass balls to kill one sister then waltz into the other's home.

He rummaged through the contents of the briefcase. As his sleeves slid up to reveal more pustulous lumps, Simone suppressed her revulsion. She hated him, despised every little detail of the man.

Lord Bromley frowned and snapped his case shut. He glanced at her and smiled apologetically. At least, she thought the sickly grin was a smile.

"I beg your pardon. But I seem to have left the necessary paperwork at my hotel room. Would you excuse me while I call my associate?"

"That's fine," Trent answered. "Can you use your cell or do you require the phone in the kitchen?"

"A land line would be perfect. Thank you."

When they were alone, Simone turned on Trent.

"What are you doing saying you're my fiancé and what's with the fake accent?"

"Don't you think it's a bit of a coincidence for him to find a Brit here? It's a plausible cover."

"Not one that I find to my liking."

He walked over and placed his arms around her waist. She pushed against his chest, but he only held her tighter.

"Gideon can see us," he said. "Act like you care."

Two can play this game, Simone thought. Sometimes it's better to fight fire with fire. Before Trent knew what to expect, she snaked an arm around his neck and pulled his face down.

"Oh, I care," were the last words she breathed before locking her lips to his. She threw all the pent up anger and frustration into her kiss, demanding his response. He tasted of danger, and the force of his hand against her back left no doubt in her mind as to whom he hunted. He ran his fingers through her hair, devouring her mouth, and teasing her lips apart.

Oh boy, this was more than she bargained for as waves of hunger coursed through her body, burning hotter and faster with each flick of his tongue. *Mine. Yours. Mine.*

She was shocked to discover his hand had crept up, brushing lightly against her left breast. He ran his thumb across her nipple, paused, and caressed once more. His touch was fire, triggering a vicious blast of desire that almost knocked her over. *Take him.*

She pulled back, away from the inferno of his embrace and gazed into raging eyes that shimmered a brilliant blue.

"You don't want to ever go there again," he said, his voice deep and menacing.

"No," she agreed. "I don't think I do." The ball of fire in her gut subsided behind the blaze of the passion he awoke. It unsettled her. *Foolish child. He is your mate. How is it possible you know nothing?*

She stepped back, putting much needed space between herself and the man who had suddenly flipped her world over. She sat at the table, folded her hands neatly in front of her and waited for Lawrence Gideon to finish his telephone call. She couldn't look behind her. She couldn't face Trent.

***

Hot. Simone had smoldered beneath Trent's touch like a volcano on the verge of eruption. She'd clung to him, aroused and uncertain. *He'd* been aroused and uncertain. Bloody hell, the pull was strong. None of his research denoted this kind of experience. The call. The act. The completed circle. That was all history detailed. No lust. No attraction. He needed to clear his head.

Lord Bromley returned from the kitchen. This was the first time Trent had been this close to him, and it was evident that his case of porphyria had advanced considerably. He was shocked to see the horrible affects of the disease.

Based upon the size of the pustules, he figured dementia was firmly in place. Lawrence Gideon covered it well, but it explained the sudden escalation of murders.

Trent stepped behind Simone and placed a hand protectively on her shoulder. She sat still as stone. If her reaction to him was an eighth of his response to her, she must still be feeling the aftershocks. His body fairly hummed with the memory of her touch. Bloody hell, he swore again.

Lawrence Gideon sat down. Simone smiled tightly, still stiff beneath Trent's touch.

"I'm sorry Miss Walker it appears that we'll have to meet again. The documentation that shows our joint lineage appears to have temporarily disappeared."

"If you'll provide me the names of your immediate family, I'm certain I can confirm whether or not my parents ever mentioned them."

Gideon paused. "It's slightly more convoluted than that. I'd appreciate your patience while I sort my paperwork out."

"However I can be of help Mr. Gideon, is fine by me. Here's my number." She handed him a business card that displayed only her work number. Smart girl, Trent silently complimented her.

"May I ask if you have any children?"

Trent immediately went on alert. He was certain Lawrence Gideon knew about Jessie's existence. If his research led him this far, it wouldn't have left that little morsel unearthed. Simone latched her fingers through his in a very unSimone-like gesture for support. He squeezed her hand reassuringly and took control.

"We are blessed with a daughter, Mr. Gideon."

"Please pardon my impertinence, but she's both of yours?"

Before Simone could protest, Trent answered for her.

"Yes," he insisted. "She is." He prayed this would hinder Lord Bromley. That it would put a small blockade in the man's personal hunt for female descendants. The lie might buy them a few days to formulate a plan.

"I see. Well then, I'm sorry to have wasted your time. I'll be in touch, Miss Walker."

"Good bye, Mr. Gideon."

Simone directed the man out the front door and escorted him to his car. When he had driven away from the house, she stalked into the kitchen. Grabbing a can of Lysol from beneath the sink, she sprayed the phone then walked to her dining room and sprayed the table.

"Don't forget the door knob." Trent said, obviously amused. "It's not contagious you know."

She turned and glared at him. With a "how dare you" snarl, she left him alone and went upstairs.

Julie Korzenko

Chapter Eight

Simone sat on the edge of her bed. Her body felt alien. Rivers of foreign sensations wove through her nerves, tangling themselves together so tightly she couldn't pluck out the good from the bad.

When she'd escorted that horrible man to his car, he'd offered to buy her lunch later today. Simone accepted. She didn't want to be a pawn. She wanted action, and she wanted knowledge. Trent believed he held the upper hand. He was wrong. Dead wrong.

There was more to Lawrence Gideon. He was the shadow as much as Trent remained the light. Simone laid her head upon her pillow and tried to reach within for the answers. *Stop ignoring who you are, Simone of Draconius. Accept your fate and let me out.*

Fading beneath the power of exhaustion, she ignored the odd words and slipped into a restless slumber. The last image to flicker across her mind was the vibrant blue of Trent's eyes which slowly dissipated into a swirl of fog.

A weight pressed against her chest. In her mind, it materialized into the image of an emerald scaleddragon. It sat upon the curve between her breasts and pushed a claw against her heart.

Simone struggled to sit. But the dragon pushed her back, its golden eye glinting from the rays of the sun that streamed through her bedroom window.

Simone was mesmerized. She stared at the ethereal image, slipping beneath its power and allowing her mind to tumble back in time. The dragon pushed harder and she fell further until her vision cleared and the memory began to play.

***

Twilight softened the mists that swirled around the base of Draconius. Seren slipped away from the mesmerizing view beyond her window and searched the dark recesses of her chamber.

The last fortnight raged with shadows. They crept from the edge of her walls, signaling an evil presence. The sense of unrest and malevolence billowed from the gray shades in waves that struck terror into her soul. She didn't understand the source.

Her dragon was hunting for Llallogen. The wizard had not been seen since the night of the spell weaving, a decade past. Seren needed his guidance regarding these dark forces.

A cool breeze tickled the edge of her linen chemise. She turned and smiled when Trynt stepped through the chamber door. He grinned, raking his eyes from the top of her head, slowly burning a path past her neck, pausing along the low neckline of her undergarment and resting on the swell of her breasts.

"You are beautiful, Seren."

She smiled and walked over to her husband, her body no longer chilled from the approaching night. She was on fire, heating beyond control for his touch.

Lifting a hand, she caressed his cheek. He wrapped his fingers through hers and brought them to his mouth, nibbling on the tender ends and running his tongue along her palm leaving a fiery kiss upon the sensitive curve of her wrist. She sighed and swayed toward him.

He gathered her within his arms and carried her to the bed, laying her gently upon the downy covers.

"Why are you dressed so enticingly love?"

She laughed softly. "You mean undressed?"

He grinned and kissed her nose. "Exactly."

She watched him unfasten the clasps of his tunic, stripping it off in a hurried tug followed quickly by his breeches.

"I was tired. The strain of Grael's absence must be more than I anticipated."

Trynt bent over and ran a finger along her temple. "It has been too long."

Seren nodded and closed her eyes allowing his touch to soothe. "I feel the shadows more, don't you?"

His lips found hers and she smiled, sinking into the kiss and wrapping her arms around his neck. Opening her lids, she gazed into the azure depths of his eyes. His power glowed and her magic answered its call.

"I feel them. But I prefer to feel you." Dipping his head, he sprinkled a trail of kisses across her neckline then moved farther down, nuzzling the thin fabric that covered her breasts. His tongue licked at her nipple, suckling and gently pulling it into his mouth. The slight abrasiveness of the fabric sent desire flaming through her system. She bit down on her lip and groaned, arching her back.

The haze of passion suffused her as Trynt ran his hand beneath the covers, pushing at the chemise that separated them. He sat back and gently lifted the gown over her head, tossing it on top of his discarded clothes. She smiled and gazed into his face. "I will always love you."

His eyes answered her and he ran a finger along the edge of her breast, brushing gently over the nipple still burning from his kiss. "And I you."

Seren sighed as he covered her body with his own. She wrapped her legs around his waist, waiting for the promise in his eyes. His lips touched hers, branding their kiss upon her soul. The heat of his breath fanned her desire, and she whimpered as only the tip of him eased inside.

His tongue searched for hers, flicking between her lips at the same time he moved slowly deeper. She gripped his back and forced her hips upwards.

"Patience, my love." He laughed against her mouth.

She sighed, relaxed her muscles and allowed him control of their pace. He braced himself above her, the raven locks of his hair falling against his face as he gazed at her. She pushed them away from the eyes that owned her heart and opened her legs wider. He grinned and entered her with maddening slowness.

Seren swallowed and fought against the urge to buck up and take him full to the hilt. As if he could read her mind, he shook his head. She reached behind and grabbed the bed post, refusing to give in to the desire that pushed her body. She was Trynt's, and he would claim her however he saw fit.

Bending his head, he kissed the area between her breasts and began to move. Her stomach quivered as he pulled himself out all the way and rubbed his moistened tip against her swollen nub. She inhaled sharply and bit the bottom of her lip.

Trynt arched his neck, sweat beading along his temple. He entered her again and filled her all the way. She rocked against him, but he slowly pulled out and repeated the caress against the most sensitive area of her body. Seren groaned as his touch sent her spiraling into the night.

He swayed his hips, rubbing against her in controlled moves, his hardness pushed and prodded with intense delight. She could feel drops of his love seep out and it added another tantalizing sensation. Trynt moved until his tip rested inside then dipped down and rocked back and forth allowing only his head to penetrate.

Seren cried in frustration, desire and need for him coursing through her body in wave after wave of passion. He brought her close to climax then eased out, placing a gentle kiss upon her lips.

"Ready?" he asked, his voice thick with passion.

"Oh God, yes!" She wrapped her legs around his waist and held on as he plunged inside her, bearing down with the force of the passion he'd held in check. He pushed deeper, and she slammed her hips up to meet his thrust. Harder and faster. They soared to the brink together. Snaking her arms tightly around his neck, she held on as the power of his love lifted her to the edge of oblivion.

Their passion exploded in a blinding second of union, and her climax ran from the core of her body into every desire-sensitive nerve as he spilled his seed. She lay exhausted; love pounded from her heart in erratic, over accelerated beats.

Seren sighed and traced her finger down the thin line of black hair that ran from Trynt's chest to his navel. His stomach tightened, and he turned to face her. Their eyes met, a wicked grin played along her husband's mouth.

"Are you not satisfied, woman?"

Seren laughed. "Never." She bent forward and touched his lips with her own. Teasing her tongue between his teeth, she inhaled as he pulled her tight against his chest. The thick cotton and heavy woven blankets couldn't hide his reaction to her love. She tossed away the covers, freeing their bodies to touch intimately once more.

Lifting her foot, she caressed his calf with her toe. He suckled her lower lip, groaning as her legs parted slightly. Seren opened her eyes and met the deep azure gaze clouded with passion. She smiled against his mouth. Their love remained strong and true after nearly a decade as Dancer and Ancient.

It'd grown as full and rich as the roses that graced their castle walls. Grael guided their missions and helped educate the masses to improve society and better man's world. But it was these moments, these seconds of anticipation before the quick rush of passion cascaded into satisfaction that Seren treasured most.

Trynt ran strong fingers down the length of her spine, cupping her bottom and spreading her open with his knee. He leaned above, nibbling her ear and kissing the sensitive skin beneath her lobe.

Her head dropped back as waves of desire flooded her body. She waited. The anticipation of his touch heated the flame of passion.

"I always want you," he whispered against her ear.

A deep chill filled the room. Seren's eyes snapped open as a dark presence slipped within the cherished walls of their chamber.

Trynt stiffened. He felt it too. They gazed beyond the boundary and safety of their bed. Seren inhaled in fear and gripped her husband's shoulders.

She watched in horror as tendrils of milky-white fog slipped beneath the slight gap at the base of their door. Slowly it rose and formed clouds of mist that billowed eerily upward like shapeless shadows. The clouds moved closer . . . toward Tyrnt.

The shadows, long and narrow, reached like dark gray limbs across the floor, their fingers crawling across the stone like ants on the march for food. They spread eerily beneath the misty phantoms that floated all around. Fear tightened within her chest, and she squeezed her eyes shut.

"Trynt what is this?"

He shook his head and moved slowly off her, careful not to disturb the evil mist. "Call Grael."

Seren focused on the ball of fire within. But she couldn't connect, couldn't spark the flame that signaled the dragon.

Her hands shook and she opened her eyes to gaze into his worried face. "Nothing."

Trynt bent his head, murmured a soft chant and lifted eyes that sparked and fired with an Ancient's power toward the shadows. Raising his hands, he focused his power and flung blue lightning at the evil.

Seren shuffled behind him continuing to attempt to raise her dragon. It was as if the mist wrapped itself around Grael's spirit and prevented Seren's access. Every bone in her body felt frozen.

Black tendrils shifted closer. They stretched across the twisted blankets in waves of pure evil. Her eyes widened as they crept closer to Trynt. No! She moved to the side, trying to reach her husband. But it was too late.

He arched his back as the gray mist reached for his chest. Fingers of black air penetrated the skin above his heart. He cried in pain. Seren grabbed for him, screaming for Grael.

His skin felt cold. She ran her hands over his shoulders and penetrated the dark mist. Placing her palm upon his heart, the tears that flooded her eyes made it difficult to see.

He collapsed against her, blood trailing from the corner of his mouth. Trynt coughed and tried to speak. " . . . love you."

Her heart shattered. "Hush, my darling. You'll be fine. As soon as Grael arrives, we'll fix this."

Tears ran down her face as he shook his head. She bent and touched her lips to his, tasting his last breath. She sobbed his name, the grief wracking her body in sharp stabs, and watched in disbelief as life faded from his eyes . . .

***

"No!" Simone sat up in bed, hitting the arms that held her.

"Simone. Wake up." Trent grabbed her face and made her focus on him. His eyes, full of life, bore into her soul. She ran her fingers through his hair, touched his cheek gently and pulled him close.

Oh God, he'd died. She knew it, with every edge of her being screaming in pain and agony for the loss of her love. And she'd failed him. Her heart felt as if it shattered into a million pieces, the power of love swept her mind. It hurt. Oh God, it hurt.

"It's okay. Hush, love. I'm here."

She wrapped her arms around his neck, allowing the tears to flow. Her sobs wracked her body, and she couldn't control the absolute power of sorrow. She'd lost him. Her love. Her life.

It vanished in a twist of evil shadows, shadows that were a mirror image of her gray-uglies.

No. This was wrong. Reality parted the veil of dreams. Jessie was her love, her life. Not this man. She pushed Trent away, refusing to glance at the eyes that haunted her.

"Please leave."

"Simone, what's wrong?"

"I asked you to leave." She pulled her knees to her chest, hugging them as strongly as she'd hugged Trent. The bed lifted as he stood.

"If you need me, I'll be downstairs."

Why did the sadness of his voice make her cringe? She'd hurt him. But oh my God, she was crazy. Dreams weren't real. This must be a manifestation of a sick mind. Tears slid down her face and fear stabbed her heart. How would she ever help Jessie if her sanity were going?

Who were those people running around in her mind?

Wiping her hand against her cheek, Simone paused and held it in place. Her skin felt warm as if the rush of passion she'd experienced in the dream were genuine. She remembered the caress and feel of the man in her vision.

Simone clung to the one thing that might help ease her mind from the dark path of insanity. The White Book of Rhydderch. She must have it. Lunacy wasn't an option.

Chapter Nine

Trent paced the outside deck like a caged lion. Last night's spectacle combined with the horror of whatever dream attacked Simone wouldn't cease nagging at him. He needed to speak with someone more versed in the calling. It all felt wrong. He needed his mother.

He glanced up. Through the pane of glass, he watched Simone mirror his incessant gait.

"Bloody hell, I can't think of my mother and look at her. That's just not right," he said to the row of cardinals perched on an aged bird feeder.

He studied the feeder. It appeared to be in the shape of a barn and had the words ROCK CITY painted in faded white on its roof. That, he had to admit, was definitely at odds with all the other tasteful things Simone scattered around her house, making him curious about its history.

Trent shook his head. He stared, once more, at the beautiful vision flittering back and forth on the other side of the glass. The power of an Ancient coursed beneath his skin, clamoring to fulfill a destiny Trent no longer saw as black and white. He needed answers.

With a sigh, he flipped open his phone. "Where are you?" he demanded, when his partner answered.

"Heading back downtown, I think."

"Right then. I need you to run a background check on Rosalyn Allen and another on the two from Paris."

"I already did that."

"I want another one run. I specifically want to know if they belonged to any covens."

"Ovens? Why would they belong to ovens?"

"Coven, you bloody idiot. Coven--as in a group of women involved in Wicca." Trent knew this was a long shot, but his gut screamed that what he'd witnessed last night was connected to this case and it stunk of black magic.

"Wicker? Like the furniture?"

Trent sighed and pleaded for patience. "Witches, Ian. I want to know if either of them were witches."

"Oh, right. Why didn't you just say that then?"

"I don't know. I guess I was trying to be politically correct."

"Really? How bloody thoughtful of you."

"Just get back to me with the details."

"Right. I'll ring you shortly. How's the calling going? Any luck?"

Trent stared into the tree line. "I'm not comfortable at all. I called the Director last night, and he denied my request to explain things to Simone."

"He's right. She has to awaken with no assistance but more importantly she has to trust you."

"That's the whole bloody problem, Ian. How will she ever trust me when she finds out I've known all along what lies within her?" Trent swore in a low voice. "No matter which way you look at it, I'm buggered."

"Build the relationship, Trent. It's what you must do. What's with the witch hunt?"

Trent heard a horn blast through their connection. "There's something here. Something more than the dragon."

"That's enough for me, then. I'll have you some answers posthaste."

"Thanks, mate."

"Trent?"

"Yes?"

"Your mother's . . . "

Trent interrupted Ian before he said another word. "Shut up and go do what I've asked."

"Don't ignore it."

He hung up before Ian badgered him anymore. Trent felt bad for snapping at his friend. They were both tired, and Ian didn't deserve the backlash of his frustration over an unmitigated desire and need.

He inhaled and realized that the scent of lemons surrounded him once more. Trent stepped off the deck and went in search of the magnolia trees. He was curious. As he glanced around, he noted there were numerous magnolias scattered all around the house.

Huge white flowers lay nestled within the deep green, waxy leaves. He bent one down and inhaled. Lemons. A shiver of apprehension tickled down his spine, causing Trent to stare into the dark depths of the woods.

Evil watched. Was it Lawrence? Or was it something more . . . something he'd never encountered before.

"Trent?" Her voice carried softly on the wind. He turned and found Simone standing in the same spot he'd just occupied. Her arms were crossed protectively over her chest, and he swore he could see a chip on her shoulder greater than Mount Olympus.

"Hi," he smiled and stepped toward her.

"Hi, yourself. What're you doing?" She spoke quietly which immediately put all of his senses on alert.

"Thinking," he ran his fingers through his hair and winked, "of you."

"That's why I came out here. I wanted to apologize."

"What for?" Trent moved closer. He stood beyond the edge of the deck, his feet immersed in the cool comfort of thick Bermuda grass. The height of the decking allowed them to be practically eye level with one another.

"Oh, let's say, for that totally uncalled for display of affection earlier today."

He couldn't help but smile. She was bright red in the face, and if she ground her toe any deeper into the unrelenting wood, she'd find her foot popping out the other side. He thought about dragging this out, then decided against it.

"It's what I deserved. I'm the one who should apologize."

"So you admit you manipulated me?"

"I admit that it appeared like I manipulated you. I honestly didn't do it on purpose."

"Am I the bait?"

Trent paused at her question. That certainly had been his plan, but things changed. Like the fact that you want to protect her, love her, and make her laugh. He shook his head in denial. She took it as an answer to her question.

"I only ask that because if I am, I want you to do something before I put myself in the line of danger," she spoke softly. He strained to hear her.

He rocked back on his heels and shoved his hands into his pockets. What was going on in that creative little mind of hers?

"You're already in the line of danger," he stated frankly.

"Nevertheless," She paused and took a deep breath. "I want you. I mean I want to finish what we started in there."

"What? You don't even know me." He cringed at the sharp edge of his words.

She flinched, and he dropped his head, avoiding her gaze.

"I know that you made me feel something I haven't ever experienced."

"There's definitely an attraction." He closed his eyes for a second, attempting to find the right answer. If he agreed, the consequences would be great. "But I think it'd be best for both of us if we kept our relationship professional."

"I'm telling you how I feel in the hope that you will do as I wish."

"And what exactly do you wish?" He spoke quietly, counting the blades of grass surrounding his feet.

"I want you to give me everything you know about my sister. And then I want you to leave."

He allowed the words to immerse themselves into his soul. It helped. She was making it easy to re-center his emotions, to distance himself. He glanced up and focused his gaze on her flustered face. She was manipulating him, and it didn't sit well. He was an Ancient. He got that. He would forever be bound to her, submissive to her. He understood. But not yet. Not bloody well yet.

"You know something, love? I've been conned by the best in the world, and you don't even come close." Trent stared at her. The pulse at the corner of his eye beat rapidly, keeping time with the inner ticking bomb that was his temper. Simone's eyes muted into an array of grays and greens with small gold flecks scattered within.

"I'm not manipulating you," she stated, her tone flat and emotionless.

"You don't call swapping sexual favors for my files and a promise to leave manipulation?"   "No. I'm sorry if my honesty made you think I was just into swapping sexual favors. It just so happens that as an independent woman I find it much easier to ask for what I want rather than wait on a man to run around playing cat and mouse for a month. It's a waste of time."

"Let me get this straight." Trent's voice deepened with resentment. "You want a roll in the sack and then a kiss goodbye?"

"Yes. I don't want any strings. There's no room in my life for anyone other than Jessie. Right now the best course of action for me is to gather as much information from you and then send you packing. I think you're more of a danger than you realize."

"To who? You or your daughter?"

Simone gasped, a flicker of doubt crossing her eyes. "To my daughter."

"How do you figure that?"

"It's hard to explain."

He stifled his retort and exhaled loudly. They could quibble like this until the sun went down, but it wouldn't change the ordeal Simone was about to endure.

"I think," he rasped in frustration. "I'm the only man standing between you and certain death."

Simone blanched and turned away. She stretched her hands to the sky, shook her arms, and faced him once more.

"I'm not on some kamikaze mission," she admitted. "I think I need to do this. I feel . . ." she smacked her palm against her chest. "I need to do this."

"I'm sorry, Simone. It's not going to happen."

"Is there someone waiting for you back home? Is that why you don't want me?"

"No." Trent answered honestly. He did want her; more than he cared to admit. "There's no one at home."

She nodded.

"I have to go to work." Her eyes skimmed down and shifted to the left. She was lying, and he knew it. What was going on?

She was the first woman to rattle him in forever. "First you proposition me, and then you abandon me? That's not very nice, Ms. Walker."

"I have responsibilities and deadlines to meet."

"What about Jessie? You can't leave her."

"Jessie will be fine."

"I don't buy that." There's no way she'd leave her daughter at home and Trent knew it. What was really going on here?

Simone exhaled impatiently. "She's coming with. Okay?"

"So am I."

"No, you're not."

"Don't make me call Sheriff Tippens," Trent threatened. He narrowed his eyes when all color drained from her face. What was she afraid of?

"He can't make me stay home from work."

"No. But he can make you take me with you."

"How?"

Trent's brain went into hyper-speed. He didn't know the American law. He was certain there must be something to do with obstruction of justice, or witness protection, or house arrest, or whatever to keep her at home and safe.

"Section 44.2a of the U.S. Federal Code states that under extreme levels of endangerment a potential victim may be detained against their will." He prayed that sounded official. She glared at him thoughtfully, and he gazed right back, raising his brow in a silent challenge.

"Look, Sherlock, here's the deal. I'm going to work, Jessie is going with me. At noon I'm meeting Lord Creepola for lunch. I'll answer his questions, take a look-see at whatever flippin' paperwork he has and verify that he's leaving the States for good then return home. Safe, sound, happy, and delightfully absent of all this British baggage that keeps arriving on my doorstep."

"You made a lunch date with a man suspected of murdering numerous women? What is this, an invitation to politely get oneself killed?"

Trent paced in a tight circle. She must have arranged the meeting when she showed the old bugger to the door. Could she truly be this naive? He rounded on her, once more, his anger making his tone escalate. "Heaven forbid you allow a knife to be plunged into your heart without first tasting the soup du jour. Unbelievable, bloody unbelievable."

He didn't understand what she was doing.

"Oh God, you're right." She said softly, her words barely discernable against the singing birds and chirping summer bugs. "That was a stupid thing to do. I'm not thinking clearly. I just want Jessie safe, and I want my life back."

"A moment ago you wanted to make passionate love to me. Now you want your life back? It doesn't work that way, Simone." He stepped closer. Her face was flushed, and she bit her lower lip.

"I didn't say I wanted to make love to you."

The words slipped from her mouth like sweet, early morning dew. All she had to do was speak and his testosterone heated beyond the boiling point. He ignored it.

No.

He supposed she hadn't said it that way.

"You don't seem to comprehend that you won't have a life to *get* back if you allow Lawrence Gideon anywhere near you and yours. He wants only one thing."

"And what is that?"

"Jessie." He stated firmly, hating himself the minute the lie left his lips. "He wants your daughter."

"No!" Simone gasped and stepped back. She covered her mouth with a shaking hand and shook her head in denial. Soft strands of blonde hair escaped the braid that had imprisoned them down her back. They danced and whirled in the light breeze, carefree and oblivious of the danger that crept slowly forward. "You said he wanted me. And I thought by giving him my cooperation we could end this damn fiasco. We'll be in a public place, for crying out loud."

"He does want you, but if you prove too difficult, he'll look to Jessie." Trent walked onto the deck and grabbed her arms. He held her face an inch from his. "He's going to attempt to kill you." And he believed every word he said to her. His gut was literally tearing itself apart agreeing with his accusations.

"I need to protect Jessie," she stammered, eyes widened and glittering with tears. "And I think it's best for your sake if you leave, you're too much of a distraction. This is more than what it seems. Call in Randy, call in the Atlanta PD. I don't care. But get the hell away from me, Trent Arnot."

He narrowed his eyes and held onto his anger. "Come with me, Simone. Allow me thirty minutes of your time and then make your decision." He swore vehemently, and wished fervently he didn't have to be this brutally honest.

"All right," she agreed. Her voice sounded despondent, and it crushed him to be the cause. "I need to make a few calls to reschedule my time. I'll meet you back in my office in about twenty minutes."

Julie Korzenko

Chapter Ten

Simone dropped the phone back into its charger. The lead weight that dragged at her heart made it difficult to find the pleasure she normally felt for work and life. Biting her lower lip, the embarrassment of a few moments ago flushed her face crimson red. She'd propositioned Agent Arnot.

Hanging her head, she shook it slowly. How could she? Her mind replayed the dream. It had felt real; her love for the man dying within her arms burned even now, teasing her emotions into a knot. She wanted confirmation. She wanted to believe she wasn't crazy.

If she could move past these emotions, then she could concentrate on finding that damn book. But the kiss she'd initiated that morning troubled her, overlapping the memory of the man with Trent's eyes. The connection intense and frightening.

She was losing her mind.

Simone inhaled a deep cleansing breath, squared her shoulders and convinced herself that if she needed to sleep with that irritating man downstairs, then she'd do it. Damn it all to hell. She'd find a way. She'd do whatever was necessary for her daughter's safety. If sleeping with Trent eased her fear about her sanity, to hell with her pride.

She crossed her legs and opened the cover of the book in front of her. Tapping the faded yellow page of the old family book, she traced her finger along the name on the first page. The Gideon Memorial. This was it. This was why Lawrence Gideon's name was familiar. It appeared her sister linked the connection to Lawrence Gideon long before Agent Arnot, and it occurred to her that Rosalyn might have met with Gideon in an attempt to gain the White Book of Rhydderch and paid with her life. She felt the rage build. *That's it, little one. Anger opens doors.*

Simone frowned, ignoring the voice, her thoughts turning back to the man downstairs. She knew her cooperation was essential in apprehending Gideon, but she believed what she'd told Trent. If he invaded her dreams, he weakened her. He must leave. Perhaps she could convince him to swap places with his partner. Without his blue eyes as a distraction, she could investigate in a pure businesslike manner. Find the book she needed. Protect her daughter. And stick a blade in Gideon's gut.

She scrutinized the memorial that lay open on her lap then raised it to her face sniffing the binder. It smelled old. She inhaled again, almost as if the faint scent of pipe smoke filtered through its pages.

Simone sighed and closed the book. She gazed out the window, allowing the serenity of the lake to soothe her troubled mind. At thirteen, her nights were filled with haunting shadows. And her days? The shame of her actions still twisted her gut.

Her days were a torture of endless hours at school, being bullied and ridiculed. Randy Tippens called her crazy, insulted her sister. He spread horrible rumors about why Rosalyn left town. Even though Simone struggled with the absence of Rosalyn, she'd defended her.

A tear slipped down her cheek as the memory returned. There were no fuzzy edges or out-of-focus moments with this reminiscence. She'd cornered Randy on the walk home from school, unlocked the thing that burned in her chest and invaded his mind, digging until she found what she wanted. His fear.

She'd used it, tossed the horror of his childhood in his face. The beatings. The rapes.

Simone's chest caught, and she dropped her head. She'd humiliated and tortured him. He had been a bully. But he hadn't deserved that. No. She'd been wrong. The shock written across his face as she tossed her threats into the air like a challenge to a duel haunted her. He'd stiffened, tears shimmering in his eyes.

Randy agreed to leave her alone if she promised never to reveal the sordid tales of his early years. She'd nodded and allowed him to leave. But the pain, the hurt of a young boy being brutalized by his father lingered. To this day, it lingered.

And since that moment, she'd listened to her sister's advice and shoved that stupid flame deep into the recesses of her soul. Whatever had permitted her to see his secrets was banished. Jailed permanently.

And now someone or something opened that cell. Because the flame burned bright once more. And it scared Simone more than the gray-uglies. And this time, it had a voice.

Simone stood up and placed the memorial on her bookshelves. Rehashing the past wasn't going to help her now. She'd already used all the tricks she'd discovered in her youth. Focus. Shove the power away. Move forward. Live.

"Mama?"

Moving through her room, she smiled at her daughter. "What is it sugar?"

"Trent's asking for you."

"I'm coming. Get your stuff together; we're going to the office for awhile this afternoon."

Her daughter nodded and left the room. Simone paused in the doorway, her memories still troubling her. She'd allowed time to heal. But every once in awhile, Randy cast a look that spoke of what she'd done. And the shame struck.

***

Trent placed his hands on the worn surface of Simone's desk. It was cluttered with rolled-up vellum and stacks of paper. He'd taken her seat. The chair of power, he grinned. He'd laughed to himself early that morning when she'd led him in here. Control was vital to Simone. He was about to take that away.

Somehow that thought didn't make him happy.

He opened his file folder, laying documents out in an orderly fashion. Frowning, he couldn't believe the audacity of the woman whose office he invaded.

"Ask for what I want . . ." Her words tripped through his mind like a canvass of brightly painted flowers. He'd never ratify how fiercely he wanted to act on her suggestion. His job was to protect her, prepare her and not have wonderful mind-altering sex. Their union was destined but guided by a doctrine older than time.

That was all.

Simple.

Cut and dry.

"Get out of my chair."

Trent blinked and focused upon the vision of Simone. She stood framed in the doorway. Her hands were on her hips; a frown slashed across her face and a smile was nowhere to be found. The sun, however, shone behind her, illuminating her golden hair and basking her in a soft array of light.

What a stunner.

His stomach clenched with desire.

"Now is that any way to talk to your soon-to-be lover." He tilted his head and brazenly scoured her from head to toe with his eyes. She inhaled sharply and steadied herself by leaning against the door. His fingers itched to be where his gaze fell. She looked soft, pliable and delicious.

"No way, Sherlock. We're not going there. You won't leave so this is now strictly business. I hereby rescind my offer. Please vacate my chair." She tilted her head and stared at him. "I don't suppose you'd consider swapping places with your partner?"

He ran his fingers through his hair. Yeah, he'd considered it. "Sorry, I'm quite happy here and no, I'm not switching with Ian." Stretching the cricks out of his neck, he pointed at the other chair. "Sit."

She sat. He fought against the smile that tugged at his mouth. Simone acted as if he'd taken away her favorite toy.

"I'm waiting. Enlighten me."

He snapped his thoughts back to the ugly task at hand. His gaze hardened, and he pulled out the first set of documents he'd laid on the desk. He spread them out and turned them one by one to face Simone. She leaned forward to examine the pages. With a gasp, she jumped back into her seat and glared at him.

"That was dirty. I already told you I believed you."

"Maybe. Did it get your attention, love? I want you to take this matter seriously." He smiled sarcastically. The name Sherlock was quickly topping his most aggravating word list.

"I am. Shit." She swore several more times. "My daughter's at stake here. I'm dead serious."

"Then I implore you from the darkest recesses of my hardened heart to lean forward and study each one of these gruesome pictures. You're not having lunch with a sheep, Simone."

"I'm well aware of that."

"He's more like a great white," Trent's words were harsh and forthright.

She stared at him with flat eyes. His heart twisted when she nodded stiffly and leaned forward once more. The women depicted within each picture had been sliced down the center, their skin peeled back, like that of a filleted fish, and a pentagram had been burned into their open and raw flesh.

The mutilation perverse.

The vindictiveness extreme.

He had to admire the way she studied each page. Her jaw was tight, and Trent thought he saw the glimmer of a tear in her eye. She gathered the documents and handed them back to him.

"Where's Rosalyn?"

He'd expected this.

"We haven't developed the pictures, yet." he lied. He could be cruel, but he'd be damned to hell for all eternity if he'd mar her memories with that specific depravity.

"Tell me about them."

"The pictures?" he said, slightly disconcerted.

"No," she shook her head vehemently. "The women. My cousins, right?"

"Correct. The first woman was found in her flat just off Piccadilly Square in London. Her name was Charlotte Benson. The local authorities contacted MI-5 when a small particle of Lawrence Gideon's hair was discovered at the crime scene."

"Why? Couldn't they handle it themselves?"

"The Bromley line is highly regarded within Parliament as well as the monarchy. They felt we were more equipped to handle the sensitivity of this case."

"Where did your investigation lead you?"

"To Paris. The twins were found just off the Rue De Rivoli. No hair this time, but we did find what could be trace elements of a soil indigenous to the land that surrounds Lawrence Gideon's country estate."

"Circumstantial?"

"Very. The third woman is an individual we've yet to identify. The database kicked her out because of the parameters of the killing and her connection to Blithewoods. She was murdered almost five years ago. Her file is still marked unsolved. If I can link her to this picture," he slapped down the shot of Lawrence Gideon and the strange woman in the countryside he'd been studying yesterday afternoon. "I could add another nail to his coffin."

"Who do you think she is?"

Trent shook his head. "I have no idea. She's your typical Jane Doe. The forensic team was unable to match fingerprints or DNA analysis."

"But you believe she's tied to Lawrence Gideon?"

"Her body was located on the outskirts of Blithewoods with the exact same markings as shown here."

Simone studied the picture, rubbing her thumb over the woman's face. "Show me the genealogy. I want to know why you believe we're next."

"You're the last of the Bromley line." Trent laid out a long sheet of paper depicting her lineage.

"See how the rest of the family continues," he ran his fingers down the left side of the sheet. "But you and then your daughter are the end of the Bromley blood."

She leaned closer, running her fingers opposite of his, until they rested lightly on two names.

Pamela Allen = Sir Lawrence W. Gideon.

|

Simone Gideon

dob: 7/17/1980

"I thought you said Lawrence Gideon was my cousin?"

"No. I said the victims were akin to your 3rd or 4th cousins. I never mentioned his relation." Trent's heart beat. This could backfire dreadfully. He might have pushed too hard. She could refuse to participate.

Simone looked up, her eyes wild with fear and disbelief. She stood and paced around the small confines of the room. He remained silent, allowing her to battle through what he could only imagine to be extremely conflicting emotions. She stopped directly in front of his chair.

He gazed into her eyes, into an angry depth of a muted green tornado.

"Are you insinuating that the creepy vampire that showed up at my house this morning is my *father*?"

***

Simone felt like she'd been thrown into the deep end of the pool in the middle of winter. She was numb, and her chest seized making it difficult to breathe. Her mind couldn't absorb her connection with the diseased man who'd murdered her sister.

She turned and walked abruptly out of her office. Space and air. Moving her arms in circles, she concentrated on leveling her emotions. She wandered through the downstairs staring into each room without really seeing.

"Simone?"

"What." She cringed as her voice rose to a level she reserved for angry words.

"Come here." Trent's voice was soft. She glanced back at him, and his eyes held nothing but compassion and concern. "Please?"

She nodded and walked to him. "This man is my father, right?"

"I believe so."

"And he has this disease?" The verbalization of her fear lightened some of the tightness in her chest. "If I remember correctly, you indicated this morning that it's genetic."

Simone watched a startled expression cross his face.

He nodded slowly and frowned. "The version of the disease that Lord Bromley has is genetic. But there's no indication that he's passed it on to you." Trent said.

"Is there a test for this thing?"

"Yes."

"And Jessie, can she be tested too?" What if she was fine but Jessie wasn't? Fear for her daughter made it difficult to swallow.

"Yes. I'll contact the laboratory that assisted my research into the disease. They'll tell me what you need to do."

"I can see how scared you are. Is there something you want to tell me?"

Simone bit her bottom lip. She didn't want to verbalize her fear. It seemed impossible to believe that the past few months were nothing more than illusions created by a diseased mind. These things she felt and saw weren't real. Her sister thought she'd stumbled upon magic when in essence it was nothing more than the manifestations of porphyria.

"You need to quit thinking so hard." Trent said. He rubbed her arms then held her hands. "I'm going to call my contact and find the closest lab. There's nothing to worry about. You don't look all bubbly and gross to me."

Simone smiled. "Not everything can be seen on the outside."

He frowned. "What are you talking about?"

She gazed into his eyes. "The other night when you came into Jessie's room I was paralyzed. I knew you were there, but I couldn't move. Paralysis is part of this disease and tingles and burning. I have all those things." He narrowed his eyes and shook his head slowly.

"Remember, porphyria is extremely rare. Even the genetic form."

Simone nodded, praying he was right. The thought of becoming a walking vampire like Lawrence Gideon frightened her more than the gray-uglies.

"Don't let this become bigger than you can handle. I understand your concerns, and I'm not belittling these symptoms. But I want you to stay focused."

"I'm focused. You've just torn my world apart, but I'm focused." Simone snorted in a very unladylike manner. Trent grinned. "I want my daughter safe. God help me, I want to see Gideon pay. It doesn't matter how we're connected. I want him dead."

Trent's eyes softened, and he nodded. "Do I get to stay now?"

"Yes." It didn't settle her stomach to think this way.

"There's my girl." He stood up. "Let's head out."

Chapter Eleven

Simone felt suffocated. The sway of the Land Rover as it drove south toward Atlanta nauseated her. Her daughter and Trent were engaged in a lively discussion about the latest chick flick. Jessie insisted that the female lead hadn't been over-the-top in her expectation of the perfect man. Trent laughed, making Simone smile. He teased her daughter mercilessly about the male lead's over-buffed physique and that the perfect body didn't necessarily lead to happily-ever-after.

"Mama, make this poor specimen of a male understand about true love."

Trent reached behind her seat and tapped Jessie's knee. "True love is the emotion a horse feels when his trainer brings him a bucket of warm oats."

Jessie groaned and slapped at his arm. Simone smiled, begrudgingly admitting that he had a way with kids.

This side of Agent Aggravator was a pleasant surprise. She could almost find the man behind the investigator. She wished fervently that the horrific facts currently performing a play-by-play--you're going to end up old, pale, and full of nasty blisters-act would cease.

The truth of Lawrence Gideon's identity made her chest tighten and stomach clench into a thousand knots. They'd barely finished their discussion when Trent received a call from Randy's office. He'd shown up on her doorstep less than ten minutes later, Trent's suitcase in one hand and a sly grin firmly in place. That's all she needed.

Simone hadn't wanted to spend any time in his presence. The memory of her childhood days and his accusation of her mental stability rang an awful truth bell. The realization that if she were crazy she couldn't possibly have read his mind had her more confused than the damn tavern puzzles Jessie loved so much.

The White Book of Rhydderch was the key. Simone bit down on her lip and promised herself that the truth was there, within its pages. She had to find it. Her sanity and the safety of her daughter depended upon it.

Reaching for her sunglasses, they clattered toward the driver's side as Trent navigated a sharp corner. Her hands brushed his arm, and she fumbled ungracefully, trying to ward off the electric shock that raced up her arm. *You are certainly the dimmest of all Dancers I have ever encountered.* She bit her tongue against blathering to her inner voice to explain itself and retrieved her glasses, slamming them on her face.

Trent pulled the Land Rover off the highway and was manipulating his way through the midtown traffic like an old hand. She frowned and realized how well he handled the vehicle.

"Don't you drive on the wrong side of the road at home?"

He flashed a quick grin that flipped her already nauseated insides upside down.

"Considering that England had carriages way before the States did, it's my personal opinion, that y'all," he mimicked her accent with unique proficiency. "Drive on the wrong side."

"A matter of perspective, I suppose. My office is three buildings down on the left."

"I know."

She raised a brow then twisted around to see her daughter singing softly to the tune playing on her iPod. "Of course, you do."

She started when he narrowed his eyes and glared at her.

"It's my job."

She hated the way he did that, one moment all relaxed and jokey . . .

the next uptight and, well, just plain British. Her father, at least the man she preferred to think of as her father, Des Walker, used to be exactly the same way.

"Fine," she answered, hoping that her indignation shone brightly.

Trent parked the vehicle beneath the glass and chrome sky rise that was home to her business. They exited the vehicle, Jessie began chatting away--oblivious to the tension between the adults, and headed into the building. He was insisting on joining her for lunch.

Simone still hadn't come to terms with her heritage. She'd yet to question him on her mother. One step at a time, she consoled herself. Trent's presence at lunch would be tolerated but only because she didn't want to be with Gideon alone.

They rode the elevator in hushed silence, a wonderful reprieve from her daughter's never-ending chattiness. She glanced at Jessie and smiled despite herself.

What a beautiful child. Her auburn hair and vivid green eyes a direct reflection of the sister she'd recently buried. How proud she was to have created such a magnificent creature. Simone smoothed several stray strands of hair from Jessie's head and bent to drop a light kiss on her forehead. As she straightened up, her eyes caught the reflection of Trent's stare in the metal doors. She didn't care how much he protested, this man wanted her. It was blatantly obvious in the heated blue depths of his gaze. If he were Superman, there'd be a hole burnt through the elevator at that very moment.

"What?" she asked because she could no longer stand the silence.

"You need to listen to me, Simone. Please don't argue anymore."

"I won't. I trust you." They alighted onto the twenty-second floor. She smiled at her staff as she stepped onto the well-worn commercial carpet. Her secretary waved to her and approached with an inch-thick pile of messages.

"Thanks, Sandy. I'll only be in the office for a few hours today. I'll try and return as many as these as possible. Those I don't reach, I'll call from home."

"I'll make a note of it, Simone." Sandy leaned forward and whispered in her ear. "There's a delicious Englishman making himself at home in your office. I tried to keep him out, but he insisted he'd be welcome."

"Another one?"

"Another, what?" Sandy asked as she glanced curiously at Trent. "Oh, I certainly see what you mean. I don't suppose he arrived in silver and on a horse?"

"Not by a long shot," Simone laughed. "Did the other one?"

"Nope. I guess you're still on the market then."

Trent stepped between Simone and Sandy and headed directly into her office. His arrogance irritated her and the back slaps and "cheerios" that filtered back through her open door did nothing to dampen that feeling.

"Jessie, honey, why don't you take your sketch pad into the conference room and work on the changes you want made to your room."

"Okay, Mama. Can I use the color and fabric samples?"

"Sure," Simone watched her daughter leave. She'd be safe here. They'd decided it was time to update her bedroom from the flower and prints of a preadolescent to a more sophisticated décor worthy of her new teen status. With luck, Jessie would relent to Simone's sense of style, and do away with the lava lamps and beads her daughter had originally suggested.

Simone stepped into her office, discovering its panoramic view of downtown disturbingly blocked by two large, stinky men. They didn't really stink, but the thought helped to block the handsome faces and muscular physiques.

"You have to be Ian," she stepped forward to shake his hand.

"Right you are, Miss Walker. It's nice to finally put a voice to a face."

"Gee, thanks. Would you gentlemen like to tell me what's going on?"

Simone looked back and forth between the two MI-5 agents. They were absolute stellar opposites. Ian was slightly shorter than Trent by an inch but his blonde curly hair was neatly combed back and resembled a well-manicured lawn compared to Trent's spiky black mop. MI-5 must have a prerequisite on their application--"Only drop-dead gorgeous need apply."

"Ian has been informed that another body was found."

"No," she gasped. "Where?"

"Boston."

"That's where Roz lived. Do we know who this woman was?"

"Umm-" Ian glanced down at a printed report and read the contents. "Ida Lackingbird. Eighty-five years old." He raised his head and looked at her. "It appears to be a heart attack and wouldn't normally come to our attention except that she was your sister's confidant."

A flash of an ancient woman with craggy hands and crackling cough crossed Simone's mind. "Do you have a picture?" She needed confirmation. Her world was disappearing quicker than her favorite chocolate bar.

Trent handed her a fax.

Simone gazed at the grainy black and white fax. Her heart sank. The last link to the knowledge that Roz held lay on a slab in some cold, sterile morgue. Even if she did find the right book, she had no clue what to look for. "I know her. Well, I don't really know her, but I've met her. She was at Roz's funeral. I have her business card at home." She glanced up at Trent. He was it, her last chance. She needed him to destroy the threat of Lawrence Gideon. Only then would she achieve the space and time required to focus on the gray-uglies.

"Ian's going to Boston to check it out. It appears that your wish has been granted." Trent said.

"Oh good. I hope it's the one where you leave here for good never to bother me again." A lump lodged in her throat when she realized what she'd said. She didn't mean it. She couldn't allow him to leave now.

He cocked his head and lifted a brow. "Wrong. It's the one where

Lawrence Gideon leaves here. He's booked a flight back to London for this afternoon."

"Doesn't that mean you have to follow him?" Maybe there was no danger.

"I'm not certain. I'll determine that cause of action after our lunch date."

Simone wasn't about to show how apprehensive she actually was. Lunch loomed before her, making her nauseated. "I still think this is ridiculous of you to attend."

"I am your fiancé. Why shouldn't I join you?" Trent stood with his legs spread apart and hands crossed over his chest. He wore faded blue jeans and a black collared sports shirt embroidered with a golden eagle. He'd changed before they'd left home and Simone thought it was a good thing he'd covered up his legs but now the tightness of his pants only accentuated his muscles . . . all of his muscles.

She moved in front of him and pointed a French manicured nail into his chest.

"You are not my fiancé."

"Lawrence Gideon thinks I am."

"Go home."

"No."

Ian chuckled and clapped Trent on the shoulder.

"I'm leaving now," Ian laughed. "You two will have beautiful children."

Simone and Trent both glared at Ian's back. They were suddenly alone, and she was standing too close. His breath touched her hair leaving behind soft tingles of desire. He pushed away from the window he'd been leaning against and gripped her shoulders. She attempted to twist from his grasp.

"Quit being a Neanderthal, Sherlock, and let me get on with my life. Obviously, if Lord Ugly-Bubbles is going home, he's not interested in the likes of me or my daughter."

"I disagree."

"He might not even be my father."

"True. But you're still my job."

Simone struggled slightly then relaxed in his grasp. She refused to meet his gaze.

"I believe, darling, we have a luncheon to attend." Trent practically picked her up off her feet and moved her to the side. He walked to her door, a wicked grin lighting his face. She stammered her indignation and swept past him into the hall. After a brief check on her daughter, she followed the self-righteous slog-of-a-man into the elevator.

***

They hadn't spoken a word on their drive uptown. Trent seemed content to play the strong silent type. It bugged her. As they walked toward the restaurant, he slipped her hand into his. She jumped at the stimulating contact. Needles would look wonderful sticking out of his eyes.

"Let go of me."

"What on earth for? I love you."

Her heart stopped. Memories of him saying those words crashed in wild abandon against her aching head. She knew he was joking; but, for a moment, a tangle of unfamiliar yearnings and sensations threatened to swallow her soul. In disbelief, Simone stopped. She stood still, an unmoving statue against the wave of hungry pedestrians. Trent looked back when she tugged on his hand. He frowned and pulled her forward.

I love you back, she silently answered. Aloud, however, was another matter. The absolute certainty scared her. How could she possibly have these feelings? She'd only known him for two days.

He's yours. Take him. TAKE him.

FREE.

ME.

No. Go away. You're not real. He's not mine. How can I feel this? "Let go of my hand, Sherlock. You're hurting me," she yelled against the din of the lunch hour race.

He released her but then slid his arm around her waist and pulled her tightly against his chest, buffering her against the wave of bodies. "Sorry. What's the matter? You're terribly pale." Trent gazed into her eyes, and she quickly closed them.

"I'm fine. I guess I'm nervous about this lunch," she lied. With a deep breath, she glanced over his shoulder and tried to release herself from his hold. Trent held tight.

She checked that her anger was sufficiently hyped and turned to glare directly into the depths of his baby-blues. He gazed at her fiercely then his face registered absolute shock.

"Your eyes," he exclaimed.

She swore silently, *did he see her emotion*? She ridiculously wanted to find a mirror to prove to herself that the "I love you Trent Arnot" flag wasn't flying for everyone else's entertainment.

"They're gold. Beautiful."

"Huh?"

"Astonishing."

Simone rolled her *beautiful* eyes and slid easily from his embrace. This time, she was the one to reach for his hand and tug him down the sidewalk.

They reached the small Italian bistro on the corner of Peachtree Street. Glancing through the large windows, Simone immediately recognized the figure of Lord Bromley. He sat at a center table for two dressed as he had been earlier that day. He was chatting amicably with a gentleman seated at the table next to him. Simone found it difficult to match this man with the killer her mind portrayed.

Trent placed his hand on the small of her back and guided her through the entrance to the restaurant. The scent of fresh bread and garlic enveloped them. Normally it would make her mouth water but today she concentrated on not gagging. Lord Bromley spied them and waved her over.

He frowned at her when he realized Trent followed. He signaled a waiter and ordered another table. Simone couldn't believe how attentive the restaurant staff appeared.

"Simone, dear, I hadn't expected the wonderful surprise of Mr. Arnot's presence."

She felt a prick of evil as Lawrence reached for her hand, kissing the top like a French count. Within a second, however, the pain had subsided. She glanced sideways at Trent, surprised that he hadn't spoken. A light sheen of sweat glistened on his face, as if an instant fever had built. His phone rang.

"If you'll excuse me for a moment," Trent said. "I have to take this call." He left them alone, but Simone noted that he didn't go far. He stepped outside the door, but kept her in sight through the large floor to ceiling windows.

She sat down and faced Lord Bromley. Faced her father. Her stomach clenched, and she breathed deeply. I am in a bubble . . .

"You appear quite comfortable here. Do you visit Atlanta often?"

Lawrence Gideon's lips twisted upward. "I'm a spokesperson for the British Red Cross, and we often travel extensively attending international conferences. Atlanta is one of my favorite American cities."

Simone was shocked. "The Red Cross? I'm impressed." He didn't strike her as the sort of individual a charitable organization would consider as a positive role model.

He shrugged as if it was an insignificant thing. "My family is quite wealthy. I was raised with the importance of giving back to those in need. Unfortunately due to circumstances, I am incapable of donating blood. Instead, I offer my time and services."

"I see. Do you find it rewarding?" *Does it balance the evil you perform by killing people?*

"Absolutely. I recently spent time in North Korea. The destruction after the train explosions in Ryongchon was devastating. Our teams did a fantastic job tending to the injured and bringing in relief supplies. It's very rewarding." He sat back and steepled his fore fingers. "But we're not here to talk about me. I want to know all about you."

Simone felt uncomfortable. She didn't want him learning anything about her. "Oh, there's not much of interest where I'm concerned."

"I find that difficult to believe. I understand you're a very well respected architect."

This she could handle. "Yes. Reflections is a solid business. I enjoy my job."

He nodded. "That's good then. Now, tell me about your parents."

"They . . ."

Trent returned. She smiled, relief loosening the band of nerves around her chest.

"Well, old chap," he said, pulling a chair out and sitting down. "What little secrets can you tell us about my future wife? Are there any skeletons I should be aware of in the proverbial family castle?"

"Skeletons?" Lawrence asked, obviously as baffled by the line of conversation as she was.

"Oh yes. With a line as old as the Bromley's," Trent looked at Simone. "Trust me, love, it's a very ancient line. There must be oodles of wonderful old family stories. Murder? Mayhem?" Trent leaned close to Lord Bromley and whispered softly. "Disease?"

Simone was shocked. Had Trent lost his marbles? He'd accused her of inviting danger in. He was downright courting it.

"Quit provoking him," she hissed behind her menu. Then raised her head and smiled at Lawrence Gideon. "I'm certain Mr. Gideon's lineage contains nothing of the sort."

Lord Bromley's eyes narrowed. "Interesting. I thought you were from the south?"

"You did? Whatever gave you that idea?"

Simone didn't know what game he played. But she felt the shield go up around Gideon. The man's face turned a deep red, flooding with anger.

"Your accent." Gideon leaned forward. "I'm curious as to the origin of your knowledge about my family. Tell me, Mr. Arnot, exactly what do you do for a living?" he spoke softly. It was difficult to discern his words among the noisy lunch crowd.

"Oh a bit of this and a bit of that. Investments mostly. I once spent a year abroad. And I love accents. It amuses me to absorb them." Trent smiled. Simone had to shake her head in amazement at how easily he'd played the English Lord. He certainly was smooth.

"I see." Bromley turned and gazed at her. She pushed away the shiver of revulsion and smiled.

"Please excuse my fiancé. He has a warped sense of humor." It surprised her that he didn't continue to push Trent regarding his knowledge of Gideon's background.

"My dear, I have a few documents here that I would like you to look at." Lawrence focused on her and reached to touch her hand with his own, pushing a stack of papers in her direction.

She nodded and glanced at the pages on the table. Frowning, she traced the lineage with her finger. If she read it correctly, his copy indicated that her mother, Marjorie Walker, was his sister. She searched the diagram for any reference to Pamela Allen, the woman Trent's genealogy chart indicated as her birth mother. But she didn't see the name anywhere.

"I recognize some of these names." She pointed to Marjorie Walker. "This is my mother."

"Wonderful," he cackled, coughing lightly into a handkerchief. "I would like to extend an offer for you to come and visit our estate. Blithewoods, although lacking in skeletons, does come with its fair share of history." He didn't seem affected by the knowledge that she was his niece. Nor did he ask after her mother's whereabouts.

Over her dead body was she going anywhere near Blithewoods. However, the differences between their two genealogies peaked her curiosity not to mention smoothed her nerves when she realized he certainly didn't think of himself as her father. "Oh, I don't think . . ." Simone began only to be rudely interrupted by Trent.

"Of course, we'll come for a visit. Isn't that wonderful, love? It's not far from Mother's."

"Well, I'm not sure," she said, glaring at him. "What with the wedding plans and all." Her eyes flashed a warning, but the arrogant-ass simply ignored her.

"We'll be in Bath next week to visit my Mum. How about we pop around then?"

"Smashing," Lawrence Gideon answered, a Cheshire cat smile twisting his lips into a perverse grin.

He made her ill, and she moved her gaze downward.

"On one condition, however," Lord Bromley stated. "I insist you bring your lovely daughter, as well."

"Oh, I . . ." Fear gripped Simone's heart. She didn't want Jessie's name to ever touch this man's lips.

"I'm certain that she'll be delighted by your request. Isn't that right, love?" Trent responded.

Simone was frozen. What was he saying? He was dangling Jessie in front of Lawrence's nose like a carrot to a horse. How could he deliberately endanger her daughter?

Simone felt him reassuringly squeeze her knee beneath the table. She wanted to backhand him from here to eternity. Instead, she gritted her teeth and smiled politely.

"Yes, sweet cakes, I'm certain Jessie would enjoy Blithewoods very much." She reached beneath the table and pinched the top of his hand.

Trent flipped his wrist and wound her fingers through his. She tugged. He held tight.

He'd not manipulate her or her daughter. This man was done twisting her emotions into a pretzel.

"I believe we need to return to your office Simone," he said, pushing his chair back and standing.

"But we haven't eaten yet." Not that she wanted to, but his behavior seemed odd.

"If we're visiting with Lord Bromley next week, I'm certain he'll be able to answer all your questions then."

"Absolutely," Lawrence Gideon agreed. Simone frowned as he rose as well and the only party remaining seated was her. Okay, both of them were acting strangely.

"Suit yourselves, then." Simone followed Trent from the restaurant. The heat of the afternoon slammed into her face as they made their way back down the street they'd walked earlier. She smacked Trent in the arm. "You never told me he was an important member of the British Red Cross."

Trent lifted his brow. "You never asked."

She snarled. "I didn't even have a chance to find out any pertinent information about Rosalyn."

"He doesn't know you're aware of his connection to her. It would've sparked too many questions I'm not willing to answer yet."

"Dammit, Trent. You're not taking us to England."

He stopped and turned to face her. "Do you want Jessie safe?"

"Of course I do but taking her across seas . . ."

He interrupted. "Do you want revenge for your sister's death?"

Her stomach flipped. He was playing dirty. "Not at the risk of Jessie."

"Then trust me."

***

Back in the comfort of her own surroundings, her confidence regenerated itself. Simone faced Trent once more.

"What are you doing making him believe we'll come to England? What's going to happen when no one arrives? Because, I'm sure as hell not going."

"Yes, you are." Trent was slouched comfortably on a plush Italian sofa that lined the interior wall of her midtown office. She'd spent the past hour returning phone calls and rescheduling the appointments she'd missed earlier that day, too angry to confront the man before her. "Right after you have your blood tested at . . ." he pulled a piece of paper from his pocket and read the scribbled words. "Emory Hospital."

"No. You might be heading back to the mother country, but I'm staying right here. Why the hell would he even think I'd agree to go to England? I don't even know the man."

Trent looked at her through sleepy, bedroom eyes and slowly shook his head. "Sorry, love, but you'll be right by my side."

She stared into his face, trying to read behind the mask in place.

"And I suppose you expect me to bring Jessie as bait? You are one cold fish, Agent Arnot."

His gaze narrowed, and she could visibly see the strength of the pulse that beat just below his jaw line when he responded. "Jessie will remain stateside. I'll not risk her."

"But you'll risk me," she stated flatly.

He stared long and hard at her face. She thought his gaze softened slightly when he met her silent plea. Not for long, however, the eyes of a hunter slipped back in place.

"Yes," Trent whispered. "I'll risk you."

Chapter Twelve

Simone drifted toward consciousness, the weight pushing against her heart familiar. It sparked alarm. Her eyes fluttered open and the vision of a wavering golden eye snatched her attention, forcing her beneath the power of the energy tossing her back through time. It felt gentle this time almost as if it guided her through the centuries, stopping at a preordained destination.

**

Elizabeth lay in bed, the hushed whispers echoing down the hall filtered beneath her door. She threw back her bedcovers and grabbed the crimson over-gown that lay in a silken puddle on the floor. Her body tingled from Rake's recent caress. The voices grew louder, and she knew her brother approached.

Henry, Prince of Wales barged into her quarters heedless of invading her space. He was to be king. "Elizabeth, I will have answers." His face burned the color of the roses her mother had imported from Denmark--blood-red. They climbed the exterior walls of Draconius in wild abandon.

"Henry, it isn't what you think." Her brother might be well educated and a fine judge of art, but his sense of self-righteousness often blocked the greater vision he would require to succeed as King of England. Charles, on the other hand, lacked no such moral standard and although no more than a decade old constantly nipped at his brother's heels.

Henry snorted in disgust. "Frederick shall be arriving in less than a fortnight. I have worked hard on this alliance with the Germans solidifying the Protestantism."

Elizabeth bowed her head. "I do not love Frederick." She spoke softly, knowing that her heart wasn't an issue

"Where is he? Where is your lover?"

"Here, Your Highness."

Elizabeth sighed in relief as Rake strode into the room. He'd only had moments to dress when Henry first arrived and wore only his breeches and a linen shirt. His blue eyes locked on her and she smiled. His love was sound. Of that, she had no doubt.

Henry whirled around and faced her lover. He pointed an angry finger. "These pagan acts shall not take place beneath my rule."

"Henry," Elizabeth said. "It wasn't his fault. The power is too much to handle. We couldn't wait. The White Book of Rhydderch says that he must claim me body and soul for the dragon to be free."

The Prince of Wales shook his head. "Nonsense. You must overlay the Red Book of Hergest in order to seek the true prophecy. Rake has done nothing but strike at my honor. Frederick has been tested and is an Ancient. Your future lies with a king."

Elizabeth shook her head. "No. It lies with Rake. If you do this, force my hand in marriage, we'll never reach the true destiny that is ours to take."

Rake moved to stand before her, his body shielding her from her brother's wrath. "It is as she said. I am the one."

"Blasphemy!" Henry raged. "Guards."

Rake spun and gripped Elizabeth's shoulders. "Run. Leave this place and . . ."

She felt his weight as he fell upon her. Elizabeth gazed one last time into the eyes that were her heart and watched the life fade in slow seconds of agony. Tears ran down her cheeks. She fell to the ground, clutching the man that was her world. Raising her head, she saw the bloody knife within her brother's hand. "What have you done?"

"You shall marry Frederick." He turned and left her chamber.

She stroked raven hair away from Rake's eyes. "I shall always love you," she whispered against his lips.

"And I you," he exhaled and was gone. Her chest seized and sorrow filled her soul. Narrowing her eyes, anger simmered and flared to life. The force within grew.

Elizabeth laid Rake gently upon the cold stone floor and slipped from beneath the weight of his body. Pulling a cover from the bed still warm from his love, she covered him and left the room.

She found her brother. The fool. Her power grew and demanded release.

"I curse you, Henry, Prince of Wales. You shall not live beyond the night."

***

Simone woke, the curse still bitter upon her tongue. Tears left a damp trail on her face, and she felt the sodden pillowcase beneath her head. It happened again. Did the men she loved always end up dead? She hadn't seen the shadows within this dream, but she'd felt them. These dreams weren't of real people. She convinced herself. They were a manifestation of this disease that ran through her veins like an alien invasion.

But what if? She remembered enough from her history course in college to recognize the characters that played within her memories. Inhaling deeply, she tried to vanquish the uncomfortable thought that her grip on reality was slipping.

She'd felt the power blaze from Elizabeth. It mirrored the same heat from her childhood and the uncomfortable burn of what lay lodged in her gut today. With a shaking hand, she pushed back the hair from her face and glanced out her bedroom window.

The horizon brightened with the break of dawn. Resigned to sleeplessness, she grabbed a pen and pad off her night stand and scribbled down two titles. The White Book of Rhydderch and Red Book of Hergest. There were two volumes. She remembered the brief conversation with Ida Lackingbird about having to read the White Book in conjunction with another volume for the answer to be revealed. Ida was dead. Another source frustratingly yanked from her access.

Jessie's future, maybe her life, depended upon Simone's ability to separate fact from fiction, reality from fantasy, sanity from madness.

Propelled by concern for her daughter, she headed downstairs unhindered by the lack of clothes she wore. She didn't care anymore. The love her heart felt wasn't real, and if it was, it would only end up killing the man with the ageless blue eyes. If he was some kind of soul mate as Elizabeth indicated, then it was obvious to Simone their union only ended in his death.

Her bare feet hit the slick, hardwood floor and she padded into the kitchen.

"You're up early," Trent said.

She jumped and spun around to find him sitting at the kitchen table. His hair was damp with sweat and he wore nothing but a pair of running shorts. Her eyes feasted on his naked chest. She inhaled, resisting the urge to lick her lips. The desire fanning her insides into an inferno wasn't welcome.

Simone lifted her eyes to gaze into his face. He pushed back from the table and stood, never once releasing her from his hypnotic stare. Trent's muscles bunched in anticipation of the kill. Hunter and hunted. She stepped back, slamming into the side of the refrigerator.

They were a hairs length from one another. Simone's breath came in short gasps. His presence sent an amazing array of fireworks skating along her skin. He leaned close, bringing his lips to her ear. She tried not to sigh, fought against rubbing her cheek against the stubble that lined his jaw.

"You should wear more clothes," he whispered, his breath hot against her cheek, sending her already raw nerves through the roof.

She turned her head, allowing him to nibble on the sensitive skin of her neck. He didn't disappoint, and she groaned softly. "So should you."

He ran the edge of his tongue across her skin and scattered soft kisses up her neck. She sighed and pulled him closer, her hands playing along the muscles that tightened beneath her touch. He smelled like heaven, and her mouth watered to taste him.

Trent found her lips and she soaked in his kiss as if her life depended on it. He groaned and moved closer, pinning her against the refrigerator. The want and need that flashed through her soul scared the hell out of her. Simone ran her fingers through his hair, tipping her head back to stare into the passion cloud of deep-azure. It would be so easy to open her legs, climb the length of his powerful body and beg him to take her.

What she felt mirrored the passion and love that filtered through her dreams. It overpowered and destroyed her. Tears welled as the memory of life fading from his eyes slammed into her. Her soul shrieked with sadness and a sense of abandonment she hadn't felt in twenty years. She couldn't do this, couldn't allow her love to endanger him. Couldn't allow herself to lose again.

"I want to go to Boston."

Trent's gaze hardened. The soft hue of love fled from his eyes to be replaced with a hard edge stare. "And you thought a hot kiss would get you there?"

"I . . ." Simone stammered. "No. I came down to tell you that I need to go to Boston. The kiss doesn't have anything to do with it."

"No? Nice try at manipulation, Simone. But I already told you this line of bait and attack won't work on me."

"You son of a bitch. I'm not manipulating you." She pushed him away from her. "It's your fault. You came on to me all naked from the waist up with testosterone leaking out of every pore." Anger was good. She hated the way his eyes were vacant of any feeling, any love. It hurt. It felt wrong.

He ran a hand through his scraggly mop of hair. God, he was gorgeous. Simone turned away not wanting him to see the tears that threatened to tip over her lashes.

"What am I supposed to do? You walk in here with a slip of silk covering your breasts and not bloody much else on." His frustration laced his words, making them come out in one hot tide.

The tension and attraction arcing between their two bodies filled the kitchen with enough electricity to fuel the entire house for the winter. Simone unfolded the rim of her boxers so it covered her belly button and tugged down her chemise. "I'm sorry," she said.

He shook his head and grunted, walking to the other end of the room. She glanced at his butt and swallowed. When he turned, the evidence of his arousal made her bite her lips. Her body tightened and a river of heat spread downward, making her want to scream. If she stripped her clothes off and demanded his body, he wouldn't refuse. She knew he couldn't.

Her eyes met his.

"It's damn hard to fight you when you look at me like that," he said, his voice low and husky. "I won't deny that every inch of me wants to be buried in you right now." He moved out of the kitchen and into the living room. "But it's not going to happen. Is that clear?"

"Yes."

"I'm going to take a very cold shower and then you and I will discuss Boston."

She sighed. Her fingers found the handle of the coffee pot, and she started her morning routine. "That'll be fine."

"Are you going to change?"

Her eyes snapped up at the sharpness of his tone. She nodded, and he retreated to the guest suite. Simone didn't understand why he always thought she was manipulating him. Bloody hell, he was sensitive. Bloody hell, she was swearing like him. Bloody hell, he'd crawled beneath her skin.

***

Trent leaned against the shower wall, head bent and shoulders sagging. He shivered as the icy flow of water sluiced down his back. His body still burned. Bloody hell, his need for Simone made him want to get down on his knees and cry. This couldn't be happening. He didn't understand the attraction; it went far beyond physical, far beyond what the chronicles claimed.

He'd felt the evil creep across the table at lunch yesterday. Lawrence

Gideon was more than a serial killer. But exactly what, Trent didn't know. Getting away from the man's aura had been the one thing that screamed loud and clear across the restaurant. He'd given Gideon enough hints as to who Trent really was that the man would be a fool to continue his attack on Simone.

Trent warmed the water to a more tolerable temperature and scrubbed away his desire, too bad he couldn't reach into his heart and yank out the emotion he feared lay there.

He blew out a thick gust of air and flipped the water off. "Bloody hell!" he yelled to the bathroom walls and punched the air with his fist.

***

Simone stared across the kitchen table at a very angry Trent.

"You're not going to Boston," he said for the tenth time that morning.

She smiled sweetly and shoved another cup of coffee at him. "Yes, I am."

Jessie danced into the kitchen, snagged a box of cereal, shook its contents into a bowl and splashed milk on top. "So am I."

Trent's face flushed a deep red but Simone didn't back down. "It's my sister's life in that apartment. I believe I have a right to see what's there."

"Ian mentioned that her friends were packing it up. They'll ship everything here. There's no need to go to Boston."

She smacked her palms on the table and stood up. "Why are you acting like this?"

He mimicked her actions. They stood nose to nose. "Like what?"

"Like an overbearing body guard." Simone ignored the crunching of cereal and giggles from her daughter.

"It is my job to keep you safe. Boston isn't safe."

"Lawrence Gideon's already returned to England. As a matter of fact, he was here when that poor woman died. I bet there's no connection."

His gaze dropped to her lips. "The answer is no."

"I'm going to Boston with or without you."

He leaned across the table. She swallowed, the air disappearing from her lungs. His eyes swept up and imprisoned her. With a wink he moved closer, touching his lips to hers. Her lashes closed and she absorbed the warmth seeping from him, the kiss soft and gentle.

Trent pushed back, breaking contact. "No, you're not." He said in a whisper and walked away, leaving her flustered and unsure. He pointed a finger at Jessie and scowled. "And neither are you."

Simone followed him out of the room. "Where do you think you're going? We're not finished *discussing this*."

"I'm off to visit Sheriff Tippens."

"Why'd you kiss me?"

Her question stopped him dead in his tracks; he turned slowly a sly grin twisting his mouth. "You were pouting. I couldn't resist."

She sputtered. "I was not pouting, and we're going to Boston."

Trent raked his fingers through his hair, and she smiled when she recognized his action as a sign of uncertainty. "Oh, bloody hell."

"We're going."

He closed his eyes and sighed. "Fine. Make the arrangements. But we're not staying longer than one night. Is that clear? We need to be in England as soon as possible, and I have a ton of loose ends to tie up here."

She resisted the urge to jump up and down and clap her hands. Instead, she smiled and shooed him off. "Go play with Randy."

He shook his head and walked out the front door. Jessie walked up and slipped her arm around Simone's waist. "Did he just kiss you?"

"Yeah," she answered. "I was pouting."

***

Boston glittered in the light of the setting sun, its skyscrapers winking in rapid fashion as the reflection of the fading day washed against their glass walls. Simone marveled at the site as the plane banked and approached a landing pattern. Older stone buildings skirted the outside of the sprawling New England city, a fortress of rock around its modern heart.

As they neared the airport, water passed beneath them at an amazing speed. Jessie gasped as the wheels hit the tarmac. She reached for her daughter's hand and smiled at her, soothing her nerves. Trent sat behind them. He hadn't spoken a word during the two and a half hour flight. She chuckled to herself. Now look who's pouting.

They exited the plane and quickly found their way through the maze to baggage claim. He'd argued that they didn't need a suitcase just an overnight bag. Jessie stared at him in utter shock. How could she travel with only one change of clothes?

He'd finally relented and allowed them one suitcase between the three of them. It tickled and alarmed Simone at the ease with which they moved as a family unit.

"Stop pacing. You're making me dizzy." She said, amused by his irritation.

"If you'd agreed to a carry on, we'd already be at the hotel by now."

Simone smiled. "Patience."

He glared and she turned away before she laughed in his face. As she watched the weary travelers grab their luggage, the reason for their trip north settled painfully in her chest. It seemed impossible that she should miss someone she hardly knew.

Her eyes swept over her daughter. She stood beside Trent, small and innocent. Life seemed terribly fragile. If Simone was infected with porphyria, what future would her daughter face? She closed her eyes and shut down the disturbing thoughts. The thought of her daughter losing the exuberance and thrill of life ignited resentment. She'd be damned if that was going to happen. Their appointment for blood work at Emory was tomorrow. It couldn't arrive fast enough.

Trent snagged their suitcase and signaled for her.

"Are you okay?" he asked.

"I'm fine. If we only have this one night, then I want to go directly to my sister's apartment."

Trent glanced at Jessie. "Do you think that's a good idea?"

She knew what he meant. It might be dangerous. They didn't know what they'd find within Rosalyn's apartment. "I'm sure as hell not leaving her alone at the hotel."

"Oh Mama, I'm almost thirteen."

"Don't remind me. But the answer still remains no. We're sticking together."

Trent nodded. "I'll call Ian and ask him to meet us there."

She ignored his clipped business tone. If he wanted to pretend they were strangers, that was fine by her.

***

Entering Rosalyn's apartment was like stepping through a portal to another dimension. Trent turned in a circle as he stared at the main living area. It was stark. White walls, white carpet, white furniture. Simone hadn't left his side since Ian had opened the door. Her fingers were currently wrapped around his arm in a grip that mirrored the unease and apprehension that twisted his gut.

"We're leaving. You're not ready for this."

"No." She gripped his arm harder. "There's nothing in here that will hurt us."

"Then why are you latched onto me like I'm the other half of your Velcro strip?"

She giggled nervously and released his arm. "This room certainly doesn't reflect Rosalyn. Then again, maybe it does." Moving to the center, she wiped a finger down a white cube that appeared to be some form of modern coffee table. "It's so . . ." Simone shrugged, apparently lost for words.

"White?" he offered.

She smiled and nodded. "Maybe I should've worn my white sundress instead of the peach one to the funeral."

"The peach one was fine." It was a major prop in most of his midnight fantasies.

Ian walked over and handed him a folder. By the look in his partner's eyes this wasn't for reading in front of Simone. "The contents are a bit odd," is all he said.

"Come on ladies, I think the other rooms will be more to your liking." Ian said.

Simone followed Ian and grinned as Jessie squealed when she entered what must have been Rosalyn's bedroom. "It's like a fairy's house," her daughter whispered.

Trent peered over Simone's shoulder astonished at the deep purples and vivid reds that splashed the tiny room with color. Everything was layered in light, filmy fabrics that sparkled with sequins. "Can I?" Jessie turned and looked at Trent, her eyes bright with curiosity.

"I don't see why not. I think it would be a fine thing for you to look through her things and see if there's something you might want to keep."

Jessie entered the room before Trent finished his sentence. Simone turned and continued down the hall. He found her standing in a tiny room that appeared to be Rosalyn's office. Although many of the shelves were empty, there still remained an astonishing number of books that all appeared Wiccan in origin.

"I always knew my sister was fascinated by spells and magic but this..." she waved her arm around the room. "This is amazing."

"Ian's digging into her background, and I'm certain he'll be able to answer all your questions after he's finished his interviews."

She offered him a soft smile. "I don't have any questions. But I am searching for something."

"And what is that?"

"A book. It's called the Red Book of Hergest."

Pain shot through his temple, and Trent ran his fingers through his hair. This twist headed down a road he didn't want to contemplate. It was too soon.

"That's an odd name."

Simone shrugged. "I know. And don't bother asking what it is because I have no clue." She moved from shelf to shelf, pulling books down and putting them back. "I don't even know if it exists."

It exists. But he wasn't about to tell her that. Together with its companion The White Book of Rhydderch it detailed a prophecy dating back to the ninth century. Her prophecy. His destiny.

"What are you doing?" Simone asked.

"Packing. Do you want all these delivered to your house?"

She shook her head. "I'm not sure. I haven't thought about it. Maybe they should be sent to my office."

"Fine." He ignored the troubled frown that marred her face. He needed to think and think fast.

* * *

Trent peered into Rosalyn's bedroom. Simone lay sound asleep with Jessie tucked beneath her arm. Her hair fanned across the pillow like a golden river. He fought the urge to enter and run his fingers through its silken strands.

An uncomfortable thought lodged in his throat. His black and white assignment suddenly seemed murky and unclear. The feelings mixed with his knowledge of what lay ahead had his mind spinning and his heart...well, he didn't know what his heart was doing.

He felt Ian's presence. Turning, he grinned at his partner embarrassed to be caught staring in the room.

"Let's go over that folder you gave me earlier."

"Sure thing." Ian raised his brow and Trent ignored the silent question.

"Don't go there."

"I won't."

"I mean it." He repeated as they walked down the narrow hall. "Don't go there."

"You've got it bad."

"I told you not to go there." Ian never bloody listened. This time, however, he refused to be badgered. "Grab us a couple of beers and tell me what you've discovered so far."

"Real bad."

He glared at his partner. Ian smiled and shrugged. "No sweat off my back. One more bit of competition out of the way. I guess you haven't had a poke yet or else we'd be dealing with another personality, right?"

Temper flared fast and furious. He slammed his partner against the wall and peered into his face. The humor twinkling back made him swear loudly. "Just as I thought," Ian said, biting back on his laugher. "Real bad."

Trent released him and pushed him toward the kitchen. "I told you not to go there. Get the beer."

Ian laughed and went in search of something to drink. He came back with two wine coolers. "No beer."

Trent grimaced but accepted it. At this point, he'd take anything to numb the feelings. "I want you to understand that I'm doing as instructed."

"After a second in Simone's company, I bet you realized you were in trouble."

"Stop being a fool. You know what I mean. I can't become emotionally involved."

"Uh-huh." Ian slugged his drink, wiped the back of his hand against his mouth and burped loudly. "That's not bad."

Trent eyed his bottle. He took a swig and grinned in surprise. "You're right." Scrutinizing the bottle, he took another swallow. "It says this is some sort of hard lemonade."

Ian put his bottle down and tossed over the file Trent had left on the coffee table. "Simone's sister was a serious witch. She belonged to one of the largest covens in the Boston area. Miss Lackingbird was her sponsor."

"Sponsor?"

"Yes. I guess you can't just walk up and join a coven; you have to be introduced through a sponsor. At least that's my understanding. Anyway, the details are in that package. This group did some weird crap. Kind of makes my short hairs stand straight."

Trent laughed. It wouldn't bother him. He was used to all this stuff from his mother. She didn't particularly care for witches, specifically the ones that dwelled around Pendle Hill. She called them the *Witches With No Lives* organization. He glanced through the folder at sheets of hand written spells and other items he couldn't decipher. With a sigh, he realized it was inevitable. He'd have to ask for his mother's assistance. He held up the file and waved it at Ian.

"My mother?"

"That's what I thought. Lady Lichfield should be a fountain of information on this subject." Ian laughed. "It's been awhile since we've had the prophecy read to us." He teased Trent.

"Very funny. That's not a real prophecy, you know. They've never been able to connect it to the Dragon Dancer legacy."

Ian waggled his brows and pointed down the hall. "She is the one."

Trent's gut twisted tighter. "I want you to hit the books some more. I think we're missing something from the chronicles."

"How so?"

"The pull and the call, it's not as written. It's harder. I feel as if she's wrapped herself around me, and I can't breathe."

Ian paused and stared at him. "It's love, old pal."

Trent glared at him. "I told you not to go there. Any details on the old lady's murder?"

"Nada. It couldn't have been our guy because there weren't any nasty stab wounds. Besides, it's really a cut and dry robbery."

Trent's raised a brow. "Oh yeah? What was stolen?"

Ian frowned. "The Red Book."

A warning flare went off in Trent's head. This was too coincidental. "I'm taking Simone home tomorrow. She has an appointment for her blood to be tested for porphyria. Wrap up your interviews then meet us at the Manor house."

"What do you think Gideon's up to with the invite to his estate?"

Trent glanced at Ian and shook his head. "I honestly don't know. But the Director and I both agree that the awakening will be smoother at home. Gideon just made the inevitable easier."

"She trust you?" Ian picked up his drink, emptied the contents, and placed the bottle on the coffee table.

Trent mimicked his actions. "She does. But for how long, I can't be certain."

"You going to wake them?"

"Nah. I figure we'll just sleep here tonight."

"Right then. I'll see you back across the pond."

Trent nodded. "Keep in touch." He followed his partner to the front door and locked it after he'd left. Walking through the silent apartment he eyed the couch.

It was sleek and sexy. Why did women feel the necessity to buy pretty sofas with wooden legs and nice curves? He craved thick overstuffed cushions.

He sat on the edge of the small sofa. What would Simone say if he told her he knew exactly where to find The Red Book of Hergest?

Chapter Thirteen

Trent walked into the small brick building that housed the Sheriff's department. Yellowed linoleum squares lined the open room with six gray metal desks placed in uniform position upon its surface. The drab conditions didn't darken the jovial mood of the men swapping weekend stories of fishing conquests and bragging about the women they'd met.

He waved and proceeded through their center into Randy's office. It smelled of stale tobacco and biscuits, an odd combination that Trent found relaxing. Maybe it made him think of the pubs at home or maybe it was such a refreshing change from the sweet scent of Simone that his nerves were able to settle. He didn't know. He didn't care.

"Back from Boston?" Randy looked up and smiled. Trent liked the man. Their first few hours together had been rocky, but once he adjusted to the rhythm of the Sheriff's schedule they'd found an affinity with one another. And respect. He might be small town, but there wasn't anything small about his commitment to the safety of its inhabitants.

Trent ran his fingers through his hair and sat in the hard backed chair facing Randy's desk. "Yes. And it was nothing more than a wild goose chase. Anything else turn up from Atlanta?"

Randy stuck a straw in his mouth and chewed on it. Trent frowned and tilted his head in an unspoken question.

"Tryin' to quit."

The defeat in Randy's shoulders spoke a million words.

"Delores?"

"Yeah."

"Still love her, huh?"

"Yeah."

Trent fantasized for a moment what it would be like to carve out a life in this quiet corner of the world. Come home everyday to a woman you loved beyond reason and a child whose every move made you want to laugh and protect her at the same time. It'd be heaven.

It wasn't in his cards.

The moment Simone realized the depth of his deception, she would hate him. And he'd leave because that wasn't an emotion that would sit well.

"Atlanta?" he asked, trying in vain to focus on his job.

"Nothing." Randy shook his head. "I found it odd though that their first call to me indicated suicide. Why would they say that? I've reviewed your file and looked at those pictures. My God, they've given me nightmares. And why haven't they turned over her belongings?"

Trent nodded and shrugged. "I don't know. Did you ask them?"

"I got some cockamamie response about misinformation from headquarters regarding the suicide and then more bullshit about misplacing her stuff. It doesn't add up."

Trent allowed a tight smile to form. "Yes, it does. They were bought. If the details of the murder had been released through the computer system they would have linked with the other bodies immediately. One you can hide. Two you can't. And three, you're going to spark a world wide investigation. Gideon's not stupid. Or maybe he is. He doesn't know that we're already on to him. At least he didn't until we had lunch."

"What did you do?"

"Not much. Just got the old boy's brain twisting with my accent and knowledge of his background. I hope I've shaken him."

Randy nodded. "Bastard." He tossed the coffee straw into the waste basked. "I didn't much care for Rosalyn, but she didn't deserve to die like that."

"What was with you and Rosalyn?"

"Nothing. She was just weird. My older brother used to say she did spells and shit like that. And then Simone . . ." His voice trailed off as he realized he'd probably said too much.

"What about Simone?"

"Nothing." Randy slid his eyes downward and to the left. Trent leaned forward and placed his elbows on the cool metal of the Sheriff's desk.

"What about Simone?"

Randy shook his head. "It was nothing. Just mean kid stuff."

Trent decided not to push any further. If it was childish behavior the man referred to then it really shouldn't concern the investigation. And if it wasn't, he wasn't certain he wanted to hear about it. The desire to know all the intimate details of Simone's life was purely personal.

"Do you think it has anything to do with Rosalyn's death?"

The Sheriff snapped his eyes up in shock. "No. Hell, no. I'm just not real proud of the boy I was."

"Okay, then. I suppose I'll head back to the house. We're out of here shortly. Ian's wrapping up in Boston, and MI-5 is working on setting up what we'll need to hopefully put an end to this man's warpath."

Randy stood and stretched his hand out. Trent accepted it and clapped him on the back. "If you need anything, don't hesitate to call." Randy said.

"You're going to be fine with Jessie?"

"Sure. We'll be okay."

***

Trent walked around to the back yard. Simone was knee deep in a flower bed, yanking and pulling at weeds. The afternoon sun blazed down, and he was grateful she'd worn a straw hat to protect her tender skin. The affection he felt as he watched each graceful move she made tightened his chest. All he wanted was to gather her in his arms and sweep her away. Love her.

He squared his shoulders and slammed down the mask of indifference he'd been perfecting the last twenty-four hours.

"I'm taking Jessie into town for an ice cream," he said, anything to put distance between them.

She turned and smiled. Her face lit beneath the shade of her hat and her eyes glowed with anticipation. "Oh yay, I love ice cream. Give me a minute, and I'll join you."

"Don't bother yourself. Just tell me what you want, and I'll bring it back." He hated the hurt that darkened her eyes and had to battle against the drop in his stomach when her face flushed with embarrassment.

She shook her head and turned back to the garden. "Don't bother. I'm fine."

"We'll be back in an hour." He turned and ran back to the house. Trent opened the back French door and called to Jessie.

***

Simone put the finishing touches on the final sketches for the Gulliver estate. Her lack of success in Boston frustrated an already complicated situation. The information contained in both the book Rosalyn searched for and the one Simone was certain her sister already possessed called to her. There was knowledge to be had, and she hated all the brick walls in her way. Trent had failed at obtaining Rosalyn's possessions.

Sitting behind her desk, she tapped an impatient pencil against the Gulliver plan's Mylar surface. She needed to deliver the prints this evening and then pack her bags.

Jessie's laughter filtered through the open window. Smiling, she realized that the gray-uglies had disappeared temporarily and her chattery inner-self silenced. Her acceptance of the disease that flowed through her veins probably calmed her symptoms. No more paralysis. The tingling, however, continued and only abated in Trent's presence. Psychosomatic, she figured.

Pushing her thoughts to the background, she gazed out the window. Trent was racing behind Jessie wielding a hose that spewed forth a fountain of cold water. He drenched the child and allowed her to wrestle it from his hands and turn the spray back in his direction. He barked in shock as the frigid water crashed into his face, running glacial rivers down his body.

His affection for Jessie was clearly obvious. They'd played basketball. Tossed the football around, and even engaged in a horribly one-sided game of croquet with Jessie triumphing. Trent insisted he was reliving his childhood. He had younger brothers and their days of horsing around had been over for some time.

Simone inhaled sharply when he peeled off his wet shirt. His chest rippled with muscles that glistened in the afternoon sun. Tossing the sodden top to the ground, he bunched his arms and faked an attack. Jessie shrieked, and he lunged for her. They rolled around the wet grass like puppies until he raised his hand, begging for mercy.

For the first time in her life, Simone wanted to be Jessie. She wanted her affection accepted and returned. It would never happen. He'd shut her out. All she was to Agent Arnot was bait. Maybe, it was the thought of her being diseased that cooled his blood.

The telephone rang. She reached over, digging the cordless from beneath the mountain of papers littering her desk. After listening to the voice on the other end, she thanked them and hung up the phone. Her heart pounded. She sat stunned, totally thrown by the call.

The details froze her mind. It couldn't be true. She'd already accepted her fate; her future . . . now it all came crashing back into her lap. Gazing at her fingers, Simone couldn't help the swell of pure joy that swamped her. To hell with everything else she was experiencing, this was one bit of news that deserved celebration.

She let out a whoop of delight.

Trent and Jessie raced to the window, shouting out questions.

"Simone, what is it? What's happened?"

She turned, smiling with happiness, one ton of trouble dropped from her shoulders.

"That was Dr. Paige's office. We're clear."

"Clear of what?" Jessie asked.

"Porphyria. We're gene free," she grinned. Happiness bubbled forth in a torrent of relieved laughter. Trent splayed his hand against the screen. After a brief second, she rested hers against it.

"Thank God," he whispered.

"Yes," she answered, trying to ignore the emotion welling from his touch. She convinced herself it was Jessie he had been concerned with. This display of affection had little to do with her.

Trent pulled his hand away, wiping it against his chest as if it burned. "In celebration, I'll cook tonight for the Walker women."

Jessie groaned, making nasty facial expressions.

"I'll have you know, Miss Jessie, that I wield a mean barbeque fork."

"How could you?" Jessie taunted. "You're English."

"Come here you wretched child," he cried. "I'll teach you a thing or two about being English."

He threw one last lingering look at Simone before racing after her daughter. Her heart lodged in her throat.

What had that meant?

***

Trent walked into her house thirty minutes later. He'd managed to dry himself off in the sun. His shirt flung over his shoulder, he followed the sound of a tapping pencil. Simone sat behind her desk, playing with the lead utensil and staring at a large print.

She was gorgeous. Her hair was twisted into a knot and held in place by a tortoise shell clip, exposing her neck. His groin tightened. Counting to ten, he balanced his libido and moved behind her. He resisted the urge to touch the baby hairs that curled around her nape.

"What's this?" he asked.

"The final plans for the Gulliver Estate."

He frowned then pointed at a circular section, bending close and brushing her back with his chest. He bent lower and rubbed his arm against her bare skin. Tingles of excitement ricocheted within the small office, and he closed his eyes to block the desire that curled an invisible fist inside him. Stay distant. He didn't.

"This marking, what does that mean?"

He could feel her tense and knew he was being unfair--to both of them. He'd successfully maintained his distance. Her brief touch through the screen had almost undone him, scorching a mile-wide path through his resolve.

"It's an observatory. Mr. Gulliver is an astrologer-wannabe, and Mrs. Gulliver is an ornithologist-wannabe. I've created a room that will satisfy both their hobbies."

"Do you always satisfy?" He whispered against her ear, attempting to keep this closeness alive.

She whirled her chair around. It slammed into his knees, and she pushed against his chest nearly knocking him off his feet.

"What are you doing?" she asked.

"I'm sorry?" He quickly regained his composure, running nervous fingers through his hair.

"Why are you coming in here acting like we're intimate lovers? You've practically frozen me out of my own home." Her face was flushed with anger, and he wanted nothing more than to bend down and taste her lips.

He'd seen the look in her eyes on the sidewalk outside the restaurant, a mirror image of eyes captured by a weaver and emblazoned upon a tapestry that hung in his family's library.

He'd snatched everything churning in his gut and scrunched them into a ball of self-preservation before they connected with her. He'd not allow them loose. Not yet. He didn't believe this destiny was more than what the chronicles detailed.

Trent Arnot, MI-5 Agent. Ancient. A man sent to release an ageless being. That's whom she needed, and that's whom she was going to get. Anything less, or more in this case, was dangerous.

"I've a job to do, Simone. I'm sorry if my professionalism hurt your feelings."

She narrowed her eyes and glared at him. "You didn't hurt my feelings."

"I'm glad. Because, I'd hate anything to interfere with your safety and this investigation."

"The latter," she said. "I'm well aware of."

"Simone, what do you want me to do?"

Kiss her, that's what her eyes begged for. He resisted the invitation.

"I want you to arrest Lawrence Gideon and get the hell out of my life."

He nodded. She continued to glare at him, shooting daggers of resentment into his heart.

"Right, then. We'd better get a move on. How do you like your steak?"

"Walking," she snapped.

He smiled tightly and left the room before she realized the extent of his internal battle. They couldn't be together. Not here.

The books said he was to be nothing more than a soldier for her, a vessel to be used to tame the rampant power that rested within her soul. He would not fall folly to the notion that their relationship would be anything more.

He hadn't fallen in love.

Trent grabbed the platter of meat off the kitchen counter and headed out to the grill

Jessie was swaying back and forth on the tire swing he'd hung up yesterday. It moved languidly like a huge rubber pendulum. Frowning, he walked to the edge of the deck. Jessie wasn't moving. The tire tilted upward and headed toward the sky, but Jessie wasn't coaxing it forward. It glided silently through the air . . . powered by an unseen force.

"Simone," he yelled, racing off the deck. The swing had picked up momentum, dipping from one end of the tree to the next. His attempt to grab Jessie as she sailed by, failed. She was motionless within the flying tire.

"What's going on?" Simone screamed, a sudden wind ripping the words from his ears.

Keeping an eye on Jessie, Trent ran backwards, reaching for Simone's hand, but it only connected with thin air. Glancing over his shoulder, he hollered her name into the storm. She was bent over, clutching her stomach, rocking back and forth. The sky ripped open, pelting them with inch thick raindrops. Each step he took forward, pushed him back four.

The tire had stopped. It hung immobile in the air, stretched from the length of the rope in a horizontal line. An unconscious Jessie draped precariously over its upper rim. Simone straightened and reached an arm toward her daughter. He heard the call, a song that soaked into his soul. The storm whipped Simone's hair into a medusa frenzy. Slowly, the hemp relaxed and the swing descended. Trent felt a lapse in the pressure of the wind and moved forward.

Battling against the invisible barrier, he hunched over forcing everything he had into making his steps count. After what seemed like an interminable amount of time, he reached the tire and yanked Jessie from its interior. With a yell, Simone dropped her arm and collapsed on the ground, an ethereal green haze fading to nothing.

The earth groaned, shooting a bolt of lightening into the ominous sky. The black thunderhead answered with a crack and bang that shook every bone in Trent's body. His power ignited, and he controlled the urge to smash the unseen force into smithereens.

Cradling Jessie to his chest, he raced to Simone. He gathered her beneath his other arm and ran with both women into the shelter of the house. The minute they entered, the storm released its hold and dissipated into the atmosphere.

They sunk to the floor. What he had witnessed was more than a culmination of wind and water. It was a message straight from Hell.

Jessie's eyes fluttered opened and she screwed her brow in confusion. She glanced from Trent to Simone, taking in their white faces and shaking bodies. "What happened?"

"Sweetheart, are you okay?" Simone's voice sounded as if it had been shaved raw by a razor blade.

"Mama, you look horrible. Why are we all sitting on the kitchen floor sopping wet?"

Trent looked into Simone's eyes. They shuttered, closing him out.

"Don't you remember anything?" he asked.

"No. I think I fell asleep on the swing. It was so hot."

"You did," Simone reassured. "A storm blew over and we carried you in."

"Huh," she answered.

"How about a shower?" Simone suggested.

Trent helped them to their feet, dismayed that Simone wouldn't even look at him. He wanted to help, but he couldn't unless she let him in. Frowning, he tried to recollect whether or not there was anything in the prophecy that spoke of this kind of sadistic power. This couldn't be by Gideon's hand. He ran a hand through his hair.

Trent absently watched Simone sling an arm around her daughter's shoulders and lead her through the living room and up the stairs, whispering softly in her ear.

***

Simone collapsed beneath the heat of the shower. The water cascaded across her shaking shoulders in a torrent of hot rain. Clutching her fist to her chest, she pressed it against her aching heart. Tears threatened to flow. Her lips quivering uncontrollably, she bit her mouth to prevent the sob that pushed to escape. Never in her life had fear ripped through her soul with such intensity.

It had almost gotten Jessie. The gray-uglies penetrated every corner of her serene back yard. In broad daylight, they had dangled her daughter in the air like nothing more than a piece of garbage to be discarded. She'd felt them, seen their tendrils flicker between the branches. Drawing in a ragged breath, Simone fought against the black future.

Slamming her fist against the marble, she allowed the sting of the shower to calm her trembling body. Breathe in . . . breathe out. The routine of scrubbing her hair and shaving her legs, calmed her slightly. She turned the water off and stepped out. Wrapping a towel around her hair, Simone snuggled into a robe Jessie had swiped from The Ritz Carlton.

A smile crept out of nowhere as she remembered the shock of opening her 30th birthday present. She'd demanded to know where her ten-year old daughter had gotten the money to buy such an expensive gift. The stammered confession and blubbering apologies had her doubled over in fits of laughter. It had crossed her mind several times since then that she might need to be saving for bail money instead of college.

Now she prayed only for a safe tomorrow.

"Jessie," she sighed. "What am I to do?"

Simone sank into the chair that normally afforded her hours of serenity. This evening, however, her dread of what life held pressed upon her chest, tightening, strangling. Tears pricked, and then ran in salty rivers down her face. She bent her head and allowed the world to shatter her reserve. She wished she was crazy. At least when she thought she had porphyria, she could believe all these bizarre occurrences weren't real. Now? Now, she had to face facts or fantasy or whatever the hell possessed her.

"Simone?" A deep voice invaded her room. She refused to answer.

Why wouldn't he leave her alone? She swiped her hand across her face, and gulped back the sobs lodged in her throat.

She refused to allow him to see her undone

Too late.

Trent crossed the room and stood before her chair. Studying her face, he swore. Dropping to his knees, he reached for her. His arms snaked around her back, and he pulled her close.

"Dammit, woman. You don't have to do this alone," he whispered, leaning his forehead against hers.

His breath was hot, and all she wanted was to reach for him. Reach for the comfort and security he offered. Her towel slipped from her head, and he ran his fingers through her damp hair.

Staring into her eyes, he growled and dropped his lips to hers. She clung to him, allowing his tongue to find hers and deepen the kiss. Her body was on fire. Desire rippled into every nerve ending, sending her senses into a tailspin. She was so worried about her daughter. Seeking safety in his touch, she melted against his mouth. The world dimmed. Her troubles slipped into oblivion.

She wrapped her arms around his neck and pulled him closer. His hands found the gap in her robe. Reaching within, he stroked her skin, tempting shivers of longing from her core. She sang for him. Her heart the percussion . . . her soul the chorus. His touch, his scent . . . it slammed into her, ringing with an awareness she shouldn't possess.

His lips branded her. She answered his passion, tasting his essence.

The early evening sun bathed him in a vibrant red haze, clouding him between past and present. His eyes burned, familiar sapphire pools, and then he snarled viciously, pulling roughly away.

She gazed at him.

Confused.

Embarrassed.

"I can't give you what you want," he said, running the hand that had recently seared her skin through his hair.

"How do you know what I want?" The aching in her heart had come back and slammed into her with the force of a hurricane. She couldn't breathe.

"You deserve a man who can love you, honestly with no strings attached."

"Maybe," she croaked. "I just need mindless sex."

"No," he insisted.

"Maybe, I just need your body."

She was lying. She wanted his body all right, craved it in fact. But now--it had to come with his love. The recollection of having been loved by this man before wouldn't allow her to accept anything less. He was her king.

He stood up. Shook his head, and turned to face the glowing horizon.

"Maybe," he whispered. "We need to forget this."

"That's the smartest thing you've said all day." Simone gathered her hurt close within, forming a bubble.

"I can do that sometimes."

"What?" she snapped.

"Be smart."

"Then why can't you see this means no more to me than a quick tumble in the sack with a boy toy." She lifted her chin and prayed her eyes wouldn't betray her.

At that comment, Trent laughed loudly. He shook his head, tipped her chin, and kissed her lightly on the nose.

"Because, love, I'm not your boy toy."

No, you're certainly not. You're more. My past. My present. She bowed her head. But not my future.

"I'd better catch your steak before it walks itself out the front door," he said, leaving her alone with her misery.

"I'll be right down," she answered absently.

Replaying the past few moments, it was clear to Simone that he cared. Her insides tingled at the thought. She realized with a start her eyes weren't the only ones that played Benedict Arnold. His sexier-than-sin blues had singed her with his need, telling a very different story than the one that escaped his lips.

He'd known it, too. Allowed it to happen.

What held him back?

His job? Maybe, she thought, biting her bottom lip. She rose and walked toward her book shelves. Simone drew out her old book.

She peered at it through the dimming light of dusk. Its leather cover contained an ancient and well-worn metal clasp. "Memorial" was embossed in gold across the brittle center of the journal.

It was time to hand this over to Trent. She needed his knowledge and his help in order to uncover the truth behind the gray-uglies. The two of them, along with Lawrence Gideon, were tied together somehow. Of that, she was certain. She didn't know where her conviction came from, but she wasn't ignoring it any longer.

It was time to find the answers.

Chapter Fourteen

Trent relished the warmth of the southern night. He loved her back deck, listening to the calls of the catbirds delivered in multi-toned constancy. The grill burned beside him.

He watched the steaks sizzle, inhaling the delicious aroma of red meat and spices. He figured he'd let his guard down enough for Simone to understand that even though he might care, he couldn't allow his emotions to rule.

"Trent?" He'd felt her presence. She'd been standing there for quite some time uncertain whether or not to disturb him.

"I'll not ask what you want, because I think I'm afraid of the answer."

She chuckled and stepped into his line of vision.

"I've never encountered anyone like you. Most men would have gladly participated in unconditional sex."

He stared at her. The thought of any other man touching her had his temper rising. Her eyes shifted color, deepening into a mixed tide of greens and blues. She was beautiful. He only had to say the word, and she'd fall into his arms forever.

That thought was enticing. The allure of companionship, of a family, was an alien land he'd never traveled. This woman could take him there. If he only said the word.

"When I take you," he said. "It'll be a far cry from unconditional sex."

"When?" she asked, her voice suddenly growing deep and frustratingly sexy.

He felt the strings tighten, fate knotting their future. "When."

"Phew," she exhaled in a shaky voice. "You've got me all tied up hither and thither. First, I think you like me. You say no. Then, I'm certain you like me. You still say no. Now, you've admitted you like me, but you're still saying no." She walked off the deck and over to the tire swing. Glancing around, she shrugged her shoulders. "I'm not certain what makes the least sense. You and me or these crazy, bizarre events."

"Definitely you and me," he grinned, attempting to lighten the mood. She returned his smile and scouted the tree that recently held the nightmarish event.

"My parents hospitalized me when I was thirteen." She moved in and out of the evening shadows.

"Why?"

"Because I wasn't sleeping. They sent me to a sleep center."

He frowned. His heart hurt for the scared little girl he saw behind the face of a beautiful woman. "Did it help?"

"No." Contemplating how far to open up, she twirled the rubber tire swing in a slow circle. "I have something for you to see. It might help in some way to explain what I've been going through."

"What is it?"

"A memorial. It details my lineage and contains several documents I can't transcribe."

"Your lineage?"

"Yeah. It stops around 1942 so it won't determine my specific connection with Lawrence Gideon just that our lineage is similar."

"When did it start?"

"1080. Rosalyn gave me the book."

Trent stared in disbelief. Why hadn't she shown this to him before? He narrowed his eyes. "You know about your connection with Gideon?"

A faint blush colored her cheeks.

"Honestly?"

"I'll accept nothing less."

"Sort of." She moved back on to the deck. "I also didn't tell you that Rosalyn was meeting Lawrence Gideon to obtain a copy of an even more ancient book."

Trent paused. "I didn't know Rosalyn purposely went to meet Gideon. I thought he'd caught her unaware, like the others."

Simone shook her head. His stomach clenched and he wondered what other secrets were hiding behind those pretty green eyes. "What else?"

"These things that are happening to me now have happened before, when I was thirteen. That's when Rosalyn left. I think she was scared. And it's what prompted my hospitalization. But Rosalyn said the answers were to be found in this book."

"Why were you keeping this to yourself, Simone?"

"Because I thought I was crazy. I thought that I had porphyria."

"What?" He was genuinely surprised. He hadn't even considered the fact that she might seriously consider the illness. Trent wouldn't deny that he'd been relieved at the results, but it was just one more thing out of the way.

"Isn't that why you've been so aloof? Afraid to get close to someone who's going to end up a bubbly puss pot?"

He laughed. "No."

"Why then?" She stared at him, demanding answers.

He ran his fingers through his hair. "It's complicated."

"Simplify it for this poor country girl."

"I can't. At least not yet. You'll have to trust me."

Simone nodded. "The White Book of Rhydderch."

Trent's body went numb. "What did you say?"

"That's the book Rosalyn was after. Together with the Red Book of Hergest my questions will be answered. And I can fight these gray-uglies that are attacking me and Jess."

"Answers to?" How much did she know? Prophecy closed in.

"Answers to who the hell is haunting me. I'm sick of this. And I'm sick of this burning pressure in here." She stabbed at her chest. "It's begging for release." She ripped her shirt off her left shoulder and he gasped in shock. "Look at that. Since the day you arrived, it's darkened and changed color to this." Simone stood still as he stepped closer. "Are you ready to run yet?"

He traced his finger around the crimson star that marred her perfect skin. He'd seen it before--in his mother's books. She was right; The White Book of Rhydderch held the answer. And his future.

"I'm not running, Simone."

She turned and gazed into his eyes. "Your touch soothes the pain. It doesn't burn so much." She swallowed and reached up to touch his check. "What are you to me?"

He held her hand and pushed her shirt back into place. "Let's eat and then we'll go over the memorial. Maybe we can find something in there."

***

"This is incredible." Trent exclaimed, gazing in disbelief at Simone. If this memorial were correct, the chronicles and prophecy needed to be revised and his mother's word accepted.

Dinner had been eaten with the Walker Talkers, his nickname for Simone and Jessie, discussing at a frenzied pace the advantages and disadvantages of living in a small town.

They sat in the living room, stuffed with perfectly prepared sirloin.

Rhythmic keyboard clicks signaled Jessie's connection to her social network account, allowing a small amount of privacy for himself and Simone.

"Pretty amazing, isn't it?" she smiled.

He scanned barely legible chicken scratch that covered more than two hundred pages of aged and cracked paper.

"Yes. This is extremely informational. Look here, Simone." He traced his finger down a lineage that spanned the years of 1826-1845. "This is where you cross Lawrence Gideon's family line."

Trent recognized many of the names. If he was correct, her heritage went directly back to William the Conqueror not Mary Queen of Scots. He frowned at the small lettering noted on a corner of the page. It referred to a document he couldn't translate and had never heard of.

"My mother can tell us what this all means," he stated in a hushed tone.

"She can read Latin?"

"Yes, but this isn't Latin. It's a language far older."

Simone sat back. He absently rubbed his hand across her knee, pulling it away when it triggered an array of unprofessional emotions.

"How does your mother know this then?"

"She's a gypsy." He grinned at her shocked expression.

"A gypsy?"

"Yes. See this line right here?"

She leaned forward, and her breath tickled his shoulder. He shifted away from her touch.

"Uh-huh. Who is it?"

"That's my family line."

"Yours? We're related?" The dismay evident in her voice had Trent grinning from ear to ear.

"No. Not by a long shot."

"I don't understand."

"I think I do. I know who you are Simone Walker."

She grabbed his arm, forcing him to focus on her. Her hair hung softly across her shoulders skimming the edge of her thin T-shirt. He reached over and brushed the silken strands back, caressing her cheek with his thumb. Her breath hitched.

"Who am I?"

"You're a myth, my love. A beautiful, glorious myth." And so much more than just his Dancer.

Chapter Fifteen

Simone pulled her Mustang convertible up the drive. The commute back and forth from the Gulliver's had calmed her clambering nerves and afforded her the opportunity to place things in perspective. Trent was being decisively vague about his knowledge of her ancestry. She'd been angry when he'd refused to explain himself.

She'd counted on a more specific answer. Maybe she was a witch and didn't know it? Or how about a connection to a past spell that meant she'd have to solve a riddle in order for the spirits of her ancestors and Trent's to rest. Simone had no doubt they were connected. She accepted that. But a myth?

Exiting her car, she paused for a few moments to soak in the jewel-laden sky. Stars twinkled on a mile of black velvet. Inhaling the evening's perfume, she fought back the pain of leaving Jessie. Randy assured her that all would be fine, but Simone wasn't convinced.

She heard the light step of Trent as he made his way off the porch. She didn't want to deal with him right now, but it appeared she had no choice.

"Are you packed?" he asked softly.

"No," she answered. "Not even close."

"Don't be mad." He held her hand and pulled her close. She wanted his comfort, but she swore it'd snow tomorrow before she'd let him know that.

"Why does everything have to be so convoluted? Why can't you tell me what the book says?" Simone hated the pleading of her voice.

"Because I need clarification."

She gazed into his face. He asked for her trust, but he wouldn't tell her his theory. It made her angry. "It's late. I'm going in." Simone pulled away from his grasp and headed into the house. She had to pack. She had to see Jessie.

Trent remained beneath the blanket of stars, staring into the night. She paused before shutting the front door. Bathed in moonlight and darkness, he called to her silently, the essence of who he was tugged at her heart. She closed her eyes and steadied herself against the need that demanded she return to his side.

She felt him moving toward her. Silently he stepped across the walk and up the stairs. Her body tingled; it wanted his touch.

"What are you doing?" he whispered into the hushed air of night.

"Trent." Her heart was racing a mile a minute, her entire being screamed for his contact, for his love. Before she could prevent it, a lick of fire escaped its prison, reaching out, reaching for the thing that was being denied.

"Stop it!"

"You can feel that?" She shook her head and stared into his eyes. Blue-fury smashed down. His anger doused her need, and she snapped the link back quickly.

"You don't need magic with me." He answered coldly. "I crave you more than any man should want a woman."

"I'm sorry." The hurt in his eyes stabbed her heart. She didn't understand.

"Good night, Simone." He brushed past her and headed to his room.

"Good night," she whispered to his back.

***

Male voices reverberated loudly up the stairwell. Simone sighed, realizing that Randy was here to collect Jessie. A shriek of joy announced the arrival of Melissa Tippens into her daughter's room, and the two teenagers began going through and repacking everything Simone had put together last night.

She peeked in and waved at Melissa.

"Jessie, make sure you have everything okay?"

"Yes Mom."

Walking into the foyer, she was disconcerted to see Trent laughing with Randy. The two men looked like they'd been best friends forever. Trent's steely blue eyes met hers, and he nodded curtly. Her heart lurched. Why had she done that last night? In one second, she'd broken the bond that had formed between them. For a moment, she'd actually fantasized that they had a future together.

"I'll leave you two alone." Trent stated flatly, heading out onto the back deck.

"Scaring the men away, again, eh Simone?" Randy drawled.

"Shut up, Randy."

He stared at her, his brows raised in shock. Shaking his head, he punched her lightly on the arm. "I'm sorry, Walker. I didn't realize."

His sincerity stopped her in her tracks. She looked at him and smiled slowly. "You never cease to amaze me, Tippens."

He grinned back. "That's what Delores always says."

"Speaking of your ex-wife, is she okay with this arrangement?"

"She'd do anything for Jessie, you know that."

Simone nodded. She couldn't believe that she'd had the gall to ask Delores to allow Randy back in the house while Jessie stayed. Her best friend hadn't demanded an explanation but agreed without any reservations. That's what friends are for, is all she said.

"Randy," she stuttered, uncertain of how to continue.

He reached out and touched her arm. "Is Jessie going through what you went through?"

Simone's breath hitched. She didn't want to believe that he'd be a bully to her daughter. That he'd cause her child the same shame he'd piled on her. "Damn, Simone, I'm sorry about the past. I can't change what I did. I was stupid. But I'd never hurt Jessie. I love her like my own."

She bit her lip and realized that the truth would only help. "She's not exactly experiencing what I did. But, I think something's after her. All I can say is they're like shadows. Watch her when she sleeps and don't leave her alone. And so help me God, Randy, if you dare call her crazy, I'll personally do something that'll wither your balls into little prunes."

He instinctively covered his private parts and stepped away from her. "You can't really do that, can you?"

She grinned wickedly. "I could try."

He studied her for a moment then gathered her in a bear hug. Momentarily shocked, Simone didn't know what to do . She patted his back. "I'm sorry, too."

"Don't worry. Jessie will be safe with us. Nothing will happen to her; I promise."

"Okay," she gulped, fighting back the sting of tears. This was the first time she'd ever been away from her daughter for more than one night. Was she doing the right thing? She had to believe so. Jessie's safety would be ensured by the downfall of Lord Bromley and by the possession of both books, white and red.

She ignored the rage that flooded her system every time she thought about Bromley. He'd killed her sister, and he'd pay for that. Somehow. She'd make sure of it.

"I hate to break up this romantic interlude, but we'll be late for our flight." Trent stood in the doorway. He was tense and looked ready to add a few more angles to Randy's nose. The sheriff obviously noticed his predatory behavior and released her from his embrace.

"You understand, Arnot, that I expect Simone to be returned to us within five days, safe and sound and emotionally equipped to retrieve her daughter." The ease of their earlier banter forgotten behind the tense situation.

"I do, Sheriff."

"Then I don't need to remind you that women tend to get a bit weepy and needy when away from their children."

"You don't."

"What are you two going on about?" Simone interjected.

"I'm trying to explain politely to our British Agent that if he breaks your heart, I'll personally redefine the meaning of Southern hospitality."

"Oh, puhlease. Both of you put away those testosterone pistols and go upstairs for Jessie's bags. I can't stand any more of this." Simone stalked into her kitchen. "Unbelievable," she muttered. "Bloody unbelievable," then grumbled even louder when she realized she sounded like Trent.

***

Trent's mind wandered as he maneuvered within the heavy traffic that swamped the convoluted highway system that wound around Atlanta. He didn't feel like speaking to the woman beside him. Vulnerability was not something he wore well.

"I'm sorry about last night." Simone said for the tenth time that morning. She was trying. He didn't want her to.

"Leave it be, Simone." He knew his voice was curt and offered no acceptance to carry on the conversation any further.

He also knew she didn't understand anything that was going on, and he hated himself for that. How would she feel if he told her the truth? Told her that everything she felt inside wasn't real. Turning off the exit Simone pointed to, he wove through the lines of traffic barely acknowledging her presence. His insides felt raw and the pain of fighting his attraction to her burned with a fierce intensity.

"You need to head to the south terminal." she said, interrupting his thoughts.

"I know that." He winced as she shrugged and turned to look out the window.

The emotion he feared was real. It wrapped itself around his heart until he could barely breathe. This was against everything detailed in the Ancient Chronicles. He understood what it meant to be an Ancient and the importance of the awakening, but somehow Trent considered that he'd remain his own man, have his own life. Following the signs to the car rental return station, he parked. They exited the vehicle, and he grabbed their bags from the back.

"I can carry mine," Simone said, the hurt his emotional isolation caused evident in her tone and stance.

He gazed at her. How next to proceed? Trent knew their destiny demanded a union, and he wanted it more than he wanted anything else in his life. But how was he to do that when the unknown offered greater danger?

Honesty.

Trent frowned and shook his head at Simone. "I'll get it."

She shrugged and walked ahead of him.

Honesty?

The word kicked its way around his mind.

***

Simone settled beside Trent. The first class seats on the Boeing 747 were roomy, but the enforced intimacy of spending seven hours knee to knee with Trent had her tapping her toes and playing with a pencil like it was her lifeline back to sanity.

The plane took off from Hartsfield without a hitch. The moment they were airborne, she picked up the sky phone and called Jessie. Everything was fine, her daughter reassured her. They were off to rent some movies and buy popcorn. A pang of homesickness knotted Simone's gut. She missed her child. How would she survive this week? Fear and need. That's how she'd survive. She feared her future and needed answers to her past.

Simone reached into her oversized travel bag and retrieved her e-reader. Settling back, she prepared to immerse herself in several hours of reading oblivion.

"I work for a secret division within MI-5," Trent grumbled from her left, startling her out of the first tantalizing paragraph.

"Come again?"

"We, I mean all of those in the division, are special."

She could see how tense he was, but this information was not doing a thing for the hordes of contentious emotions currently dancing the can-can in her stomach. What did this have to do with the price of beans?

"And I need to know this because?" Her insides were scrambling to find a foothold. Because," he turned dazzling blue eyes in her direction. "I knew everything about you before we met. Our futures are one."

Simone inhaled sharply. "You knew what *myth* I was before you arrived in the States?"

"Yes. But there's something I don't understand. Our connection. It's too strong." He reached for her hand and held it lightly within his. She stared down at their intertwined fingers and suddenly saw years of this type of intimacy.

She understood his confession. He was trying to explain his reaction to whatever lay inside her. It didn't really matter. She'd sworn to keep it locked away from now on, praying that her conviction would be enough. "I don't know what happened last night."

"Me neither. We'll find the answers, though. Together."

"Tell me more about this secret division."

He gazed into her face. "Myths and legends are based on fact. You're not the only myth walking around, you know." He glanced down, his gaze forcing her to look at him.

"I'm not? Well, I suppose that's good news." She sighed, trying to hold onto her temper.

He grinned. "We all have callings. You awoke mine."

"How?"

"Do you feel a presence, Simone? Something buried deep inside?" He leaned his forehead against hers. "This power you hold in, it's real. And it's very dangerous."

She stared at him for several minutes. He held her gaze, waiting for her answer. "She speaks to me."

Trent frowned. "And me."

Irritation flared. "Who is it? What is it?"

He paused and then exhaled. "My legacy is that of an Ancient. It is our duty to tame the power within you."

Did he understand the danger of which he spoke? Her dreams educated her on the power of the Ancient and the weakness. "Which means what?"

"It means, Simone, that you and I are linked together for the rest of our lives. This bond we feel is something that has been preordained. It's not of our own choosing."

Simone sighed. "I have no power over you, Trent. If you want to go, then go."

"Sorry?"

"You allow this so called destiny its power. It controls your every move. I can't fight that. Won't fight that. Beside there's a huge loophole in this entire scenario of yours."

"And what would that be?" he asked.

"Free will." Simone sat back in her seat. Glancing out the window, she watched the horizon slip into night, her insides frozen like the crystalline clouds floating below. This destiny he spoke of meant the end of his life.

He reached for her hand, once more. She held on but didn't look at him. She didn't know where they could go from here.

***

The flight to Heathrow was an interminable suffering of silence. Instead of pulling her closer, Trent had managed to erect a wall that rivaled the Tower of London. He ran his fingers through his hair, attempting to loosen the strain threatening to kick into a full force migraine. What had he said?

He'd wanted her to know the truth. Understanding his reservations regarding their relationship should make her happy. Right? Instead, she'd spent the entire flight hugging the window, leaning her head against its cold glass. His arms should be comforting her, his shoulder, her pillow.

Trent stared at her sleeping form. Hair fell across her cheek, creating the illusion of a silken veil. She was curled in a tight ball. He frowned, ignoring the sudden stab to his heart. What was he feeling? Scared. She was in danger, and he was delivering her right to the devil himself.

What kind of man did that make him?

You allow destiny to hold the power. Simone's words hit their mark. She was right.

Leaning over, he gathered her in his arms and pulled her tightly against his chest. She mumbled sleepily and snuggled against the warmth he offered.

***

Simone slowly rose to the edge of consciousness. Her dreams had been laced with murmurs of love and promises of passion. She realized with a start that she lay within the arms of the man who'd been the central focus of her midnight fantasies. How had that happened?

His chest rose beneath her cheek. He tensed when she moved the hand that rested lightly on his lap. Stomach tingling and heart lurching, she glanced up. Electric blue passion stared back.

Her breath hitched as he lowered his head and gently kissed her lips.

"I'm sorry," he murmured.

She fought against the need for his touch. "For what?"

"This."

He draped a blanket over them and pulled her hard against his chest. His heart pounded against her skin, as he held her close seeking every inch of her neck with his tongue. Fire licked through her belly and roared downward in flames of desire. Running her fingers through his hair, she brushed her cheek against the late evening stubble. He moaned and moved them closer to the window.

The cabin was quiet; its few occupants sleeping the flight away.

His fingers snaked beneath her shirt, snapping open her bra. He cupped her breast, trailing a finger lightly over her nipple. Her stomach clenched. Flattening her palm against his chest, she pulled back slightly, searching his face. He grinned and slipped his hand lower, unfastening her jeans.

"What are you doing?" she gasped.

"Shush, you don't want to wake anyone do you?" He winked wickedly and ran a finger beneath the rim of her panties.

He shifted her onto his lap. She was powerless to do anything but clutch at his neck and hold on. He touched her gently, sliding his finger into her silken wetness. Biting her lip, she buried her face into his shoulder. She opened for him, helpless to prevent what she so desperately desired.

He rubbed maddeningly slow, but she couldn't move her hips to urge him on afraid people would know that he was driving her to the brink of oblivion. He devoured her mouth, inhaling her moans, touching her, pushing her toward release.

His breath was hot, his need obvious. She ran her hands down, seeking him. Pinning her tighter to his chest, he prevented her reach, flicking his fingers instead, sending her into a spiral. Writhing with desire, she gasped as his pace increased.

"Come on, love," he growled. "Let go."

His tongue singed her mouth, keeping time with the movement of his hand. She couldn't stop. Turning and straddling his lap, she allowed him access to all of her. He slipped his finger inside, moving in and out, offering only a hint of what she truly desired.

She pressed her mouth hard against his, matching his pace and demanding more. Trent held her tighter, pulling her down, and rubbing her against him.

His hips moved up.

She wanted desperately to undo his pants and let him loose to plunder her.

He refused.

He pulled away, and she whimpered against his lips. Devouring her mouth with fiery lips, his fingers dove within her; she moved her hips, not caring about anything but release. He stroked, pushing into her core and tripping her through the gates of paradise. In a shuddering breath, her body convulsed, one, two, three times, the sensations rippling over one another in wave after wave of endless cascading pleasure.

As the fog of passion cleared, she was mortified at what had happened. She realized in dismay that Trent was breathing heavily, holding onto her for dear life. He was rock hard, pulsing beneath the confines of his jeans.

She maneuvered beneath the blanket, zipping her pants back up and attempting to secure her bra. Her hands were shaking so badly the clasp kept slipping away. He pushed her fingers away and fastened the hook for her.

"That can't have been much fun for you," she hissed.

With a sharp in-drawn breath, he swallowed, and his chest rumbled with a deep chuckle. "Says who?"

Snapping her head up, her eyes connected with the amused blue-sea of smug male arrogance. She went to slip beneath the blanket, her fingers trailing down his chest. He inhaled sharply and pulled her up motioning with his head at the arrival of the stewardess. She swore in annoyance.

"Next time . . ."

He nodded and kissed her gently. "Next time, I'll let you run the show."

"I'm embarrassed," she admitted sheepishly.

He grinned, fighting hard not to laugh in her face. "Why?"

"There're people around. They could have heard."

"And what do you think they'd have done? My bet is they'd be damn jealous. But if it makes you feel any better, take a look around and see for yourself. Everyone is sound asleep."

She peered over the seat, and he was right. The five individuals who occupied first class were all snoring gently.

"You're incorrigible."

He hugged her tightly. "I'd never do anything to harm you or your reputation." This time she heard him laugh and punched his arm.

"I'm going to return the favor, Trent Arnot. You can count on that," she threatened.

"Promise?" he smiled, and the rakish gleam in his eye sent her insides into turbulent somersaults.

"Yes." The sudden emotional closeness warmed her.

He gazed into her eyes and smiled softly. "I don't know where we're going." He sighed in resignation. "I wish I could fight it."

She grinned. "We're going to England, and I don't want you to fight this anymore. I don't want either of us to ignore it. Something in here," she tapped his heart. "Needs something in here." She tapped her heart. Frowning slightly, she tried to ignore the cloud that suddenly passed across Trent's eyes.

He shook his head. "This isn't going to be easy."

"Relationships never are." She laughed out loud when he grimaced at her then patted his cheek. "It's okay, Sherlock. I'll be gentle." Simone worried her bottom lip. For all her brave words, she didn't truly understand what they faced. There were too many doubts and too many questions. But if she put her best foot forward, pretended that they were normal people entering a normal relationship, maybe Trent would believe that as well.

She sighed and rested her head upon his shoulder. He stroked her hair and kissed her forehead. They'd work this out. Positive thinking equaled positive outcome.

***

Stepping into the quiet, reserved interior of the Four Seasons Hotel, Simone sighed wearily. The flight had landed on time, but after wading through customs, grabbing a cab, and maneuvering the busy London traffic, jet lag kicked her painfully in the butt.

Trent registered them and the bellhop led the way down the plush, blood red carpet and into an elaborate gilded elevator. She'd felt another shift in the gears of their relationship, but she couldn't tell what it was.

Entering the large suite, she looked longingly at the door she assumed led to the bed. The far wall was floor to ceiling windows draped in heavy gold brocade. A sitting area invited her weary body to slump into the luxurious sofa. She resisted. Sleep. She needed sleep. If she'd had all her wits about her, Simone was certain the little escapade on the plane would not have happened.

Then again, she'd have missed the best orgasm she'd had in her entire life. Thoughts of having Trent, all of him, caused a flash of desire to spark despite her exhaustion.

"Is everything to your satisfaction?"

"Fine. Please have room service deliver some coffee and croissants." Trent tipped the bellhop and closed the door. He turned and pierced her with dark blue eyes.

"It probably would've been a safer idea to have separate rooms."

Her stomach clenched, and she felt the tendrils of desire fan and spread deep into her core. "I . . ." she stammered, not knowing how to respond.

He crossed the small space that separated them and gathered her in his arms.

"I want you," he said. Dipping his head, he trailed a line of kisses across her brow and down the side of her neck. He flicked his tongue in her ear and she melted into his embrace. There was no denying this man.

Her body, her soul, her heart, he had it all.

"Well, well, I see your emails were right on the mark, Agent Arnot."

Simone jumped back and faced a woman adorned in the hotel's service clothes. Frowning in confusion, she watched as the intruder wheeled a cart laden with coffee and steaming croissants. Trent had stilled and turned slowly to face the woman.

"Deputy Director Hilliard, may I introduce Simone Walker." He ambled toward the food cart and pulled it into the center of the room.

The woman reminded Simone of a ferret. She was compactly built, rather buxom, but she walked with an arrogant, self-righteous jaunt. Kathryn Hilliard provoked nothing but dislike.   "This is yours?" She asked Trent, pointing directly at Simone's chest.

Simone gasped and glared at the offending rodent.

She could see the anger in every movement Trent made. He poured coffee for Simone, liberally lacing it with cream and handed the cup over. She accepted with a smile and resisted the smug look that wanted to come into play when he purposely ignored the Deputy Director.

"You're quite a successful woman, I understand." Kathryn Hilliard walked over and poured her own coffee, glaring at Trent.

Simone scrutinized the woman's less than flattering outfit. She smiled and shook her head in dismay. "More so than you, I see. I do hope that outfit is a cover and not just a poor choice of attire."

"Charming," the deputy hissed. "Simply, charming." She turned to face Trent, and the intimate glance she gave him had Simone's insides burning with jealousy.

He's yours. Fight for him. A wave of rage flowered upward, searing a trail of heat from the pit of her soul.

Simone's thoughts were shocked into silence. Her inner self had been so quiet for several days she'd almost forgotten the disconcerting voice.

"Trent is well aware that his connection to MI-5 has been hidden. As Deputy Director General of MI-5, my presence here would alert unnecessary attention. Besides, Trent and I often indulged in undercover fantasies, didn't we lover?"

"You're out of line Deputy Director," Trent stated flatly.

She shrugged. "Trent. I don't need to remind you to remain professional, at all times, do I? He refrained from commenting about acting professional. "Understood."

"We can't allow emotions to cloud your judgment, can we?"

Simone saw his jaw tighten and wanted to rip this woman to shreds.

"Not a problem."

"Then what I saw as I entered this room was simply practice, is that right?"

"Kathryn, that's enough," Trent warned. "You might be my superior officer, but I'll not have you insinuating something that doesn't exist."

Simone's heart shattered. What was he saying?

"Good, then. I expect a full report on my desk by tomorrow morning." The ferret exited the room, leaving Simone feeling as if she'd arrived at a birthday party to discover she'd missed the cake.

"Are you all right?" Trent asked softly.

"Fine, why wouldn't I be?"

"You seem angry. Don't let her get to you. She's just jealous."

"Right. Just jealous."

He grinned and walked to her. Caressing her cheek, he bent his head and whispered in her ear. "Where were we?"

"I'm not sure," she responded icily. "Somewhere between wanting and not existing."

Chapter Sixteen

Trent stepped back, stunned at her reaction. "Simone, I was only protecting you. Kathryn would sink her teeth into our relationship like a shark on chum."

"Relationship?" she coughed. "I can handle Kathryn Hilliard." Simone crossed her arms and glared at him.

He ran his fingers through his hair and sighed deeply. There was no graceful retreat in sight. Tilting her chin upward, he stared into the kaleidoscope depth of her eyes. Their multicolor speaking of a destiny he was trying desperately to understand.

"This," he touched his forehead. "Is what will save your life." Placing a palm over his heart, he smiled. "Not this." Trent knew he'd made a fatal mistake. He needed to step back, become Agent Arnot once more, at least until Gideon was sorted.

He silently berated himself for touching her. It hadn't been enough. He craved more.

She narrowed her gaze and moved closer. "This," she grabbed his crotch, sending him up a ladder of lust. "Won't see the light of day until this," she rapped on his heart. "Comes along."

"As far as this goes," She slapped his forehead with her palm. "I've yet to determine if there's anything in there." Simone cast him a final murderous glance then stormed into the bedroom, slamming the door behind her.

He turned to stare out the window. London traffic swarmed around the hotel. Red double-deckers scattered haphazardly among the mass of black roofs creating an affect of splattered blood. His eyes soaked in the familiar scene of a city he adored.

As Big Ben tolled in the distance, he consigned himself to the futility of moving toward an intimate relationship with Simone. Above all else, she must be kept safe. His feelings weren't important.

Trent walked to the breakfast cart and lifted one of the silver domes that Kathryn had tapped her crimson nail upon. Shaking his head at her histrionics, he retrieved the file that lay hidden within.

Sitting on the edge of the sofa, he flipped open the file. The papers within detailed the plan to infiltrate Blithewoods. He studied Kathryn's directions. Everything appeared in order, but he didn't trust her. Leaning back, his mind whirled around how he would manage keeping Simone safe, arresting Lawrence Gideon and consummating what was ordained in the chronicles. The release of what lay within trumped all cards, even the Queen of Hearts.

Stripping his shirt off and unbuttoning the top snap of his jeans, he sank into the overstuffed pillows of the couch, and rested his head against the back, sighing in relief. He was exhausted. Though the clock displayed the time of ten a.m., his system was on Georgia time and four in the morning represented the fact that he hadn't slept in close to twenty-four hours.

It surprised him that Kathryn was jealous. She'd stepped beyond protocol with her attempted intimidation, and he hadn't liked it one bit. His response regarding Simone was an attempt to protect her. If the vulture found a kink in his armor, she'd slice and dice until nothing was left of him or of Simone. Kathryn had never considered that she might not be his Dancer.

Pausing, he inhaled deeply. He could smell Simone--on his hands, on the shirt he'd draped across the arm of the couch, on every item she'd touched within the hotel suite. It made him restless. He wanted to knock down the door separating him from his desire. His body screamed for her touch. But that was out of the question. He must concentrate on the case and the release of the One.

Closing his eyes, he focused and drifted uneasily into sleep.

***

"Trent," Simone whispered unsure as to whether she should wake him. She'd slept for four hours, lost within the fantasy of this man. The piercing ring of the phone had lodged her out of her dreams, forcing reality back into play. She'd listened to the wheezing of the voice on the other end and confirmed their commitment to visit Blithewoods the day after tomorrow.

She quickly jumped into the shower, scrubbing the remnants of travel from her skin and hair. The hot water pounded back the fear Lawrence Gideon's call ignited.

Simone wrapped the luxurious Egyptian cotton robe tighter around her waist, looking down at the one man who steadied her. Raven strands swept back from his forehead in a crest of jagged stakes. Long lashes rested peacefully against his olive skin, concealing the cobalt fire that claimed her soul. His chest rose steadily, and she swallowed tightly as her eyes followed the line of hair that dipped beyond his unbuttoned pants.

With a soft sigh, she ran her fingers through his hair. He looked innocent and vulnerable, and her heart hammered painfully with the love she was desperate to have returned.

She gasped as he snaked an arm out and dropped her onto his lap, hugging her close. She pushed back, trying to find her balance.

"I know, I know," he grumbled. "All my body parts have to line up perfectly before I can play." He rubbed her back, sending little licks of fire up and down her spine. "And I agree."

"I'm sorry I locked you out of the bedroom," she whispered against his neck. The rest and steaming water from the shower had patched her hurt.

"You are?" His eyes snapped open, and he pierced her with one of his breath-stopping burn-her-clothes-right-off-her-body stares.

She swallowed back the desire to lean in and kiss him. "Yes."

"Good."

Trent slid her off his lap, and Simone bit down on her whimper of dismay. "I suppose we need to get ready?" she said, trying not to sound disappointed.

"I'm going to take a shower. Why don't you get dressed and order something to eat?"

She nodded and watched him walk into the bedroom. His phone rang as he shut the door, the deep tenor of his voice filtered from the bedroom. Simone checked her watch which was set to Eastern Standard Time. It was ten p.m. back home, and she knew Jessie would still be up as there was no school in the morning.

"Hello. Mama?"

She grinned at the sound of her daughter's voice. "Hey, sugar."

"Hey, Mama." Simone heard Jessie yawn and stretch. "It's late." her daughter said.

"Not for me."

"Where are you?"

Simone settled against the cushions of the couch, allowing the sound of Jessie's voice to wash over her. It steadied her, reminded her of the reason she was here. "In London."

"Cool. I miss you."

"Same here." Simone said. "Are you feeling all right?" The sofa smelled of Trent's spicy cologne. She ignored it.

The answering groan calmed any fear Simone might have. "I'm fine. Randy keeps asking me the same question. You sure my blood work came back okay?"

Simone laughed. "Yes. It did. I'm sorry if I'm alarming you. I'll let you get ready for bed."

"Okay."

"I love you, sugar."

"Love you too, Mama."

She disconnected. Jessie was fine. She felt a thousand times better knowing that nothing happened during the dark hours of the night. Maybe Trent was right. The shadows used Jessie, they didn't target her. Distance could be a positive thing. If Simone continued to think that, then the days spent apart from her daughter might not feel so empty.

***

Trent sat on the edge of the bed listening to Ian's voice. The connection went static and he swore. "Hold on, Ian. My battery's dying. Let me call you back on a land line."

He spied his briefcase piled on top of the suitcases. Snapping it open, he grabbed his charger, plugged it into the wall and connected it to his mobile. He snagged a legal pad and pen then went and sat down at the desk. Picking up the phone, he punched in Ian's mobile number.

"About time," his partner said.

"Sorry, mate. Start back at the beginning so that I can take notes."

"Okay. I finally received the box of Rosalyn's personal items from Atlanta PD. There wasn't much, just a small overnight bag with standard clothing and her purse." Trent heard him rustling through items. "In her purse, I found a set of keys. One of the keys belongs to a safety deposit box. After much deducing, I determined what bank and what branch."

"How'd you do that?"

"I went to the institution listed on her checkbook."

"Much deducing, my ass. Please continue amazing me with your brilliance."

Ian snorted. "I called up my good buddies in the Boston PD, and we went and retrieved the contents from the box."

"And?" Trent leaned his head back, impatient for a shower.

"I found Simone's birth certificate."

That caught his attention. "What did it say?"

"Her parents are Pamela Allen Drake and Simon Drake. She was born in Bath within the Parish of Blithewoods."

"Drake?" Trent's heart stopped. He picked up the base of the phone and moved to the bedroom door, cracking it open. Simone sat on the couch, talking on her cell phone. The smile that lit her face, pierced his heart.

"Yeah. Is it possible do you think? I mean, the chronicles paid no credence to this. But your mother . . ." Ian knew the prophecy as well as he did. It'd been the root of many pub jokes and late night ribbings.

He ran his hand through his hair, turning away from Simone. "It doesn't mean anything. A myth about a myth." Trent finally said.

Ian didn't respond.

Trent frowned and repeated his last statement.

"If you say so," Ian sighed. "But this legacy of yours could possibly be taking a new turn. Thinking outside the box wouldn't be a bad thing. You need to clear your head and look at the big picture."

"I'm trying."

"Trent, why is Lawrence Gideon targeting Simone?"

He struggled to clear his thoughts. "Who was Pamela Drake? She must be connected with the Bromley's if Simone was born in Blithewoods Parish."

"I'll call the rectory and see what the good Father has to say."

"Fine. Was there anything else in the safety deposit box?" Trent didn't think he'd be able to squeeze a personal visit into the rectory so it was just as well Ian called.

"Not that I can make sense of. But she did mail herself a package from Atlanta. I think you need to see it."

"What is it?"

"A personal journal. Do you have a fax in the room?"

"Hold on." Trent looked around the bedroom. He walked into the main part of the suite and spied the fax in the corner. Waving Simone back to the couch, he scribbled the number down and headed back into the bedroom ignoring the silent question in her eyes. He rattled the number off to Ian.

"Okay. I'm sending over some pages now."

"Right. Call me after you've spoken to the priest."

"Will do."

Trent hung up and walked back into the living room. "Sorry about that," he said to Simone and softened his words with a smile. "I was on the phone with Ian."

"It's okay. Are you done in the shower?"

"Haven't even started, why?"

"I need to get in there for my makeup and stuff. Actually, I'll just go grab my clothes and toiletries and dress out here while you get ready in the bedroom."

Trent nodded absently his attention focused on the pages spitting forth out of the fax machine. Rosalyn's writing was easily discernible. He quickly scanned the pages, her words were frightening. Grabbing the sheets, Trent walked back into the bedroom to study them further. Simone's exasperated cries as he slammed the door behind him didn't penetrate.

June 4

I can feel the spell waning. Something must be wrong. I need to visit Simone, she must be very confused. Could it be Jessie? Could I be that far off base?

Trent flipped the sheet to the next page.

I saw you today for the first time in twenty years. How you've grown. What a beautiful woman. I fear for you. My dinner with Lord Bromley didn't go as planned. I'm mailing this journal home because I saw my death in his eyes. Simone, know that the gray shadows surround Lawrence Gideon. His aura is nothing but blackness and shade. He is pure evil. He will come for you! Of that, I have no doubt. He hides his cause well. I couldn't see beyond the end of my own life. Does he control your gray-uglies or do they control him? That is what I feel you must learn. It will be the only way to defeat him. I will try to help. I love you. I have always loved you. Don't be sad. My spirit lives on in the heavens. I will try and return.

Bloody hell. This was damn creepy. She'd seen her own death? He didn't doubt it, the proof rested in his hands.

Folding the two pages in half, he shoved them into one of the pockets of his briefcase. Running his fingers through his hair, he swore. This entire case was riddled with complications and mysteries. He almost wished he'd never met Simone. Never been called.

Opening the bedroom door once more, he glanced at Simone. She sat on the sofa, arms crossed against her chest. His anger built. Did she know how controlled their lives were?

"Simone."

She turned and gazed at him. The kaleidoscope green of her eyes shone brightly behind unshed tears. His anger disintegrated beneath the tide of love that filled his heart. How could he resent her?

"What?" she said.

"I'm sorry I shut the door in your face."

She stood and stalked past him. "I'll just grab my clothes and get out of your way."

He nodded, unable to formulate any more words. Right now he needed the distance; he didn't think he could handle any hint of intimacy.

***

"I don't understand what these documents are saying." Simone looked sideways at Trent. He maneuvered a sporty black car expertly through the winding roads of the English countryside. Swerving to miss a pothole, he flashed a half smile. He'd decided to show her the pages from Rosalyn's journal.

"Me neither." He paused and slowed the vehicle before swinging it around a hairpin turn. "What does she mean by the gray-uglies? You've mentioned them before, but I didn't really understand."

Simone's heart skipped a beat. "You're going to think I'm even crazier than you first thought."

Trent grinned and shook his head. "Love, you can't possibly imagine what I'm thinking. But I assure you, crazy doesn't come close."

"Oh, I guess that's good then." Simone glanced at him. "The gray-uglies are a term I used as a kid to describe the things that came for me."

He narrowed his eyes. "Explain."

"Well," she sighed. "It's a bit difficult. They're like shadows that creep down the wall and under doors."

"Wraiths?"

She bit her bottom lip and frowned. "Wraith is a term created from fantasy novels. They're not real. But if you want to describe them like that, then I won't argue."

He nodded. "Do you feel them around Lord Bromley?"

Simone leaned her head against the back of the seat. "Yes."

"Me too."

She sat up, her stomach flipping. "Come again?"

"I feel them as well."

"How? I mean why?"

"That doesn't matter. What is important is Rosalyn's belief that the key to destroying the threat of Lawrence Gideon is the understanding of whether or not he drives this force or it manipulates him."

Simone looked at Trent. He was keeping something from her. "The

White Book?"

Trent nodded. "I think that's a perfect place to begin."

"What exactly did my Memorial show you? You called me a myth. Why is that?"

He reached over and squeezed her knee. "You'll see. Be patient."

Simone fumed silently. Her impatience was growing and the scar on the back of her shoulder itched mercilessly, making her irritable.

"And the spell? That's why I'm feeling all these strange things lately. She's removed some sort of protection from me?"

Trent shrugged. "I honestly don't know."

"Do you think there's a possibility Lord Bromley is my father?"

Simone prayed he wasn't. The mystery surrounding her parentage had left many sleepless hours.

Trent's face brightened. He smiled, flashing all his pearly whites at her. "I know that for a fact he is not your father."

"What?"

"Ian found your birth certificate among Rosalyn's personal effects."

Simone allowed his words to sink in. "You didn't tell me her stuff had been found. What did it say and was The White Book among her things?" Simone's chest hurt. Why hadn't he mentioned this before?

"Drake is your birth parents last name. And no . . ." He turned and offered her a tight smile. "The book wasn't among the items the police department handed over."

"Why didn't you tell me any of this?" She couldn't believe he'd keep this information quiet.

He glanced over and smiled. Her heart stuttered, but she glared at him.

"I wasn't keeping it secret. I wanted your impression on Rosalyn's notes first, that's all. The birth certificate slipped my mind. Does the name Drake ring a bell with you?"

Simone worried her bottom lip. "Are they dead?"

"I don't know. Ian has copies of adoption papers signed by your mother. Her name was Pamela Allen Drake. He's also putting a call into the priest that handles the parish at Blithewoods. He's a whiz at the history of the Gideons. He'll confirm Ian's documentation."

Trent looked closely at her. "So does Drake mean anything to you?"

"No. Should it?"

She frowned again when he suddenly went quiet. What was it that he wasn't telling her?

"Do you think Lord Bromley knows all this?"

"I'm counting on it."

She studied the journal pages once more, and it suddenly dawned on her what was bothering her.

"This is eerie. The way Rosalyn wrote it as if she knew she was dying." Simone paused and in a rush of words told Trent about her midnight visit. "Rosalyn came to me when she was dying. It's beyond my ability to comprehend how she managed to speak with me. I thought it was a dream."

Trent shrugged. "She was a witch. We don't really know what level of power she held."

Simone snorted. The words were unreal. "Oh come on, you can't possibly be serious?"

"Dead serious." He swung the vehicle around another hairpin turn.

Simone needed to change the subject, and fast. "At least your boss provided us with a nice ride. I've never been in a Roadster before."

"It's mine."

"Yours?" She'd assumed he made a normal government salary. Not poor, but certainly not rich. This vehicle would have cost him more than twenty thousand pounds.

"It was a gift from my father for my thirty-fifth birthday."

"I thought you said your family owns a pub."

"They do," he grinned. "Among other things."

The countryside melted away the dark and edgy secret agent persona. This was her Trent, the man that ran around her backyard chasing Jessie with a hose. His eyes sparkled, and he smiled easily. She reached across the small space separating them and touched his hand. She couldn't reconcile her love with the ever present pinprick of mistrust not to mention his yo-yoing between man and agent. But she could let it rule.

"I want you to promise me something." Her heart beat rapidly, and she prayed he'd take her seriously.

He linked his fingers through hers and squeezed. "Anything."

"If something goes wrong at Blithewoods, and I don't make it--I want you to make sure that Jessie is taken care of."

He slammed on the brakes, punching her painfully against the seatbelt.

"Nothing," he answered slowly, after the car screeched to a stop, "*nothing*, is going to happen to you."

"I know you'll do your best--but accidents happen. Delores is Jessie's godmother and guardian. But I want her to have someone special looking out for her interests. I want her to have you."

"This is foolish." He tilted her chin and refused to allow her to drop her eyes. "I promise you that no one will hurt my girls."

She looked into the sapphire depths of his eyes. His girls? The possessiveness sent warm flutters of security skimming around her insides. He cared, she knew. But was it possible that he loved?

He leaned over, kissing her gently. More words were conveyed as his lips tenderly touched hers than could be spoken out loud.

"Okay," she whispered. "I'll hold you to that promise."

"I was going to wait until we reached Bath before telling you this, but I want to ease your worry." Trent released her and looked out the windshield, furrowing his brow. "You're not going anywhere near Blithewoods."

"What?" She sat back in the seat and stared in shock.

He pinned her with a stare that attempted to rebuke retaliation. "I'm not endangering you."

"He's expecting me. How're you going to set the trap without using me as bait?"

"I've already informed headquarters that a new plan is being set in place. I'm not using you as bait. I won't risk it."

"Like hell you won't! I didn't fly all the way across the Atlantic Ocean to be hidden away in some closet. I'm going to Blithewoods in the morning with or without you. This sucker is going down, do you understand me? Down." She was breathing heavily. How dare he?

Trent's muscles clenched in anger, but she refused to succumb to his Neanderthal behavior.

"You're not going."

"Yes, I am."

"No," he insisted.

"Yes." She cringed as he banged his hands against the wheel.

"Don't you get it?" he growled.

She wasn't about to allow him the risk of failure, when they had achieved this much. "Get what?"

"It doesn't matter."

"It matters very much to me," she whispered.

"Not me. I only care about you. I won't risk you."

"Oh," she sighed, shaking her head. He'd tilted her world once more. "And I care about you." She reached across and touched his knee. "But I choose to risk me."

"Simone . . ." He ran his fingers through his hair, and she grinned knowing that she'd won.

"No, Trent. This is my choice. Either you can stand beside me or you can call Ian and have him come with, but I'm not leaving England without putting Lawrence Gideon's head on a stick." She grabbed his arm. "He killed my sister, and he threatens my daughter."

Trent stared into her eyes, his gaze unwavering. "Then you might not leave England at all."

"If that's the case," she whispered, her stomach clenching in fear. "You'll help Jessie?"

"Bloody hell woman. Why are you being so stubborn?"

"You're the one that made me realize that in order to secure the safety of my daughter, I need to be here."

"Are you talking about what I said in your office?"

"Yes."

"I lied. To you and to myself." He gathered her into his arms. "I could never risk you. Never."

"I'm going to Blithewoods," she murmured against his chest.

"We'll discuss this later." He kissed her forehead, sat back and pulled the car onto the road, driving the rest of the way to Bath in silence.

Simone chewed her bottom lip nervously. A visit to Blithewoods without Trent would be like walking through the desert without water.

Simone rested her head against the window, absorbing the scenery as Trent skirted Bath. They continued past the ancient city once occupied by the Romans and sped across narrow streets into the open countryside beyond. It was chilly. She slipped a black cashmere sweater over her head as rolling hills of muted greens chewed at her memory. Her brain synapses must be on overload, she mused, because the familiarity of the surroundings was startling.

Large brick pillars loomed ahead. Simone gasped as her eyes absorbed the image of gigantic marble dragons. The beasts raised their heads to the heavens, crying their fury into the sky. Stunned by their wingspan, she craned her neck for a better view. Trent swept the vehicle between the aged pillars. She leaned forward and inhaled sharply as the dragons appeared to follow them with their milky eyes.

"Where are we?" she asked. *Home.* She felt a lick of excitement and deep purring within.

Trent echoed her inner voice. "Home."

"This is what MI-5 considers a cover?"

"No, love. This is what Trent Arnot returns to when he's not busy chasing bad guys. I figured it'd be simpler to delete my connection with MI-5 and become the man my mother always hoped I'd be." He grinned.

"And who is that man?" she said with a smile.

"Trent Arnot, the eldest son of the Lord and Lady Lichfield. I invest in the stock market, own several valuable race horses, and have a half-interest in a new, but extremely promising, French vineyard."

"Are you serious?"

"Absolutely."

"I would never have guessed. Why didn't you tell me?"

"You never asked." He smiled to soften his words, but they hinted of more secrets yet to be unveiled.

She watched his home emerge from the early evening mists. Three stories of ivy-laced brick rose upward, reminding Simone of what she'd always imagined an English Manor House would be.

"Pub ownership must be very lucrative," Simone said.

His teeth flashed in the dark recesses of the vehicle. He drove the

Roadster around a circular drive and parked in front of the dwelling. Two wings that angled back, dropping to two stories, flanked the home. Cornices were adorned with more stone dragons, each one facing a different direction.

"And you thought my house was amazing? This is incredible."

"Your home is an original piece of art. This . . ." he waved his arm in a circle. "is simply a place. It doesn't contain passion or personality. It's a testimony to the heritage and history of England."

Home, little one, we're home.

She smiled at the sheer happiness emanating from the voice. Simone didn't agree with Trent but wasn't about to begin another argument. The double front doors opened, spilling soft yellow light onto the yard. A petite, raven-haired woman bustled out, running toward Trent, and wrapping her arms around his neck in a fierce hug. Returning the embrace, he smiled sheepishly over at Simone.

"Mum, this is Simone Walker. Simone, this is my mother, Francine Arnot, Lady Lichfield."

"Stop being so formal, Trent. Let me have a good look at your fiancée."

"Oh no," Simone stammered. "That's just a cover story. We're not engaged."

"Really?" The elder woman gathered Simone's hands and squeezed lightly. "You're the one, and I won't be told otherwise. It has certainly taken long enough. Finally, the beginning and not the end."

Simone shook her head unsure of what this woman meant. It must be jetlag, she thought. What was she rambling on about? She glanced up to find Trent staring at his mother as if she'd lost her mind.

"That's a legend, Mum, not fact."

"Honestly, Trent, you can be terribly stubborn. What differentiates myths and legends from fact? Hmmm?"

"Proof," he responded automatically, as if the question was asked him on a daily basis.

"Right, my dearest son. Here's your proof." She smiled at Simone and pulled her toward the house.

"Where?" Trent sighed, following them. "Where's my proof?"

"It's right before your eyes." Francine Arnot responded. She hurried them through the door and led them into a circular sitting room.

Simone soaked in the antiquities scattered around like they were no more valuable than furniture bought at your local discount shop. She wasn't an expert, but she was certain that Sotheby's would salivate at the opportunity of an estate sale. Sitting cautiously on the edge of a Louis IV settee, she scanned the room. Her eyes resting on an ancient tapestry hung above the fireplace.

She gasped and rose to get a better look. An emerald dragon gazed intensely from the depths of the aged, woven hanging. The artist, whoever he'd been, had captured the complex and variegated color of the beast's eyes . . . eyes that were a rainbow of gray, green and gold.

Eyes that were a reflection of her own.

Julie Korzenko

Chapter Seventeen

"What's this?" Simone asked pointing at the dragon.

"We refer to her as The Empress," Francine responded, walking to stand beside her. She smiled as she cupped Simone's chin in her hand, turning her face to the side to study her. "You have her look about you."

"I apologize if I offend you, Lady Lichfield, but she's a dragon."

"And you? Simone Drake, what are you?"

Simone looked at Trent who glared at his mother and shrugged, shaking his head at Simone.

"I believe my name is Simone Walker," she said, trying to remain polite as she stepped back from the woman's touch. All politeness aside, this was crazy.

Francine Arnot clucked her tongue and smiled sadly. "Don't you have any appreciation for the past? For history? Or are you like my son?"

"I have tremendous appreciation for history, but your son can be a bit overwhelming." Simone couldn't suppress her smile as Trent's mother laughed heartily.

"I'm pleased you two have finally connected. It's been a long time coming. Too long. The powers are weakening even as we speak."

Trent held his hand up and silently begged Simone to keep quiet. It wasn't difficult. She had no clue how to respond to such an outrageous statement.

"Mum, why don't you fetch father. We'll meet you in the dining room shortly. I'm certain you'll be able to answer several questions that have been troubling us."

"All right, son." Lady Lichfield swept out of the room, oblivious that her behavior would appear bizarre.

"Trent, I . . ."

He placed his forefinger against her lips and shushed her. "I know she sounds crazy, but she's extremely bright and well versed in the history of this area and that includes Blithewoods. Put her odd words down to the fact that she's a gypsy, all right?"

"Yes, but . . ." She shook her head in confusion, her stomach knotting with nerves. "I hadn't expected to land in Oz."

His chest rumbled with a deep chuckle. "I survived my childhood and ended up relatively normal. If it gets too crazy, just click your heels, and I'll whisk you away to a better place."

"I'm clicking," she whispered.

"Don't be such a wimp, Walker. Hear my mother out, okay?"

She gazed into his face, longing to run her fingers through his hair. Not wanting to break the fragile bond they'd formed on the car ride, she held back.

***

Simone glanced around the dining room in awe. She sat at one side of a massive marble table that glittered and sparkled with the reflection of an ornate, gilded chandelier swaying above its center. Trent was deep in conversation with his father.

She watched Lady Lichfield move gracefully around the table, filling platters with slices of roast beef that smelled of garlic and onion. Her stomach rumbled, and Simone smiled apologetically at Trent's mother.

"A good appetite is a compliment to the chef," Francine whispered as she passed behind Simone.

A gigantic emblem of a fire-breathing lion adorned the far wall, catching her attention as rich crimson hues wavered in the light, creating an affect of motion. She sipped tentatively at the crystal goblet, pleasantly surprised by the crisp white wine. She'd feared a heady, sweet almost sherry taste and was gratified as a dry, vanilla essence slipped down her throat.

Her nerves tingled. Simone was finding it increasingly difficult to contain the sparks of power that wanted to leap from the recesses of her soul. She absently rubbed her left shoulder.

Ever since stepping into Trent's home, a hammering of paranormal proportions constantly hounded every nerve inside her. The voice replaced by something that rattled her skin. She tried concentrating on comforting thoughts. Visions of Jessie and their home floated before her eyes, masking the dread that was a permanent knot in her stomach.

Allowing the rare meat to melt within her mouth, she swallowed and focused on consuming her meal. Several painstaking minutes passed, and she folded her napkin on the table. Unable to contain her curiosity any more, Simone turned to Trent's mother and decided to dig for information.

"Lady Lichfield, what can you tell me about my parents?"

"Which ones, dear. I'm familiar with them both."

"How about both sets, if you don't mind." The wine burned a path to her stomach, and Simone fought against its lulling presence. If she relaxed, she was afraid of the consequences.

"Your father was Simon Drake. Your mother was Pamela Allen Gideon, Lord Bromley's sister."

Trent interrupted Simone. "Are you certain about that Mother?"

"Yes. Positive."

"What happened to them?" Her mother must have dropped her surname when she left Blithewoods, Simone thought.

"From what I can uncover, it was a rather scandalous affair. Simon Drake was married to another woman when your mother became pregnant with you. She ran away and stayed with your adoptive parents,

Marjorie and Des Walker. Relinquishing her parental rights, she begged them to take you to America. I don't know why."

"She never married Simon?"

Francine shook her head. "I don't believe so, dear, why?"

"Trent, didn't Ian say my mother's name was Pamela Drake?"

"Yes, I believe that's right. He'll confirm everything tomorrow."

She nodded, wondering if that was at all important. She turned back to Lady Lichfield, who swirled the light yellow liquid within her glass and gingerly tasted the wine. A smile of satisfaction crept upon her face, and Simone realized with a start that Trent's mother was truly beautiful. Battling back her normal tendency to refrain from unpleasantness at the dinner table, she continued her interrogation.

"Whatever happened to her?"

Trent's mother glanced at her husband, who shook his head.

"I'm afraid dear that they're gone. Both of your parents have been dead for many years."

"How?" Simone sensed there was a major piece of the puzzle being withheld.

"They were murdered," Lady Lichfield rested her fork against the side of her plate and turned to her son. "Trent, darling, would you please pass the butter?"

Simone sat back, her face stinging from the verbal slap. She leaned forward and grabbed the woman's wrist.

"How were they murdered? And are you positive that my father is not Lawrence Gideon?"

"I believe Lawrence Gideon killed your parents, and yes," Francine whispered. "I am certain he's not your father. He's evil. The same way you are light, he is darkness." Her eyes were clear of any lapse from sanity. Simone shook her head. This woman and Rosalyn would've been a perfect match with their half-truths and riddles.

194

Attempting to absorb this information, she mulled over what she'd just learned. Lady Lichfield was purposely being evasive, and the loose ends were innumerable. Nothing fit.

"Who was Marjorie Walker?" Simone asked.

"Your mother's cousin," Francine answered.

"Lawrence Gideon was my mother's brother?"

Lady Lichfield leaned against the back of her chair. She stared at Simone and nodded slowly.

"Why would he kill his sister?"

"For the same reason he wants you, Simone."

Blasts of electric fire sizzled to the edge of her fingertips. They burned. She bit her bottom lip, imploring the power to remain buried. Jets of electricity jolted down every nerve, and she was certain that if she were to raise her arms and let loose all she held at bay, the house would rock on its ancient foundations.

"Simone, are you all right?" Trent asked. She looked into twin pools of ocean-blue and abruptly her inner volcano ceased to rumble. Smiling, she nodded and turned to study Lady Lichfield.

"Is there a reason you're being rather lax in detailing the history of my family?" she asked. Trent chuckled and shook his head.

"I warned you, mother. There'd be no evading the truth with Simone."

"There's more to this than your parentage, Simone."

"Then tell me, Lady Lichfield. Tell me why Lawrence Gideon killed my sister or is that cousin? Enlighten me as to how I am to go about helping your son arrest him and free my daughter from danger." Simone felt every muscle stretch beneath her skin.

"Arrest Lawrence Gideon?" Francine laughed. "Is that what you believe you are here to do? Your destiny has brought you to these shores. You must sacrifice more than you're willing before Lord Bromley ceases to breathe."

"Mother," Trent yelled, slamming his fist against the table. "That's enough. Stop frightening Simone and explain yourself."

"She's not ready." Lady Lichfield tossed her linen napkin on the table and left the room.

"I resent this . . ." Simone yelled, racing after Trent's mother. "You have no right to withhold what you know."

Francine Arnot whirled around and stalked back. She raked coal-black eyes over Simone and snarled. "You have no idea of who you are, child. Don't dare to presume that I retain my knowledge out of selfishness. You must be prepared or else the death of my son is unavoidable."

Simone was speechless. What madness was this?

"I would never cause your son harm," she whispered.

"No?" Lady Lichfield asked. "When you look into his eyes what do you see?"

"The past," Simone blurted before she had a moment to think of what she said.

"And when you dream, what do you see?"

Simone's eyes filled with tears. How could she know?

"When your pride decides to take backseat to fate, you will be ready. Until then . . ." Francine turned and walked down the hall. "You are welcome to remain beneath my roof. I shall guide you as I see fit."

***

Simone rested her head against the pillow frustrated and angry by Lady Litchfield's riddles. Would Trent visit her tonight? She prayed he would but figured the agent side of him would outweigh his emotions. His brain had been chewing on the ramifications of her connection to Lawrence Gideon. If she knew anything at all about Trent, he'd be on the phone to Ian demanding immediate confirmation.

Closing her eyes, she placed her hand over her heart. The weight was there, pushing her beneath the waves of memory. She struggled to remain in the present but the heaviness forced her under, backward in time. Past Elizabeth. Past the image of Trynt's fading life.

***

Mist clung in swirls of damp air along the pebbled shore of Llynnau Mymbyr. Seren hastened down the worn footpath that wove around the edge of the still lake in twists and turns threatening to send an unwary traveler into the cold depths of water. She was grateful for the full moon that shone above the craggy peaks of Snowdon.

Her chest tightened in anticipation.

The light cast a luminous tint to the drifts of white gracing the cap of Dreigiau Rheol. She prayed the lunar crown that encircled the moon was a symbol of luck for this eve and not the normal predilection for storms.

She paused to listen to the night. The soft mewing and shuffling of one of the many sheep herds that grazed along the valley could be heard in the distance. Its normalcy helped soothe her nerves. At this stage, she couldn't yet decipher the voices of the congregation that gathered beyond the next slope.

Seren grabbed a fistful of finely woven cotton, lifting her kirtle in an attempt to free the hindering fabric from her legs. The long tunic slapped against her skin, its thread sodden by the thick mist which coated the ground in a layer of chilled dew.

She moved forward, trying to force herself past the urge to spin on her heels and dash in the opposite direction. The scent of burning wood wafted across the lake, and her eyes traveled beyond the moonlit slope to the soft glow of a burning pyre.

She was almost there.

Her fingers traced the top of the emerald green dragon embroidered upon her tunic, trailing down the ridge of the neck that crossed her heart. The golden piping that outlined the length of a collar signified her status as Dragon Dancer.

As one of the chosen, this was her destiny. To be friend, teacher and servant to the great beasts that dwelled within the caverns of Snowdon.

A comfortable life full of riches, wisdom and knowledge suddenly seemed a very distant memory. Tonight she must bend to a power greater than the love that flooded her heart. She didn't know what lay ahead.

Her future cut short by the cruel invasion from the barbarous men of the Norse. They threatened to flood her land, searching for gold and dragons. The legend and myths surrounding the creatures brought the savages to the shores of Glamorgan Shyre. It wouldn't be long before hordes of blood thirsty murderers swarmed from the south and invaded the sacred Cambrian Mountains.

Seren imagined the destruction and pillage of Dreigiau Rheol, its riches and secrets horded by a race incapable of understanding what they held. The slaughter of her kind and her protectors was imminent. Prophecy did not lie.

A sudden breeze skipped across the black waters and snatched the filmy fabric of her head rail, tossing it to the ground. Seren grabbed for it, swore softly, and unraveled the twisted cap. Her loosened hair cascaded across her shoulders and danced in the night like a nest of serpents. She smoothed it down and secured the head rail in place.

Before she could resume her travel, a haunting cry pierced the air. She swallowed against her fear. Wizard Llallogen called forth the dragons.

She swayed as the heat of her magic sparked and fired. Seren felt the power of the beasts as they swept from the depths of Snowdon. A smile touched her lips and she inhaled the night, one with the dragon. They flew past the highest ridge of Dreigiau Rheol, exhilarating in the freedom of flight.

She laughed with delight as the one that claimed her as Dragon Dancer somersaulted, then dove in playful aerobatics. A sadness filled Seren's heart. The power of a Dragon Dancer went far beyond the wealth brought to her table. It was a connection to an ageless soul of wisdom.

That connection would soon change.

On this eve, Llallogen was to spin a spell to save the magical creatures. As one of the last remaining Dancers, she'd become a vital key in this mission of mercy.

"Seren," a deep voice called from the edge of the muddy trail. She swung around and her gaze fell upon a tall man dressed in a simple tunic adorned by a small woven emerald dragon that mirrored her own.

A warmth spread from her insides, bringing a flush to her cheeks. "Trynt."

He stepped from the shadows and embraced her. His arms held her tenderly as she rested her cheek against his chest. The scent of cinnabar and ale swept around her, making her heart hurt with the thought of never feeling this loved and wanted again. He tipped her chin with gentle fingers. Their eyes connected, igniting a passion the elders would frown upon.

"I shall be yours for all eternity." Trynt spoke softly. His barely contained anger laced the loving words into a demand. "They shall not separate us."

A pang of despair tugged her heart. If only it were true.

They walked hand in hand, their bodies parting the mists in waves of milky air. At the top of the ridge, Seren inhaled a quick breath. The scene spread below sent a shiver of apprehension entwined with excitement running along every nerve, causing her hands to shake.

A pyre cast an eerie glow among the humans gathered around its fiery rim. Tunics heavily embroidered with multi-colored dragons shimmered in the orange light, undulating as their wearers moved in a graceful circle about the beacon.

A soft melodious chant reached Seren's ears. With a habit built by years of servitude to the dragons, she began to hum along. The tune fed her power, and it wasn't long before she felt the full awareness that signaled the arrival of Grael.

Come, little one. A voice boomed through her mind.

Her dragon.

Her destiny.

She pulled on Trynt's arm. He paused and looked down into her face. The sapphire blue of his eyes burned her mind. "I shall always love you," she said, allowing her full emotions to shine in the words.

His chiseled features softened beneath the force of a tender smile. "And I you." He bent and touched his lips to hers. Seren wrapped her arms around his neck and held him as close as possible, allowing his warmth and strength to seep through her cloak and wrap around her heart.

This night would change all.

She stood on her toes and framed his face with her hands. Her eyes soaked in every plane and angle before she touched her lips to his. The warmth of his breath as he groaned and pulled her closer stirred her passion, but she banked it and turned the kiss gentler. She absorbed every nuance and branded his taste into her soul. As she slipped from his embrace, a lone tear chilled her cheek.

Seren stepped before Trynt and led him down the steep embankment. The fire burned brighter, reaching for the sky with red, angry fingers. Her eyes focused on what lay beyond. A circle of dragons, Grael at the center, waited on their human counterparts.

For each dragon there was a Dancer. Their lives forever twisted together. It had been this way for hundreds of years, neither existing without the other.

The human link tempered the dragon's endless quest for knowledge, teaching them patience. Over time as they learned from the infusion of man's compassion, the dragons lessened their greed and focused on wisdom and the nurturing of the world wherein they dwelled.

They were no longer the beasts that nightmares fed off or the creatures the Norsemen hunted.

At the edge of the circle, Trynt moved left to stand with the other chosen males. Seren touched his cheek lightly and proceeded toward Grael. A golden eye bore down upon her, its weight both prison and life.

Grael's massive head snaked around and rested upon the ground at Seren's feet. *Break the tether that man has on your heart.* Her voice resonated within Seren's mind. She nodded, sweeping her lashes down to hide the tears that refused to remain unspent.

Seren knelt and stroked the sleek scales that encased her oldest friend like an emerald suit of armor.

"I am your Dancer, you are my dragon. Forever we are bound. For always we shall remain." She spoke softly and swallowed past the lump in her throat caused by the splintering of her soul.

This must be done. Grael bellowed, causing a stab of pain to Seren's temple. The dragon raised her head and shrieked into the night, the sound echoing ominously along the hills.

Seren lifted her eyes and watched Llallogen enter the clearing. His crimson cloak sparkled with silver spun stars. White hair flowed in abandon down his back, and the ruby eye of his staff blinked menacingly beneath the full moon.

"It is time," he cried to all present.

Fear coursed a path from her toes to the tip of her scalp. She searched the night for one last glimpse of Trynt. He stood a head taller than all the men within his group. His raven hair, tousled by the wind, created a breathtaking frame for the vibrant blue of his eyes that gazed at her from across the field. He nodded at Seren, touching his fingers to his lips then placing his hand over his heart.

He'd been chosen as an Ancient, his bloodline as old and powerful as her own. Magic would bind the Ancient to the Dancer, allowing his power to temper the fierce will of the dragon and prevent the death of the Dancer.

But he wouldn't be her Ancient.

He'd belong to someone else. Her destiny lay with his older brother. Grael was Queen and demanded the most powerful Ancient as her own.

Llallogan signaled for the Dragon Dancers. The women stepped forward and gathered before the wizard. Bowing their heads, they joined hands and formed a circle.

The fire smelled of death. It spoke to Seren of a future without her love, a future of heartache. Smoke filled her eyes, and she blinked back the tears. She must be strong. It was her duty.

Emotions filling her soul reminded her of the eve of her thirteenth birthing day when Wizard Llallogen collected her from her village. She'd been marked. A small star above her left shoulder signified the magic that lay buried within her soul. It seemed, once more, the wizard claimed her future.

Llallogan raised his twisted and gnarled staff high above his head. In the flickering light of the fire, it reminded Seren of a writhing snake. He began to sway beneath the power of his magic.

His spell wrapped around the dragons. Seren gasped as Grael faded into the night. Her physical shape melted into nothing more than an ethereal shadow. Grael's sadness at being transported into the metaphysical pummeled Seren's mind, tears spilled over her lashes as visions of a thousand years of the dragon's life flashed before her.

The heat of the spell wove around Seren's ankles, insinuating itself into her skin and entwining with her soul. She disengaged from the circle and grabbed for her throat. Her breath burned in her chest. Outside the death grip on her body, she heard the cries of the other Dragon Dancers. She groped to reconnect with the circle. Tears blinded her vision, and she stumbled to the side.

Her fingers found the nearest woman then lost their hold as Grael slammed into her body with a force that rivaled the bloody Norsemen. Dropping to her knees, Seren bent beneath the power of her dragon. She fought to hold onto herself, to remain separate. But Grael filled every inch of her being.

The dragon demanded too much. Seren felt herself slipping into a darkness that offered no return. She panicked. Tilting her head to the sky, she exhaled in a curdling scream of pain and horror.

A shadow blocked the bright pinpoints of the stars. She closed her eyes, praying for relief from the spirit that tore at her body and soul. A soft kiss touched her lips. Seren raised her hand as the pain softened. She reached for safety and pulled her Ancient closer, locking on with everything she had. Tears tore down her cheeks as she felt the dragon recede beneath the influence of the man before her. The possession complete, the power tempered.

As the ravaging beast calmed to a background roar, the scent of cinnabar and ale wafted across the night. It couldn't be. Seren's eyes flickered open, and she gazed into Trynt's face. His eyes glowed as the power of an Ancient coursed through his blood. A tentative smile lessened the worried frown, and he knelt, pulling her tightly against his chest.

"Trynt," she said softly, her body drained of all energy. "How?"

"Llallogan isn't the only wizard within these mountains." He rocked her gently.

She swallowed, her heart flooding with love. The future felt forever. Grael raged within the deep recesses of Seren's soul, but she chose to ignore the dragon. She glanced over Trynt's shoulder at the wizard bearing down on them with long strides, causing the flush of safety to banish. His body was taut with anger.

"What have you done, you fool!" Llallogan screamed. He pulled Trynt from her, icy fingers of the night sending shivers along her arms. The wizard slammed his staff against Trynt's chest and bellowed his outrage into her lover's face. "You've gone mad!"

"I am hers!" Trynt stood his ground, veins popped against his brow testimony to the fierce warrior that he was. "No one takes my woman."

"This has nothing to do with love." The wizard spat on the ground. "You have bound yourselves together forever."

"And we shall love for all eternity." Trynt pushed past Llallogan. He reached down and Seren grasped his outstretched hand. She stumbled upward and turned to face the wizard.

"What can possibly be wrong with our union?" she asked, alarmed at the crimson bloom suffusing Llallogen's face.

He swept his arm around, encompassing all in the small valley. "These dragons, these Dancers, these ancients are all tied to you. You have their queen. Without her they will not exist."

Seren frowned. "I do not understand."

"Prophecy is truth. You have played with elements beyond your comprehension." Llallogan bent close and reached for Seren's hand. "Is it done? Is it too late?"

She couldn't help the smile that spread across her face. "Yes, Wizard. It is done. Trynt is my Ancient." She stepped close and placed her hand upon his arm, allowing the power of Grael to sweep through her touch. "Grael is well."

"For now, Seren. That is true. But what of the next generation? Your soul will not remember this love. As the power of the dragon burns for release, the next Dancer will be lost unless she finds the ancient with," Llallogen pointed at Trynt, "his soul."

His gaze bore into both of them before he bent to one knee and drew a circle in the dirt. Reaching within his cloak, he retrieved a small velvet bag. With a flick of his wrists, Llallogen cast the bag of bones into the dirt. Sparks flew from the small area, playing around Seren then dancing to Trynt.

Llallogan slumped to the ground. "The corruption of my spell speaks disaster for the race we sought to save." He looked at Seren and then sent a scathing glare at Trynt. "Grael's fate and that of her brethren now rely upon the unpredictability of the human heart."

Chapter Eighteen

Rays of stubborn sunlight insisted on pushing Simone to the edge of consciousness, panic making her heart beat ten times its normal speed. What did it mean? What was that dream about?

A cool hand soothed her matted hair from her face, and she fluttered her eyes open.

"Trent," she gasped. "What are you doing?"

He smiled and kissed her lightly on the forehead.

"I'm waiting for my Sleeping Beauty to arise. It's almost ten o'clock."

"It's that late?" She tried to calm her alarm at the distressing visit to the past. It was too much. If these were real memories, then her life wasn't her own. The fire that burned within was another being. Is this what he knew? Is this why he didn't want her?

"It's the jetlag. Your body still thinks it's four a.m."

Simone sat up. She glanced down and yanked on her T-shirt. Trent's hand stopped her, gliding gently beneath the rim of the well-worn cotton and skimming her skin in a gentle caress. She closed her eyes and inhaled deeply. He rubbed a thumb lightly across her nipple, and she melted.

"We can't," she whispered, but she desperately wanted his touch. She wanted him to wipe away the memories and claim him as her own. He wasn't a ghost. He was real.

"I know, but I'll be damned if I don't try." Bending down, he traced the path of his hand with his lips, igniting her nerves with a fire that flashed directly to her core.

Simone gasped and pushed him away. Frustration was written across every muscle of Trent's body, and she wilted beneath the heat of his want.

"We really can't, Trent," she pleaded. Where had the professional disappeared to? "Ian's expecting us in Bath by noon."

"I know," he said. Rising from her bed, he crossed the room and stared out the French doors. His fists were clenched tightly, and he punched the air. "I hate England."

Chuckling, Simone padded into the bathroom. "Other than the fact that your mother walks a fine line between sanity and lunacy, I find England absolutely charming." Before closing the door, she raised her hands to ward off what she knew Trent was about to say. "I know, I know. She's a gypsy."

***

Bath. Simone inhaled the scent of fresh baked bread and woolen merchandise. The cobbled side streets yanked at her brain like she was nothing more than a fish on a hook being reeled to an alien destination. Stepping into the worn and ancient alley, she held Trent's hand and hurried toward the other side of the narrow road.

Moving into the center of the street, she faltered. Her foot sank within the paved stone of the road and reality faded, as the air grew thick and impenetrable. Figures wavered before her, their blue jeans shimmering into tailcoats. The clambering of horseshoes against rock screamed louder than the hum of engines.

She grabbed for Trent's arms, but an invisible weight prevented her hands from moving. Simone pleaded silently for help. Sapphire eyes shone from his chiseled features then suddenly muted into a face she recognized only from her dreams.

A white face.

A lifeless face.

"Simone?" Trent's voice was far away. She tried to focus but kept slipping further back in time.

Her heart caught as shadows crept from the darkened alleyways. They crawled forward, clawing with misty daggers across each stretch of cobbled rock.

She was floating through time.

The black wraiths slithered closer, reaching evil tentacles toward Trent.

"Oh God," she cried. "They're coming for him." They suddenly took shape. The shadows didn't want her, they wanted Trent.

Panic ripped her soul.

Stabs of heated power burned the back of her eyes, and she reached for it, pulling it from the deepest core of being.

Concentrating on the turmoil raging within, her mind flung the power up and out beyond her physical being. She stumbled beneath the waves of pure white force that blasted from her soul.

"Simone," Trent yelled. His voice closer this time. She locked her eyes onto his face and rode the wave upward . . . away from the shadows, away from the past.

The world came to life. A horn blasted loudly in the background, and the voices of humanity rose in a welcome crescendo. She breathed in deep, ragged gasps, feeling as if she'd been rescued from the bottom of the ocean.

Searching within the alleyways, she saw they were empty of shadows, empty of evil.

"Simone," Trent held her tightly to his chest. "What happened?"

Focusing on his cool gaze, she smiled thinly. "Don't know."

"You scared the hell out of me."

"Scared myself," she gulped and looked around. They were on the other side of the street, and Trent was cradling her within his arms.

"I felt your power," he whispered against her hair.

"It was certainly something," she sighed. "I think it's time your mother was up front with me. If she understands these things, she needs to tell me."

"She's doing what she feels is best. I have no control over that, but I trust her."

"Do you believe she knows what's happening?" Simone wondered if his mother's prophecy matched the events detailed in the dream.

"Yes." He nodded. "And she's scared."

Her stomach clenched. Lady Lichfield knew the truth. She understood that Simone's soul was here to claim Trent. And upon doing so, his life would end as it had ended in the past.

"That doesn't make me feel any better."

Trent grinned at her and kissed her on the nose. "Tell me what just happened."

"I left Oz," she felt her lips tremble, and fought against the tears that wanted to fall. "And I sure as hell didn't end up in Kansas."

She gazed into his eyes and drew strength from their depths.

He frowned, his face creased by lines of concern.

"Let's see what Ian's come up with. We'll try and understand this later."

Simone looked at the street they had recently crossed. "I don't want to walk on those stones again, okay?"

He nodded and swore beneath his breath.

They walked slowly, hand-in-hand, to the entrance of a pub. The masthead depicted a battle between St. George and the Dragon and read in large black letters "Dragon Fire" with a pint of frothing ale painted against the foreground.

Trent led her down steep, stone stairs and through a thick wooden door. It took Simone a moment for her eyes to adjust to the dim interior, but the scent of yeast and polished wood embraced her in a blanket of familiarity.

"Welcome lad and lassie," Lord Lichfield bellowed from behind the bar. Simone smiled earnestly, finding it slightly disconcerting to match this man with the somber gentlemen she'd met last night. Lady Lichfield finished pulling a draught and glanced in their direction. Her eyes widened as she absorbed Simone's presence, and she scurried in her direction.

"Simone, is everything all right?"

"I'm fine, ma'am." She was unnerved at the concern that laced the older woman's voice.

"Your dra . . ." She bit her lip and clamped her mouth shut.

"Excuse me?"

"Your dreams must have been difficult last night. You look very tired."

"It's just jetlag, Mum, stop pestering her." Trent hugged his mother affectionately and hustled them all to the back of the pub. "Where's Ian?"

"Where do you think, lad?" his father boomed. "He's over at the bar, chatting up the ladies."

Simone chuckled, following Trent to a large round table nestled against the far wall. Waving her into a chair, he departed to extract Ian from the clutches of the entire female contingent within the pub. She sank into the chair feeling as if she'd run ten miles and then climbed Mount Everest.

A shimmer of power lingered within, sending jolts of heat down her arm. She laced her fingers together alarmed that they trembled violently.

Francine gripped her shoulder, and she gazed up into the woman's face.

"I'm concerned for you. Are you certain everything's all right?"

"I'd feel a whole lot better if you'd tell me whatever it is you're holding back," Simone challenged. She desperately wanted the truth, needed to understand the vision from last night.

"I can't do that," Lady Lichfield responded. "At least, not yet."

"Then when?"

"When everything is in place." She patted Simone's cheek and walked back to the bar.

Within the crowded and raucous room, solitude wrapped a strangling arm around her neck. It choked and suffocated, suffusing her in the isolation of distrust.

What did these people want from her?

If Lady Lichfield new about Simone's power, why wouldn't she explain it?

Not even the reassuring sight of Trent's broad shoulders could dampen the surging fear of the unknown.

***

Trent found Ian flashing his MI-5 identification and telling tall tales of adventures they'd never been on. He grabbed his partner's shoulder, apologizing to the mesmerized women and dragged him back to the table where Simone sat.

He glanced at the array of pork pies and hot steaming chips his father had delivered to the table. Simone only picked at the food, a troubled expression written across her face.

He settled next to her and slipped an arm around her back. She smiled and snuggled closer, her eyes lighting as she spotted Ian.

"Hey there, stranger. Any news from Boston?"

"Hi ya, Simone. Welcome to England. Don't listen to this old thug, we don't eat all Americans."

"Really?" Simone answered, trying to suppress her smile. "What DO you do with them?"

"Well, no . . . I didn't mean . . . That didn't sound quite right."

Trent snickered at Ian's discomfort and switched the subject. "Tell us more of what you've uncovered."

"I've confirmed that Pamela Allen is Simone's blood mother."

"Lady Lichfield seems to believe that my mother never married Simon Drake." Simone interjected.

"She did. However, it was after you were born."

Trent motioned for Ian to continue.

"Rosalyn Allen was not their child. She was Simone's cousin, Marjorie and Des Walker's daughter."

Narrowing his eyes, Trent verified that Simone wasn't too rattled by the news then turned to question Ian. "Rosalyn was Marjorie and Des's natural child?"

"Yes. According to the beginning of her journal, she left home abruptly at the age of eighteen when her parents refused to tell Simone the truth about her heritage. A firm believer of Wicca, she became a member of one of the oldest and most respected covens in Boston." Ian glanced down at his notebook then looked back at Simone. "She dedicated her life to the study of Dragon Dancing."

"Dragon Dancing?" Simone asked. Trent's heart clenched, and his mouth suddenly felt dry. He noted the paleness of her face as she digested the information but there was no shock.

"Dragon dancing. It stems back to the age of the druids when dragons dwelled beneath the rocks of Snowdon." Ian sat back and gazed from Trent to Simone. "You haven't told her yet?"

"Not yet." He glared at his partner. "I wanted to separate the facts from the fairytale."

"It's much more than a fairytale," interjected Francine, settling in a chair next to Trent. "And you know it Trent. A person is born a Dragon Dancer. It's a gift not a learned craft."

Simone reached for his hand. Her touch sent bolts of electricity up his arm, and he silently smoothed the jagged nerves. Squeezing back, he tilted his head and smiled. "It's a bit much, eh? Accepting all this mumbo jumbo?" He wasn't certain how she'd react.

She shrugged. "How are you connected?"

"I'm stilling working through that." Trent said, unnerved by her easy acceptance.

"Dragon Dancer and Ancient," she whispered.

"What?"

Simone blanched and covered her mouth. "Nothing."

How could she know? "Did you say Ancient?"

She shook her head. "I'm still unclear as to why Rosalyn left when she did. That doesn't make sense. There must be more to it than the truth about my parentage. Besides, what does all this have to do with Lawrence Gideon? Whether I'm his niece or his daughter, I'm still related. Right?"

"What happened right before Rosalyn left?" Francine questioned, leaning forward and scrutinizing Simone.

Trent frowned as Simone's expression shut down. He narrowed his eyes, searching her face. Pulling her tighter into his embrace, he kissed her forehead. "Simone, whatever you're not saying could be very important. Please, tell me what happened that night. You've alluded to these gray-uglies but not much more. What made Rosalyn run?"

"No," she said, shaking her head. "I can't discuss it."

"Balderdash," Francine blurted. "You're holding something back, and I need to know what it is. What are these gray things Trent is referring to?"

Simone rose from the table, and the despair written across her face squeezed his heart.

"I . . ." She spoke quietly to his mother. "Can withhold whatever information I choose. You, Lady Lichfield, are certainly not assisting me by remaining closed mouthed about my history. All your ramblings have done nothing but confuse me and increase my distrust."

Trent glared at his mother and raced after Simone as she wove her way between the crowded tables and out into the afternoon sun.

He caught her before she stepped on to the main street.

"Easy there, love. I thought you didn't want to cross this road again."

She jerked from his touch and hastily retreated pressing her back against the side of a Scottish wool store.

"I can't stand this anymore," she whispered, shaking her head.

"Simone, what is going on?"

"Trent," she moved to his side and grabbed his arm. "Would you think I'm crazy if I told you that whatever is haunting me is really after you?"

He bent and kissed her cheek. She smelled lightly of jasmine, causing his pulse to quicken at the memory of her silken skin. "With everything else that's been going on, I hardly think a few gray-uglies would scare me."

"They're real and very dangerous."

"Tell me about it, love." He pulled her against his chest, and the feel of her pounding heart sent a shiver of fear down his spine. She was petrified.

"They're not after Jessie or me. The shadows will come for you. I think it must have something to do with this burning in my chest and the birthmark on my back. You're in danger."

"Why do you say that?"

"When I stepped on to those cobblestones, I fell back in time. And they were there. Waiting for me, reaching across the stone and threatening you. Just like all the other times."

Trent wasn't certain what to make of this last statement. Simone reached up to his face and ruffled his hair back. "When I look into your eyes," she whispered. "I fall back in time. I see you as you were a thousand years ago then four hundred years ago."

"It's because of who we are," he sighed.

"Then who I am is no good for you, because every time I see the mirror of your face you are dead."

His heart pounded beneath the weight of fate. It was closing around him like a swarm of honeybees. He held her tightly, smoothing her hair, whispering sweet words against her head. "We'll be all right," he reassured. "Everything will be all right."

He felt the sobs shake her shoulders and could do nothing more but continue to soothe Simone. It was true. His mind reeled. Everything his mother had told him was true. How could the chronicles have been wrong?

Chapter Nineteen

Trent strode down the hallway. His mind focused upon the disquieting luncheon in Bath. He sighed. As usual, Lady Lichfield had spent the past twenty-four hours invoking the mystical cadence of a loon. It had done nothing but infuriate Simone. Her emotions were now in full charge. They'd returned from Bath, her feelings locked tightly away from his reach.

She insisted on spending time alone in her room. He decided to come clean about the entire prophecy, even the areas he was guessing at. If nothing else, it would ease her mind about his safety. The gray-uglies weren't after him. There was nothing in any of the books regarding that.

Bath affected her. He didn't understand what she felt, but he was certain it bordered the realm of terrifying. The need to dig beneath her skin and expose whatever it was that frightened her was driving him mad. He wasn't thrilled that fate appeared to be in control at the moment, but he'd do whatever was required to keep Simone safe.

Knocking gently on the mahogany door, he waited impatiently for her to answer. He leaned against the jamb, crossing his arms, and tapping his foot. After what felt like an interminable amount of time, he knocked again.

"Bloody hell," he swore at the offending barricade. He knocked one final time, and when it went unanswered, he was unable to prevent himself from trying the knob. It turned easily, and he pushed the door inward.

"Simone?" he whispered into the darkened space.

A quick scan confirmed the room was empty. A sudden blast of cold air slammed the door shut behind him. He walked over to a pair of French doors that stood open, their pale, sheer curtains blowing gently in the wind. Walking into the brisk night, he glanced around.

His step faltered and a rush of emotions held his breath at bay.

Simone was below.

She wore a silken nightgown that shimmered gold over every curve of her body. Within the inner gardens, her feet rested lightly upon thick grass. The scent of roses in full bloom tickled his nose.

Her arms rose to the stars, weaving a magical dance to her own silent song. She twirled beneath the moon, the image of a dragon floated around her, wrapping ethereal wings protectively about and mirroring Simone's dance.

She was radiant beneath the emerald glow of the massive beast.

It was breathtaking.

It scared the hell out of him.

Goaded by fear, he raced down the steps and into the garden. She turned to face him.

"I can't stop it," she cried.

The transparent dragon stood behind, challenging him to interfere. It bellowed silently, whipping the air into a frenzied dust storm with the beat of its translucent wings.

Simone locked eyes with him.

Solid gold spheres flashed across the distance, piercing his heart.

He sucked in sharply as another pair of gold orbs forced themselves within his line of vision. The ghostly dragon radiated power. Her luster growing stronger with each step he took forward.

"Simone," he bellowed against the din of the wind.

"Mine," a hiss escaped the dragon spirit.

"Simone," he raged. "Lock her away."

"How? How do I do that?" She was fading into the mists as the dragon took form.

The vision wavering before him lay in blatant testimony to the existence of the powerful legend. This was his destiny. His heart lurched as he realized what needed to be done, what fate demanded.

"Simone," he said. Her name stolen from his lips by the wind.

He was her soul mate, the one man that could balance the power of the dragon.

It was his legacy to temper the essence of the beast by claiming Simone as his own. Branding her heart with his love, forcing the spirit back to its lair. It was why he was born.

To protect her.

To protect the power.

A stab of regret pierced his heart. In sudden clarity, Trent realized why he had denied himself full understanding of his destiny. This woman had woven herself into his heart, empowering his love. But it was nothing more than fate's hand at work. She wasn't truly his.

The dragon lay like a shadow within Simone, waiting . . . counting the seconds until her vulnerability fed life to its force. How foolish he'd been to ignore all the facts, ignore the path that led him here tonight. If he'd bothered to gaze as deeply into her eyes as she had his, Trent would have known.

He would have seen the inevitable, recognized the futility of honest love. His fortune had been cast more than a thousand years before.

"Trent," Simone called. "I can't fight her."

"Don't fight, love." He stepped before her and gathered her within his arms. The power of the ethereal spirit burned his soul. "You need to accept her. We need to accept her."

The dragon faded slightly, rising above them, and spreading her wings in an emerald umbrella. She bent her neck around and speared him with one golden eye. He ignored her, focusing on Simone.

She was resplendent in the light of her dragon, her eyes flashing gold, reflecting the luster of her gown. He smiled softly.

Trent didn't know what the future held, or what he could offer her. But he swore silently to the creature above, he'd show Simone what his heart felt--even if it was only what destiny decreed. He'd love her until her mind was dizzy and her heart beat for him, and him alone.

Lowering his head, his lips claimed what his soul desired. She trembled beneath his touch. He held her close, and whispered in her ear.

"You are mine."

She gasped as he nibbled and teased, tasting the sweetness of her skin. The dragon danced above, her shadow casting rays of emerald against Simone's skin. He traced the shadows with his tongue, slipping the gown from her shoulders. She was on fire and writhing beneath his touch like a dancing flame. Trent kneeled, peeling the rest of the silken dress off, and revealing her naked flesh to the night.

She ran her hands through his hair, bending down to brush her breast against his lips. He flicked his tongue across her nipple and grazed his cheek against supple skin. Reaching up, he pulled her toward him, trailing kisses from her navel downward. His heart beat madly. She stopped and tilted his head upward. Golden rays beat down upon his face.

"It's my turn, Trent."

"No, it's our turn," he said, pulling her down and spreading her upon the soft grass as he cradled her head upon his hand. "I'm going to love you like no man before."

Her eyes widened and streaks of emerald highlighted the golden orbs. She nodded and opened herself to his touch. Soft and warm, each inch of her naked flesh demanded his caress. He ran his hand across her breasts, fondling her nipples and trailing kisses behind his fingers. She dragged his sweater off his body, and moved her fingers across his skin. Reaching down, he discarded the rest of his clothes.

The cool air tantalized his inflamed senses, sending pulses of desire down his spine. He'd never wanted a woman as strongly as the one beneath him. *This was more than destiny.* He longed to believe that, but if he accepted those words he would risk everything. Could he trade his soul for his heart?

They lay together, flesh against flesh. Two hearts pounding for one another, insisting on unity. He felt the weight of the dragon upon his back, urging him forward, insisting he claim what destiny demanded was his. Simone was ready for him, her soft whimpers pleading for his entry. He raised himself above her and stared into the golden pools of her eyes.

"This is what the forces demand, do you understand?"

She furrowed her brow and shook her head.

"They say I am to claim you," he growled, fighting against the urge to plunge into her.

Simone reached a trembling hand up and caressed his brow. "I don't know about that, but I know the only thing that is important."

She wrapped her legs around his waist, forcing him to dip down, to feel the wetness and warmth she offered.

"What's that, love?" he whispered, holding himself back.

"I love you," she answered, grabbing him and pulling him into her.

He groaned, unable to prevent fate. Moving slowly, he delved into her depths, feeling her heat close about him. She gasped as he pushed deeper. Their hips moved fluidly as one, like they had done this a thousand times before.

He was home.

She moaned, increasing the rhythm. He devoured her mouth, tasting and inhaling her as he buried himself again and again. He couldn't stop, his heart felt as if it would burst. Releasing all control, he pounded faster, feeling her breath hitch and muscles tighten.

Simone met him thrust for thrust. He answered her demands, diving deeper and swifter. Trent paused, kissed her tenderly, and reached down to caress the center of her. She screamed, bucked wildly, and threw her head back, her body shuddering in waves of shattered release. His soul spiraled into oblivion as her heat convulsed around him, pulling him over the edge and into the cascading climax.

His world tilted precariously as he fought to recover control. Simone sighed and pushed gently against his chest, forcing him to roll on his side. He took her with him and nestled her within his arms.

"Well done," a voice hissed as the dragon faded back within Simone. He shook his head, and held her tighter. Tears pricked the back of his eyes. An amazing thing transpired but he felt like he'd made a deal with the devil.

"Trent, who am I," she whispered.

"Mine." He kissed her damp hair, loving the way it fell across his skin. It felt like a million soft kisses.

"You're my Dragon Dancer."

***

Simone was angry. She'd finished showering and yanked a brush harshly through the tangles in her hair. Tangles caused by the grasp of an infuriating Englishman.

He loved her.

She knew it, but why did it feel wrong? Trynt and Seren had been in love, so had Elizabeth and Rake. What was wrong with her? Maybe he wasn't supposed to be her Ancient.

He'd carried her back into her room, laid her gently on the bed, kissing her passionately, then left without a word. Not one word.

What complicated emotions were rolling around in that man?

The memory of their passionate union beneath the stars flipped her tummy into another swell of raging hormones.

Leaning forward, she peered at her reflection. Wide gold flecks dominated her eyes. The essence of the dragon within spread into every nerve ending, and it took her several seconds to battle the desire to release her.

She wanted to allow the power to wash through her and spread into all corners of her soul.

No. Simone swore. Outside, as she relinquished to the power of the dragon it'd scared the heck out of her. She'd felt as if she was being sucked into a black hole. The world dimmed until Trent wrenched her back, loving away her fear.

"Grael," a voice echoed in her mind.

"What?" she whispered.

"My name is Grael."

"Oh great," Simone said. "Now I can hear it out loud."

"I could always talk to you, child. You chose not to listen."

Simone stared into the mirror. Her eyes shimmered a vibrant gold, making her gasp in alarm.

"Who are you?" she yelled at her reflection.

"I told you. Grael."

"And what are you doing inside me?" Simone demanded.

"What has happened over the generations that you don't know about me?"

Simone studied the mirror. The dragon shimmered all around, her wings spread in barely visible wisps. Her essence occupied the entire bedroom. But, Simone wasn't afraid.

"Why don't you scare me?" Simone asked, narrowing her eyes at the ghostly apparition.

The dragon's face split into a menacing grin. "Your heart is his. I can no longer control you. Why don't you know this, Dragon Dancer?"

A loud knock prevented Simone from continuing the line of conversation. Closing her eyes, she pulled the creature's spirit back within and snapped shut the invisible cage. Simone walked over and opened the heavy wood, facing an extremely irate Trent.

"Why didn't you answer?" he demanded, clenching his fists.

"I didn't hear you," she snapped. Simone wasn't about to show him how his very presence sent her heart skidding and body melting.

He relaxed and leaned against the doorjamb. "I was worried," he whispered and pulled her into his arms.

"What's happening to me?" she asked.

"Nothing . . ." He looked deeply into her eyes. "That I didn't want."

Frowning, she wondered what the hell he was talking about.

"I meant what I said outside, Trent."

"What was that, love?"

"I love you." She grew alarmed when he closed his eyes and sighed deeply.

"You believe you love me, sweetheart, but it's not real."

"Damn you, Trent Arnot. Who do you think you are to tell me whether or not what I feel is real? You . . . arrogant, no-good, lying, sack of manure. Go stuff yourself."

She whirled around, slamming the door behind her. Heaving in great gasps of air, Simone tried to make sense of what he had said. Ignoring the hammering on her door, she decided that she needed to take control. She smacked her palm with the hairbrush and yanked on the doorknob, ducking the fist that shot in her direction.

"Damn, Simone, I almost hit you." Trent shook his hand and wriggled his fingers. His knuckles were bruised from the abuse of the wooden panel, and she couldn't prevent herself from taking them and wiping away the sting.

"I'm sorry I yelled," she snapped, dropping his hands as if they burned her skin. "I need to speak with your mother."

"Okay," he tilted her chin up and searched her eyes. "I'm sorry, too." He gathered her to his chest and hugged her tightly.

"Grael's quite miffed that I don't know who she is." She resisted the urge to relax and allow life to settle back in place.

"Who's Grael?" he asked, smoothing her hair back from her face.

She prayed he'd stop touching her. Her body was not listening to her new resolve of taking control. "She's the one you refer to as the Empress." She inhaled sharply when he pushed her away to examine her face.

"She told you her name?" Steely blue eyes met her startled gaze. Agent Arnot slammed into place, eliminating the warm and comforting presence of her lover.

"Yes," Simone stammered, fear slicing through her soul. A soft laugh reverberated within, mocking her in notes of fluted music.

"You're right. You need to see my mother." He pushed the door closed and hurried her down the hall. Simone clutched her hairbrush as if it held the power of a pistol, despairing at the thought of listening to the crazy ramblings of Lady Lichfield. She wasn't at all certain she wanted to hear what Trent's mother had to say.

Trent pushed upon a set of wooden swinging doors and led them into a mammoth kitchen. A fire roared in the far left corner, held in check by a massive stone hearth crowned with a thick wooden mantle. Scattered in easy chaos were pictures in various sizes.

The heat seeped into her chilled body, and she walked closer to examine the people that smiled brightly into the camera lens. There was a family portrait, and Simone was amazed to see two other Trent-like figures surrounding Lord and Lady Lichfield. She frowned, trying to remember when he'd mentioned he had brothers.

It was a handsome family.

"Where are your other sons, Lady Lichfield?" Simone turned and studied Trent's parents.

They sat at a heavy wooden kitchen table, nursing crystal goblets full of blood-red wine.

"France," she answered, sipping lightly at the liquid.

"Both of them?" Simone asked.

"All of them." she answered.

Trent stepped forward and glanced over at the picture Simone had been studying.

"Hmm, Devon isn't in this shot, is he?" He looked into Simone's eyes and smiled. "You'd like him. He's not at all like me."

She smiled back but prevented her fingers from touching his face tenderly.

"Is everything all right?" Francine Arnot asked.

"The dragon has introduced herself to Simone." Trent announced, guiding Simone to the large wooden table.

Lady Lichfield's eyes widened. "It's happened? You're connected."

"Yes."

Trent's mother faced her and stared. "When?"

Simone felt her face turn bright red. "Awhile ago." She turned to Trent and glared at him, mortified to be discussing their sex life in front of his mother.

"It's the only way." He said, an apologetic smile tilting his lips upward.

"What does that mean?" she asked, a bit afraid of the answer.

"Our union as Ancient and Dancer. Sex." Now his face blushed. "It's the only way to ignite the bond."

"I see," Simone sighed.

"If I remember," he furrowed his brow and poured her a glass of wine. "There is something within the old books that details an instance where a dragon speaks its name as a pretence to serious danger."

"Yes, son, you're right." Lord Lichfield answered. "When a dragon reveals its name to a Dancer it is to empower the Dancer in order to have her battle a danger which would threaten all dragon kind."

Lord Lichfield rose and walked out of the room, muttering to himself only to return a second later with a large, leather-bound book propped within his arms.

Simone sat gazing desperately around. What on earth were they going on about? She couldn't untangle her thoughts from Trent's admission that he made love to her to connect to her dragon.

They were all bent around the aged manual, combing its pages for an item she could only guess at.

"Interesting," Grael hissed. "I know the scent of these humans. Is it possible you managed to be claimed by the right Ancient?"

"Shut up," Simone snapped. "You're all crazy."

"What?" Trent glanced up and furrowed his brow in confusion. "Did you say something?"

"No. Well, yes, actually. I told Grael to shut up."

Francine stood and walked over to stand directly in front of Simone. "Grael, you say? What did she want?"

"She said she remembered your scent. She said I had been claimed by my Ancient." This was preposterous. Wasn't it?

Lady Lichfield frowned and gazed at her husband who only shrugged in return. Trent walked over and knelt beside her chair. "I know this is all a bit much to take in. And Grael's right, I think. That's the twist in the prophecy that isn't mentioned in any of the chronicles I've been studying."

"Oh," she whispered, unnerved slightly that he hadn't known everything until tonight. She'd assumed he was like his parents-steeped in the lore of witches and warlocks.

"I'm a gypsy," Lady Lichfield interrupted. "I was raised by gypsies and taught their ways in this world. When Trent's father swept me off my

9

feet, I became Lady Lichfield on the outside. But in here," she tapped her chest. "I will always be gypsy. We believe what most people label legends."

"Which is just the way I like her," Lord Lichfield interjected. "I met Francine when she was only nineteen, and I was a graduate student determined to uncover the secret of the Pendle Hill witches. Francine's ancestors dominated that area and recorded many facts about the original fourteen persecuted witches. Your lineage, Simone, sprouts from one of the first to be tried and hung. Luther Draconius was his name. Later, the surname was shortened to Drake and his ancestry goes further back to a time when dragons roamed the earth."

Draconius. Where had she heard that name? Simone stifled her laughter at his last sentence. "Terrific. I'm not only a dragon but a witch."

"No, my dear," Francine whispered. "You've never been a witch or a dragon and neither was your ancestor. It has been your destiny to hold the essence of the dragon within."

"I believe that part having had a recent tête-à-tête with Grael. But, I don't understand it." She wasn't ready to explain her dreams. Let them tell her everything they knew, and then she'd decide how much information to impart.

"Dragons haven't been able to exist within this plain since before the ninth century," Francine continued. "They were hunted and killed by mankind. Their wisdom threatened by extinction. A spell was cast and the physical dragon faded into an essence that was bound directly to a Dancer."

"Please," Simone asked. "Tell me specifically what a Dragon Dancer is." She wanted to know how much truth lie within her visions. What Lady Lichfield discussed was eerily familiar.

"In the age when dragons wore their physical forms, they were able to communicate with gifted humans. These people cared for their needs and worked as their representatives. It took years for the dragon to understand the ways of human compassion and over time they learned and made it their drive to protect our world. Their humans were called Dragon Dancers because of their ability to understand the intricate workings of the dragon's mind. When the dragons were subjugated to an ethereal form, the Dancer was linked with their spirit forever."

"Are you saying that my soul and that of Grael's are intertwined?"

"Yes."

"Why?"

"In order to preserve their wisdom and their power. Good and evil battle on many different plains. For us to have lost the guidance of these special creatures would have tipped the scales, so to say."

"Why has she never shown herself before?"

"You would have died. Without the protection of an Ancient, her spirit would have disintegrated you."

Simone narrowed her eyes and glanced back and forth between Trent and his mother. *And here the confusion begins.* "Why are you telling me this now? I have been asking for the truth."

"Because, my dear, Trent has fulfilled his destiny."

Her heart clenched and the pain that ripped through her soul almost drove her to her knees. *This was what he had meant when he'd accused her of not really loving him. He believed everything of this prophecy. And the one thing that was left out was the love between Dancer and Ancient. That never filtered through time.*

"This is," she inhaled deeply, "slightly unbelievable."

"If you had remained in England with your family they would have taught you how to dance with Grael. How to bring her alive and use her powers. You would have called upon her to find your soul mate and change your life and the lives of all of us. It is a great honor . . . this gift of yours."

"No," Simone shook her head. "I am responsible for myself and my actions. I would never use a power to manipulate my life." She turned and looked purposely at Trent. He raised an eyebrow but remained silent.

"Maybe," Francine shrugged. "Maybe not. It makes no difference. Grael has exposed herself, and the only thing standing between you and sudden death is my son."

"What are you saying?"

"The power of my son will hold you on this earth until it is time to leave. Without him, the pull of Grael's spirit will kill you and send your soul back to the heavens to wait for another return to earth. And the awakening will have failed. Again."

"There's only one kink in your carefully schemed lore," Simone answered flatly. "Your son and I have no future together. When I have put Lawrence Gideon in the hell he belongs to, I'm returning to the States."

Francine raised a brow and cocked her head to stare at Trent. She smiled and nodded in understanding then looked back at Simone.

"He can be stubborn sometimes," is all she said. Simone's heart dropped. She'd wanted his mother to confirm what her heart felt, but she didn't. She didn't say that he loved her.

"*It's not enough,*" Grael hissed.

"Tell me something I don't know," Simone retaliated silently.

"*Stupid man,*" the dragon spat.

"Now that, my scaled ghost, is something we agree on." Simone's mind whirled with everything she'd been told. It was all a muddled mess of fact and fiction. She sat back and thought. Trent and his parents were back pouring over the book that apparently held all the answers to her problems. He'd refused to look her in the eye, embarrassed she figured by what his mother had said.

"I think," she spoke loudly. "I'd like to take that book you have and read the background information for myself. Lady Lichfield have you had a chance to transcribe that document from my family memorial?"

The Arnot's turned and stared. Francine smiled brightly, flashing a set of pearly whites that looked amazingly like Trent's.

"Yes, my dear, of course you may have this book. There's another in the library you might find of interest as well . I'll leave it for you. You are perfect, darling, simply perfect. I couldn't have picked a better match, if I'd tried. The language in that document from your memorial is very old. I'm having difficulty with some of the wording, but I'll let you know as soon as I've deciphered it."

Simone smiled, ignoring the woman's reference to her son. She held her arms out for the book. Francine handed it over. Simone glanced at the title. A buzzing hit her ears as she gazed at the cover, stunned by the title. The Red Book of Hergest.

Brushing past Trent, she headed out of the kitchen and back to her room. His voice echoed up the staircase, pleading with her to wait. Closing her eyes, she paused and held her breath. Rage and distrust washed over her. He'd lied all along, led her around like a stupid puppy.

She was a fool.

"Simone, hold up." He reached her quickly and turned her to face him. "Are you angry?"

"Angry? No, I think that's too tame a word." She laughed harshly. "I'll get back to you after I have a conversation or two with Grael."

"An intelligent human? Is that possible?" A soft hiss mocked her.

"I'd like to be there for you," Trent whispered, the sapphire depths of his eyes staking her heart.

"No," she shook her head, refusing to give in to her emotions. "I've been alone in this quest for a long time, haven't I? Why change now?"

His eyes clouded over. With a shrug, Trent released her and spun on his heels. He walked down the long corridor and out the front door, slamming it behind him and rocking the crystal sconces lining the front hall. Wincing, she walked up the remainder of the stairs and into her room.

Simone laid The Red Book of Hergest at the end of her bed, not even contemplating the fact that Trent's family owned it. She wondered if the other book Lady Lichfield referred to was The White Book of Rhydderch. If so, she wanted to read that as well. Damn Trent. Damn him to hell. He'd played her.

She quickly changed into an old T-shirt and sweatpants. She twirled her hair into a loose bun, securing it with a clip. Nestling between her pillows, she opened the aged journal to the place Francine had marked. An ink etching of a fierce, winged creature headed the yellowed page. Beneath the drawing, large letters scrawled the chapter heading.

Dragon Dancer

Llallogen weaves magic and might

Dreigiau Rheol cannot fight

The winged creatures fly no more

As is decreed by ancient lore

They dance the night with tempered souls

Fulfilling fate and powerful roles

Wisdom and magic must prevail

Or darkness will lift and evil wail

The Ancient claims his Dragon Dancer

And blocks the force of necromancer

Three souls entwine, with love divine

The power of three, their destiny

Simone studied the page. It was a pretty read, but what did it all mean? She raised her brows then widened her eyes when she realized the answer lay within.

"Grael? Are you there?"

"Yes," a bored hiss replied. She materialized within the room, curling around the bed posts.

Simone stared and smiled. It was easier having a conversation when

Grael was present. At least she didn't feel like a looney talking to herself. "Who was this Llallogen this paragraph talks about?"

"A great wizard."

"Like Merlin?"

The dragon rumbled with laughter. "He's known by many names."

"You mean he was Merlin? As in King Arthur and the Holy Grail? I thought that was a myth." Simone asked, surprised to hear a name from her fantasy novels.

"And what did you think we were?"

"Oh, right. True." Simone nodded, suddenly realizing that an entirely new portion of life had opened itself upon her.

"Who were the Ancients?"

"An old line of humans who'd lived since the dawning of time. Their power is special and unique. They were well hidden within the population and only drew together during the darkest of days."

"What happened to them?"

"The spell linked them with the Dancers. They were no longer a separate race."

"Then, what happened to you?"

"After the spell was cast, we melted into the universe. We became creatures of unearthly matter, destined to reside within the soul of our Dancer, never to breathe fire or fly the skies." The dragon's sadness was over whelming, it pulled at Simone's heart.

"Why?"

"It was believed that as each Dancer's soul passed from one generation to the next, the soul of the Ancient would as well. Together these essences would allow us our freedom. They'd be strong enough to withstand our demand at life and temper our need to be independent. Then, and only then, could we escape our prison and fly among the heavens."

"I don't understand," Simone frowned, trying very hard to comprehend what Grael meant.

"Without a soul mate, the Dancer would die if the power of the dragon were released."

"Each Dancer has an Ancient. One specific soul mate?"

"Only the two that twisted the spell."

"I still don't understand."

Grael sighed and Simone felt her exasperation. "Your soul and that of the one that resides within the Ancient who paces like a caged animal down the hall are the only two that must intertwine."

"Why is that?"

"You were beginning, you will be end."

The dragon spoke in riddles. Simone inhaled deeply, trying to wash away her impatience. Instead of sorting through the maze of twisted words, she continued her questions. "How often do these souls find one another?"

"Rarely. In their attempt to find ever lasting love, they failed to recognize an important element."

"And that was?"

"The human heart cannot bend at the whim of a spell. It is too strong. Seren was my Dancer and Trynt the man she loved beyond time. He warped the spell so that their souls would only ever find one another. Trynt's arrogance blinded him to the force of each individual heart."

Simone's gut kicked. She thought back to Grael's response in the kitchen and her recent reference to Trent. "I am that Dancer. I am this Seren?"

"Yes."

"And Trent contains the soul of her Ancient, the one who warped the original spell?"

"Yes," Grael cried. And Simone couldn't hold at bay the joy and excitement that flooded from the dragon in waves. She stared hard at the pages before her. Grael was leaping around the room like a kid with a new toy.

"Grael," she whispered. "How do I make you go away?"

Julie Korzenko

Chapter Twenty

"Go away?"

Simone laughed out loud at the shock resonating from Grael. "Yes. Can I not set you free or something like that?" She cursed her stupidity for not writing her dreams in a journal. Closing her eyes, she tried to remember exactly what it was that Seren said about Grael being gone. She sighed with frustration and glanced at the dragon.

The spirit of the beast filled her room. She must have been beautiful in life, the faint shimmers of emerald scales only a shadow of the luster blood and breath would've given them. Grael snaked her head around to gaze thoughtfully into Simone's face. "Why would you want to do that?"

"I'm scared." She answered truthfully. "I don't want this." An expression of hurt and disbelief crossed the dragon's golden orbs.

"Why ever not? This is an honor. Your power is stronger than any before you. I can feel it. The shadows feel it." She leveled a look at Simone that sent a river of fear flooding her soul. Grael nodded. "You are afraid. And so you should be." Snaking her neck around, Simone felt her slide behind her shoulders and glance at the book laid out on the bed. "Why do you read this?"

"I'm looking for answers."

A soft laugh echoed within the room. "You read man's words when you have the source of truth before you?"

Simone frowned. The dragon was right. She was reading tales

handed down through the ages and translated many times over. She pointed to a paragraph within The Red Book of Hergest. "It says here that dragons are deceptive creatures and must be dealt with accordingly. Their wile and intelligence only seek to better their position and wealth. Dragons cannot be trusted."

"True." Grael slipped away, dissipating into thin mist. She didn't know where the dragon went, but she felt alone. The ball of fire didn't burn as painfully as it once had. It was as if the creature could separate them at will and disappear.

Simone shook her head and rose from the bed. Her body ached. Checking her watch, she realized it was early morning. Padding to the French doors, she opened them and inhaled the crisp English dawn. It came early in this part of the world, the sky already bright with light and fading the stars to a mere memory.

The chill air sent shivers skittering along her skin. Blowing out a breath of air, she rubbed her arms and shut the doors against the morning. If there were no more answers to be gained from the dragon, then she might as well find the other books Lady Lichfield referred to.

She crept to the library. Ignoring the anger that swept away her exhaustion, Simone picked up The White Book of Rhydderch that waited for her in the center of an antique monastery table. The trestle-legged table was constructed of French oak. She'd been searching for a piece just like this to add to her growing collection of Middle Age furniture. Scrutinizing the furniture, her architect's eye discerned the dense grain and perfectly joined wood that indicated the table was authentic and probably more than five centuries old.

She ran her hand across its waxed surface curious as to whether or not it had been around during the time of Elizabeth.

A hand written note lay on top of the large leather-bound book.. *The two volumes must be used together. Good luck. Francine*

Trent had known about the existence of these books and never told her. Had that been the only thing he held back, or was their more?

Simone narrowed her eyes. Betrayal and mistrust were unwelcome emotions, but she couldn't help what she felt. She left the library and returned to her room. It no longer soothed her. The isolation and disadvantage of being the last person to understand the details of the past fortnight encircled her, cutting her off from the rest of the inhabitants of the manor house.

Fire scorched her neck. She clutched at the neckline of her T-shirt, tugging at it and peeling it from her skin. Pain wrenched her stomach heaving its contents upward. Gagging, she gripped the edge of the bed.

A blast of heat spread from her chest, running the length of every nerve ending. It hurt. She gasped and fell to her knees. Grael shrieked, pulling and tugging at every corner of her soul. She infiltrated and decimated. Simone's temple throbbed and stabs of pain jammed into her eyes in hot flashes. Her body flushed with heat then fell to an unbearable bone-chilling temperature.

Tipping her head back, Simone screamed for Trent. Through the veil of terror, she heard him answer her call, an unearthly cry of rage and vengeance. She struggled against the will of the dragon, but as each second ticked by her body faded beneath the power.

***

He heard her. Felt her terror. Trent raced down the halls of Draconius. Slamming his shoulder against the heavy wooden door, it inched open. He pushed harder breaking through the resistance caused by Grael. Sliding between the narrow gap he'd made, Trent faced the dragon.

She filled the bed chamber. Her will and power flowing into every crevasse of the room. Her jaw opened and he saw a line of jagged teeth as she sneered at him. Simone cried. The glint in Grael's eyes challenged him, dared him to perform the duties of an Ancient.

He swore at her and dropped to his knees beside Simone. She tugged at her clothes as if they burned her skin. Ripping her shirt up and over her shoulders, Trent tossed it away. He then stripped the rest of her clothes off and threw them over his shoulder. His heart caught. Simone writhed and fought against Grael.

He knocked her hands away and ran his fingers across her skin. The heat of the dragon burned through her entire body. As he caressed, she quieted. Her breathing slowed and the heat receded.

Trent blinked back the tears that blurred his vision. He'd never been more scared in his entire life. Gathering her into his arm, he kissed her forehead and smoothed back her sweat-soaked hair.

***

A touch, soft as a feather, soothed the knifing pain to her temple. Gasping for breath, she inhaled a spicy scent that helped her reach forward beyond the blinding ache and pull Trent closer. His lips touched hers, and she moved closer taking the safety he offered. Her instincts told her to seek his body, to absorb the power of his soul.

He smoothed his hands across her skin washing away the ache that wracked her nerves. She surrendered to his touch, eyes closed and mind concentrated on nothing but the feel of his gentle fingers.

"Simone?"

She inhaled and gazed into his eyes. They shone with power, the blue deep and bright. "Thank you," she said unsure of what she meant.

He grinned, causing her to frown. What was so funny? "You're welcome."

Pushing up on her elbows, she glanced around mortified that she lay sprawled upon the carpet her clothes torn from her body and her naked flesh tingling from his touch. No wonder he was so cocky.

"I," she stammered. "We didn't?" Kneeling, she gathered her shirt up off the floor and pulled it over her head. The invasion of her soul left her feeling dirty and embarrassed.

Trent sat back, leaning against the foot of her bed. "No." He reached for her hand and tugged her close. "But if you'd needed me in that way, I would have done whatever was necessary to ease your pain."

"I don't understand this."

"Simone, until you accept who we are and what this damn destiny is all about, I'm afraid Grael's essence will be stronger than yours. That's what I'm supposed to do. Temper her will."

Listen to your Ancient. The dragon's voice boomed through her head, stabbing at the back of her eyes. She flinched and backed away when Trent moved closer alarmed by her reaction. She shook her head and used the edge of the bed to help herself to her feet, her legs shaky and exhaustion making her muscles resemble wet noodles. Trent jumped up and tried to help but she pushed him away.

"No. I need space. Please, go away." She tried to catch her breath. Simone felt used. The blame couldn't be pinned on him, but his presence reminded her that she held no control. Disgusted at this insane predicament, anger flooded her system.

It wasn't how Grael brought her down in sixty-seconds flat and ravaged her brain until she passed out that filled her with bitterness. It was her heart. The stupid organ betrayed and murdered. Trent only had to gaze into her eyes to cause a fatal wound, the confusion and enforced detachment that floated there as deadly as the power of her dragon. She wanted him to feel what she felt. She needed him to feel what she felt.

Unconditional love.

But he wouldn't do that.

He'd always hold back that level of intimacy she desperately desired because he'd feel a pawn . . . the Dragon Dancer's puppet. A soul manipulated by prophecy.

***

Simone woke slowly from the comfort of a deep, dreamless sleep. She stretched and yawned, inhaling a cleansing breath. The scent of spice still lingered in the room, and she sat up to see if Trent had returned after she'd collapsed in bed.

He hadn't.

Her clothes still scattered the floor like pieces of a jigsaw puzzle. She slipped from beneath the warmth of the covers and gathered all the discarded items into her arms. Dropping them on a chair, she proceeded into the adjoining bathroom.

Sitting on the edge of the claw foot tub, she ran a hot steamy bubble bath. Her body begged to be pampered. Before sinking beneath the enticing water, Simone went to the mirror and wiped off the fog. She stared at her reflection.

"Shit."

Her eyes glowed a deep golden yellow, gone were the flecks of gray and shade of green. She felt Grael waken, the tingle and burn along her nerve endings still raw from the early morning attack.

"No!" She scrunched her face up and pushed with every ounce of mental energy she possessed. Focusing on the now familiar emerald dragon, she shoved the essence of the dragon into it and kicked it away. Snapping her eyes open, she sighed when they remained gold. At least her nerves were soothed. And she'd managed that without Trent. Feeling a bit more empowered, Simone ignored the echo of Grael's laughter.

She climbed into the oversized tub and sank into the hot embrace of water and jasmine scented bubbles.

Before she had a moment to relax, the weight of the dragon pushed on her chest. A flickering thought of here we go again crossed her mind and then nothing but vivid blue sky.

**

She flew in graceful arcs through the snow capped peaks of the Cambrian Mountains. Snowdon lay ahead, the craggy ledge of Dreigiau Rheol waiting. Its ancient rock a solace to a race all but forgotten.

Grael twisted and spiraled, her soul full of joy. The air washed over her scales in waves of chilled pleasure. Diving toward the valley, her heart skipped a beat as a large male lifted his head and roared at her. She slowed, lazily circling the green pasture he sunned himself in. Deep sapphire winked in and out as her shadow played against his scales.

He stood, pulling himself upright and spreading his wings. He was magnificent, almost twice her size.

She twisted on her side and swooped closer. He raised his snout to the sky, bellowing a call that lit a fire within Grael.

She answered, heat lacing her shriek with a deep crackle. He leapt from the earth and tore toward her, roaring her name. A moment of confusion caused her to hesitate then the nature of the beast seized her, and she met the male midair. They danced, swooping and twirling, their turns becoming sharper and cleaner as their hearts beat as one.

He suffused her. His power greater than her own. The love that spread through brilliant blue orbs touched her soul and she answered it with the passion he demanded. Mating had never been like this, an overwhelming need, a lick of flame that bound them together for eternity.

Settling upon the ground, Grael bent beneath his will. She succumbed to his insatiable desire and allowed her body to be caressed and loved until pleasure made her sink against the sweet grass in exhaustion.

***

Simone rose from the bottom of the tub, gasping and sputtering for air. Gripping the edge of the white porcelain, she allowed the tears to flow. Her shoulders shook beneath the sobs that wracked her body. The wail of sorrow that echoed from the depths of her soul spoke of a passion she understood.

A love stronger than time.

She released the hold she had on Grael's prison and the dragon sprung forth from deep within. Instead of the fire and pain Simone sought to ease the rending of her heart, Grael slipped out with the barest whisper of heat.

Her force enveloped Simone and ethereal wings wrapped around her body. The dragon rocked her gently and keened softly into her ear. Her voice sang of love and laughter, pain and sorrow.

"Get dressed, little one. You have much to learn."

Simone stood and ran her hand across the shimmer of scales, feeling only a slight tingle as her fingers skimmed the spirit. "All right." She swallowed the lump in her throat and went to dress.

Pulling on a faded pair of jeans and well-worn football jersey sporting the dolphin and bright aqua of her favorite team, Simone shook her head at the constant jabbering of Grael. The dragon seemed mesmerized by her clothes, or lack thereof, and wanted to know when the female stopped layering in fabric and began wearing breeches. She peered over Simone's shoulder as gold earrings were put in place and remarked at their smallish size. Didn't she know that a Dragon Dancer needed to present herself as a prodigy of wealth and wisdom?

Simone chuckled.

"Be quiet," she finally said. "You're giving me a headache."

Grael blinked once and then sank into silence, an expression crossing her face that Simone figured was a dragon pout.

Surveying her room, Simone felt suffocated. It was probably because Grael filled every corner with either a wing or claw. She stepped onto the balcony outside of the French doors and inhaled the day. She'd slept the morning away.

Reaching her fingers to the sun, she stretched to the left then to the right. A tingle of awareness skittered up her back. She turned and Trent stood upon the terrace to her left. She held her hand up to prevent him from moving closer, then turned and headed away from him.

She didn't feel like dealing with those emotions yet.

Moving with long strides, she skirted the rose garden. Memories of the night before flushed her cheeks and melted her insides. "Not going there."

"Where aren't we going?" Grael asked.

Simone pointed at the horseshoe shaped garden. "There."

"Why? I think your last visit was quite pleasant."

A snort escaped Simone's nose, and she bit back her laughter. "Tell me what happened last night." She felt shock resonate from the dragon.

"You do not know?"

Frowning, she hated this feeling of being stupid and lost. "No."

"The human anatomy is very different than a dragon's but I'll certainly attempt to explain what occurred."

Simone felt even more confused but decided to remain quiet. She sat on the edge of a wall and watched a stable hand exercise one of the Arnot horses with a lunge line. He pulled the long lead in a circle, nipping the mare's hooves with a thin whip. The animal moved from a leisurely gate into a crisp trot.

"A sexual act between male and female takes place when the male penetrates the female. If this is done with the prowess of a dragon, then the female achieves great satisfaction. That would've been the part where you screamed."

Simone rubbed her eyes, ignoring the burning blush of embarrassment. Nothing was sacred anymore. "What the hell are you talking about?"

"I'm explaining last night."

She laughed out loud reaping a curious stare from the horse handler. Simone waved, eliciting a formal nod from the man. "Not that part of last night. I want to know about the part where you nearly killed me."

"I'm relieved you understand the intricacies of mating. You had me concerned." the dragon said.

"I know all about mating, and I'd appreciate it if the next time I choose to participate in that sport you'd kindly disappear."

Grael snorted. "I have never encountered a Dancer such as you."

"Yeah? That makes two of us."

"I attempted to show you my strength and the affect it will have upon you if you turn away from this Ancient."

Simone sobered, her mind chewing on what the dragon said. "But you chose to show me. Does that mean that you don't have to drown me in all that pain?"

Grael was silent for several minutes. "No. The longer you are away from your Ancient the easier it will be for my spirit to overtake yours. In the end, your body won't survive and our souls are once more tossed into the heavens."

"That's not true."

"Dragon's don't lie."

"That's also not true." Simone remembered what the tales of their past disclosed.

"How did Elizabeth survive?"

"She didn't. She died as did all the rest."

Simone knew better. "The Elizabeth in my dreams was Elizabeth Stuart, sister to Henry Stuart, Prince of Wales and daughter of King James VI of Scotland later to be titled King James I of England. She did, in fact, marry Frederick in 1613. And her brother, Henry, died in 1612 as she predicted. I've done my homework. Elizabeth died at the ripe old age of sixty-six. How was that possible?"

"The Winter King was an Ancient."

"I don't understand. If Trynt warped the original spell so that only their two souls would only ever unite, then how can a Dancer merge with another Ancient?"

"In order for the rest of my brethren to feel the power of life, Seren and Trynt's souls must become one through the magic of Dancer and Ancient. But any Ancient can use his power to calm my spirit."

Simone frowned. This wasn't at all what she'd expected. She thought she'd found a loop hole. Unwilling to give up, she argued with Grael. "Still, Elizabeth lived thirty years beyond Frederick."

Silence.

"Grael?"

After an interminable lapse in time, the dragon finally answered. "That is the truth."

"How did Elizabeth escape your spirit?"

"It was a terrible mistake."

Simone's heart skipped. The possibility of freedom existed. "How did Elizabeth set you free?"

"Freedom is not mine to have. The only way to banish my soul is to transfer it."

"To who?" Simone asked, it didn't outline anywhere in the volumes within her room that this was a possibility.

"Enough!" Grael screeched and smashed through Simone's mind with enough fury to force her off the wall and onto the grass. Breathing against the pain, Simone fisted her hands in the thick green blades and battled against the will of the dragon. There was information there that she needed. "I will not answer you," the dragon insisted.

"Yes," Simone panted, heat searing her nerves. "You will."

A hand warmed her shoulder, and she reached up entwining her fingers with Trent's. She didn't know how he knew she needed him, but his presence allowed her to fight Grael. The dragon weakened.

"You will tell me."

"It was a horrible time."

Simone's heart melted as fear and sorrow leaked from Grael's spirit. She held on to Trent. "I'm sorry, Grael. But I must know."

The dragon lashed against her and flashed an image that froze Simone in place.

Shadows, long and gray reached for Grael's spirit. Elizabeth laughed as a man wove a spell around her and tethered the dragon to the wraiths. Evil was everywhere. It pulled at Grael and ripped her soul apart, bleeding it dry of goodness. Chained to this man against her will, Grael existed in a world of foul deeds until the death of the one who'd once cherished her.

Simone felt the tears slip down her face and heard Trent whisper her name.

"These shadows, they exist today."

Grael calmed and settled against her mind. "I have felt them. I fear they will always be a part of us. Elizabeth sold our destiny for fine art and freedom."

"Where do they come from?"

"I do not know."

"But they didn't begin with Elizabeth. I saw them enter Seren's chamber and kill Trynt."

Simone felt the dragon's confusion. "Trynt died because of the blackness of the spell he wove."

"No. Trynt died from the clutch of the shadows."

She didn't understand the sudden panic that entered Grael. "I know nothing of this. How can you?"

"I saw it."

"In a dream?"

"In my past."

Simone frowned. Why didn't Grael know this? Wasn't she the one who sent her spiraling through time? She moved away from Trent without glancing at him. His hand dropped from her shoulder and in the distance she heard him turn and walk away. He couldn't hear the conversation taking place within Simone's head, but he would've known something was going on. He hadn't questioned, simply done his duty. It worried her at how easily he'd succumbed to prophecy. Was he not willing to fight?

Grael surrounded her. Was it possible for other people to see her? Trent could. At least, he saw her last night.

So many mysteries.

Simone battled the curiosity that poked at her to unravel the clues. All she needed was the knowledge of the gray-uglies and their purpose in her life.

"Where's Llallogen?" Grael asked.

Simone gazed at the dragon. "Dead would be my guess."

"Nonsense. Wizard's don't die."

Considering the past twenty-four hours, Simone figured that she shouldn't be surprised at this fact.

"Where's the one that built the barrier against me?"

"I don't know what you're referring to."

Grael's body twitched, and she flipped her tail like an annoyed cat. "On your claiming day, I awoke only to be wrestled back to sleep by a spell."

"I'm still in the dark here. Claiming day?"

The dragon sighed. "Your thirteenth birthing day when the star upon your shoulder burned with the need for my release, when you no longer reside as human but step into your destiny as Dragon Dancer."

"Is that what the scariest night of my life was all about?"

Grael snarled. "Now I'm in the dark, as you say."

Simone lowered herself to the grass. She plucked absently at the grass, twining the thin blades through her fingers. A breeze blew from the east, bringing with it the sweet scent of rose blossoms and memories of Trent's passion. "The shadows were there that night. The heat in my chest that scared my sister must have been you trying to break free."

The dragon wrapped her tail around Simone. "The witch wasn't scared. I think we could do with her counseling. Where is she?"

"Dead," Simone said out loud.

Grael was silent. Simone felt her chest tighten and figured it was a spirit hug. "Thanks," she replied.

"You are different than all the rest." Grael's head swam before her so that they were eye to eye. "It's more than your power. You are old, which might be the answer."

"Gee, thanks. In this day and age, thirty-three isn't considered old."

The dragon shrieked and spun into the air, a cyclone of emerald and gold. Simone jumped to her feet, fear kicking her in the gut. She searched the area. "What is it Grael?"

The dragon settled back around her. "Sorry. I had an awareness."

"Is that anything like having a moment?"

"You are not alone," Grael said, her eyes blazing in yellow shadows. "There's a hatchling."

Jessie. Simone backed away from the ethereal spirit. "My daughter must be left out of this."

"Your child has made you wise, Dragon Dancer. That is the difference. I must go in search of Llallogen; we need to know more about the shadows."

"Okay. Go ahead. I'll wait right here."

"Impossible. We must travel to Snowdon." The dragon floated on the air, a cloud of shimmering scales. Simone felt the anticipation of traveling to a place Grael felt safe wash through the chill air. She shivered.

"As in Wales? No. I don't think so. I need to be here, to help bring down a very bad man. Can't you go alone?"

"Not without you, Dragon Dancer. Unless . . . "

Simone wanted her gone. If there was a way for just a moment's peace, she'd snatch it. "There must be a way. Elizabeth was able to set you free. I know . . ." She hurried on before the dragon's fear came back. "What she did was wrong. But maybe we can use it in a positive way."

"The soul of a dragon can be taken but never freed."

"Taken? How?"

Grael lifted her lip and bared a row of jagged teeth. Simone was suddenly grateful she only had to contend with the spirit of the dragon. "You are not ready to know that secret."

"Damn it, Grael. If it will help keep my daughter safe then I'm ready."

"Your child is not in danger."

Why didn't that comfort her? She blew out a mouth full of hot air and paced in a tight circle. "Can't you go all metaphysical and seek out Llallogen. Didn't you do that with Seren?"

"I can . Your sight into the past is very powerful."

Simone frowned. "Are you not responsible for that?"

"Somewhat. But you know more than I can show; you are the first Dancer to hold the memories of all the rest."

Simone inhaled sharply and decided to deal with that later. In the meantime, Grael needed to leave. She needed to breathe and think clearly.

"Go away like you did during Seren's time."

Grael wrapped herself around Simone, warming her. "It's dangerous. You could die."

Julie Korzenko

Chapter Twenty-One

Trent stood upon the concrete balcony outside his suite, gripping the baluster until his hand blanched a deathly white. He swore loudly to the rising sun. He'd spent the entire night walking the estate and keeping a watchful eye on the soft light emanating from Simone's window.

She'd shut him out.

His head hurt. A tightening in his chest squeezed painfully upon his heart. Why didn't she want him? The feel of her wrapped around him beneath the sparkling sky had touched a part deep within that had nothing to do with destiny and everything to do with Simone.

Punching the air, he swore violently. Was that true? Could it be possible that if fate lifted her hand, Simone would still love him?

He frowned and searched deep within. His heart and mind were at complete odds with one another.

One screaming to be released . . . the other demanding an action that chilled his very soul. If he were to deny destiny and sever all ties with Simone, she would die.

That was not an option.

If he relinquished control of his life to fate, then wouldn't he be living a lie? How could he stare into the eyes of a woman who only loved him because they were tied together through some twisted spell? They would both know it was false. The thought of being her pawn, being submissive when he wanted to control struck a foul chord. He frowned when the shrill ring of his phone echoed in the room. Striding inside, he snatched it from his desk and answered it with a brusque hello.

"It's Ian. We're in place."

"Is she with you?"

"Deputy Director Do-You-Then-Screw-You?"

Trent couldn't suppress his grin. "That would be the one."

"I still don't understand your reluctance to hand over all that incriminating evidence you have against her," Ian argued. Here we go again, Trent sighed, argument number one that had plagued their friendship over the past three years.

"I've told you my reasons."

"They're stupid, mate."

"Ian, I'm not Kathryn. If I were to do as you suggest, I'd be crawling on the ground like the vermin she is. It's not me." Trent rubbed a hand across his forehead, raking it back through his hair.

"She's mad as hell, man. And that spells out danger."

"Ian," he snapped, his temper coming to a heated boil. "I'm well aware of what Kathryn is capable of, but I'm following orders."

"Why?" Ian asked, his voice an octave higher.

"Deputy Director Hilliard will make a mistake that will either kill her or get her fired. Either way, I don't care."

"Since when?"

Since I've fallen in love.

"Since now."

There was silence on the other end while Ian digested Trent's words. "Yeah, Kathryn's here and stalking about," he finally said.

"Make sure she stays within sight. I don't want her getting in our way."

"Right-o. Are you on schedule?"

"I guess. It's only six a.m--we're not expected at Blithewoods until noon. We'll be by your way around ten-thirty. Hang tight, partner."

"Trent?"

"Don't go there."

"I won't."

"Fine." He didn't want to hear his partner reiterate the thoughts that slammed around his brain.

"Don't be a fool."

Damn, he went there again. "What's done is done, mate. I have no control over anything."

"Simone's no Kathryn. She'll not treat you like you are hers to control."

Trent shook his head. "I hear you." His voice held no joy.

"You're being a fool."

"Guilty as charged," he agreed softly.

***

Simone followed the wonderful aroma of fresh brewed coffee through the heavy wooden doors and into the kitchen. Smiling at Trent and his parents, she paused for a quick moment as her eyes absorbed her man.

He looked awful.

She felt wonderful.

"Your eyes," he sighed.

"I know. They retain this color when Grael is around."

"She's here?" he asked.

"Yes."

Simone's heart pounded. If she did this, it would change everything. From this moment on, the power that resided within would be diminished to a small spark that would only flame upon a deep need. Grael cautioned her about the danger of not being able to reconnect. They'd both decided, however, that an answer must be found regarding the gray-uglies.

It saddened Simone to learn that Seren hadn't lived beyond the night Trynt was taken by the shadows. The grief Grael felt over the death of her first Dancer remained lodged within the essence of the dragon and revenge coalesced into the dragon's agreement to fly free.

Shutting her eyes tightly, she released the last tendril of restraint. Grael screamed within her mind and flew from the bindings of Simone's physical body.

The kitchen echoed with startled gasps. Pans rattled and a blast of heated air whirled around the four humans. Grael's spirit filled the cavernous kitchen, and with one last screech for all to hear, she melted from the room into the expanse of the sky beyond. Simone rocked to the beat of her powerful wings, inhaling the scent of the mists that the dragon flew through.

"Simone," Trent yelled.

She snapped herself back to her own body, blinking rapidly. Grael was gone. Her soul ached at the loss, and a prick of fear tickled her neck. What if she couldn't bring her back?

"Sorry," she sighed. "We've been practicing all night, and I still find it hard to resist the pull of freedom whenever I set her free." Simone squared her shoulders. She glanced into Trent's face and knew she'd made the right decision. This separation served both the needs of dragon and Dancer. She would prove to Trent her honest love.

Remove the stamp of manipulation.

"She's gone?" Francine interjected.

"Yes."

"I don't understand," Trent whispered as he guided her to the kitchen table. His touch sent shivers racing down her spine, and her face flushed as memories of the other evening flooded her mind.

"This defies all that we've researched, Simone. Are you certain that you're safe allowing that dragon to roam free." Francine sat stiffly at the head of the table, waiting for Simone's response.

"Yes, I'm safe. The role of being a Dragon Dancer doesn't mean that Grael must remain a part of me always. She has the will and the right to her freedom. The spell wasn't meant as a prison but as an alternative way to maintain their control upon the positive forces circling our world."

Simone pulled a piece of paper from her pocket and flattened it against the table. She and Grael had worked through this all night until the dragon had finally conveyed the meaning of the spell into something Simone's mind could grasp.

Creating three wavy lines, Simone wrapped them around one another like a braid.

"This is a picture of our souls. Grael's is the large line in the middle, Trent's is the Ancient to the left, and the fine strand is me, Dragon Dancer. Which," she looked at Francine and grinned. "I find to be a stupid name. I don't dance with Grael; she trips through my mind like a six-week-old puppy. No grace. No balance. But we're all intertwined, like a helix."

"Oh, but you could dance, Simone. The books say the Dragon Dancer walks with the wind and weaves wonderful magic." Francine sat forward, her eyes bright with a fantasy Simone was about to smother.

Simone's grin faded, and she narrowed her eyes. "You're relying on words written by an individual who knew nothing about what he wrote. He wasn't a Dancer or an Ancient, was he?"

"No," Francine admitted, sitting back into her chair. "It was written by the historian of our tribe. Each generation would transcribe the journals of the last in order to retain the truth."

"I'm telling you the truth, Lady Lichfield." Pointing back at the paper, she continued her lesson.

"Our physical bodies die upon old age, and we reenter the plain of spiritual existence until our soul is cast down into a new form. Apart from Grael, our memories die with our bodies." Until me, but Simone chose to leave that tidbit out.

"Yes, that is as the book describes," Francine agreed.

"Llallogen's spell of connecting the dragons to Ancient and Dancer was tainted."

"Love, what are you saying?" Trent asked.

"There are two souls that must find one another in order for the spell to come to fruition. Grael's Dancer and that of the Ancient who loved her when this spell was woven must unite. If they don't forge together, then the dragon is caught in perpetual lethargy never allowed the freedom that the wizard desired. Grael has spent generations trapped within my soul, never allowed to fly, or speak, or find others of her kind. She's been living in death."

"I don't understand," Trent whispered. "Why doesn't she just break free of the Dragon Dancer?"

"Because that would kill the Dancer, and the entire process begins again."

"If they don't find one another, what happens to the Ancient and the Dancer?"

"They die." Simone pierced him with what she hoped to be a threatening look. "If the Ancient and Dancer fail to unite, their spirits are cast back to the heavens until the next rebirth."

"Aren't the Ancient and Dancer destined to find one another?" Francine asked.

"That's the thought that prompted our ancestors to spin this thread into the spell. Apparently, the first Ancient loved Grael's Dragon Dancer with a passion that refused to be manipulated. He wove his own magic into our two souls." She pointed at Trent. "And linked us together forever. According to Grael, we've done a really lousy job of joining. There are many dragons caught between heaven and earth, entombed and enraged. Until we become one, they won't awaken within their Dancers."

"So," Trent murmured, "the spell doesn't force them to find one another, but once they do, it weaves its magic?"

"I suppose you could say that," Simone answered, a sudden chill washing over her. "At least I think that's the right way to put it."

"Until now," he stated.

"That depends," she answered, gazing into his eyes. "I understand the past, Trent. Our souls have connected. They have loved but their fate hasn't been a kind one."

"Probably because you can't force something to exist that doesn't lie within the heart."

"No. You're wrong. It's about shadows and evil. Light and darkness. Love and despair. Two people determined to battle whatever force for their love."

He narrowed his eyes and tilted his chin. "You don't know what lies within your own heart. How could you? The presence of magic exists there, warping your vision of the world."

"No." She shook her head. "There is no magic now. My eyes see very clearly."

"And what do they tell you?" he asked, leaning forward and gazing intently into her face.

"It's all about choices," she whispered. Images of lifeless eyes haunted her mind. Their souls had been separated for over five hundred years. Grael showed her, and it pierced her heart. Seren and Elizabeth weren't the only Dancers to lose their Ancients.

The curse of the shadows followed their souls and tainted every relationship. She couldn't allow that to happen here. "No more discussion on this, we have a more pressing emergency. Or had you forgotten?" The dragon was a miraculous part of her but it didn't dim the fact that Rosalyn died at the hand of Lawrence Gideon or that Jessie might still be in danger.

"No," he smiled tightly. He gathered her hands in his and kissed the tips of her fingers. Little fires sizzled into her palm, and she sat back drawing both hands away from him and resting them in her lap.

"Which brings me to our dear friend Lawrence Gideon," she said.

"What about Bromley?" Trent asked, slipping instantly into his secret agent mode.

"He's after Grael."

"Why?"

"During the witch hunts of the sixteen hundreds a rumor began. It said that the power of a Dragon Dancer could be swapped from one family member to another but only by the death of all other members of that line."

"Okay, that confirms my theory that he's eliminating all descendents of the Gideon line," Trent stated, furrowing his brow in deep thought.

"Yes." Lady Lichfield interrupted. "The translation of your documents details that fact. It says that a spell was woven by the witches of the Pennines to allow the transference of the dragon to the last remaining heir within the existing ancestral line."

She paused looking from one Arnot to another. "It's false."

"What?" everyone cried in unison.

"It's not true. The rumor was started by Elizabeth Stuart. She created it as a cover for a darker side of this prophecy."

"And that would be what?" Trent asked.

"I don't know. I haven't deciphered anything that deals with the specific details of our destiny. There's lots of prose but not much meat. But Grael does admit that there is one person who can steal the power of the Dragon Dancer."

"And who's that?" Francine asked.

"She wouldn't tell me," Simone admitted, feeling the heat of a blush creep up her face. "She said I wasn't educated enough to hold this knowledge. I was kind of hoping y'all might know."

"No," Trent answered, shaking his head. "All of this is a complete revelation."

"Oh well," Simone sighed. "It doesn't really matter now, anyway."

"Are you aware that dragons are manipulative and deceitful?"

"A dragon might be all powerful and full of endless wisdom," Simone grinned. "But they're nothing compared to the force of a thirteen year old girl. Grael understands the rules." Her stomach flipped. She prayed she was correct.

Trent laughed and flashed a brilliant smile in her direction.

"This is not funny, Trent," Francine snapped. "She has allowed an extremely erratic and powerful force loose upon the world. This might have deadly consequences."

"Lady Lichfield," Simone attempted to mask her irritation by speaking slowly. "I have done nothing more than allow Grael her chance to aide us in the battle that we face."

"You have tipped the balance," Trent's mother yelled.

"So be it."

Simone stood her ground, refusing to bow down to the insecurity that had her stomach in knots.

"Who will protect you against Lord Bromley? With the power, you had the chance to capture this man."

"I don't need any special powers for that. I have your son."

"She's right, mother." Trent stood and held his hand out for Simone. She took it and rose to her feet.

"Is it time to go?"

"Yes. Kathryn and Ian are waiting in the field across from Blithewoods. We need to get you wired and in place."

"Okay. Let's do it."

"Simone," Lady Lichfield called. "You are a strong woman, of that I have no doubt. Now don't be a stupid one. Call back Grael. You have the power."

"I'm sorry Lady Lichfield, but I no longer have that capability," Simone insisted, keeping the intricate details of recall to herself. She felt the last link disintegrate more than ten minutes ago. Grael was free.

"What nonsense is this? A Dancer can never be free of the dragon."

"That, Lady Lichfield, is where fiction separates from fact. Don't believe everything you read." Simone started to follow Trent, but a hand grabbed her arm.

"The dragon's dangerous, you know." Trent's mother clung to her, and then glanced at her husband for support. He nodded sadly and shrugged his shoulders.

"That's where you're wrong, ma'am. She's only as dangerous as you allow her to be."

"You need her. Destiny demands it."

"Destiny will not rule me," Simone snapped.

"What about my son?"

She switched focus and stared into the depths of Trent's eyes. His blue gaze was unwavering, and she answered directly to them. "I want more than what fate dictates. Grael is gone. She'll not return, therefore, you have no need to remain by my side. Do you remember when I told you that without your heart the rest wouldn't happen?"

"Yes," Trent whispered, his face paling slightly.

"The other night everything lined up perfectly but your arrogance defined it as destiny. Grael is no longer a part of me. See?" She bent close, allowing him to peer into her eyes. "It's just me, Simone Walker. Architect and mother." She spun on her heels and exited the kitchen. Her heart hammered against her chest, and she fought against the need to run back to Trent's arms and pound him until he recognized his own love.

It was there. He only had to look.

***

Trent mulled over Simone's words. She was holding back. And before he acknowledged anything as the truth, he'd dig out her secrets.

"Trent," his mother said, a bitter edge to her voice. "Snap out of it."

"What?"

"You're looking like you've just lost your best friend when in fact you've gained something far more valuable."

"What are you going on about mother?"

"I know who can steal the dragon from the Dancer."

Lady Lichfield shoved him back into the kitchen and sat him at the table like she'd done a million times before while imparting family history.

"Why didn't you tell Simone?" His gut was twisting and instinct told him he wasn't going to like the answer.

"Because it's you, dearest. The man who owns her heart can own her dragon."

He froze. "I don't believe I own Simone's heart," he whispered harshly.

"Why do you refuse to accept your role in history? Generations of Arnots have come before you and acknowledged their responsibility to the Dragon Dancer. You must do the same. It is written."

"It's been centuries since any notation of the Dragon Dancer has been recognized. Don't you understand? If what you say is true, Simone isn't in love with me. It's a trick, a mockery of some ancient spell."

"You're a fool if you believe that, son. She loves you. She gave up Grael for you."

Anger flared fast and hard, and Trent stood up abruptly, pointing an accusing finger at his mother. "So she says. Don't you manipulate me, Mother. This will not rule me, do you understand? I make my own choices." He left the room, controlling his urge to run. Where had Simone gone?

***

Simone stared out the window, allowing her thoughts to flow. Wrapping her arms around her waist, she grimaced at the knot in her stomach. Her heart was raw with the need for Trent's love. She'd never been to this place before, never needed anyone other than herself.

A soft knock interrupted her musings.

"Come in," she called, turning and facing the door.

"Hey," he said, his voice low and alluring within the confines of her room.

"Hey, yourself," she didn't move. She scanned his face, searching for that one emotion that would make the sun shine for the rest of her life. "Do we need to leave?"

He grinned and eased his way across the plush Oriental rug. "We have a few minutes, want to fool around?"

She reached for him, wrapping her arms around his neck. It suddenly didn't matter that their future together was questionable or that her emotions ran deeper than his. This man wanted her, and it was a call she couldn't resist.

"Yes," she sighed, her mouth raised for his kiss. He growled and seized her lips. His hands were everywhere, touching, teasing, arousing. Her shirt slipped from her shoulders, and he deftly undid her jeans, stripping them away. She stood before him, covered in only her lace undergarments. His eyes were hot and a pulse beat widely against his throat.

"You were supposed to say no," he spoke gruffly, his voice tinged with desire. Stepping back, he pulled his own shirt off, revealing well-defined muscles that rippled with each movement of his arm.

They stood for a moment. Their eyes were locked, each searching for something.

"I believe," Simone whispered, "it's my turn." She placed her hands upon his chest, pushing him backward until the bed touched his legs. She grinned and slowly unzipped his jeans.

His hand stopped her right before she released him.

"No regrets?" he asked, staring intently into her face.

"Not a one," she answered with a half smile then slipped her hands around his waist and pushed his pants down. He gasped as her skin brushed against his full arousal. Pushing him farther back, he fell upon the bed.

She slid one bra strap down then the next in a slow tease. He smiled, and then snatched her arm, pulling her roughly on top of him.

"I'm dying here." With a flip of his wrist, her bra was gone.

She sat up and straddled his waist. The hardness that pressed upon her bottom tantalized her. Simone savored this moment, loving every inch of the man sprawled beneath her. She nibbled, caressed, stroked, and kissed until he burned and groaned with want.

He would remember her touch, remember every inch of her. When they were a thousand miles apart, she needed to know that no woman would ever love him like she did. She was enticingly slow with her seduction, running her tongue around his nipples and trailing the thin line of hair downward.

Trent snaked his fingers through her hair pulling her up until their lips touched. "I can't hold on much longer," he gasped. She smiled against his mouth and wiggled out of her silk panties.

She lowered herself gently down, he shook his head, grabbed her thighs and surged upward entering her with the full fury of his desire. There would be no more leisurely pace as he rocked his hips madly. She met him thrust for thrust.

He filled her again and again, until their pace was nothing more than a frantic race to the end. Sweat streamed from their bodies and gasps of pleasure escaped their lips. He held her hips as she rode him, each jolt within searing her soul, branding her heart.

She would never love another man.

Simone tilted her head back, luxuriating in the feel of him. His hands moved from her hips, and he gently trailed his fingers against the softness of her most intimate spot. Her eyes flew open, and she looked down into his face. He growled, caressed, and pulled her hard against him as their passion exploded.

She collapsed upon his chest, drawing ragged breaths in great gasps. He swore softly and held her tenderly, running his hand up and down her back.

"I don't know . . .," he whispered.

"Shush," Simone interrupted, unwilling to listen to false platitudes. She slid off him and snuggled to his side.

"I need to tell you something," he insisted, "about the link with the dragon."

"What about it?" Her voice hitched, and she prayed that he'd recognize her sacrifice.

"You asked earlier about Grael's reference to some other person being able to take her power."

"Oh, that," Simone sighed, trying to hide her disappointment. "I've decided I don't want to know who it is. If something were to happen and that person took Grael, it would be too tempting to snatch her back. I'd hate to be responsible for another individual's life."

"What're you talking about?" Trent asked.

"Grael mentioned something about once she was taken the only way to get her back would be through the loss of the other person's life. I don't know. It's all very confusing."

"Are you sure you don't want all the answers?" Trent rolled over and gazed into her eyes.

She stared back and smiled. "No, I don't want all the answers. All I want is honesty. Promise me you'll never lie to me, Trent. That you'll never say anything untrue?"

He stared at her and shook his head. "I can't do that, Simone."

"I was afraid you'd say that," Simone said, her tone dead and flat. "It's this destiny crap, isn't it?"

He nodded and kissed her nose. "We'd better get dressed. Ian's waiting."

"Okay," she smiled sadly.

***

Trent's mind churned over everything Simone said downstairs. If only life were as easy as the spoken word. His phone rang and he grabbed it off the bed.

"Arnot."

"I have something you need to know about." Ian's hushed voice sent alarm springing along every section of his nerves.

"What?"

"Kathryn's done it again."

Trent narrowed his eyes and tried to hold onto the bitter churning in his stomach. "What has she done this time?"

"Charlie just rang to say that he and one other guy had been called into her office and told to head to America. She wanted them to take Jessie into protective custody and use her as bait."

The cold chill of anger crashed against him in a vicious wave. He didn't know how he'd manage the next few hours in Kathryn's presence without killing her.

"I'll get back to you, Ian. I'm placing a call to the Director General."

Trent heard Ian exhale in relief. "It's about bloody time."

***

"What are you doing?" Trent asked as he slid behind the wheel of the Roadster. Simone had taken a quick shower, grabbed her purse, and gone to the convertible to wait for him.

"Making notes," she sighed. "We've a much better idea of Lawrence Gideon's motivation now than we did back in Atlanta. I'm just trying to see if I can guess what his next move might be."

"Simone, look at me."

She shook her head, swearing at the tears that threatened to fall.

"Okay," he sighed. "I'll let you hide for awhile longer, but you will talk to me when this is all over."

She nodded and continued scribbling in her pad.

"What have you deduced so far, Watson?" he persisted.

She grinned and glanced sideways, gazing at him through the shelter of her lashes. "I figure, Sherlock, that he's going to show me his and then ask me to show him mine."

"What?" Trent said, braking sharply at the end of the driveway.

"He'll shock me with the revelation that the Walker's weren't my real parents then wait to see how much I know about my heritage," she quirked her brow, challenging him to disagree.

"For a moment there I thought you were discussing body parts," Trent flashed a heart-stopping grin.

"And that would bother you?" she asked, holding her breath.

"Do you really need to ask that?" he gently held her chin and forced her to stare into his face.

"Yes," she whispered.

"I didn't lie the other night, Simone. You are mine." He bent close, consuming her mouth with a hungry kiss.

"But," she gasped, trying to breathe from the onslaught on her lips.

"You didn't say it wasn't destiny." Her body trembled for his touch, and she cursed her weakness.

"Doesn't change the fact that I want you," he said, pulling her tightly against him.

She melted against him, accepting what little she could have. She ignored the pain his words caused her heart. He released her suddenly, pushing her back into her seat. "Stay over there, or we'll never make it to Blithewoods."

Julie Korzenko

Chapter Twenty-Two

Trent turned the car onto a major motorway and sped in a northwesterly direction.

"It makes sense," he said.

Simone rested her head against the back of the seat and closed her eyes. She felt as if someone had slammed a needle into her arm and drained out all the energy, leaving her weak and vulnerable. If this was the power of love, she didn't want it. "What does?"

"Your theory regarding Lawrence Gideon." He tapped her knee, and she entwined her fingers through his allowing the warmth of his touch to replenish her soul.

"Why do you say that?"

The bottom line came down to Grael. Lawrence Gideon held no proof that she was the Drake who possessed the dragon's essence. She believed this.

"Ian unearthed a sketch in Rosalyn's files."

"Oh?"

"It details the ritual that Bromley's been playing out on his victims. Apparently, the twisted knife work is an incantation to invoke the essence of the dragon. When the dragon didn't appear, he killed the girls."

Simone shuddered. She couldn't imagine being Rosalyn, knowing the method of death that awaited her. It must've been terrifying. Lawrence

269

Gideon's carefully constructed tapestry was beginning to fray. Simone needed to find the thread that would unravel it all together.

"When we arrive at the rendezvous, I'm going to let Ian set you up."

"What are we hoping to accomplish today?"

"I'd like to get beyond the normal touristy areas of Blithewoods, get a peek into Bromley's inner sanctum. We might see something that will allow us to question him regarding your cousins and sister. If we're lucky, maybe we can trip him into an unwitting confession." He glanced at her and shook his head. "I don't think that'll be the case though. He's smart."

"Me neither," she nibbled her bottom lip and concentrated on her pad of paper.

Frowning, she realized the predicament that her stubborn pride placed her in. Sending Grael away might have been a benefit to her heart and the quest for answers, but it certainly left her vulnerable to Lawrence Gideon. Trent's mind must have been working along the same lines because he suddenly swore loudly and pulled the vehicle on to the side of the road.

"Can you not call Grael back?" he demanded.

"No," she shook her head. "I can't." *At least not yet,* she finished silently.

"Damn it, Simone, look at the position you're in now."

"You'll protect me, Sherlock. I trust you." She patted his knee and offered a reassuring smile.

Thirty minutes later, he maneuvered the sports car onto a field of softly rolling hills.

Simone glanced around, noting that the area was empty except for a rundown caravan that looked as if it had been salvaged from a post-apocalyptic gypsy reject pile. The door crashed open. Paint chips and small slivers of wood flew into the air as it banged against the side of the metal van. A horse grazing in the field beyond flicked its ears and neighed softly at the interruption.

Kathryn Hilliard and Ian McAllister exited the wagon arguing loudly.

"I will not be left in the dark," the Deputy Director of MI-5 stated loudly. Simone took in her pin striped skirted suit, panty hose, and three inch spikes, shaking her head at the inappropriate attire. If this woman were a member of the team, wouldn't she have worn something that would have allowed her to actively participate in the mission? She wouldn't be able to take a step larger than a small rabbit in that outfit.

"Kathryn," Ian pleaded. "Please understand that by monitoring activities from the wagon, you'll play a vital part in this operation."

"Let me handle this," Trent stated, walking over to his partner and boss. "Why don't you begin wiring Simone?"

Ian sighed in relief and dove back into the wagon, signaling with his hand for Simone to wait where she was. Trent guided Kathryn back toward the beaten-up camper and pushed her inside. Simone stood in place. She'd been left to stand alone outside not privy to the inner workings of MI-5.

She took the quiet moment to perform a mental check on herself. An emptiness waged war with relief. Grael's absence saddened her more than she'd anticipated. The bang of the wagon door startled her from her internal reflection, and she smiled brightly at Ian.

"Are we ready?" she asked, moving to stand beside him. He spread out an array of wires and miniature microphones on the hood of Trent's car.

"Yes," he said, mumbling something about hotheaded agents and ball-less wonders.

"What was that?" she laughed.

"Nothing, Simone. Would you please unbutton your shirt? I need to snake the wire beneath your bra."

Simone shrugged and figured it was all in the name of duty. She unbuttoned her black cotton shirt, untucking it from the waistband of her linen pants. Ian quickly ran the wire and snapped the tiny microphone in place. His hand barely touched her skin.

"You're a pro at this," she stated, slightly startled that he hadn't even batted an eye at her naked flesh.

"Trent would kill me if I didn't picture you as an eighty year old woman with spotty skin and deflated breasts."

She burst out laughing and fixed her shirt. "I understand perfectly Quasimodo."

He grinned. The man probably had a mile wide path of broken hearts sprinkled all over England and Europe.

"I want to talk to you about your sister," Ian said.

"Cousin, you mean."

"Sister at heart," he reiterated. "I received a call yesterday afternoon from one of the women within Rosalyn's coven. I left the transcript in the wagon for Trent to read."

"Why don't you give me a run-down on what the woman said?"

Ian nodded. "Rosalyn changed her name to Allen when she discovered that Lawrence Gideon was searching for you."

"What time period are we talking about?"

"I believe it was right after leaving your parents home. Apparently, the night of your thirteenth birthday, Rosalyn confronted her parents. She implored them to tell you the truth."

Simone frowned. "And what truth would that have been?"

"Your parents received a warning from your blood mother right before she died. She sent a letter detailing her brother's illness and his fascination with an old family myth."

"The Dragon Dancer myth?"

Ian shook his head. "No. Something about stealing the power of the dragon. I'm not sure. She didn't really know because this story was passed to her through Ida Lackingbird, and she felt the old woman hadn't told her everything."

"My parents knew about this whole prophecy thing, and they never told me?"

"I'm not certain. Remember this is all hear-say. My guess is they believed your innocence would protect you. Rosalyn took the name Allen, left the house, and spent her life researching details on Dragon Dancing. According to this woman, she was protecting you."

Simone sighed. Her whole life had been a sham, and she hadn't even known.

Ian crossed his arms over his chest and cocked his head, a slight grin teasing his lips upward. "You must be some lady to be able to wrench Trent out of his self-imposed exodus from the female population," He interrupted her thoughts, holding his palm out for her sunglasses. She handed them over.

"I don't know about that," she answered with a lopsided smile. "Things are terribly complicated."

Ian tilted his head. "Isn't that always the way with love?"

"Maybe," she agreed. "But I'm not certain we're at that level yet."

"Oh, I believe you're way past that level. Here try these," he said, handing her the sunglasses. She slipped them on and frowned.

"It's not sunny, Ian. I can't see a thing."

He leaned over and pushed them up until they rested on top of her head. He quickly arranged her hair and stepped back to study his handwork. "That's perfect. Can you hear me?" He mumbled into a speaker she didn't see, but his voice boomed loud and clear against her left ear.

"Yes," she giggled, "perfectly."

"I could whisper sweet nothings, but I'm rather attached to my face just the way it is."

She sighed and fidgeted with the glasses.

"Don't be nervous, Simone," Ian said as he headed back to the wagon.

"He'd die for you."

She stared at his retreating back, allowing the words to sink beneath her skin.

He'd meant to comfort, but instead, he'd terrified her.

Static and garbled words tickled her ear. Simone reached up to remove the glasses, but a voice she knew suddenly boomed clearly.

"I don't love her, Kathryn," Trent stated harshly.

Shock washed over her, numbing her mind and draining her emotions to her feet. Her heart stopped. Squeezing her eyes shut, she inhaled and focused. The verbalization of her insecurity more painful than she'd expected.

"This mission is extremely important to our division, Trent. It's the first awakening in centuries. If you threaten its positive conclusion because of personal emotions, I'll have your badge."

"She needs to trust me explicitly for this mission to succeed. I haven't done anything less than what you would have done in my position."

"Is the child in place?" Kathryn asked.

Jessie! Simone's heart twisted and she fought against the alarm that fired through her system. Was this evil woman speaking about her daughter? Searching the perimeter, Simone spun around. She needed to reach her daughter.

"Yes," Trent answered. "She's in the states and everything is going as planned."

Oh God, Simone cried silently. *What have I done?*

"Make sure your seduction doesn't cloud your brain, Agent Arnot. Remain distant," Kathryn said.

Tears burned the back of Simone's eyes, and she shook her head, attempting to deny the folly of her heart. She inhaled. Focus. Forming a bubble, she channeled her worry and other emotions into its center. A clear head needed to remain in place if she were to complete today's assignment and get her butt back to Atlanta pronto.

"It won't." Trent's voice filtered through the protection of her imaginary force field.

"If I hadn't stolen your file and redirected the focus of the enemy, our entire operation would have failed." Kathryn's voice wove through the remote connection.

Simone wanted to rip the sunglasses from her head and stomp them into smithereens. Only a perverse curiosity prevented her from performing the act.

"One thing I don't quite understand, Kathryn, is how you managed departmental approval? We never use children."

An evil snicker jammed into her ear. It sent shivers of revulsion skimming down her back.

"That, lover, is sweet. I didn't."

Trent chuckled and she heard the turning of the doorknob. She quickly jammed the glasses on her nose to mask her hurt and climbed into the Roadster. Simone watched Trent exit the wagon and walk with long, graceful strides in her direction. He was the epitome of the hunter poised to kill.

Mission. Seduction. Success. Jessie. She was a fool.

The words rocked around her mind, blasting holes in everything wonderful the past week had held. Everything had been a lie, except her destiny. She wasn't his Dancer. He'd already found his future.

For a moment, she had kidded herself into believing that they would succeed . . . that their souls would unite with true love. What pile of dirty laundry that fairy tale had been. All he'd been concerned with was the successful capture of Lawrence Gideon. In order for that to happen, he needed her trust, he needed her daughter. He'd manipulated her from the first moment they'd spoken.

The hunter killed.

***

Striding to the Roadster, Trent's relief flooded every corner of his being. He passed Ian.

"Did you get it?" he asked.

His partner grinned. "Every morsel."

The tape-recorded session of Kathryn's unwitting confession was clutched in Ian's hand and he waved it in triumph. "Will you use it?"

"Bloody hell I will, the nerve of her sending Robert and Charlie stateside after Jessie. If you hadn't received that call from Charlie, I don't know what I'd have done. Simone would kill me if she thought I'd placed her daughter in danger." The mere thought of Jessie being exposed to this type of threat curdled Trent's stomach.

A deadly grin spread his lips. The Director General agreed with Trent that under no circumstances was the child to be involved and asked Trent for irrefutable evidence to Kathryn's treason. Trent complied without hesitation. From the moment Kathryn realized she'd never be a Dragon Dancer, her mind splintered. She'd manipulated Trent, almost killing him on their last mission. The bitch barked up the wrong tree this time, and it was about to come toppling down on top of her.

"Good job, then. We got her." Ian said. "Go take care of Simone, she's twitching with nerves."

Trent nodded. "Thanks, Ian. I owe you one."

"Yes, you certainly do."

It had been difficult to lie. Trent was amazed that Kathryn hadn't seen beyond his words and unearthed how he truly felt. How the only thing that moved him forward through this ugly investigation was the thought of Simone's safety and that of her daughter's.

Sliding behind the wheel, he grinned at her and leaned over for a kiss, but paused. She wasn't being receptive. She sat stiffly in her seat, her fists clenched together in tight little knots. Her eyes were hidden behind black sunglasses that were entirely out of place on this gray morning.

"Simone? Are you all right?"

"Yes," she said, gazing anywhere but at him. "I guess I'm just nervous."

He sighed in relief. "It'll be all right, love. Here . . ." He reached for the glasses, intending on pulling them off, but her hand slapped his away.

"Don't touch them," she said.

"They look ridiculous. You can't walk into Blithewoods wearing those."

"I'll move them to my head before we enter the grounds. Right now, they're helping," she said.

Running his fingers against her cheek, Trent soothed her. "Headache?"

"Yes, I suppose that's what you'd call it."

He frowned when she scooted closer to the door. Then suddenly it dawned on him what the problem was.

"It's Grael isn't it?" Dropping his hands to his lap, he observed her closely. "I can't imagine what it would feel like to lose a part of myself." Yes, he could. If she walked out of his life, he'd be left empty, half the man he was before he'd feasted on the sight of her dressed in a flimsy apricot sundress. He narrowed his eyes as she jammed her shoulder against the window glass. "Are you certain you want to continue this mission?"

Accepting her curt nod as a refusal to argue the issue again, he shrugged and started the car. He pulled onto the main road and turned toward Blithewoods. "You'll be okay, love, trust me."

"You got that right, Sherlock," she mumbled beneath her breath. "I'll be just fine."

Trent glanced at her once more and decided her nerves and anxiety over the forthcoming meeting were getting the best of her. Didn't his mother always become snappish right before she entertained, scurrying around the house and ordering everyone to put away *that* or clean *this*? He shrugged and figured she'd be fine once they began their meeting with Lord Bromley.

***

Simone watched the fields flash past her window as Trent drove around several corners until Blithewoods came into view. Sheep grazed lazily against the rolling hills.

She couldn't breathe.

Her heart was lodged like a football in her throat, and it hurt to swallow.

Reaching into her handbag, she pulled out a chocolate bar, quickly unwrapping it, and shoving it in her mouth. Small shards of milky delight melted against her tongue, easing the stab of hurt.

"What's that?" Trent asked.

"A chocolate bar," she mumbled, licking the crumbs from the corner of her mouth.

"Do you have anymore?"

"No," she lied. She'd be damned if she'd pass over her only Band-Aid. Resisting the urge to wrap her arms around herself, she prayed silently for Jessie. The thought of hugging her child to her chest almost unleashed the torrent of tears threatening to fight their way past her lashes.

Her daughter was everything, she reminded herself. Lawrence Gideon had to be arrested. As long as he remained free, Jessie's life would be in jeopardy. The Lord of Bromley didn't know it was Simone he was after. She firmly believed that this visit to Blithewoods was another test, another angle to approach unsuspecting descendents into revealing the dragon. But she wasn't unsuspecting. She was in control.

"Oh, too bad. I could really use a sugar fix," Trent spoke, interrupting her thoughts.

"Sorry," she answered, hardening her heart and building her resolve.

"I could always pull over and kiss the chocolate off your lips," he said, flashing a grin.

She shook her head and pointed to the entrance of Blithewoods. "It's time to go to work, Sherlock."

Simone glanced at the vast lands surrounding the estate. Wrought iron fencing, thick with ivy, enclosed the property immediately adjacent to the main building. Peaks of stone were barely discernable above the fence, and she found herself leaning forward to obtain a better view.

This was her past. Her mother had grown up here, and the butterflies careening around her stomach were testimony to the anticipation of walking upon the same path as her ancestors.

Trent maneuvered the vehicle to the entrance, stopped before the closed gateway, and pressed a button on the side of a brick pillar. Announcing their arrival, he drove through gates that swung slowly inward.

Traversing a narrow stone drive, the car finally pulled up before a massive manor. It sprouted turrets from each corner and appeared to have once been encased by a moat.

The expanse of rose gardens caught Simone's eye, and she couldn't help but admire their beauty. An array of colors encompassed the mansion in a robe of botanical brilliance. This was much larger than Trent's family home. Its brick and mortar exterior spoke of a history stretching more than five hundred years into the past.

Climbing out of the car, she turned to absorb the essence of the castle, for surely that's what it would have been considered during the reign of the ancient monarchy.

Trent reached for her hand, tugging her into his arms. He bent to kiss her, misty fog parting beneath the noon sun and shining brightly against his raven hair. Melting beneath his touch, she accepted the love he offered until a blast of cool air froze her in place, snapping reality back in place. She pushed him away violently.

"What are you doing?"

"What do you mean? I'm kissing you. As your fiancé, that's definitely acceptable. Besides, this part doesn't require any acting ability whatsoever. Why are you pulling away?"

"I'm not comfortable with this type of public affection."

"No?" he wiggled his brows and grinned devilishly.

"No," she stated flatly, suddenly distracted by Ian's voice summoning her. "Ian says he can hear us loud and clear and that you should behave yourself."

"Where's the microphone?" Trent asked, raking across her body. She fought against the sudden blast of desire that ignited beneath his scrutiny.

"In the glasses."

He frowned, stepped back, and then quickly leaned forward, snatching them from her face. He swore loudly, tossing them into the car. Pulling her away from the vehicle, he stared hard into her eyes.

"You heard?"

She nodded unable to speak. His eyes were sapphire depths that swelled with an emotion she longed to call love but couldn't make fit with his harsh disposal of her daughter. He had used her she reminded herself, reinforcing the bubble protecting her heart.

"I didn't mean what I said, Simone," he sighed, pulling her into his arms. "I was trying to trick Kathryn into revealing she'd gone rogue. I've got it all on tape."

"What?" her voice hitched in a sob. She was desperate to believe but Jessie's vulnerability remained her greatest concern.

"Oh God, you listened to every blasted word I said against you?" he held her tighter, resting his chin upon her head. Swearing softly when she nodded, he continued in a rush. "I was only playing to Kathryn's personality. It didn't even cross my mind when Ian walked past me with all his paraphernalia--that you were connected. He was setting everything up for two-way transmission. I would never hurt you."

"Huh?" Simone rolled her eyes at her inability to speak more than one syllable responses, gasping to catch her breath.

"I was able to trick her into a confession by using tactics only she would understand. She's been twisted ever since she was forced to acknowledge that she wasn't my Dancer." He tilted her chin upward, his gaze intense and steadfast, pushing against her resolution of indifference. "I'm finally doing what I should've done months ago. I shouldn't have protected her as long as I did."

"Why now?"

"She stepped too close to something I cherish." He kissed her forehead and hugged her fiercely. His heart beat loudly and his arms trembled as he held her. Love burned through her mistrust and doubt, promising a future he hadn't yet voiced.

She nodded against his chest, her heart and mind struggling to unite. She trusted him. But she didn't trust Kathryn Hilliard. And no matter how many vows of safety Trent made her, it was her responsibility to protect Jessie. Never would she expose her daughter.

That meant returning to Atlanta. Would Trent support her decision? Closing her eyes, she inhaled his scent. This would be a defining moment, one she wasn't certain she was ready to face. She prayed he wouldn't make her choose. Because he'd lose. They'd lose. Jessie was everything.

"Are you okay?" he asked.

"I will be," she whispered, frantically roping in her conflictions.

"Ready to face the big bad ugly blister boy?"

She grinned at his description of Lawrence Gideon and nodded. Walking back to the car, her insides continued to kick around like an angry mule. Retrieving the sunglasses, she placed them on her head. A sudden blast of profanity smacked her ear--Ian had not been pleased with the break in communication.

Pushing her doubts and insecurities into the farthest recesses of her heart, she focused on the task at hand. It was time for work. "I apologize for the interruption of your regularly scheduled programming," Simone stated in a robotic voice. "But technical difficulties could not be avoided. We now continue without further commercial interruption," she glanced at Trent, inhaled deeply, and stalked to the front door.

Julie Korzenko

Chapter Twenty-Three

The door opened before she had a chance to knock. A pack of women, talking excitedly about what they'd discovered inside poured from the entryway. Cameras pointed at the beautifully landscaped grounds. They ignored Trent and Simone and headed in the direction of the church.

"What was that?" Simone asked.

"Blithewood's Great Hall is open to tourists."

"I see." They stepped within the shadowed recesses of the building. Simone gasped at the intricate carvings of the staircase which swept from the foyer area up to the next level. The balustrades were etched with angles and symbols that sported the family's numerous coats of arms. She inhaled sharply as her eye skimmed the posts. Simone bent and traced her finger along the length of a giraffe's neck that twisted upward to a mouth wide open as if the creature called the coming of guests.

"This is gorgeous." She glanced up at Trent. "The artist has created all these animals to appear like heralds."

"I believe this was built during the reign of Charles I." Trent led her up the staircase.

"It's fascinating."

Trailing her fingers along the beautiful curves, Simone followed him trying not to gawk at the surroundings.

The stairs appeared to be made from oak, but centuries of wear polished them to a deep bronze. Her architect's eye noted nuances a layman couldn't possibly see. Although the staircase dated back to Charles I, when she entered the Great Hall there were Elizabethan and Regency additions that graced the hardwood paneling and fireplace mantel.

"This is beautiful." She said to Trent. He smiled and pulled her down a side hallway before she had a chance to scrutinize the walls more carefully. There was a gold plaque upon the door that read "Private Residence." Trent pressed the button located to the right of the plaque.

The door swung open and they entered a room decorated with the modern conveniences of the twenty-first century. A young woman sat behind a large cherry desk. Simone took in the color of the bland gray suit and hair twisted into a tight bun. The lack of jewelry didn't hide the expensive cut of the clothes nor the silky luster to the woman's hair.

"Ms. Walker and Mr. Arnot I presume?" The woman asked, typing rapidly upon her keyboard and squinting at the computer screen.

"Yes. We have an appointment with Lord Bromley."

"He is expecting you. Let's see . . ." She peered at the monitor. "He is in the orangery."

Simone raised her brows and craned to see what the computer displayed. It acted like a security camera with different views of the manor house. Interesting.

The receptionist stood, smoothed her skirt and stepped away from the desk. "If you'll please follow me."

They traipsed after her down another hall and through large French doors that led to the back of the manor house. Outside, they followed the length of a concrete walk that was covered by ornate arches and roof lines.

"This is the orangery," the woman said. "It was used as a centerpiece for the gardens. During the eighteenth century most of the fruit trees that were gifted from other monarchies were stored within a small greenhouse at the edge of this stone walk."

"So much history." Simone said not quite sure how to respond.

"Blithewoods is a British treasure. Its history dates back to the first century."

"I see."

They stepped off the stone walk and headed across the lawn. Simone's eyes were immediately drawn to the man who stood at the edge of the grass.

Lawrence Gideon stood within the shadows of a huge oak tree, cloaked from head to toe in black. A turtleneck, gloves, and wool slacks covered every body part except his face. Noting thick sunglasses, Simone mused she probably could have worn her own and fit right in with the vampiric dress code of Blithewoods.

"Please come join me," Lord Bromley waved his arm indicating they should step forward. "Welcome to Blithewoods."

Lacing her fingers through Trent's, she moved toward Lawrence Gideon. Laughter echoed from behind him and a group of dancing people caught her attention. They were dressed in unusual attire.

A man held a long pole topped with a makeshift horse head. Its mane crafted of yarn. The plastic eye glittered back and forth as the man rode the hobby horse in wide circles chasing a woman adorned in the roughly hewn cotton of a maid's outfit from the fourteenth century. She held a hand firmly against the white cap that threatened to shift from her head and tossed a cheeky grin at another man.

This gentleman was garbed in head to toe silk. His bright colored diamonds and slippers tipped with bells denoted his jester status. He tumbled along the grass and executed a perfect flip to the delight of the bystanders.

Simone shook her head in amazement as a mass of people swarmed from behind a tree, dashing in front of the man on the imaginary horse. Each individual sported a large rack of antlers and pranced about with high steps.

"What's this?" she asked.

A smile twisted his face upward, puckering the small boils that lined the left of his lip. "Each fall this area celebrates a ritualistic dance. This year I am hosting the grand event in honor of the Red Cross."

"How admirable." Trent said.

"I hope to raise a goodly amount. But don't let me bore you with my trivial charitable contributions. You must be weary from this unseasonable heat."

Simone frowned at Trent. It wasn't hot. "We're fine."

"Come. Let's retire to the library."

"Thank you for your kind invitation Lord Bromley. I'm honored to visit such an ancient and historic manor home."

He smiled causing small pustules around his mouth to pucker and ooze. Dabbing away the pestilent liquid with a handkerchief, Lord Bromley waved to the dancers. They waved back and returned to the orchestration of intricate moves. He appeared so normal it unnerved her. She bit down on the automatic reaction to grimace.

They entered the manor through a separate set of French doors and crossed into a narrow hallway of sorts.

Trent scanned the room discretely. Simone gazed at his face, mesmerized by the casual smile that contradicted his intense eyes. If his hair could stand any straighter, it'd be a lethal weapon.

"Where is your daughter, Miss Walker?"

"Please, call me Simone. After all, we are related," she smiled nervously, ignoring his reference to Jessie.

"Lord Bromley, this visit is a pleasure," Trent interjected, pulling Simone back to his side and snaking a protective arm around her waist. He smiled, but the deadly gleam sparking from his eyes left no doubt in Simone's mind that Agent Arnot was in control.

Lawrence Gideon nodded and led them through an arch and another hallway, this one twice the width of the passage they'd recently left. Trailing her fingers across the walls, she marveled at the masonry.

"When was this part of the estate built?" she asked Lawrence Gideon.

"All records indicate around the late fourteenth century. However these lands were granted to our ancestor, Hervey Gideon, during the conquest in 1086."

He paused before a glass dome that encased a slew of family seals. He pointed to a horned goat surrounded by Latin script.

"That is the seal of Sir Lawrence Gideon, my namesake. He reigned as Lord of Bromley in the early thirteenth century. It is believed that he is the one who commissioned the erection of this castle. This family seal remained unchanged until the reign of Henry VIII."

"Fascinating," Simone whispered. A leaping stag drew her attention. It was inlaid in golden detail upon a wooden oval, highlighted by the hint of a silver dragon.

"And this? Whose seal is this?"

Lawrence Gideon tensed. "That," he spat. "Is not of our heritage."

"Then why is it within this case?" Trent asked.

"It is a Draconius seal," Lord Bromley said, inhaling sharply. "And it's here, Mr. Arnot, because it's extremely valuable. I am a collector, and it makes a fine addition. Don't you agree?"

"Yes," Trent responded, narrowing his eyes.

"Do you recognize the Draconius crest, Simone?" Lawrence Gideon asked.

"No, I'm afraid I don't."

She moved away from the display case, trying to shake the haunted castle feeling that suffocated her.

"I have something quite unusual for your consideration," he said.

Trent held her close by his side. The warmth from his arms assisted in easing her nerves, but it couldn't eliminate them totally. Something or someone was hiding within the shadows. Crossing the hall, they entered a large library. Three walls were adorned with floor to ceiling bookcases. Their trim ornate, displaying extravagant hand carved rosettes.

A fire flickered against the fourth wall, casting shadowy flames across crimson curtains. Heavy velvet covered windows that flanked either side of the massive stone hearth. Bright burning logs providing the only light. Within the center of the room a large glass case presided. Simone gasped when she realized what lay within. Taking her hand, Lawrence Gideon pulled her toward the display.

"This is a cross that was hand made for Mary Queen of Scots. Her son, James VI, requested its creation for his beloved mother."

Simone hoped that the shock of seeing her drawing come to life went unnoticed. She detected the sarcastic tone in Lawrence's voice and rattled her brain about the history of the Scottish Queen. If she remembered correctly, James VI was chosen by Queen Elizabeth to hold the throne after his mother's abdication. She didn't believe the young King was at all sorrowful over Mary's demise.

He was also Elizabeth's father.

Peering at the ornate cross, its every detail identical to the drawing she'd reluctantly handed over to Trent, Simone felt a sting of recognition that had nothing to do with that penciled sketch.

"Is that so?" she said, hating the silence of the room.

"Yes. Richard Gideon, our ancestor, was Queen Elizabeth's Steward. This is truly fascinating, isn't it my dear?" Lord Bromley peered at her from above the rims of his glasses and continued in his dry, nasal voice. "As her deputy lieutenant, the eminent Lord Bromley became sole charge of the captive Mary. They spent many hours together in confinement."

"I see," Simone said not really understanding where this line of conversation was heading.

"No, I don't think you do. Needless to say, Mary was a beautiful woman, and it wasn't long before she worked her magic upon the unsuspecting Richard. They became involved and nine months later she bore a son."

"Really?" she asked, honestly fascinated at this bit of history that wasn't recorded in any book she'd ever read. "How long was Mary held captive?"

"Sir Richard began his role at Tutbury Castle in 1584 and then moved with Mary to Chartley in November of 1585."

Lawrence Gideon walked toward an antique trolley and drew them each a measure of scotch. Handing over the cut crystal, he sniffed and tossed the amber liquid back. Neither Simone nor Trent touched theirs.

"Richard," he continued, "quickly whisked the child to safety, fearing for both of their lives. He left Mary under the charge of his old and trusted friend, Marmaduke Darrell."

"Then what happened?" Simone encouraged.

Lawrence Gideon turned and retrieved a yellowed sheet of paper. Its age apparent by the thin reed and dark stains around the documents edge. Simone accepted the sheet, furrowing her brow in confusion.

"Read that," Lord Bromley insisted.

She scanned the page more intrigued by its age than its contents. "This is about the death of Mary?" Simone whispered, handing the letter to Trent.

"Yes, my dear. On the seventh of February, Mary of Scotland walked through the dreary grounds of Fotheringay to lay her head upon the wooden block. Laced between her fingers was the rope that held this cross. Kissing its jeweled handle, she said her last prayer and waited for the sharp cut of the axe to end her life."

Disgust pummeled every nerve ending Simone could feel. The closeness of Lawrence Gideon, the vivid picture he painted . . . it all felt dirty and diseased. She watched as he reached within the display case and retrieved the cross. Caressing its jeweled surface, as Mary must have done, he then put it close to his cheek.

"This," he handed her the cross. "Is our heritage."

"You expect me to believe that Mary Queen of Scots conceived a child when she was forty-odd years old? And what I'm assuming here is that this illegitimate child is our ancestor." Simone was forced to accept the historic jewel. It was heavy, laden with rubies, emeralds and diamonds.

"Yes, that is exactly what I'm saying."

The fire flickered softly, sparking rays of purple streaks through the clear diamonds and across the polished wooden floor. She glanced up to discover Lawrence Gideon frowning.

"I won't steal it," she stated, trying to absorb all the information he'd just imparted. It still seemed farfetched.

"Of course not, my dear. Do you feel anything from the cross? Does it hurt your palm?"

Confused, Simone glanced at Trent who just shook his head. "No. It's certainly heavy, but as for feeling anything unusual, I'd have to say no." She failed to mention the memory that kept tugging at her mind.

"Ah," Lord Bromley sighed. "I know that was an odd question but you see the cross was crafted from the blood and anger of the witches persecuted by Mary's son, James VI. He fed it with evil, hoping to damage his mother's soul."

"Why would he have done such a thing? That's ghastly."

Simone couldn't begin to understand the motivation behind James.

"I suppose he had his reasons," Lawrence muttered. "Porphyria can muddle anyone's mind."

She narrowed her gaze. "I'm not following you Lord Bromley. Are you insinuating that James was afflicted with porphyria?"

"As was Mary Queen of Scots. The historians have insinuated this fact for years. Are you familiar with the disease, Simone?"

"Yes, as a matter of fact I am."

"Then you've already noticed that I suffer from an advanced stage," Lawrence Gideon swept his arm across his body. He turned to Trent and smiled sadly. "So you see, Mr. Arnot, you were quite correct when you indicated that our family indeed is riddled with skeletons and disease."

"I apologize, Lord Bromley. I certainly meant no disrespect."

Lawrence nodded and moved to sit before the fireplace. Simone and Trent followed. Settling opposite their suspect, they watched as he filled a pipe and lit it. The sickeningly sweet aroma of tobacco assaulted Simone's nose. Mesmerized, she watched a tendril of smoke curl into the room, vanishing within the folds of the velvet curtains.

"Do you know who your parents are Simone?"

Simone's heart caught. She couldn't believe she'd guessed properly. "Yes," she stated flatly. "They are Pamela Allen and Simon Drake. Pamela was your sister."

If he went any paler, Simone figured Lawrence Gideon would be dead. She'd one-upped him, but it didn't dissipate the awareness of danger rattling her nerves.

"Quite correct," he whispered. "Your mother was certainly the rebel, changing her name and then insisting on marrying that man."

"What is your purpose of seeking me out, Lord Bromley? If you've known for all these years that I existed, why are you contacting me now?"

He stared at her for a long time before answering. Her shoulder burned, warning her of danger. "Death is a difficult master to serve, Simone. I face many more lonely days ahead before succumbing to its rule. But this disease will force it upon me."

"I don't understand."

He leaned forward and tapped her knee. She shivered. "You are my last heir. You and your daughter. This will one day become yours."

Simone frowned and shook her head. "No. I don't want any of this." Time to make an offensive move. "Why were you interested in my sister, Rosalyn?" Simone asked.

"She was a member of the Boston Red Cross and involved in a research project I was funding for them." he answered. "How do you know that I had any connection with your sister?"

"I wasn't certain until now." She didn't believe him. He sat back against his chair.

"You're very smart, Simone. Tell me, how did you end up being a Walker?"

She didn't take the bait. He was attempting to startle and unnerve her. She pursed her lips, pretending to think. "I don't know. I thought maybe you might be able to answer that for me."

Lord Bromley stood and refilled his glass. "Your mother and I had some differences. She fought her legacy and the responsibility of being a Gideon. After mother and father died, she constantly went against everything that our parents had decreed in their trust. She ran away. I couldn't find her and when I did . . ."

Simone followed him to the antique cart laden with scotch and whiskey decanters, grabbing his arm and gazing into his eyes to search for truth. "You killed her."

Chapter Twenty-Four

Lord Bromley disengaged her grip on his arm. "You make unsound accusations."

Simone pushed further. "What about my other cousins?"

Lord Bromley froze in place, his mouth slightly open as if he'd been about to take a swig of scotch. "What other cousins?" He moved and sat back down in his chair.

Simone returned to her place beside Trent. "The women found murdered. The women with the same M.O. as Rosalyn's. One was in Paris and another in England. I'm surprised you don't know about them." She leaned forward, tapping his stash of books piled on the coffee table. "Your research as in depth as it is."

"M.O. as Rosalyn?"

"Modus operandi," Trent answered.

"You are aware of the horrible way in which my sister died aren't you?" She watched Lord Bromley's throat move as he swallowed.

"No." He finally said.

"What about the other women?" Simone asked.

"I know about them. They were relatives so, of course, I was informed. I'm startled, however, that you do." Lawrence Gideon narrowed his eyes and scanned Trent, a feral gleam lighting the blood shot orbs. "Who are you exactly?"

"Just who I claim to be," Trent answered without batting an eye. "I'm surprised you weren't familiar with my family name."

"Arnot? No, I'm not familiar with it. Where are your estate holdings?"

"About thirty kilometers south of here."

"And is there a name for your parish?"

Trent frowned and nodded. "Draconius."

Simone sat beside Trent, stunned. Why hadn't he told her? Another lie, she realized. She quickly snapped her mask in place and pretended that this was information she'd always known. Lawrence Gideon leaned forward and pointed a finger at Trent.

"You are not who you appear to be young man." His mouth twisted in anger and puss trickled down to his chin.

Simone screamed inwardly, squirming uncomfortably at the horrible vision of Lawrence Gideon. Fear quickly distracted her.

Shadows, long and narrow, crept from the corner of the room. She glanced at the bookcases to see if their bound contents were causing this illusion. Scooting closer to Trent, she realized that the gray-uglies were making an appearance.

Her eyes widened when the wraiths pulsed upward, forking into thin tendrils that lurched forward in awkward staggers. She clutched Trent's hand, and he squeezed back. He didn't see them, but the tense muscles in his arm proved he sensed them.

They formed themselves into wraiths, dark gray shadows of evil. Hollow eyes glared accusingly and craggy fingers reached for her. Swaying closer, they stretched their hand over Lord Bromley, caressing his body. She thought a smile flickered momentarily upon his face.

"I'm sorry, Lord Bromley," she heard Trent speak. He sounded far away, but his warmth against her skin told her he still held her hand. "I believe we must take our leave. Miss Walker has several more appointments this afternoon." He rose and pulled her up into his embrace. She staggered slightly.

The evil presence wavered then melted back into the innocence of a simple cast of darkness brought on by the dancing flames. She blinked several times. "Yes," Simone agreed, her voice slightly shaky. "We really must be going. If you think of anything that might help me in finding my sister's killer, please don't hesitate to call." She stopped before exiting the library. "Because the person responsible will pay for her death."

"Of course," Lawrence Gideon agreed, not bothering to rise and show them to the door. "I believe you can find your way out."

"Yes," Trent said, furrowing his brow. He quickly hustled her down the hallway and out the front door, signaling for her to remain quiet until they reached the safety of his Roadster.

She fumbled with the door handle, and Trent reached around lifting her hands from the car. She frowned as he pushed her forward and marched her around the car.

Slamming the door shut, Simone collapsed into the passenger seat. She'd been on the wrong side. With a toss of her hair, she decided it was just as well things wouldn't be permanent for her and Trent. If they were to live in England, it would take her years to overcome her tendency of climbing into the wrong seat.

"What do you make of that?" she said, as soon as Blithewoods was nothing more than a blur in the rearview mirror.

"I didn't like it one bit. He seemed as eager to be rid of us, as we were to leave. What was going on with you? You stepped upon some dangerous territory." He looked across the seat and narrowed his eyes, scrutinizing her. "The gray-uglies were there, weren't they?"

"They made an appearance," she sighed, and rubbed her forehead. She could feel the beginning of a massive headache.

"I felt them. Could you determine where they originated from?"

"What do you mean?"

"Rosalyn indicated we needed to find out if Lawrence controlled them or not."

Simone thought. "I'm not certain. They came from the shadows but I did note that they seemed to pat or caress him, and I thought he responded with a smile. But I could've been imaging it."

"Oh," he said absently, lost in thought.

"I kinda hoped they were drawn to Grael and would disappear when she did. But," she quipped, "I'm wrong again."

He parked the car back in the field surrounding Ian's gypsy hideout. "Hand me those glasses and the wire, and I'll give them over to Ian."

She handed over the glasses and quickly unbuttoned her shirt. Unclipping the wire from her bra, she pulled the miniature speaker and recording device from her chest. With a quick flip of her wrist, she twirled it all together and handed it to Trent.

"Ian wired you up?" he said, his face suddenly a shade darker.

Surprised, she glanced up and met a heated gaze that sent a line of fire straight to her center. His eyes blazed cobalt fire, instantly igniting every inch of her body. Swallowing the lump in her throat, she nodded. "He said he pictured me as a little old lady with wrinkled balloon breasts or something to that affect." A nervous laugh escaping her lips

"And how did you picture him?"

Was he jealous? Simone couldn't believe her ears. "As Quasimodo, you idiot."

He smiled, visibly relaxing in his seat. He tenderly touched her cheek, then reached down and stopped her from buttoning her shirt. "I'll do that," his breath hot against her skin.

She stopped his hands and stared him straight in the eye. "Why didn't you tell me my other ancestral home happened to be your current residence?" These bits of information that kept being left out were becoming troublesome.

"I don't know. I suppose I didn't want you to think we were related."

"Are we?"

"Not in blood." He grinned, a wicked glint lighting his eyes. "Our families formed a strong union during the sixteen hundreds. According to our legend, we were the protectors and the Drakes were the protectees. Somewhere things became convoluted, the families fought, and Draconius became the property of the Arnot's." He shrugged. "Simple as that."

Simple as that, my ass. There was more, and she was determined to discover it. She remembered when Ian unearthed her surname as Drake, Trent had a funny look on his face.

Gathering all the technical paraphernalia together, he exited the vehicle. Simone sat still absorbing this last piece of the puzzle. Why did everyone else know so much more than she?

Her mind whirled.

She was a Drake, the protectee. He was an Arnot, the protector. Had their souls always been recycled as Drakes and Arnots? That was truly bizarre, even for this group of whackos. However, if that were the case, then it would certainly explain Trent's insistence that the hands of fate were manipulating them. And hadn't Elizabeth referred to her manor house as Draconius?

The pieces of the puzzle clicked into place and for the first time in a week, Simone saw everything through clear glass. She slumped against the seat, her heart feeling too heavy to stay in her chest. It hurt.

He wouldn't allow himself to love her. This was his job, his *calling*. As each piece of the puzzle snapped into place, Trent understood the gravity and unnatural force behind their union.

With a stab, she realized her fantasy of a perfect future together was just that, a fantasy. He might never love her in the manner she needed. He couldn't. Simone swallowed, bending her head and worrying her bottom lip. She wasn't certain "settling" was a word in her vocabulary.

Her breath caught as she watched Trent saunter back. The wind ruffled his hair, tossing its spiky ends into a mass of waves. Tight jeans and navy polo shirt hugged every ounce of his flesh. Her pulse raced. Her hands itched to run across his chest and delve into the most sensuous areas only a lover knew.

He was gorgeous.

As he retuned to the car, she quieted her thoughts and centered her mind on Jessie.

"Ian and I are going to stake out Blithewoods tonight. There didn't appear to be an excessive amount of security. We'll be able to disconnect the security system in place easily enough."

"Okay. Do you want me to come along?"

"No, you'd only be a distraction, albeit, a nice distraction, but a distraction nonetheless." He smiled and offered a half laugh.

She smiled and nodded absently. Her thoughts wrapped around what he might discover at Blithewoods and how long he'd be away from Draconius "Isn't this illegal without a warrant?"

"We won't be able to use any evidence we find. It's my hope that we'll only discover the next direction Lord Bromley's going to take. I think you got to him today. He's going to react." He shrugged and focused on the road. "I've got an agent driving in to watch over you while we're gone."

"Is that necessary?"

"You're still alive, and I choose to keep it that way." His look squelched any form of argument. She sighed in frustration, her heart hurt.

"What are you sighing about?" Trent flashed a naughty smile.

She didn't think she was ready to explain herself. "If you must know, Sherlock," she spoke slowly, attempting a creative excuse. "I was thinking of a bubble bath."

"For two?"

She laughed. "That might be a bit difficult considering you'll be hunkering up to Ian tonight."

"Damn," he pouted then smiled again. "How about waiting until I get home?"

"Well . . ."

"Please? I promise it'll be a fast trip...a quick mission...we'll be in an out in no time."

"As long as you don't bring that mentality to the tub, I'll wait for you." She snorted and then giggled when he ruffled her hair.

He flashed a heart-stopping smile and pulled her to him for a mind-blowing, two second assault on her mouth. He released her in time to avoid running the car off the road.

"Trent, where do you see us in five years?" She fought back tears, desperately wanting this to be real.

He glanced at her and ran one hand through his hair. "Honestly? I don't know. I'm trying to work through this the same way you are."

Simone bit her bottom lip. "Do you care?"

Trent reached over and gathered her against his chest. He kissed the top of her head and whispered against her hair. "That doesn't begin to describe how I feel about you."

She closed her eyes . A tear tipped over her lash and soaked into his shirt. His answer should satisfy her, but it wasn't enough.

"I need to go home."

"Home?"

"To Jessie. I'm worried that Kathryn will do something behind your back." Simone pushed away from him and glanced out the window.

He was silent. The time dragged out, each second a painful twist to her heart. "All right." He finally said, his voice low and thick. "We'll leave tomorrow."

She gazed into his eyes. "Thank you."

Julie Korzenko

Chapter Twenty-Five

Simone walked with slow steps through Lady Lichfield's rose garden, allowing the pungent scent of crimson petals to soak into her senses. It didn't soothe.

Closing her eyes, she envisioned the dragon. It grew larger in her mind until fire licked at her soul and burned her nerves.

Simone glanced up and saw Grael weaving through the air. "It worked."

"This was not our agreement," the dragon said, flicking her tail and moving in circles around Simone.

"I'm sorry. I have to leave England. Can we continue our separation?"

Grael settled before Simone and rested her head upon the grass. "It is no matter. My mate has not awoken nor no other."

"That isn't a surprise. I told you, Trent won't love me like his ancestor loved Seren so this union could possibly be falsified. We've failed you again." Simone sat down and crossed her legs. "However, my daughter needs me."

"There are no more dragons." Grael hissed, ignoring Simone's last statement.

Anger tightened her chest. "You obviously didn't look hard enough."

Grael tipped her head up and stared at the gray sky. Rain threatened to fall at any moment. "I searched. There is one out there whose heart beats only for me. If he'd been awakened, I'd know it."

The sadness that laced her words dampened Simone's temper. It was unfair to unleash her frustrations on Grael. She reached for the dragon. Her fingers touched only air but the connection tingled and she attempted to soothe the dragon's shattered spirit. "What do we do now?"

"I don't know. There is something out there that blocks my vision. It is tied to the shadows."

"I felt them again."

The dragon turned a golden eye on Simone's face. "Where?"

"At Blithewoods. They reached for me then disappeared. Lawrence Gideon has this cross that dates back to the seventeenth century that, somehow, is connected to everything." She absently picked at the grass, trying to work through all the angles. "I feel it."

"Describe the cross."

Simone closed her eyes and envisioned the jewel encrusted work of art. Each intricate edge seared her mind with detail and design. Grael slipped away, her link becoming weak. In a panic, Simone stopped her vision and searched for the dragon.

She was nowhere.

"Grael?"

Standing, she spun around unable to control the fear that scattered goosebumps up and down her arms. Where was the dragon? A flash of heat caught her right above her heart, forcing her to her knees. Grael viciously penetrated her mind. Simone imagined the dragon's talons were what clawed inside her head, but through the blinding pain she understood their intent. Closing her eyes, she allowed the memory to wash through her

* * *

Elizabeth hurried along the cobbled path. Shadows cast by the late afternoon sun, reminded her of the ones invading her room at night. These were innocent, those were not. The hem of her silken gown brushed against the cold stone, making soft sweeping noises that echoed through the massive arches. It was November and she'd worn a thick linen chemise that hung lower than her emerald dress. She was rushed and refused her maid's assistance in correcting the length. With a sigh, Elizabeth realized her attire would need rearranging prior to supper.

Time became more precious. Peering through the entryway to the chapel, she sighed in relief. The object she required lay within its glass prison. A pedestal made of intricately carved wood supported the display case that was a cube no bigger than her forearm.

Moving among the polished wooden pews, she flattened her palms against the slick material of her gown and smoothed away invisible wrinkles. The lace that edged her bodice and wrists itched her skin, a reminder of the marriage festivities later in the evening.

Frederick arrived as planned. Her brother no longer worried or concerned over her seemingly improper actions. The curse rang true this past eve, and the last word to grace Henry's lips had been her name. His whispered plea for his life went ignored. She'd watched, the shadows already enticing her with their power, as the life slipped from her murderous brother's face.

His death-glazed eyes didn't strike at her heart. That corner of her soul now lay barren, cold and lifeless without the warm breath of her love, without Rake.

Elizabeth knelt before the oblong glass case. She gazed beyond the jewel-encrusted cross cradled within and watched the last light of day slip behind the hills beyond Draconius. The stained glass filtered its rays in a myriad of muted color. A whisper of chill air swept down the aisle of the rectory and tickled the base of her neck. Her hair was coiled tightly upon her head, held in place by pearl tipped pins, leaving the tender skin upon her nape bare and vulnerable.

In less than a fortnight, her life would no longer be hers. A man she didn't know would own it. She must accept him. If she refused, then the dragon that rested within would destroy her soul and scatter its tattered remains into the stiff wind that blew with a vengeance from the craggy peaks of Snowdon.

She felt him. The wizard that had tainted the original spell. Shadows and grayness leaked through Draconius, taunting and praising. Their origin smelled of the west, of a place never spoken aloud. A tip of ice once known as <u>Dreigiau Rheol.</u>

Only the memory of her love for Rake prevented her from stepping across the fine line between good and evil. The tales passed through generations of Dancers spoke of that which was not light. For the grayness was evil. An evil that existed tangled within the souls that yearned for one another.

Her life had never been hers to rule.

Did it hinder? Elizabeth thought so. Did it crave? Of that, she was certain. But for what?

She believed it prevented the union of their souls and attempted to gain the power of the dragon. This was only theory. The true answer lay within the bitter ice of the Welsh mountains.

Elizabeth tilted her head, the song of the dark calling her.

Separated they were weak. Rake and Elizabeth were not the strong, united Ancient and Dancer they'd envisioned.

She wasn't certain that Frederick would be able to prevent her crossing beyond the border of all that was good and true. This temptation must cease.

The thought of yet another Dancer experiencing the heartache and loss of a love more powerful than time itself rendered her slightly mad.

The glint of the setting sun on the cross brought her attention back to what she had to do. She gazed at the rubies and emeralds pushed into the ornate carving beneath the glass, a blanket of shimmering angles embedded in the smooth and polished grain of mahogany. Her grandmother's legacy.

After its creation, King James had become obsessed with the destruction of those who fashioned the jeweled cross. Her father, intent upon uniting England and Scotland and wiping the countryside of infidels and the devil's strumpets, fell prey to the power of evil.

He'd recently returned from a personal visit to the Pennines, crimson blood fresh upon his hands. If such a forthright man could bend beneath the power of the hunt, then what of her? She already held death within her fingers.

Elizabeth felt the spell wrapped around the object.

It reached for her beyond the glass. Had it been the horror of what her father wrought upon his own mother that fed this object its power? She didn't know.

She prayed it would be enough. Wrapping pale fingers around the wooden legs of the glass case, she raised herself and lifted the lid. She laughed at her father's arrogance in his monarchy that prompted him to leave such a treasure unlocked and unguarded. Or maybe it wasn't arrogance, maybe the spells contained within warded off theft . She didn't know. She didn't care.

Blackness surrounded the jewels. Pulling fire from deep within, she called upon the soul forever destined to entwine itself with hers. The dragon surfaced, casting a golden glow to the dim interior of the parish.

Raising her hands to the glory of the Lord, invoking the prayers her vile brother once spoke daily, she reached beyond her plane of existence and found the spirit of her love. Elizabeth latched on to that soul, dragged the strength of magic embedded within the cross, and wound her heart through that of the dragon, casting her spell into the air.

Power leaked from the crucifix, a familiar touch. An icy sting of needle-like fingers that penetrated her soul, leaving behind a bitter chill.

She collapsed to the stone floor, her body weak and breath ragged. It was done.

They may call her insane. Another victim of the reign of the Mad Monarchy. But she knew different. The shimmering magic of her dragon, rested once more. Its taste slightly tainted by the evil imprisoned within the cross. An evil she now connected with the wizard to the west. It had the same feel, the infinite kiss of death that the shadows promised.

How right it all seemed now. She'd used the shadows against themselves. Evil twisted the Dragon Dancer prophecy once more, but at her hands. This time, she prayed, for the better. The next Ancient and Dragon Dancer to unite would never face the heartache of separation. They would live forever, safe from human fallacy and greed.

Immortal.

***

Simone stumbled to her feet. "What?" she yelled at Grael. "What has she done?" Turning to gaze upon the castle, she searched for Trent. Did he feel her anguish? "Is this the truth? Have you shown the truth?" Her eyes welled with tears as she spun and faced the dragon.

"It is truth."

"If, by any chance, Trent and I found happiness and love we would become immortal?" Simone felt like she was hyperventilating. This went beyond prophecy and destiny and straight into the hottest corner of hell. If she'd held onto the fantasy that Trent might love her, it was gone now. She couldn't ever allow it. How do you commit someone to immortality? How would she ever live with her actions?

Shaking her arms she paced in a tight circle. Her mind reeled with what she'd witnessed. "Why? Why would Elizabeth do that?" Grael encircled her, attempting to use her essence as a soothing touch. Simone stepped away shaking her head. "Don't." she said.

"Seren, be still." Grael said.

Simone whirled around and pointed at the dragon. "I am not Seren. She might have once been keeper of this soul but she's been dead now for over a thousand years." Was that a tear in Grael's eye? Incredible. "Are you crying?" Simone struggled to right her world.

"I cry for her, yes. But more, I cry for you. You are lost and because of that, so am I."

"I want to make sure I understand what I've seen. If, and this is a huge if, Trent and I were to successfully become Ancient and Dancer, then we would be rendered immortal?"

Grael undulated on the air; ripples of emerald scales flashed a foot above the ground. "Yes."

"And you didn't feel the need to tell me this before?"

The dragon spun straight up then dove toward Simone. She didn't flinch.

"What do you want from me? I haven't roamed the earth since Elizabeth's time and then it was in loneliness. The loss of her Ancient prevented my brethren from waking. I haven't seen my love in over a thousand years and you, you small little child, toss the heart that longs for you away like it's worth nothing more than a pebble. You want my help? Then accept the soul that fate has handed you."

"Never." Simone backed away. "Never."

"You are a fool."

"Do you not understand, Grael? Immortality isn't something to take lightly. What would happen to me? I'd be like Duncan Macleod. Forever watching the people I love die of old age. This can't be the truth."

"Who is this Macleod?"

"A highlander."

"You would never be like his sort. The Scottish are filthy men, seeking only gold and war."

Simone gazed at the dragon. "What are you talking about?"

"This Macleod person."

"He's not real, Grael." She stood up and paced in a tight circle. "Just an example of what immortality means, lost people scouring the earth in search of redemption and a way out of the manacles that bind them to this plane of existence. I don't want to be Angel."

"As an immortal, you'd never reach angel status. That's not a concern. Immortality is freedom, little one. It is a gift."

"It's a curse." She fell to her knees and sunk her fingers in the damp soil "Do you see this earth? Where will it be in a hundred years? Will it still hold the power of life? For all we know it could become a concrete skyscraper that houses a million people. I've witnessed what advanced civilization can do. Hell, I'm part of it. I create from steel and beam, wood and glass. I build upon virgin ground, watching as trees that are more than five times my age fall to the ground. I don't want to see the damage we'll cause in another five hundred years. I don't want to watch death in all its cruel facets."

Grael leveled one golden eye on her. "You cannot stop the advancement of time or man."

"No, I can't. But I don't have to witness it. What did you find when you flew the peaks of Snowdon?"

The dragon dropped her head. "Things I did not understand."

"A hydro-electric power plant, for one!" Simone said. "I've researched Snowdon. Within the caves that used to house your brethren now beats the heart of civilization. How does that make you feel?"

"Sad." Grael's eyes glimmered with unshed tears.

Simone nodded. "Sad," she echoed. "Doesn't begin to describe it for me. I wouldn't be able to stand the sight of everything that brings me joy vanish beneath the progression of man. Or watch my daughter grow old, marry, die. And then witness the same of all my grandchildren and great-grandchildren. My heart would wither and freeze until I didn't feel anything anymore. Didn't care. Didn't love." She settled more comfortably on the grass. "And then what's the point of being immortal?"

She gazed at the manor house, longing for the comfort of Trent's embrace. Bending her head, she fought against the tears. "I'm leaving England."

"And your Ancient?"

Tears welled and Simone didn't bother to stop them falling. "He can never know this. I'm leaving alone. He'll be better off without me."

"That is foolish, Simone. The three of us must work as one." Grael spun in a circle and screeched her frustration.

"Never. I can't risk this. What if he wants immortality? Where does that leave me? Where does that leave Jessie? No. I won't risk it." She rose and walked away from Grael. "Will you remain here?"

"I haven't found Llallogen."

A thought tickled her mind and she glanced at Grael. They met golden eye to golden eye. "Can he reverse this spell?"

"Of immortality?" The dragon tipped her head and considered Simone's question. "He is a great wizard. If he can do so, will you change your mind and accept your Ancient?"

Simone's gut burned. "I don't know. I don't think so. He'll never forgive me for leaving him." She shook her head at the arguments about to spout from Grael. "Trust is like a silken thread; once broken, it can't be rewoven. I understand the outcome of my actions and accept them. But I can promise that the next generation of Ancient and Dancer won't be tethered by these spells and magic. They'll have an honest chance at happiness."

She knew her words saddened the dragon and her heart felt heavy for the mate Grael longed to find. But her daughter came first, above all else. Above her love. She would find her happiness in Jessie's eyes. It would be enough.

"I'll seek the answer to your question."

Simone turned and headed into the house, releasing her hold on the connection with the dragon.

"Little one," Grael called. "If you need me, I will come." Simone nodded and continued walking. "But it'll hurt beyond anything you've ever experienced."

Her step faltered once. "I doubt it," she said, pushing a fist against her heart. "I doubt anything can hurt worse than this."

***

Simone closed the door to her bedroom, careful not to allow it to slam. She didn't want to disturb Trent. His voice carried up the stairs as he worked through the evening details with Ian. Its deep timber called to her, and she resisted the urge to walk down the circular staircase, perch upon the edge of his chair and place a hand upon his arm. Touching, connecting.

For now, the two volumes on the antique side table that graced the wall adjacent to her bed held the information she required.

The gray-uglies. She'd seen enough glimpses into her past lives to understand they were connected somehow with the original spell. If Seren knew of them, somewhere within The White Book of Rhydderch and Red Book of Hergest their origin would be revealed. If they were an aspect of Lawrence Gideon's threat, she needed to know how to battle them.

Picking up a chair from the small writing desk, Simone moved it over to the side table. Careful of the glass lamps and aged doilies, she laid the two books side by side and grabbed a notepad from her briefcase.

Lady Lichfield assured her that the translations from Welsh to English were made with detailed accuracy by Trent's ancestors. This was not the same version as the more modern transcripts first published by Lady Charlotte Guest in the nineteenth century. Her version called Mabinogion, detailed twelve myths and legends including Arthur's tale.

What Simone held in her hands was truth and prophecy passed from the time before the Dragon Dancer through the early fifteenth century. If she sought answers, it was within these two volumes.

Skipping the section marked Dragon Dancer, Simone decided to concentrate on the period that followed Llallogen's spell.

She skimmed her finger down the pages, her eyes glazing quickly beneath the strain of understanding Welsh terminology not transferable into English. It became a guessing game. After thirty minutes of reaping nothing more than a migraine, Simone pushed away from the desk in disgust.

She rubbed her fingers against her forehead and rotated sore shoulders. As much as she hated it, she admitted to needing help. The thought of seeking out Trent's mother left an uncomfortable rumble in her gut. Lady Lichfield cared deeply for her son, and Simone felt like a traitor to the hospitality of Trent's family.

The thought of her daughter having to be exposed to the evil shadows that followed Simone like a faithful dog, spurred her forward. She'd seek the aid she needed, at whatever consequence.

Simone opened the bedroom door and squealed in surprise.

Lady Lichfield stepped through, sweeping into the room without asking for permission. "You needed me?"

Wide-eyed, Simone stared at her. "How'd you know?"

Trent's mother smiled, showing a beautiful array of white teeth. "My crystal ball cleared up."

"If it's all right with you, I'd rather not ask about that."

Lady Lichfield laughed, her chest rising and falling beneath the soft fabric of her Tshirt. "My dear, you are precious. What can I do for you?"

Simone smiled and accepted her offer. "I'm trying to read these two volumes but the Welsh is making it extremely difficult."

"I see." Lady Lichfield walked to the side board and scanned the pages that lay face up. Simone stepped next to her and wondered what thoughts lay beneath the frown marring the elder woman's face. "Why are you interested in this text here? I thought it would be the prophecy of Dragon Dancer that you'd be concerned with."

"No. I don't much care about that."

The sharp gaze Trent's mother leveled in her direction twisted Simone's gut.

"I see," the woman said. "This details the origin of a spell that . . ." Lady Lichfield paused and leaned closer. "Oh my God, Simone do you realize what you've uncovered?"

"If I did, Lady Lichfield, I wouldn't have needed your help."

The woman waved her hand . "Stop being so bloody defensive. This is an unusual twist, but it's workable. Definitely workable."

Simone rolled her eyes to the ceiling. She must walk around with a stamp on her forehead that said *speak to me in riddles.* "What have you found?"

Trent's mother sat in the chair that Simone pulled over. She flipped ahead a few pages in The White Book, and then flipped the Red Book to the very beginning. "These two volumes were written at different stages in time. Rhydderch was created in the early thirteen hundreds with its counterpart, Hergest, not coming to light until much later in that century. Although to the casual observer it would appear that each volume is separate, detailing different legends, that's not what they are."

Simone didn't interrupt. Instead, she grabbed her pad and began taking notes.

"These words you were unable to translate here in The White Book are directly correlated to the same page and line in the Red Book. See?"

Simone leaned forward as Lady Lichfield grabbed the pen and pad Simone held and began jotting down a group of Welsh words. "If we translate this now, it'll make sense."

"Do you understand what they say?"

Lady Lichfield studied the legal pad for a moment then raised her eyes to Simone. The worry that etched their hazel depths frightened her. "Yes. I can read it."

"And?"

"If you don't mind, I'd like to go forward a bit more to fully comprehend what this has to do with the Dragon Dancer prophecy."

Simone frowned, she needed the answers now. "How long will that take?"

"A few moments."

"Oh, okay." She sighed in relief and felt the longing to be beside her daughter strengthen.

Simone lay down, the softness of the pillows called her name. She closed her eyes as Lady Lichfeld began reciting the translation, her words swept her back in time, visions flooding her mind.

***

"Llallogen, you must correct whatever Trynt did to your spell." Seren begged, battling against the rage of Grael that pushed against her mind like burning embers. She was losing her struggle against the dragon's will and would soon join her lover in the heavens. But first, she must destroy the evil he inadvertently sparked.

Llallogen placed a comforting hand upon her shoulder. He squeezed tightly and shook his head from side to side. "Trynt dealt with a force that my magic cannot fight."

Panic spread through Seren. This couldn't be so. "He has paid with his life, is that not enough?"

"The spell he wove the eve of the casting promised your souls to be forever linked and in return for that promise, the wizard who mastered its creation wrapped it tightly with his own spirit."

"I do not understand."

"There will always be a shadow following you. This wizard was strong, and his essence is very prominent within the spell that binds you with Grael. There will always be a shadow attempting to gain control of the spirit that now fights against its restraints. God help us if the dragon becomes bound to an evil such as the thing that seeks your life."

***

Simone opened her eyes and turned to gaze at Lady Lichfield. The woman's frown mirrored her own . "Did you see that?"

Francine nodded.

"How?"

"You are easy to read." Trent's mother shrugged. "When you crossed the threshold to this home, your visions were clear to me. It's one of my gifts."

Simone sighed. Weird and weirder, but who was she to argue? "Great," she said, pushing up on her elbows. "That dream indicates that I am being haunted."

Trent's mother laughed softly. "I don't suppose you have any clue as to how to battle these shadows?" she asked.

"Nope. And I fear that Grael has been bound to evil in the past. She mentioned an episode during the time Elizabeth Stuart lived in The Hague."

"What do you believe happened?"

Simone frowned. "I can't be sure, but I think it has something to do with a cross that I saw in Blithewoods."

Lady Lichfield nodded. "Mary's cross."

"Yes."

"It's evil or at least has been purported to be evil."

Simone swung her legs over the side of the four poster bed and slid to the ground. "I don't know about that. I felt something, but it didn't scare me like the shadows. They must be the wraithlike things I call gray-uglies."

"A link to a wizard's spirit," the older woman said, worrying her bottom lip.

"Yes. A spirit determined to steal the dragon's power at all cost."

"Why?"

Simone stared at Trent's mother. "I don't understand what Grael is, but I know she's very powerful. What the magic of a dragon can unleash is beyond my comprehension."

"Where is she now, Simone?"

"Searching for Llallogen," and hopefully finding me another ancient. Simone had no desire to die before she'd had the chance to watch her daughter grow and become a woman.

Lady Lichfield rose and hugged Simone, the woman's lips brushing lightly against her cheek. "Everything will be fine. Trust in your destiny." Trent's mother swept from the room with the same grace she'd entered it, leaving Simone disconcerted and more determined to reach Jessie.

Chapter Twenty-Six

A soft knock on her bedroom door startled Simone from her continued scrutiny of the volumes on her table. Rising from the hard back chair, she stretched her back and went to open the door. Trent stood on the other side. He was clad in black jeans and black shirt, his hair the same shade as the rest of him. Only the vivid blue that poured from his eyes broke the head to toe darkness. Without saying a word, he reached for her.

She moved within the circle of his arms, wrapping herself tightly around his body. His heat suffused her and she sighed when he whispered her name.

"I won't be long."

Simone nodded against his shoulder not trusting her voice. She fought the tears that threatened her eyes. He didn't know this was their last embrace, their last taste of a passion.

She pulled away and touched her lips to his in a gentle kiss.

"Until tonight," he said and stepped away.

She nodded and closed the door, her heart splintering into tiny shards of glass.

***

Simone finished packing her last shirt. Trent and Ian had left for Blithewoods over an hour ago and her taxi was due to arrive within the next fifteen minutes. Pushing down on her overstuffed suitcase, she paused.

Her mind filtered through images of the past week spent with Trent.

His touch that burned her skin with a desire no man had ever stirred before, the scent of spice and ale that surrounded him always. She ran a finger down the edge of the bed, the smooth fabric of the coverlet reminding her of their love.

Moving into the bathroom, Simone gathered the last of her toiletries. She zipped them in a cosmetic bag and returned to her suitcase. Pushing the bag into the outside pocket of her suitcase, she shoved and punched it out of frustration.

After one last glance around, the inevitable couldn't be detained anymore. Her hand clutched the suitcase, and she went in search of Lady Lichfield. The scent of sizzling onions originating from the direction of the kitchen clued Simone in to her whereabouts.

"Lady Lichfield," she called, as the wooden doors swung open.

"Yes, dear? What can I do for you?" Trent's mother stood in front of the commercial sized stove, stirring a pan full of vegetables, curry, and shrimp. A steaming pot bubbled loudly, waiting for the rice that sat upon the counter.

"I owe you an apology," Simone admitted, a sudden pang of reluctance at having to leave this safe haven tightened her chest.

"No, child. I believe I'm the one who owes you an apology." Francine dropped the wooden spoon, flipped off the stove, and turned to face Simone. Wiping her hands upon the bright red apron that wrapped around her trim figure, she moved away from the heat of cooking. "You were right when you suggested that we not believe everything we read. It's been a long time since an elder was about to council our younger generations, and I'm afraid that I just became too reliant upon the words of others."

"No," Simone said, "you were absolutely right." She walked over to the older woman and grabbed her shoulders. "Don't you see? We can't escape our destiny. For whatever reason, we are placed upon this earth to perform a task. If my task was to be Dragon Dancer, then so be it."

"I don't understand," Francine said shaking her head and covering Simone's hands with her own. "What are you saying?"

"I can't remain here. You've seen the past through my eyes. You must realize what a threat I am to Trent. Until these shadows are vanquished, they will hunt him."

"Simone."

She held up her hand. "No. Hear me out. I'm returning to the states, hopefully Lord Bromley will follow. I'm going to seek the help of my sister's coven. I'll find a way to destroy the shadows and avenge her death." The lie crossed her lips easily, but she didn't know about her eyes.

"You can't go without my son."

"Yes, I can."

"You'll die."

Simone shook her head. "Grael will find me another ancient."

"It cannot be so," she gasped. "My son might be pig headed and obstinate, but I know he loves you. You are the one. I'm certain of it."

"Don't you see?" Simone continued in a rush. "I *am* the one. But it's all wrong; the spell is tainted . I can't ever walk the path your prophecy has laid out. I am freeing him of his obligation. He must not follow me, do you understand?" She laced her fingers through Francine's. "Do you understand?"

"Ah, my poor little bird. You don't really get it, do you?" Lady Lichfield gathered her in a fierce hug. She might be six inches shorter than Simone, but the power and comfort she offered amazed the younger woman.

"Yes, I'm afraid I do," Simone cried. "If I stay, he'll make a commitment that he doesn't want. That I don't' want. I can't allow that to happen. I won't allow it to happen."

"How do you know he doesn't want to spend the rest of his life with you?"

Simone sighed. "That's the point. It wouldn't be a life he chose, it would be one that was manipulated." She smiled, irony tickling her funny bone. "And it wouldn't be a short one for that matter."

Francine narrowed her eyes then nodded, stepping back and smoothing Simone's ruffled hair. "Everything will be all right, you'll see." She pulled a piece of paper from her apron. "Here, take this. It might help you see things as I do."

Simone accepted the note pushed into her palm and turned to leave. "I've called a cab; it'll be here by now. I'm returning to the States. When everything's safe would you give Trent a message for me?" Simone fought hard against the tears that threatened to spill. Lady Litchfield's eyes were bright as well, and she realized with a sense of shame that she'd never truly afforded the woman a chance. "I want you to tell him that I have no regrets. The days he spent with me and my daughter will be treasured for a lifetime." She spun on her heels and raced from the kitchen.

Bumping into Lord Lichfield as she rounded the last corner, Simone hugged him fiercely and shook her head refusing any conversation. "I've got to go," she cried.

"Your car is here," he said as he enveloped her in a bear hug. "We'll see you soon."

"No," she whispered, "I don't think so." She kissed his check and left the Arnot household.

No regrets, Simone, no regrets, she mentally convinced herself.

***

Trent lay on the ground, swearing softly as the damp soil soaked through his shirt. Blithewoods was quiet...dead quiet. As in, no one home quiet. It sent a shiver of apprehension snaking down his spine. *Where is old blister-boy?*

"Ian, what's your location?" he spoke softly into the two-way radio.

"I'm past the exterior security block. Give me a moment, I'll cut the sensors then we'll start our party."

Trent relaxed a moment. Simone would be waiting for him, and he was going to take what she offered. He'd battled against himself all evening. Was it fair?

He wanted her.

He needed her.

Damn. She was his everything.

The chaste kiss he'd received before leaving Blithewoods chilled him to the bone. Dread filtered into his soul as he wondered what rattled in her brain, what attacked her emotions.

"I'm in," Ian's voice interrupted his musing. Trent rose from the ground, brushed off his clothing and vaulted over the wall.

He skirted the parish and walked the length of the concrete orangery. The centerpiece of the garden was an oblong building of stone columns. To the left was a closed room surrounded by glass but the remainder of the walk was open, an inviting place for royals to sit out of the sun and watch lawn games.

Racing across the yard, he joined Ian opposite the French doors that led to the library they were in earlier that day.

He grinned when Ian deftly broke the lock and waved Trent in. They were silent, moving like ghosts. The house was quiet. He frowned and motioned for Ian to head into the hall. He went one direction and his partner the other. After twenty minutes, his radio crackled.

"Trent, I'm sorry to say but this place is silent as a graveyard. There's no one home."

"Where are they?" Trent asked, moving in Ian's direction. He found him in what appeared to be Lord Bromley's office.

A quick glance at the conference table shoved beneath the portrait of Gideon's ancestor sent a stab of alarm between Trent's shoulders. He moved over and ran his finger along the spine of a book he knew well. The White Book of Rhydderch. Lifting the leather volume, he glanced at what he feared lay below. The Red Book of Hergest.

Laying the first volume to the left, he flipped open the cover of the Red Book and glanced at the name scrawled upon the cover.

Ida Lackingbird. Rosalyn Allen's sponsor and the woman that had drawn their investigation to Boston.

"Look what we have here Ian?"

His partner peered over his shoulder. "Got him." Ian said and clapped Trent on the back.

"It's still circumstantial. How do you suppose he managed this?"

"Simple," Ian said. "My guess would be that he hired someone to steal the book. The crime scene definitely mirrored that of a break and entry. The poor old lady just happened to be home at the time."

Trent nodded. There was a sheet of paper marking a section in the book. He turned the pages and gazed at the yellowed page. Upon its surface an inked image of the cross he'd shown them earlier was drawn . Frowning, he scrutinized the page trying to decipher a few of the Welsh words.

"I can't read this," he said. "I'll be right back." Trent jogged out of the office and down the hall. He pushed open the door to the library and walked to the glass case he and Simone had stood around earlier that day.

It was empty.

Swearing out loud, Trent ran back to the office. "Gideon had that cross in his possession. I don't know what the prophecy says in there but I don't think it bodes well for us."

"I've refrained from asking this but I can't help it now. Are you finally committed to your calling?"

Trent gazed at his friend. "You know I didn't think I'd every say this, but yes. I am."

"And now?"

He shrugged. "And now my future lies with Simone."

"Why doesn't that make you happy?"

Raking fingers through his hair he sighed, "I suppose I can't help feeling that one day she's going to wake up and realize she doesn't love me."

Ian chuckled. "Why would she do that?"

"Because if she really stares hard at what the prophecy outlines, she'll see what I see."

Trent moved to stand next to his partner. Ian was rifling through a pile of papers in the garbage can.

"And what is that mate? What will Simone see?"

"She'll see that magic controls her heart and then she'll reject it. She'll reject me."

Ian shook his head. "I think you need to give her a little more credit. Simone doesn't seem the type of bird to dive at any old worm. No, my friend. I have no clue what she sees in your ugly mug, but she wants you with or without your screwy destiny."

Trent laughed, praying his partner was right.

"This looks like a faxed copy of a flight confirmation," Ian said, holding up a piece of paper.

"Where to?" Trent asked already guessing the answer.

"Atlanta."

"And Jessie," he stated flatly. "Let's go, we need to contact headquarters and make sure they notify Sheriff Tippens.

The two men sped from the estate. Driving at a rapid pace, Trent dropped Ian at the gypsy wagon and proceeded home. Noticing the lack of light, he realized Kathryn must have left for London. One more obstacle removed from his path.

Simone would panic and insist on returning to Atlanta tonight. He didn't know if that was possible. She'd be very alarmed, but hopefully with the knowledge that Jessie was safe with Tippens, he'd be able to reassure her.

He'd only been gone from Draconius several hours, but it felt more like days. Time spent away from Simone dragged indefinitely. Spurred on by another rush of panic for Jessie, he spun his wheels turning into the estate's entrance.

Trent ran from the car and into the house yelling for Simone. His mother met him in the hallway a look of sadness across her face.

"Where's Simone?"

"Gone," she said, shrugging.

"What do you mean gone?"

"She left two hours ago for the airport. She's gone home, son. I'm sorry."

"No," he couldn't take this in. His chest constricted and he fought to breathe. She was heading straight into danger, and he wasn't there to protect her. He snatched his cell phone and dialed Ian's number.

"Ian get us to Atlanta, pronto."

"I'm already working on it partner. It looks like we can fly out of here in about six hours."

"That's too late, we need to leave now."

"Why?"

"Simone's gone." Saying the words, stabbed at his heart.

"What do you mean?"

"She's gone home. To Atlanta."

"Bloody hell, Trent. Why'd she do that?"

Trent stopped and thought. He didn't know, and as he turned his gaze on his mother another pang of fear ripped his soul.

"Mother? Why did Simone leave?"

"She said she finally understood everything and that the two of you couldn't be together. It would lead to an unacceptable ending or something like that." She walked over and caressed his check.

"At least she was finally honest with herself," he laughed bitterly, trying to hide the hurt that burned his heart. She'd finally understood that destiny ruled her heart. That she didn't love him. He sighed and shook his head. He'd known the end would come. "This is a bloody horrible time for her to admit that she was a pawn in a game of chance," he said, running up the stairs to pack his bags.

He shook his head, trying to clear the panic. The sooner he was in Atlanta the better he would feel. He refused to acknowledge the pain that wracked his soul.

She didn't love him.

She hadn't ever honestly loved him. When he realized that she was a Drake, his heart had admitted that there was no way her emotions were true. As the days continued and her mystery unfolded, each step confirmed his belief.

The power of fate was too strong. Their hearts were linked by one thing and one thing only. *Magic.*

He should be thankful. If she'd told him one more time that she loved him, he would have relented and accepted whatever wicked hand pushed them together. He would have taken her false promises and added them to his truthful ones.

He would have married her.

He screamed his rage at destiny.

***

Lord Lichfield approached his wife, trying to scowl and bite back the laughter that wanted to escape. She was something, this little gypsy of his.

"Didn't you leave an important part out?" He wrapped an arm around her slim body. The feel of her skin still sparked the flames of desire, even after forty years of marriage.

"And what would that be darling?" She smiled into his face, tenderly caressing his cheek. He waggled his brows.

"The little fact that Simone would have been unable to allow Grael her freedom if she didn't truly love our son?"

"Oh," she sighed, "that part. They'll figure it out. Those two are so determined to believe that the other feels trapped, that I doubt they would have listened to me."

"You gave her that old piece of paper?"

"I did."

"Do you think she'll realize that it's stubbornness that holds our son back and not her?"

"I do."

"I'm certain you're right," he sighed.

"Trust me, dear. The love they hold for one another is as deep as ours. What a relief it is to know that at least one of our sons has found happiness."

"I love you," he whispered, nuzzling her ear.

"And I love you," she smiled, accepting his kiss and melting beneath his touch.

Lord Lichfield watched his son pound back down the stairs, scowl at him, and slam the door as he left. Shaking his head, he smiled to himself.

Life was good, he mumbled, *life was very good indeed.*

***

Simone leaned against the back of the seat as the cab pulled into the outskirts of London. The many lanes of traffic circling through the city reminded her of a swarm of red ants intent on piling a mound high above the water level to protect their queen. Hundreds of people walked among the historic buildings, flooding together in waves of hot bodies to cross the streets.

Glancing at her hand, she caressed the paper Lady Lichfield had given her. She could recite its contents, she'd read it so many times.

The dragon will once more roam the earth as one Dancer and one Ancient entwine together beneath the power of the spell. Drake and Arnot forever twisted in a knot that neither Heaven nor Earth can separate.

It was written in bold script, repeating itself over and over until the two lines covered every inch of the page. The anger of a teenage boy battling against a prophecy his mother insisted he learn was present in every scrawled letter.

At the end of the page, one word mocked her. *NEVER!*

She closed her eyes, a bitter laugh burning her lips. If only their problems were this simple.

***

Simone tossed the plastic hotel key on the dresser, stepped out of her shoes, and sat down on the edge of the bed. She'd arrived at Heathrow and discovered that the first available flight to Atlanta departed at three the next afternoon. It was now almost nine, and her stomach screamed loudly about its lack of fuel. Picking up the Four Season's directory, she perused the room service menu.

The menu was creative and sumptuous. She wasn't hungry. Yes she was, the rumbling in her stomach insisted. Food wasn't appealing. Life without Trent wasn't appealing. Shaking her thoughts away, she made a quick call downstairs, ordered mini Lobster Burgers and a pot of tea, and prayed silently that her system would hold them down.

She hurt.

Every emotional fiber stung and burned.

This was pure torture.

The last time she'd allowed herself to feel this way had been in college. When she discovered the suicide note left by Jessie's father, the abandonment and bewilderment left her temporarily unable to function.

The next day, a truck arrived at their rented apartment and strangers packed his belongings and left her alone with her grief and her unborn child. His parents refused her calls. They purposely denied her access to his funeral, blaming their son's death on her.

She'd never spoken to them again.

Alone at twenty, Simone swore never to become vulnerable, never to become open for this type of invasion into her soul.

Until now.

Trent Arnot flashed his mesmerizing sapphire eyes and demanded her heart.

Hadn't thirteen years of self-imposed independence taught her anything?

Yes.

It taught her that the only important thing in this life was her daughter.

"Jessie," she cried and picked the phone up once more.

She listened to the ring trill several times then a breathless voice answered.

"Delores?" she asked.

"Simone, sugar, how are you?"

Simone closed her eyes, blocking the tears that sprung as she allowed her best friend's drawl to seep in. "I'm fine. Would Jessie be around?"

"You don't sound fine, honey. What's the matter?" Delores

demanded.

"I'll be home tomorrow," Simone sighed.

"He did it didn't he? Randy'll rip him a new you-know-what if that man steps one foot upon American soil."

"Did what? What are you talking about?"

"He broke your heart. Randy said you'd fallen in love. He said you were head-over-heels. He said that British fella would hurt you."

Simone sat up more alarmed by her friend's reiteration of Randy's words than by the fact that she was right. "Since when do you listen to what Randy says?" Oh wow, she smiled to herself. What had her living arrangements done? "Delores? What's going on over there?" Simone asked when her last question was met with total silence.

"I'll get Jessie," her friend finally said.

Simone chuckled. Delores had obviously seen the change in her ex-husband. She'd always been sad about their divorce, but it had been for the best. When they split five years earlier, Randy was self-centered and arrogant. Without his wife and child, he'd grown up. She now saw that he'd learned that sacrifice for the family was an important aspect of marriage. Sacrifice. That one little word meant more than the dictionary could ever define.

If her friend wanted to spend the rest of her life with the pain-in-the-butt Sheriff, then she'd support her. Especially considering the fact that he had somehow managed to do an about turn and morph into a responsible adult.

"Mama? Are you there?"

Her daughter's voice brought forth a rush of tears, and Simone wiped them away quickly not wanting her to worry. "Hey, baby. How are you?"

"I miss you," she whined, stirring another fresh batch of salty rivers.

Sniffling, Simone squeezed her eyes tightly. "I'll be home tomorrow afternoon. How's that?"

"Is Trent coming with you?"

The hitch of excitement in Jessie's young voice shattered whatever few pieces of her heart were left. Damn, she swore silently. It hadn't occurred to her that Jessie would be hurt because of her foolishness. "No, sugar, he won't be coming with me."

"Oh," Jessie mumbled. "When will he be back?"

"Sweetie, it's not like that. He was only doing his job and now that job is over. I couldn't help him."

"I don't understand Mama, I thought . . ."

Simone could hear the frustration and confusion in Jessie's voice. *How could I have been so stupid,* she berated herself. "Jessie? I'm sorry. I'm truly sorry for any pain that I've caused you." Simone's eyes stung once more.

"Oh no, Mama, don't be sorry. I love you and can't wait to see you. Just you and me, remember? Against the whole world."

Simone hiccupped and smiled beneath her tears. Then started laughing when she heard Randy Tippens swearing up a storm in the background, threatening Trent with all sorts of bodily dismemberment. She shook her head and thought how wonderful it would be to be home. These were the people who loved her. These were the only ones that counted. "I'll see you soon, baby. Would you ask Delores to drop my car off at our usual spot in the airport?"

"Sure, Mama. I love you."

"I love you more."

***

Stepping from the cool airport into the staggering humidity of Atlanta, Simone inhaled deeply. She was home. She stopped briefly, shedding her jacket and readjusting her luggage. With a quick jog, she crossed the busy traffic into the soothing shade of the daily parking garage.

Several years ago, she and Delores had worked out this routine. Her black Mustang was in the block of parking spots they always used. She had to walk a bit farther, but there was never a chance of not having an available space.

Slipping behind the wheel, she revved the engine, opened the top, and sped out of the airport and into the late afternoon rush hour. It would take her more than two hours to reach her house, but she didn't mind. She smiled and waved at other cars, grinning from ear to ear. Home.

A quick call to Jessie via cell phone confirmed that Randy would be dropping her by after supper. Delores had insisted. *Go home*, she'd said. *Take a shower, relax, and then be ready to be tackled by your daughter.* Simone couldn't wait.

Finally free of traffic, she sped up the twenty mile length of 575 and off into the country roads. Over the roar of the wind, she could hear the ruckus being kicked up by the late spring birds. She inhaled the wonderful scent of newly cut grass and rolled hay and basked in the warmth of the sun beating upon her shoulders.

Pulling into her drive, Simone absorbed everything. Her Magnolia's were heavily laden with flowers. In the morning, she would cut some branches and scatter them around the house. The lemon scent would smell heavenly. She realized that it was time to replace her pansies with cosmos and impatiens. And the garden, she recognized with a jolt, needed serious work. Wow, she'd not even been gone a week and her entire estate required trimming and cutting back. There must have been a deluge of rain.

It would be good to dig her hands in the soil. Her plants would come alive beneath her tender care, and she'd reap the rewards with fresh vegetables and beautiful bouquets.

Parking the car in the garage, Simone gathered her purse and packages that contained an assortment of gifts for Jessie and decided to come back for her suitcase later. She walked across the pathway and stopped before her front porch.

Trent Arnot leaned against the ornately trimmed post, glaring fiercely into her face.

"Trent," she said, her voice breathless with surprise. "What are you doing here?"

"Might I ask you the same question?"

Chapter Twenty-Seven

The cold anger that laced his words stopped Simone's heart. He was furious with her for leaving; but if he only knew what the cost of her love would be, he'd never have crossed the ocean to find her. "You have to leave. I don't want Jessie involved."

"I already told you, Jessie's not involved. I would never risk her."

"I don't want you here."

"Really? Maybe you should have considered that before you threw yourself at me yesterday. Or was it the day before? I can't remember. Seduction and prophecy tend to muddle my mind. I can't always keep my priorities straight when under that spell."

Simone went numb.

She didn't want to hear these bitter words prompted by his hurt and what he thought was her betrayal. But the alternative was to come clean and that wasn't acceptable. "You're good, Sherlock," she said, ignoring the painful twist in her heart. "Real good. You almost had me fooled." Feed the anger and he'll go away.

He narrowed his eyes, their ocean depths swirling into a watery storm. "You were a little slow on the uptake, Watson, but I'm glad to see you finally caught on."

She gasped. This went beyond cruel. "I suggest you leave, before I call the police."

"No can do, love. Besides, I believe the police are already on their way."

"And why would that be?"

"Because Lawrence Gideon is back in Atlanta. As long as he's here, so am I. I won't crowd you this time."

His sad smile pulled at her heart. Something flittered within the azure depths that spoke the fallacy of his words. Simone frowned. The memory of their first few days spent together, before this intense tangle of convoluted feelings, threatened to spring forth another bout of tears. She swore silently. Never, in her entire adult life, had she cried this much. "I suppose there'd be no reason to crowd me. You've already gotten what you wanted." Keep him distant.

He pushed away from the pillar, clenching his teeth in anger. Simone stepped back. He strode down the stairs, leaning close and whispering hoarsely within her ear. "I haven't come close to getting what I wanted," then jogged past her as the sound of police sirens assaulted her ears.

She whirled around as a cruiser skidded to a stop in her driveway. Randy Tippens stepped out and spoke hurriedly to Trent. Scanning the car, she walked closer looking for Jessie. The two men turned and headed in her direction. Trent's face was white, and she widened her eyes in alarm as his hands shook slightly. Randy reached her first and gathered her in an awkward embrace.

"Where's Jessie?" she asked.

"Simone," Trent interjected, pulling her away from Randy. Randy snatched her back tossing a warning glance at the MI-5 agent.

"Stop yanking on me like a rag doll and tell me where my daughter is!"

"Jessie's missing."

Simone froze. She narrowed her eyes and glanced from Randy to Trent. This was a trick. It had to be. "What have you done with her?"

Trent frowned and shook his head.

"What have you done with my daughter?" Tears welled and her knees buckled. Randy reached for her and pulled her into his arms.

"Simone, I have to leave. I have to find out what's happened."

She nodded and swallowed. "Where was she? How did this happen?"

Randy shook his head. "I'm not sure. I'll find out more information. Delores drove them to the grocery store. Jessie went to the ladies room and never came back."

Kidnapped. Simone's world tipped to the left, righted, and flipped over as fear clutched her heart. She turned to Trent, and the anguish written across his face clearly spoke of the affection he felt for her daughter. Randy left to receive an update from his deputy. She stood alone, her arms wrapped tightly around her waist, an uncontrollable shaking racking her body. Trent stared into her face.

"Come here," he whispered.

She shook her head.

"Come here," he repeated.

Tears fell, snaking a salty river down her cheeks. She shuffled forward, and he crossed the distance in two strides, wrapping her within his arms and crushing her to his chest.

"You did this, Trent. You did this to Jessie."

He froze and pushed her away.

"How could you say that?"

"I heard you," she cried. "When you were talking to Kathryn, remember?"

He frowned and then looked up at her through narrowed eyes. "I explained that conversation, Simone. It was a ruse."

"No," she replied hotly. "How am I to believe you when everything you've told me from the very beginning has either been full of lies or absent of the full truth. You set her up."

"The only person set up, is Kathryn. She's currently sitting in jail faced with felony charges. She went against direct orders by planning to involve your daughter."

"I don't understand." She wanted to strike out at him, to blame him for this mess. If this was his fault, then he'd fix it. He'd know how to find Jessie.

"Simone," Trent pleaded. "I would never harm you or your daughter. Please believe me. I don't know how many times I have to repeat myself on that subject. I love Jessie."

She narrowed her eyes and allowed him to pull her closer.

"I'm sorry," he exhaled. "I'm so very sorry. I'll find Bromley and personally put a bullet between his eyes. I should have made sure I went to Jessie before you. But I couldn't. I had to see you."

Simone squeezed her eyes. It was too much. Gazing into his face, the worry and love that shone from his haunting eyes gutted her. "You have to go," she whispered. "I'll handle Lawrence Gideon."

He stared incredulously into her face, shaking his head. "What on earth made you say that?"

She sighed and reached up to trace a finger across his chin. The risk of their acceptance of one another was too great. He must leave. A sudden flash of gold caught her eye. The setting sun was reflecting against the lights on the police cruiser, glittering fiercely into everyone's eyes.

Simone knew what had to be done. She glanced up and grabbed Trent's attention. "You can't remain here. You'll die." She spoke rapidly, preventing his interruption. "It always happens that way. I think it's some part of the twisted prophecy. And if you don't die . . ." Simone stopped, not wanting to explain the aspect of immortality. "Lawrence Gideon can't hurt Jessie until he's dealt with me. Remember? He thinks she's the one."

Trent nodded. "I know," he whispered, his voice hoarse with an emotion she couldn't read. "But I'll be dammed if I'm going anywhere. I don't care what you say will happen."

"You'll die," she insisted, wishing he would take her seriously.

"Then, I die." He released her, turning and walking toward Sheriff Tippens. Another police cruiser pulled up her drive, and the men began unloading monitoring equipment. Ian exited the last car, talking animatedly into his cell phone.

She knew what they were doing. In the belief that Lawrence Gideon would call here, they were going to bug the lines and record his messages. They were right. He wanted her, and he was going to get her. Squaring her shoulders, Simone crossed the front yard and headed for the back. She stood in the center of her carpet-like grass and tilted her head to the sky. Small bats flew back and forth consuming unsuspecting flying insects.

A purple haze spread across the horizon, the gloaming had settled upon her small corner of the world. It brought pain and anguish she'd never imagined possible.

Squeezing her eyes tightly shut, Simone dug deep within, searching and unburying.

It was there. The emerald dragon.

With an effort that had sweat pouring from her brow, she focused inward sinking into a realm deeper than one she'd visited before. Grael was far away.

Lightning flashed across the horizon, wind skidded around the house and thunder shook the ground. Raising her arms, she screamed to the heavens.

"Grael."

Her plea was answered.

Splinters of jagged light assaulted the sky and deafening drum rolls echoed across the valley. The link sliced her soul. She staggered back, kneeling beneath the onslaught of sensations. The pain was intense; she battled against the power that shattered her nerves. The dragon had been right. The farther apart they were, the harder it was to reconnect.

In the place where a broken woman had recently stood, Simone raised her head and embraced the power. Her body tingled, her eyes burned. Lawrence Gideon was going to die.

She *was* a Dragon Dancer. And instead of stuffing Grael's magic into a corner she allowed it to flow in abandon through her soul.

"I hadn't expected this," Grael hissed. Her annoyance shimmered within Simone like turbulent air.

"Lord Bromley has Jessie," she answered silently.

"Ah, the human fool who believes he can gain my power by your death," annoyance instantly replaced by concern, "let's fly." She screamed, breaking free of Simone's physical constraints. This time the dragon didn't streak through the air alone, she pulled on Simone's essence.

Simone held tightly to the dragon's visceral form. They spun upward, through the trees and into the night sky.

Her eyes scanned the ground below. Men were scrambling beneath the onslaught of the sudden storm, confusion written across their faces. Except for one. Trent stood aside, his hand shielding his eyes from the buffering wind and searched the sky. She watched as he raced around the house to find her body sprawled on the grass. Simone didn't care. She would fly with the dragon until she found her daughter.

"Where are you going, Grael?"

"I'm following her essence. Your spawn is as much a part of you as am I. I'll find her."

They dipped across the tree line and banked to the left. Simone watched the blur of leaves sway beneath the powerful current of the creature's ethereal wings. Trying to focus on where Grael was going, she blocked Trent's anxious calling.

"Tell your mate to be quiet, I can't concentrate."

"He's not my mate, and I can't tell him a thing. I'm with you, remember?"

"Haven't you learned anything?"

Simone bit back her mental retort and gasped as she realized where they were going.

"I know where Jessie is, Grael. We need to return, now."

The dragon swung around in a dizzying turn that took Simone's virtual breath away.

She could fade back to her body and leave Grael to the skies, but she wasn't ready for that yet. She needed her power.

Slipping once more into her skin, Simone opened her eyes and stared into the shocked depths of sapphire pools. He held her fiercely to his chest, yelling into her face.

"What have you done?"

"I know where Jessie is." She wiggled from his grasp. "Come on let's find Lawrence Gideon while we have the upper hand." Struggling to her feet, she accepted his hand and stood.

"Hello, Grael," he said, the disdain clearly evident within his voice.

"She says we don't really need you," Simone answered, walking into the house.

"Dancer," Grael whispered in her head, "why are you angry with your Ancient? This is the first time in over four centuries your souls have reunited. You should use his power."

"Use him?" Simone stuttered. "What power?" She could feel the dragon's confusion and shook her head, silently beseeching the beast to be quiet.

"I thought you were going to study the books," Grael said.

"I did."

The dragon hissed again. "Obviously none of the right segments."

"Where are we going?" Trent called, running to catch up with her.

"To my favorite camp grounds. It'll take us almost an hour to reach them so we have to hurry."

"Did you see Jessie? Is she all right?"

Simone couldn't believe what an idiot she was. She should have checked on her daughter. "Grael?"

The dragon flew from her mind, leaving her breathless. Simone turned and confronted Trent.

"Grael's gone to check."

"You need to stay here to take Lawrence's call. Tell me where the site is, and I'll rescue Jessie."

"He doesn't even know I'm back," she cried. "He won't be calling here."

Trent furrowed his brow. "You might be right, but he's slicker than a snake. I wouldn't be surprised if he's monitoring the flights."

"I'll forward the calls to my cell phone, okay?"

He stared at her long and hard, the deep blue depths of his eyes penetrating her skin and searching her soul . "Don't dance off with Grael, again. You bloody-well scared me to death."

She couldn't help the grin. Is that what she'd done? Danced? It had been invigorating to feel the world through the dragon's mind, the complexity of color and scent difficult for her human senses to absorb.

The power that rippled along her skin when Grael was in her presence hinted at the amazing depths of magic the dragon and Dancer possessed.

Need for the safety of her daughter allowed her to accept the destiny of Dragon Dancer. Her breath caught when she realized that if her resistance to Trent lessened, she'd be unable to control her heart. She'd take from him what it desired. His soul.

***

Trent maneuvered Simone's Mustang along the narrow, back roads of the Oconee National Forest. Heavily wooded land encompassed the majority of the foothills at the base of the Smoky Mountains.

Simone's golden eyes reflected with disturbing brilliance the presence of her dragon. He didn't know what force now guided her heart. Bloody hell, he loved her beyond reason. And it killed him to know he was going to use that love and twist it into something more calculating than Kathryn's double cross.

He was going to steal Grael at the one moment in time when Simone needed her most.

Darkness had fallen, casting eerie shadows from the hundred foot trees that clung to the edge of the narrow road.

A hairpin turn focused his attention back to the road. Tippens and the rest of the Sheriff's department were approaching the campsite through the official Ranger entrance. If the plan went accordingly, then Jessie would be safe in her mother's arms within the hour.

The car hit gravel, and he slowed to a crawl. Simone peered through the window. Her head bobbed back and forth, and she muttered beneath her breath. Grael must be hounding her with questions.

"Pull off here, Trent. If we want to catch him by surprise, we'll have to walk the remaining mile."

He pulled the vehicle into a small parking area. Campers and tents jutted out from both sides of the road. Their fires snapped and crackled and soft laughter filtered through the evening air. "Are there this many people within your campsite?"

"No," she shook her head. "I camp by a creek that is part of the Appalachian Trail. It's not considered an official site. There won't be anyone for miles."

"How do you think he discovered it?" Trent asked, curious about this side of Simone he'd never seen. He didn't consider her a rough-it kind of gal.

"Everyone in town knows I camp here. He'd only have to ask."

He nodded and grabbed a backpack from the trunk. Holstering his gun, he handed Simone a small pistol which she handed right back. "I detest guns."

"Don't be ridiculous. You need protection."

"I have Grael," she insisted.

His heart clenched.

"There's something you should know, Simone," he whispered.

"What?" she asked, heading into the darker depths of the forest, moving as silently as possible.

"It's about Grael."

She sighed and turned to him. "I'm going to use her power. You have to trust me on this."

"I know that, love. I expect you to accept every aspect of this prophecy," he stared at her for a long moment, her eyes glowing brightly in the night and held back on the desire to lean forward and kiss away the frown of concern for Jessie. "I'd never ask of you what you couldn't give, but I have to explain a part of the legacy that might help us."

She narrowed her eyes, golden liquid heating his heart and causing a want that had the power to mar his better judgment, his greatest fear suddenly in control.

"How can I convince you not to come with me?" she pleaded. "I can't allow you to be mine, if that's what you're asking from me-- anything else I have is yours."

He frowned, definitely confused. "What are we talking about?"

She sighed and tugged on her ponytail. "This," she shrugged and waved her hand between them. "It's not enough for what this prophecy demands."

He stood back, crossing his arms over his chest. He checked his watch and verified they were still on schedule. Tippens' men would be in place within the hour, and then they could move forward.

"You're trying to change destiny, right?" he asked.

"I'm trying to do what's best for us."

"What happens when it doesn't work?"

She chewed her bottom lip. "I'm not certain I understand what you're saying."

Neither was he. "If you die because of your refusal to follow what history tells us we must do, then what happens to me?" How would he survive without her by his side? He wouldn't.

After tonight, Trent would be her enemy. If he survived, he would own Grael. Simone would never forgive him.

"I'm confused . . ." she began, interrupted by the crackle of his radio.

He answered Tippens and verified their location. With a wave of his hand, he signaled Simone to follow him. They needed to reach the site.

He wove his fingers through hers, reveling in the intimacy. Trent focused on Jessie. The despair becoming minimal compared to the anger he directed at Lawrence Gideon. The man was going to pay. He'd taken from Trent.

A vision of Jessie's laughing eyes and memories of her girlish squeals hardened his heart. He squeezed Simone's hand, reassuring her with a tight smile his resolve to rescue her daughter.

Forty minutes later, Simone held her hand up.

Dropping to the ground, they belly-crawled their way to the edge of a ridge. Simone inhaled sharply and scrambled to her feet.

"Grael," she shouted to the empty night air.

The dragon shimmered around her and peered at them with golden orbs that matched Simone's eyes.

"Find them," Simone commanded, as the ghostly beast flew into the night. Trent's stomach twisted as another knot of fear yanked and wound around his gut.

"They're gone," he said, confirming the cause of Simone's anguished expression.

He wasn't certain what to do, but he closed his eyes and shut out the noise of the approaching vehicles. Trent opened his heart, focused on the love he felt for the woman beside him and cast the power buried within into the night. His breath caught as he felt it link with the essence of Grael.

"Ancient! Be gone."

"I'm sorry." He wove his magic around the emerald light that shone from the dragon, snapping the thin line that linked her with Simone.

Julie Korzenko

Chapter Twenty-Eight

Trent narrowed his eyes and searched Simone's face. She was on the verge of collapse. He held her hand and helped her down the ridgeline and into the recently abandoned campsite. He'd radioed Tippens and the slamming of car doors, bellowed orders and flashing lights indicated they'd arrived. It would take them several minutes before they reached the ravine.

He forced Simone to sit down. Proceeding with caution, Trent scanned his surroundings. The remnants of a fire smoked within a pit, its coals dampened by water. There were piles of leaves pushed to the side and a cleared area where chairs had been set out. He figured Lawrence Gideon had only recently vacated this site.

Tippens reached his side and directed his men to set up lights. His forensics specialist arrived with her bag of equipment and quickly went to work.

"I reissued an APB to cover all the counties within this area," Randy said.

Trent nodded and frowned. "What game is he playing?"

"I don't know Arnot, but I'm not liking this one bit."

"He wants Simone," Trent said.

"Are you sure?"

"Yes. He can't complete this insane ceremony without her." Trent quickly filled the Sheriff in on what they'd discovered at Blithewoods.

"Is Jessie normal then?" Randy asked with a shake of his head.

"What do you mean by that?" Trent responded.

"She's not like Simone. She's not, ummm . . ." he shuffled his feet and refused to meet Trent's eyes.

"She's not what?" He persisted, a sudden understanding dawning on him.

"Weird, you know. Special?"

"Jessie's a normal thirteen year old girl, if that's what you're asking. As far as Simone is concerned, I can see by the look in your eyes that you don't deserve my respect." Trent clenched his jaw. He wanted to deck this guy, but he needed him.

"I was only a kid," he defended himself.

"I'm sure you were," he spun on his heels and headed in Simone's direction.

"Hey Arnot," Randy called. "At least I didn't break her heart."

Trent ignored him. What the hell was he going on about? He certainly hadn't broken Simone's heart. But, he now understood why she'd always fought against what lay within her soul. It was one thing to be raised by a mother who shoved ridiculous prophecy down your throat on a daily basis and another to be an innocent caught in the clutches of its power.

If he had listened to his mother and accepted his future maybe Simone could have seen him differently. The thought that his pride and ignorance might have cost him the love of his life stabbed deep within his gut.

Trent watched as Simone grabbed hold of Ian's hand. She clung to him with the desperation of a hungry child. Ignoring the grip of jealousy constricting his chest, he hurried in their direction.

Trent paused, the call of Simone's dragon rippled across the night. He knew without a doubt what was needed. His mind focused, and he gathered his power. As if sensing his next move, Grael bellowed in his direction. He saw the golden tendril that linked the beast to Simone and with a sharp blast of energy, snapped it clean with blue fire. The dragon screamed in fury and fought the bonding. But he won. He knotted a ribbon of blue fire into the golden strands of Grael's spirit and held tight.

He inhaled deeply and switched focus to the issue at hand. "Ian, would you kindly inform headquarters about this latest development? I 'm going to take Simone home."

His partner nodded and then flipped open his cell phone. Trent peered into Simone's ashen face. "Has she come back?" He spoke softly making sure no one could hear.

"No," she cried. "I can't even feel her link."

"What? Is that normal?" Couldn't she tell? He needed to confirm that Simone wouldn't turn on him before he had a chance to reach Gideon.

"I don't know. I'm not particularly up-to-date on all the ins and outs of being a Dragon Dancer," she snapped then bit her lip.

He pulled her into his arms and hugged her. "Let's go home," he whispered against the top of her head. "Maybe things will be clearer there." Grael screeched and slammed against his head. Simone nodded, her head moving against his chest. Trent pulled them up the ridge, mentally chewing on the disappearance of Jessie.

They drove in silence, both lost in their thoughts. Worry and concern for Jessie overriding any attempt at light conversation. He prayed they'd be in time. As Trent pulled into the end of Simone's drive, he noted a soft glow lighting the back of the house.

"He's here," she whispered, leaning forward and gripping the dashboard like it was a lifeline.

He reached over, caressing her chin with his thumb and turning her so that he could study her face. He peered into the depths of her variegated eyes.

"Where's Grael?"

"I don't know," she admitted, a frown knitting her brow.

"Stay here," he mumbled, turning off the ignition. She'd find out soon enough.

"No way," she answered, quietly exiting the car and latching on to the back of his shirt. "That bastard has my daughter."

"There's something I need to tell you," Trent whispered, slowly making his way up her drive. He figured now would be a good time to explain about his ability to wrestle Grael from her mind. The dragon was currently screeching her defiance at an insane mental decibel level that threatened to crack his brain.

He had been silently imploring her to be quiet, but she refused to listen. Simone's reference to a six-week old puppy pouncing around your head was an understatement.

"Just find my daughter," she said. "We'll talk later."

They reached her front porch.

Low chants resonated from the back of the house. Pausing, Trent signaled Simone to stay on the porch. She shook her head violently, insisting on joining him. He turned his blazing eyes on her face no longer able to control the soul of the dragon, and her look of absolute shock told him that his normally blue gaze now glittered gold.

"What have you done?"

"I took Grael." He stated simply. "Remain here while I deal with Lawrence Gideon. I have what he wants."

"How could you do that?" she sat suddenly. Her shoulders slumped and a tear snaked down her cheek. "I don't understand."

"The one who loves the Dancer is the one who can gain control of her dragon." His heart clenched as he repeated what his mother had shown him within The White Book.

"How cruel life is?" she whispered, pulling away from him.

"I have to go," he insisted. "Stay right here, I'll explain later."

"Trent?"

"I know, love. We'll work this out." He raced around the house and into the back yard. He understood that if she ever wrestled the dragon from him, he would die. It was a risk he gladly took.

Lawrence Gideon had lashed an unconscious Jessie to the tire swing. He stood within the clearing of grass, a ring of candles surrounding him. Trent chastised Grael with a sharp word. He was amazed that the dragon immediately ceased her complaints. It was the presence of Jessie, the beast sensed; it appeared to calm her.

"Lord Bromley," Trent spoke quietly. His gun rested firmly within his fist.

The man turned slowly around. He was dressed, once more, all in black and his profile became muted with the night. His eyes, however, burned their feverish insanity into the center of Trent's soul.

"Mr. Arnot," he said his voice low and rattling with phlegm. "How predictable."

"I believe you have something of mine?" Trent asked, glancing at Jessie. She didn't appear to be harmed, but it was difficult to tell with the shadows. A movement from the corner of his eye caught his attention. Simone walked through the house and came to stand upon the back deck. Her arms were straight out in front, and she grasped a wavering gun between her hands.

"Go back inside Simone and call Sheriff Tippens. I'll handle this."

"I think you've handled enough, all ready, Agent Arnot. It's time Lawrence Gideon and I had a little coming-to-Jesus-party." She stepped down, continuing to point the gun at Bromley's chest.

He sneered. Bending over, he picked up an item from the bag at his feet. Simone and Trent both disengaged the safety on their weapons and aimed to fire.

"Where'd you learn to use that weapon?" Trent whispered. "I thought you detested guns."

"I do. Randy made me and Delores take a weapons class a few years back."

"You need to go into the house. Gun or no gun, I can't protect you and grab Jessie at the same time."

"If you hadn't stolen Grael, I wouldn't need protecting." She countered an angry huff to her voice.

"Excuse me," Lawrence Gideon interjected. "Can we put the bickering aside for the moment? I have a function to attend later this evening."

That snapped Trent's attention back to the task at hand. "I'm sorry to be the bearer of bad news, but I don't think you're going to make it."

"Oh," Lord Bromley murmured, "That's where you're wrong."

"Sorry, blister-boy, but I have to disagree." Simone retaliated as she stepped around Lawrence Gideon and went to her daughter's side.

Lawrence Gideon grinned wickedly and tossed an object at her face. She ducked and it slammed into her shoulder. Wincing slightly, Simone ignored it. Her attention remaining focused on Lawrence Gideon. Trent frowned when he realized it was Mary, Queen of Scots' jewel encrusted cross.

Simone kicked it aside and glanced at Trent. They both shrugged. He stepped toward Bromley, intent on apprehending the man.

As he passed Simone and Jessie, he reached down and scooped up the cross.

Grael screeched madly in his mind. His body felt as it was being ripped apart, forcing him to his knees. Shadows, dark and gray, moved forward from every corner of the yard. His eyes watered and fear clutched at his heart.

He had to fight this.

Simone was in danger.

Grabbing for his gun, he swiped at the tears that were blocking his vision. He inhaled sharply when his hands came away bloody.

What was going on?

Simone screamed, and the world spun.

Unearthly fingers stretched forward, seizing his body in a deadly embrace.

***

Lawrence Gideon bellowed his anger at the sky. Simone spun on her heels and aimed the barrel of the gun at his chest.

"What have you done?" she yelled. The vision of Trent's bloodied face, burning her senses. In the darkened night, she had barely been able to make out the ghostly apparition of Grael twisting in agony, slamming her head from side to side. She didn't know if Trent was alive.

"He has the soul!" Lord Bromley said. "Your efforts to deceive are wasted. The wraiths will kill."

"The wraiths?" Simone's eyes widened. "You're responsible for the gray-uglies?"

Lawrence didn't respond.

"What have you done?" she screamed at him.

"That cross will steal the dragon's soul." A smile twisted his face. "And then its power will be mine."

Simone shook her head. "You've left a bloody trail of bodies in search of your dragon. Was it the shadows? Did they tell you what to do?" Find the source of the wraiths. She repeated this to herself, remaining focused. "The shadows have been around longer than that cross, haven't they?"

"The cross is pure evil," he insisted. "I fed it with the blood of a Dancer. The shadows are drawn to its power and do its bidding."

"What are you talking about?"

Lord Bromley laughed. "Are you so vain to believe you're the only Dancer to exist?"

Simone narrowed her eyes. "I know I'm not."

"The gray tendrils showed me. They led me to a woman that lived not far beyond the boundaries of my home. I worked her over for more than a week, but the dragon that lay within her wouldn't appear."

"Who was this woman?" Simone was certain it was the Jane Doe.

"No one important. She wasn't even of pure blood, but I lured her into friendship and unearthed her knowledge of the old tales. She confirmed the prophecy. The shadows liked her."

"You murdered her like you did my sister. They never caught you."

Lawrence shrugged. "Case unsolved. It made me brave and maybe a bit careless. After all, your Ancient has been rather persistent. But no matter. The wraiths stole the dragon scent from that woman empowering them and have hunted you and your kind ever since. As we speak, they're tearing your loved one to shreds hungry for another dragon soul."

She ignored her panic and need to help Trent. "The wraiths do your bidding? How will you use the dragon's power if they seek to destroy it?"

"Not destroy, my dear. They want the power and control. And in order for that to happen, it must channel through me."

Simone sifted through this information. "How is this so? The cross was fed with magic not shadows."

Lawrence Gideon smiled, the lopsided twist of his lips an evil slash against his face. "There is a great power behind those shadows. It knows. It tells."

"Tells what?"

"Spells and magic."

"You're the one who has done all this? Spun this evil? Twisted a benign cross into a weapon?"

"Perhaps." He edged closer. "You're braver than your mother. When I took your father's life, she blubbered like a new born infant. What a weakness. It removed all the challenge from stealing her last breath."

"You are mad."

"Maybe. But not for much longer. Step out of my way; I will have the dragon's soul!"

Simone narrowed her eyes. She glanced at her daughter and confirmed that Jessie appeared all right. Her body was draped over the tire swing, but her eyes were open and attentive. She nodded at her daughter and turned her attention back to Lawrence.

"Dementia," she stated with a slight smile, "comes in all shapes and forms. Yours, I'm afraid, will be the death of you."

"No one has been able to stop me." He laughed madly, sending a shiver of revulsion skittering down her spine. "My search for you has been enthralling. Who'd ever have guessed that the beast lay within the soul of my silly sister's offspring? It's been a delightful journey."

"You killed them all? You killed all my cousins because of some stupid power you believe you can gain?"

"I want to be whole," he hissed, spittle smacking Simone in the face. She grimaced and wiped the offending saliva from her cheek. "The dragon will cure my disease. I've spent my life traveling to foreign countries, dedicated to the well-being of others. I deserve this."

"You are one sick flea, Lawrence Gideon. It disgusts me to know that we're related in any manner."

He lurched for her, and she staggered backwards, her foot snagging on a root. She fell to the ground, her gun flinging out of her hand and firing wildly into the night.

She landed with a jolt beside Trent's body. Bromley had retrieved her gun and now pointed it at Jessie.

"One shot," he cackled, "then two." Twisting around, he waved the threatening barrel at her face. "And the dragon will be mine."

Simone felt a hand close over hers. She gripped Trent's fingers; they were moist with the blood that seeped from his eyes.

She stared at the only man she would ever love. Why had they wasted so many precious moments?

"I will always love you," he said, attempting to pull her closer. Her heart clenched, and she fought back the pain that twisted her soul.

How long had she waited for those words? Days? Weeks? Centuries!

He was dying.

"And I you," she answered and kissed him gently on the lips. He exhaled softly, his breath warm against her mouth.

The heat lasted a brief second. His last breath, her taste of power.

Trent's eyes fluttered closed, and her soul split. The pain wrenched her heart and poured through her entire being.

He slid from her embrace, leaving her arms empty and cold. Simone tipped her head back to the sky and screamed her loss. Grael slammed into her body, spreading magic through every nerve.

The dragon penetrated Simone's soul, feeding the fire of her grief. Her anger at her enemy knocked down the final wall that separated Dancer from dragon. She welcomed the fury of the beast. Embraced its essence.

Her chest constricted, the world spun in a dizzying array of noise, scent and taste. The grass felt thick and smooth beneath her hands, and she heard the distant echo of a whippoorwill as if the bird sat upon her shoulder. Grael whispered in her ear.

"Stand up, little one."

With a sob, she struggled to her feet. "I don't know what to do."

"You are a Dragon Dancer."

The dragon flashed images within Simone's mind.

Seren stood alone upon a hill top sheathed in snow. She raised her hands to the heavens, undulating to the rhythm of an unseen power. Sparks scattered around like a swarm of fireflies. Grael rose from the earth beneath the first Dragon Dancer and flew into the night, the dragon's grief washed from the past and embraced Simone. Seren collapsed upon the ground, her power spent. Her life gone.

Elizabeth molted into the scene, dancing with abandonment. Fire singed the ground and licked the hem of her chemise. Simone inhaled sharply, recognizing the evil that followed her every step. The shadows. Elizabeth laughed at them, opening her arms and embracing the swell of darkness. Through the black shadows, the woman's pain called to Simone.

And she understood.

There was evil, and there was good. She possessed a power that was craved by both light and dark. It filled her soul, caressed her mind. There were choices to be made. She could lie down as Seren did and follow her lover into the night or turn her hatred and anger at love's demise and embrace the evil that haunted her every move.

"That's right, little one." Grael's voice was soft, patient.

"I'm not Seren, and I'm not Elizabeth."

"Choose!" The dragon demanded.

She felt the passing of Trent. He moved through her, with a blast of love that swept her heart and cleansed her mind. Closing her eyes against the emptiness that lay behind her, she turned and faced her enemy.

Biting back tears, she raised her hand in Lord Bromley's direction. He would pay.

"You wanted dragon?" She screamed against the wind that suddenly whipped around them in a cyclone. Simone glanced at Jessie. With a wave of her hand, she formed a barrier between her daughter and the man intent on taking her life. Memories washed through time, and she listened to her instincts.

Grael laughed. "That's right, Dancer. Destroy this putrid scrap of meat."

Lawrence Gideon held his arms up, shielding his face from the power that sprung forth from her in waves of anger and grief. Bolts of lightening streaked around the huddled man, slashing him like bullets.

She cocked her head and grinned. Flipping her wrist over, Simone opened her hand. Air tingled against her skin as she cupped her fingers. It tightened, feeding off the rage that dwelled within her heart. A glowing ball of fire formed, and she lifted her arm sending the blazing orb speeding toward Lawrence Gideon.

It connected with his chest, shredding his clothes and burning through his skin. He staggered and dropped to his knees. She approached, her steps sure and deadly.

"You won't kill me," his words bubbled slurred by a froth of blood.

"You are evil." Simone straightened her shoulders, glancing in disdain at his quivering body. "This is not killing. It's exterminating." She spun on her heels and headed toward her daughter. Jessie stared into Simone's face, an expression of awe and horror crossing her innocent eyes. Simone smiled and pulled her daughter from the tire swing. Holding Jessie tightly against her chest and blocking the child's view of Lawrence Gideon, she lifted her chin and gazed into Grael's golden eyes. "Finish him."

The dragon grinned, a wicked and deadly light sparking within the beast. Grael spun into the night, paused and dove toward the bloody mangled mess that was Lawrence Gideon.

Grael laughed in delight as fire tore through the night, engulfing the quivering man. The dragon didn't stop until Bromley lay at her feet, a crimson sack of smashed and burnt bones. Simone sighed and released her daughter. Closing her eyes, she reached within her soul and wove magic through her heart. She spun in a circle; arms spread wide imitating the dance she'd performed as a child. The gray-uglies melted into the night. She felt their evil tide wash beyond the hills and into oblivion. Without a vessel, they were incapacitated.

She collapsed beside Trent, cradling his body within her arms. This was too high a price to pay.

"No," she screamed to the heavens. "You can't take this man." Tears flowed in rivers. He loved her.

He loved her.

Chapter Twenty-Nine

She held onto Jessie. Simone wasn't certain who was comforting whom. The paramedics briefly managed to resuscitate Trent, but it appeared fleeting. Ian was rapidly firing instructions. His white face and clenched fists testimony to the lack of hope.

"What happened, Simone?" Randy asked, genuinely puzzled. "Lawrence Gideon looks like he's exploded from the inside out."

She offered him a watery smile and shrugged. "It must have been his disease. He had Porphyria."

"Por . . .?"

She held up her hand to block the rest of the questions and followed the stretcher to the ambulance.

"You have the power," Grael whispered softly. "Or are you giving up as Seren did?"

"What power do I have Grael?" she responded, despair twisting her heart. She sat down on the grass, pulling Jessie with her. Burying her head in her hands, her body racked with sobs.

"The power of a Dragon Dancer. Come," the dragon beckoned, "and dance with me."

Before Simone could argue, the creature sprung free of her physical constraints and soared into the night sky. Simone clung to the link, anything to escape the pain of watching her lover die. She had done that once tonight. She didn't believe she could survive the second time.

Her body collapsed against her daughter, free of the spirit that made it whole. She watched as Jessie caressed her cheek and stroked her hair, comforting Simone. Why wasn't her daughter panicked? As the child lifted her chin and gazed into the night, Simone smiled. Jessie's eyes followed the essence of her mother.

With a gasp, Simone saw Trent. He stood before her in all his glory, glittering a brilliant blue as he made his way toward her. His love blazed brightly from a soul she recognized on many different levels.

Grael embraced them in a graceful waltz. They danced across the heavens, wrapped within one another. The freedom of being one with her love, enveloped Simone. She held tight. Their love was the power. It was the key.

"Seren." The name floated around the stars, sweet music to her ears. Her heart and soul answered without hesitation.

"Trynt, my love."

"I'm sorry."

The essence she knew better than her own, faded into the night.

"No!" Where did he go?

For centuries their souls waited, wanting nothing more than to love again. She grieved for all that was not to be then drew from her heart the love for Trent, releasing it into the heavens not wanting to live without him by her side. Not even the thought of Jessie was enough to bring her sorrow under control.

Grael screamed, tipping her head back in anger.

The dragon stopped the ballet and glared at them. "Are you giving up? Ancient and Dragon Dancer--together as one are a greater power than even I."

Simone stared at Grael.

"You have a choice," she hissed.

Simone spun into the air, chasing the fading blue of her love. Wrapping her essence around his soul, she committed herself without hesitation.

Focusing on Trent's sapphire eyes, her heart beat rapidly. He nodded. Did he understand what it was she asked? Was he willing to live forever?

He reached for her, offering his soul. She didn't waver this time but captured everything he presented.

No matter what consequences lay ahead, it was his heart she wanted. He entwined his spirit with hers, a smile of acceptance lighting his face.

Grael bellowed to the heavens and suddenly Simone plummeted back to earth.

The dance finished. The prophecy fulfilled.

***

"We have a pulse and it's strong."

Simone lifted her head, gasping for air.

Before she could move, icy fingers pulled at her chest. She clutched at her daughter as they penetrated her skin, spreading in slow painful rivers through her body. The heat of Grael offset the bitter cold but Simone struggled to draw air into her lungs.

What was happening?

A sudden flash of awareness brightened her vision. Her surroundings sharpened in texture and she saw it all. The earth, the stars, the intricate web of souls and life.

Scanning her backyard, the music of night trickled forth. Its rhythm and beat pulled her in, and she closed her eyes reveling in the symphony of life. Spreading her fingers, she touched the soil and felt the pulse of Mother Nature. Her heart skipped and she gazed around in astonishment.

Staggering to her feet, she made her way to Trent. He sat on the edge of the stretcher, his head bent.

She touched his shoulder.

He glanced up and pulled her roughly against his chest. "Do you feel it?" he asked.

"Yes."

"It's beautiful." His hand stroked her hair and she wrapped her arms around him, holding tightly.

"That it is."

"I love you," he said. The ice that lingered in her veins melted from his touch. His lips found hers and she sank beneath the power of his kiss.

Running her hands through his hair, she pulled back slightly. "And I love you."

He nodded and grinned, they both laughed together.

"I gather that we have a long time to figure out all the answers."

She frowned. "How did you know?"

"Grael told me."

"Sneaky dragon."

"I don't care. You're all I've ever wanted. The prophecy be damned."

Simone kissed him and pushed away the paramedics. "I hope you still feel that way in a few thousand years."

He laughed. "You know I will."

Epilogue

Simone pushed open the French doors of her suite and stepped onto the terrace. She inhaled the chilled air and basked in the warmth of the afternoon sun. Draconius lay before her in all its stunning glory, the green hills that rolled across the horizon ending where sky met earth. If she never left here again, she'd be fine.

Behind her, Trent sat on the bed.

She prayed with all her might that Grael would find Llallogen and have an answer that she could offer Trent. But the dragon had been gone for almost a fortnight and as she watched billowing white tents being raised across the estate, anxiety kicked at her stomach.

"Immortality isn't such a bad thing." He stepped up behind her and wrapped his arms around her waist.

Simone leaned against his chest. "Yes, it is." His embrace calmed her nerves.

They'd been back in England for less than a month. She'd hardly seen him between his constant visits to MI-5 headquarters wrapping up the Bromley case and her meeting with endless bodies of people to answer questions regarding the wedding Trent's mother planned. In addition, they'd both spent hours pouring over the chronicles, editing and correcting the fallacies.

She gazed around at the white tents that draped in graceful swales of gauze and linen. This was her last night as Simone Walker. Tomorrow, she would become Simone Arnot.

"We're alive and together. It could be worse."

Simone squirmed around and glanced at his face. The warmth and love in his eyes hadn't faded but a slight frown marred his brow.

"I've been trying to work through my feelings. How can you be so blasé?" Her original thoughts regarding immortality still troubled her. What would the world be like a hundred years from now?

"What *are* your thoughts?"

"I'm not thrilled."

Trent smiled softly. "Me neither. But I'd rather spend eternity with you than a second without." He leaned forward and seized her lips with his mouth, his hunger for her apparent in the rough edge of his kiss. "Don't ever leave or try to break this spell."

She panicked. "I'd never do that. My love for you is strong and true."

He smiled and added a gentle kiss. "As is mine." She sighed, relieved that he accepted so easily.

"Grael is seeking Llallogen." They moved back to stand against the railing, trying to clear the way for the men carrying load after load of flowers. Lady Lichfield was in the process of transforming Draconius into a fairy land for their wedding.

"The wizard?"

"Yes."

"Is he still alive?"

Simone laughed at his response. "Apparently a wizard never dies."

"I didn't know that."

"Me neither."

Trent's fingers traced the edge of her chin. "And what will Llallogen do for us, love?"

"I pray he'll find a way to remove the immortality spell from our souls. I'm really not wanting to watch my child die of old age. And . . ." She paused, a pang of jealousy sticking in her gut. She'd received a phone call this morning that should've brightened her world. Instead, it made her realize all that was involved in being immortal. In being a magical creature that never aged and couldn't die. Her body would never grow old, never move forward in time.

Delores had apologized, gushing that she couldn't make the wedding. She was pregnant. She and Randy were renewing their vows the second Simone and Trent returned to the States. Pregnant? As she was frozen in time, Simone would never again feel life flourish inside, and the sadness swelled around her heart.

"And what?" Trent asked, knocking her from her thoughts.

She gazed into his eyes and whispered softly. "And I'd really love to have your child."

His face softened. He tipped his head and stared at the sky then drew in a deep ragged breath. When he glanced back at her, his eyes were bright with unshed tears. "Me too." Trent placed a kiss upon her forehead then lazily trailed his lips down her cheek until he nibbled at her lip. "It doesn't change my love."

"Grael will find the wizard. I know she will."

A door opened on one of the other terraces and Lady Lichfield waved at them. "Come on you two, we have a lot to discuss and time is short."

Trent chuckled. "I can't believe she just said that."

"If she only knew." Simone laughed and allowed her fiancé to lead her toward the dining room. The family waited. They'd decided to keep the secret of their immortality. There were too many other issues that needed resolving.

Simone followed Trent through the French doors. The room was filled with several Trent-like men. She smiled and moved among them, searching for Jessie. She found her daughter perched next to one of the Arnot brothers.

"Christian, don't let her monopolize your time."

Trent's brother grinned. "Your Jessie is precious. I'm a bit jealous that my big brother found you first."

"Flirt." She moved past him and found Francine arguing with the youngest Arnot.

"Devon, I don't care whether your head is ready to split open. You're going to sit at that table and listen to what we have to say. Now where's your older brother?"

Simone smuggled a laugh when Devon rolled his eyes. "Which one?"

Francine glanced around the room performing a head count. "Kane?"

"I'm here, Mother." The last Arnot son strode into the room. Francine waved her arms and everyone began to take seats around the dining room table.

Trent held out his hand and Simone moved to his side, sitting down next to her daughter. It'd taken Simone a few days to feel comfortable around all the men that swarmed through Draconius, sending the halls echoing with their laughter and constant pranks on one another. It was a wonderful family. One she was grateful to be a part of.

Jessie loved it. They spoiled her mercilessly.

"Okay, everyone. The reason we're here is that I'd like to review one more time the formation for tomorrow's bridal procession . . ." Everyone at the table groaned and banged their heads against its polished surface. They'd spent the past week practicing and perfecting the routine until Simone was certain she could perform it in her sleep. "Just kidding." Lady Lichfield laughed. "Simone, why don't you start?"

Simone inhaled, glancing from one set of startling blue eyes to another. "Well, there's really not much to say. You're all well versed in the prophecy. The concern that Trent and I have is that the wraiths are tied to us and will become a danger to other Dancers and Ancients. We're still learning about the power that surrounds my family and yours." She paused, taking a sip of water from the glass Trent handed her. "Without understanding what it means to be Dancer and Ancient, we're walking blind down a path that's buried in our past. I want to warn all of you that should you feel an awakening of sorts or anything odd, that you let us know immediately."

Trent leaned forward and interrupted her. "Simone and I will be leaving to go back to the States following our honeymoon. We must all stay in contact regarding any unique activity."

Francine nodded. "I agree. I shall finish translating the combined text of The White Book of Rhydderch and the Red Book of Hergest. Hopefully, it will shine a light on what we don't understand."

Devon pushed away from the table. "Do you really believe that what happened to Simone and Trent will happen to us?"

Trent shrugged. "The power of Ancients is strong in this family. We don't know. But it would be foolish to ignore the possibility that it might."

Simone nodded her head in agreement. "The wraiths will not be after Trent and me. They'll be searching for another weakness."

Everyone began talking at once. Simone frowned and reached across the table to tap Devon's hand.

"What's wrong?"

He smiled, his face so much like Trent's it startled her. "Nothing. Just a stupid headache. I probably drank too much wine last night."

"Maybe," she laughed. "But it was good. Your first harvest, right?"

"Yes. I'm very pleased with how that particular year is aging. In another five years, it'll be spectacular."

Trent squeezed her shoulder and they stood up. "We'll be outside if there are any questions."

The fresh air washed over Simone's face. It felt wonderful. They walked the length of the balcony and descended onto the soft grass, making their way through the rose garden and leaving the hectic activity surrounding the house behind.

"So what of the other dragons?" Trent asked. "Has Grael found anymore?"

Simone sighed. "She says they awaken slowly. But that they'll be drawn to me through some link in the original spell. Grael wants us back here after the holidays."

"But what about your work?"

She shrugged. "I think this is more important, don't you?"

"Yes."

"Besides, I have another small detail to take care of."

Trent smiled and nodded. "I concur Lady Bromley."

She groaned and shook her head. "Please don't call me that. I'm going to turn Blithewoods over to the National Trust."

"Are you certain? It is your heritage."

Simone nodded. "It's also the heritage of this country. I believe it'll better serve everyone as an historic site and not a private residence."

Trent hugged her tight against his chest. "I love you."

A happy shriek filtered from the grounds below. She turned and waved at her daughter. Trent's father had turned her loose on one of his horses, and they cantered through the maze of bodies preparing for the wedding ceremony tomorrow.

"She loves it here," Simone said. "Your parents have been wonderful."

"In all but blood, she is my child Simone. I'll have you know that without a doubt. I love her very much."

"I know you do. I'm just amazed at how lucky we are."

Trent laughed. "And do you believe luck has anything to do with this?"

She grinned and shook her head then stood on her toes and framed his face with her hands. Her eyes soaked in every plane and angle before she touched her lips to his. The warmth of his breath as he groaned and pulled her closer stirred her passion, but she banked it and turned the kiss gentler. She absorbed every nuance, his soul now forever one with hers.

"Ancient."

"Dragon Dancer."

He dropped his head and with his next kiss demanded the passion she'd held back earlier. Simone wrapped her arms around his neck and pulled closer.

"Marry me?" he asked.

She smiled and gazed at the brilliant emerald gracing her left hand. "I believe I already answered that question."

He nibbled her lip. "I just wanted to make sure."

"I will always love you," she whispered against his mouth.

"And I you."

She heard the distant echo of the past, but this time her heart filled with love at the truth of their words and promise of the future.

"Even without our prophecy, I would have found you Simone Walker. I would have known you were mine."

Simone's heart leapt. "I have no doubt."

"Immortality doesn't scare me as long as you are by my side."

Trent bent and kissed her, fanning her desire. His lips sizzled against hers and she raked her fingers through his hair. Gazing into his eyes, she nipped at the edge of his lip. "I have no fear of the future." She smiled as she remembered the last lines of the Dragon Dancer prophecy.

Three souls entwine, with love divine

The power of three, their destiny . . .

Julie Korzenko

Sneak Preview

RETAINER

(Summer 2012)

Chapter One

Blood comprises only seven percent of the human body weight. In Dane Grant's darkest memories, however, it burst from his brother's body in a flash flood of crimson liquid. The past frightened and tortured and taunted. Dane acknowledged this, accepted it, even. But today, rationalization didn't seem to be helping. He was home and his nightmare reality.

With an over exaggerated sigh, Dane banged his head against the leather of the steering wheel in an attempt to clear cluttered thoughts and calm the vice grip of insecurity. He slid his fingers through the cool metal of the handle and opened the truck door, stepping down onto cracked, oil-stained concrete. Dane inhaled spring, the air heavy with lemony scented magnolia. With a purposely detached gaze, he studied Main Street.

Bethany, a small town nestled in the midst of the sprawling peach farms of Northeast Georgia, appeared a quaint and picturesque village where rocking chairs scattered oversized front porches and violet clematis climbed with wild abandon around iron lamp posts. The old courthouse with its red brick walls and weathered brass dome anchored the center of town.

Dane's gaze rested on the yellowed marble steps and rusted hand rail of the legal building. Despair and defeat hadn't been a part of his being in a long time. It flared to life now, and its taste swelled bitter in Dane's mouth. He shifted his focus and observed the ebb and flow of a place where generations of well respected families thrived and ruled their tiny fiefdom. In historic Britain, he'd be considered a marauder, an evil worthy of being drawn and quartered. He wondered, absently, what punishment lay before him. It certainly wouldn't be any worse than what this place had already doled out to his family.

Dane shut the truck door, pushed the electronic remote until a high pitched beep signaled the vehicle's security, and stepped onto a brick sidewalk. A small, one-story cottage was his destination. Humidity hadn't yet claimed the air, and he spent a few precious seconds appreciating the smog-free environment. This was certainly a far cry from his utilitarian government issued metal desk in Atlanta and most definitely lacked the polish and sheen of the old fire station he'd refurbished in midtown.

"I can do this," Dane spoke the words out loud, adding conviction to his thoughts. "It's just a town. Nothing more."

A sign hung suspended between two white-washed posts. The Worley Law Firm it boldly declared in thick black letters. Dane poked the wooden board bearing the last name of his childhood friend and smiled ever so slight as it rocked back and forth.

He dismissed the oak barrels overflowing with pastel shaded pansies and opened the glass front door of the converted house to office. A soft chime signaled his presence, and he nodded to the receptionist sitting behind a tall mahogany desk. She was cute in a cheerleader kind of way with a perky ponytail that bobbed when her head tilted.

"Dane Grant," he stated. "I have an appointment with Caleb."

The receptionist offered a bright smile. "Caleb has been delayed in court. But his associate, Rae Collins, is prepared to meet with you."

Dane frowned. "I'd rather wait for Caleb." The girl was young, and he immediately regretted his stern tone as a flush of embarrassment colored her face red.

"I'm afraid that's impossible. He's in trial in a county about forty-five miles south of here." She offered an apologetic nod. "I think you'll be very happy with Attorney Collins. She's been with us for almost three years now."

He sighed in frustration but softened his voice. "Well, I guess my back's against the wall on this one. Tell Miss Collins I'll be happy to see her."

The receptionist lowered her voice, stood halfway out of her chair and leaned forward. "Attorney."

Momentarily distracted by the sudden appearance of cleavage, it took Dane a second to refocus. "'Scuse me?" He averted his gaze and focused on the clock behind her desk.

"She prefers Attorney Collins."

Dane shrugged a shoulder. "Whatever. Would you let her know I'm here?"

Perky Cheerleader who in Dane's opinion wore inappropriately low cut sweaters smiled and pointed toward the waiting room. "Certainly, please have a seat."

He settled into one of the silk brocade arm chairs and glanced absently around the room. The rebel yell echoed around the tiny sitting area. It hollered from civil war paintings and screamed out of a bronze statue of General Lee riding a saddled horse and waving the confederate flag high above his head. There was a small water color painting of a cotton field being harvested by a gathering of slaves which startled Dane enough that he stood up to further investigate.

He stared at the aged frame, his brow rising at the impropriety of such a picture and most definite political incorrectness. It tugged at something in his mind, but he didn't have time to ruminate over the memory. Dane heard a door open and turned, holding the picture in his hand. He waved it at the woman who walked into the reception area. "Caleb needs to toss this away."

She glanced at what he held and arched an eyebrow. Her eyes sparkled and Dane's mouth dried as their olive depths momentarily mesmerized. The woman flashed him a wide, easy smile and held out a perfectly manicured hand. A soft floral scent with vanilla undertones filled the waiting area. "Mr. Grant, thank you for your patience. I'm Rae Collins."

Dane's voice failed him. Silky black hair grazed the edge of a perfectly shaped chin which led to full lips shimmering with a soft pink gloss. He coughed to hide his embarrassment at gawking, and his gaze lowered to a pair of astonishing breasts pushing enticingly against a cream silk camisole she wore beneath her suit.

Dane didn't normally fall prey to feminine wiles but the entire package that was Rae Collins left him slightly disturbed.

"Um, right, sorry." He accepted her hand shake and appreciated the strength of grip. "Dane Grant. Nice to meet you."

She grinned as if his whirlwind thoughts were screaming out loud and signaled for him to follow her. "Put that horrid picture down and follow me. If you think that's bad, you should see the ankle chains in Caleb's office."

Dane shook his head, picturing what his partner in Atlanta would have to say at the blatant racism on display. "Last I checked, Caleb knew we'd freed the slaves."

"He's taken on a bit of historic collecting, I'm afraid."

"I see."

Rae tossed a smile over her shoulder at the tone of disgust in Dane's voice. "My office is just down the back hall. It's not as lavish as Caleb's, but it'll suffice."

Dane averted his eyes from the sensuous sway of her hips and refused to glance down at the length of leg stretching from beneath a rather short hemline. The fact her appearance disarmed him caused a wave of panic. He must be more unnerved by the purpose of this meeting than he realized and that wasn't acceptable. His agenda didn't include being sidetracked by a sexy little pixie.

Her office was a tiny space but bright with late morning sunlight. Rae directed him toward a barrel shaped leather chair and settled behind her desk. She popped wire-rimmed glasses onto her face and flipped open a blue folder. "Caleb's notes indicate that you want to legitimate your son?"

"Yes, ma'am."

Rae nodded, removed her glasses and offered Dane a point blank stare. "How much child support are you currently paying?"

"None."

Her demeanor iced. "How old is your son?"

Dane decided if she judged that quickly, then he wasn't about to make this easy on her. "Twelve."

"Has child support services served you with a past due support claim?"

"No, ma'am." She tapped the edge of her pen against the desk, and Dane hid his smile. He found her righteous indignity attractive.

Rae tossed the pen down and leaned back against her chair, resting her elbows casually on the upholstered arm rests. "Mr. Grant, you're going to have to be a bit more forthcoming with me. If I'm going to place myself in front of a judge and fight for your father's rights then you'll have to give me a damn good reason for it. Right now, the mother of your son has every legal stand to deny your claim and prevent you from ever having access to the boy."

"His name is Hunter."

A frown of frustration heightened by a flush of anger colored her face. "Excuse me?"

"My son's name is Hunter."

"I know that," she snapped. "Why now, Mr. Grant? Why the sudden interest in Hunter?"

Dane leaned forward, resting his forearms on the top of his knees and studied Rae Collins. Beyond her visual beauty, he liked what he saw. Compassion and dedication were as much a part of this woman as her hair and eyes. Caleb's sudden court appointment might actually work in Dane's favor. "You judge me incorrectly, Miss Collins."

"I prefer Attorney Collins."

Dane grinned. "I know."

Rae narrowed her eyes and tilted her head to the side. "Have you just played me the fool, Mr. Grant?"

He quirked a brow at the soft southern drawl that dragged his name out a beat too long and felt an honest smile twist his lips upward. "I suppose, ma'am, you could say that. And I prefer Special Agent Grant."

Her eyes sparkled with interest. "Tell me your story."

"Now, see, I figured at some point your smarts would start to show." Dane laughed out loud when her back straightened, eyes widened and anger tipped her fingers into a rapid tap dance on the edge of her desk. He held up a hand, pleading forgiveness. "Sorry." His voice sobered. "I never knew I had a son, Attorney Collins."

"Never?" Skeptism edged her tone.

"Never." Dane sighed, settled into his chair and thought for a moment before selecting the appropriate version of his tale. "I left this town over twelve years ago. I figured I'd gotten away for good." He reached into his pocket and removed a slip of paper tossing it on the desk. "Apparently not."

"What's this?"

"Police report. My high school sweetie hasn't faired too well these past few years. Apparently she's helping support the meth ring y'all can't seem to get a handle on."

Rae studied the report, slid it into the folder and turned her attention back to Dane. "What makes you think Hunter Johns is your son?"

Dane smoothed his hand over his scalp, feeling the soft edges of his crew cut. "She phoned and asked for money. Told me he was mine."

"And you believe her?"

Dane stood and placed the palms of his hands on the edge of her desk. "Do you know what happens to the poor and indigent in Bethany when they can't pay legal fees?"

Rae stood and Dane recognized her refusal to be intimidated. "Can't say that I do. But I suppose they go to jail."

Dane dropped a check payable to the firm in the amount of five thousand dollars on Rae's desk. "You've been retained. Please draw up the legitimation paperwork."

"What kind of visitation are you seeking Mr. Grant?"

Dane stopped and gave her his best Bureau stare-down. "No visitation. I want sole legal and sole physical custody. The boy's coming with me back to Atlanta." He pushed the chair out of his way and exited Rae's office.

"Wait, Mr. Grant…Special Agent Grant -- that's going to be impossible." Rae rushed after him and grabbed his arm. "Absolutely impossible."

His patience slid away. "Do it." Dane moved toward the waiting room. "Please."

She frowned and shook her head emphatically. "You don't understand. This is an extremely conservative county. No judge is going to allow this."

"Get me Lathem," Dane stated. "And he'll order it."

"Mr. Grant, I have to be upfront with you and tell you that you're going to be spending a lot of money for nothing. The best scenario will be weekend visitation every first, third and fifth week and perhaps if over time your son wants to sign an election affidavit we might be able to modify custody. But now, with no history or relationship, this'll never happen."

Dane nodded. "I appreciate your candor. However, it won't change my mind."

Rae sighed in exasperation. "Even if I manage to have Judge Lathem assigned to this case, what makes you think he'll place you in his favor?"

Dane opened the door to leave the firm. He turned and stared into his lawyer's distraught face. "He owes me," he stated, allowing his own frustration to flatten the words.

FOR MORE INFORMATION ON UPCOMING RELEASES

PLEASE VISIT MY WEBSITE

www.juliekorzenko.com

MY FACEBOOK PAGE

Julie Korzenko

MY TWITTER

@juliekorzenko

AND

MY BLOG

https://juliekorzenko.blogspot.com